For Love and Money
The Literary Art
of the Harlequin Mills & Boon Romance

Humanities-Ebooks Genre Fiction Monographs
Series Editor: John Lennard

For Love and Money
The Literary Art of the Harlequin Mills & Boon Romance

Laura Vivanco

HEB ☼ Humanities-Ebooks

Copyright

First published by *Humanities-Ebooks LLP*,
Tirril Hall, Tirril, Penrith CA10 2JE.

This PDF ebook is available from http://www.humanities-ebooks. co.uk and from MyiLibrary.com. and EBSCO. A Kindle ebook in reflowable format is available from Amazon.com. The Pdf is recommended for its superior performance on larger devices such as the Kindle DX and the iPad.

A paperback is available from Lulu.com and from all booksellers.

The author and publisher have used their best efforts to ensure that external URLs given in this book are accurate and current. They are not, however, responsible for any of these websites, and can offer no guarantee that the sites remain live or the content appropriate.

ISBN 978-1-84760-195-7 PDF
ISBN 978-1-84760-196-4 PAPERBACK
ISBN 978-1-84760-197-1 KINDLE

To every Harlequin Mills & Boon author who has ever been asked "When are you going to write a real novel?"

Contents

Acknowledgements

My funding body and our child have been a great source of encouragement and technical help. Their belief in my work has kept me going on days when I was mired in the Slough of Despond.

It has been a pleasure to be published by HEB. John Lennard's enthusiasm, efficiency and attention to detail have made this a better book. Any remaining errors and omissions are, of course, my responsibility and not his.

I am grateful to be part of a community of romance scholars and I would particularly like to acknowledge the vital roles played by Sarah S. G. Frantz (President of the International Association for the Study of Popular Romance), Pamela Regis (Vice President of IASPR and the author of *A Natural History of the Romance Novel*), and Eric M. Selinger (Executive Editor of the *Journal of Popular Romance Studies* and founder of the 'Teach Me Tonight' blog) in ensuring that the field is a lively and expanding one. Sandra Schwab marched ahead of me, slaying baggy dragons, An Goris made me aware of John Lennard's *Of Modern Dragons* and Kerstin Frank's introduction to the thermodynamics of Georgette Heyer fired me with enthusiasm for metaphors. I can only wish to match jay Dixon's vast hoard of knowledge about Mills & Boon.

Over the course of writing this book I corresponded with a number of HM&B authors, including Pamela Browning, Julie Cohen, Jennifer Crusie, Jessica Hart, Marion Lennox, Nicola Marsh, Sandra Marton, Sabrina Philips, Michelle Styles, Claire Thornton and Kate Walker. Their kindness is much appreciated.

The readers of the 'Teach Me Tonight' blog made me believe there was also an audience for this project. Many of them gave me new perspectives on, and information about, romances. Joanna Chambers read and commented on sections of the book.

Alan Deyermond remains an inspiration. I miss his incisive comments and value the encouragement he gave me as I began work on this project. My conversations with him, Louise Haywood and Iona McCleery encouraged me to believe that in stepping from Hispano-medievalism into popular romance scholarship, I was not taking one giant leap into a totally unrelated field.

I would also like to acknowledge the use, on the cover, of an adapted version of J. Herrera's *Diseño 3D, rosa roja* which was made available online under a Creative Commons Attribution-Share Alike licence. The remixed version of the rose featured on the cover of this book is therefore available for use under the terms of that licence.

Abbreviations

AD: Anno Domini ('year of the Lord')
AIDS: Acquired Immune Deficiency Syndrome
BBC: British Broadcasting Corporation
BC: Before Christ
ESP: extra-sensory perception
HIV: Human Immunodeficiency Virus
HM&B: Harlequin Mills & Boon
IASPR: International Association for the Study of Popular Romance
M&B: Mills & Boon
MS: manuscript
NHS: National Health Service (UK)
N.Sh.OED: New Shorter Oxford English Dictionary
OED: Oxford English Dictionary
RCMP: Royal Canadian Mounted Police
RWA: Romance Writers of America

Introduction

When the editor of *A Companion to Romance: From Classical to Contemporary* (2004) "observed that: 'Romance exists in *degenerate* form in works of the Mills & Boon type'", Lynne Pearce responded:

> what is most degenerate is also most *defining* [...]. Like it or not, it is the template originating in these mass-produced romances that has become the twenty-first-century's base-line definition of romance. (521)

The term 'romance', which "finds its origins in the French word *romanz*, meaning simply literature written in the vernacular, the romance language of French" (Saunders 2), has, however, been applied to a great many different types of literature:

> The word's spectrum of meaning has to be wide to include *Troilus and Criseyde*, *The Faerie Queene*, *The Mysteries of Udolpho* and *Lord Jim*, all of which have been called romances. Keats and Hawthorne both claim the word for one of their works [...]. One problem in discussing the romance is the need to limit the way the term is applied. (Beer 4–5)

In this book the problem has been resolved by taking the novels published by Mills & Boon and Harlequin as "*defining*": unless qualified in some way, any mention here of 'romance', 'romances' or 'romance novels' should be understood as referring to "works of the Mills & Boon type".

Mention will, however, be made of some of the works that have been recognised as relatives (some more distant than others) of the romance novel. Jean Radford, although she concedes that:

> It is possible to argue about 'romance' [...] that there is no historical relationship between Greek 'romances', medieval

romance, Gothic bourgeois romances of the 1840s, late nineteenth century women's romances and mass-produced romance fiction now—except the generic term. (8)

nonetheless affirms that it "is also possible [...] to give some weight
to the claim that romance is one of the oldest and most enduring of
literary modes which survives today" (8). If the claim is accepted,
then popular mass-market romances, including Harlequin Mills &
Boon (HM&B) romances, have extremely "deep taproots that lead all
the way back through literary history to medieval romances, and to a
pre-literary oral culture" (Holmes 6).

The "Greek 'romances'" to which Radford refers "were all written
by and for the Greek-speaking population of the eastern Roman
Empire, in the first, second and third centuries AD" (Williamson
25). They include Heliodorus and Longus's tales of "Chariclea and
Theagenes, Daphnis and Chloe [...] just a few of the lovers from
centuries past who had delighted" (S. James 15) the heroine of
Sophia James's *One Unashamed Night* (2010). Their presence in this
novel is one indication of modern authors' awareness of the literary
ancestors of HM&Bs; further proof of this awareness can be found
in Chapter 3.

What unifies texts:

> from *Tristan and Iseult* to the Harlequin series, is first the cen-
> trality of the love plot: what drives the plot, what motivates
> the turning of the pages, is the question of whether and how
> the two primary characters will achieve, or fail to achieve, a
> lasting union with each other. (Holmes 6)

Romance novels, however, as published by HM&B and as defined by
the Romance Writers of America (RWA), have both "a central love
story and an emotionally satisfying and optimistic ending". Or, in
the words of Daphne Clair and Robyn Donald (both prolific HM&B
authors), they tell "a story in which the plot is driven by a sexually
based emotional relationship between two people. And for most readers there has to be a happy ending—or at least the strong implication
of future happiness" (1).[1]

---

1   The RWA definition focuses on the two main aspects of romances but some

Mills & Boon, or Harlequin as the company is known in Canada
and the US, has a unique relationship with romance:

> Mills & Boon, the United Kingdom's leading publisher of ro-
> mantic fiction, is one hundred years old in 2008; and its parent
> company, Harlequin, celebrates sixty years in 2009. Over the
> years, both firms have become household names, their books
> enjoying the almost unique distinction of being requested by
> publisher, rather than author. In 1997, the phrase 'Mills &
> Boon', meaning a type of popular romantic novel, was added
> to the Oxford English Dictionary. (Bowring and O'Brien 8)[1]

Ken Gelder has also stressed the importance of the publisher's brand:
"Harlequin and Mills and Boon have long been synonymous with
romance, and it can certainly seem as if the brand name of the publisher overshadows the writer, who is quite literally subsumed into
industry" (44).

It would be wrong, however, to believe that all HM&B authors are
"subsumed" into the company. In Mills & Boon's early years its list:

> included the great and the near-great, some of whom were giv-
> en their first big 'break' by Mills & Boon: P. G. Wodehouse,
> Hugh Walpole, Victor Bridges, Jack London, E. F. Benson,
> Georgette Heyer, Denise Robins, and Constance Holme were
> all published by the firm. (McAleer, *Passion's Fortune* 3)

This is also true of HM&B in more recent decades: the company has
numbered among its authors Sally Beauman, Jennifer Crusie, Victoria Holt, Jayne Ann Krentz, Mercedes Lackey, Rosamunde Pilcher
and Nora Roberts.[2] In addition, there are plenty of HM&B authors

---

analysts of the genre have attempted to identify smaller constituent parts of the
novels. Pamela Regis has described "eight essential narrative events [which]
provide a romance novel with its basic structure" and "Three other narrative
events [which] are frequent but not essential" (38). George Paizis has also ana-
lysed "the building blocks of the narratives" (*Love* 6).

1 An indication of Harlequin's status as a "household name" in North America is
provided by Kay Mussell, who has noted that "Criticizing a film, novel, or television program as a 'Harlequin romance' has become an automatic phrase of
contempt by reviewers who may never have read a romance" (16–17).

2 As 'Vanessa James' Sally Beauman wrote nine romances for HM&B in the
1980s. Jennifer Crusie's career as an author began with Harlequin in the early

who, while they remain virtually unknown to the general public, are 'stars' to the publisher's regular readers. This is a fact of which HM&B is well aware and "As readers begin to develop a preference for certain authors, so new reading programs are made available to cater to these demands" (Harlequin, *Harlequin 30th* 12).[1]

Nonetheless, the fame (or notoriety) of the Harlequin and Mills & Boon brands has led many to think reductively of HM&B books as merely marketable commodities produced by a company whose "success has been reinforced through the application to the publishing industry of techniques developed in other areas of commerce" (Paizis, "Category" 130). Joseph McAleer, for example, states that:

> The Mills & Boon imprint, like any successful commodity in a mass market, stands for a quality product, a kind of guarantee of an easy, thrilling, and satisfying read with an obligatory happy ending. This flavourful confection, wrapped in a brightly coloured paperback cover with a dreamy scene, is to many addictive in its escapist nature. (*Passion's Fortune* 2)

Thus, although HM&B romances have been described as "an economic art form" (Jensen 32), they have rarely been judged positively as a literary art form. Rather, as Ann Curthoys and John Docker commented in 1990:

> For most of this century romance fiction [...] has been high literature's Other, a negative icon, what not, what never to

1990s. 'Victoria Holt' was, like 'Jean Plaidy' and 'Philippa Carr', a pseudonym of Eleanor Hibbert (1906–93), who wrote romances for Mills & Boon in the 1950s and early 1960s as 'Eleanor Burford'. Jayne Ann Krentz, who also writes as 'Amanda Quick' and 'Jayne Castle', wrote for Harlequin in the 1980s and early 1990s. Mercedes Lackey was already well known for her fantasy fiction before the first of her Five Hundred Kingdoms series, *The Fairy Godmother* (2004), was published by Harlequin's LUNA imprint. As 'Jane Fraser' Rosamunde Pilcher wrote ten novels for Mills & Boon between 1949 and 1963. Nora Roberts has recently been described as "a publishing phenomenon. She writes five books a year—a hardcover novel, a paperback trilogy, and a paranormal suspense under the pseudonym J. D. Robb" (Gagne-Hawes). According to Roberts, discovering Harlequin romances was a "wonderful moment in my life" ("The Romance" 198). She began her career writing category romances for Silhouette prior to its acquisition by Harlequin in 1984, and she remained with HM&B for many years.

1   Such 'star' authors include Betty Neels, whose novels have been reprinted in special "Collector's Editions".

be. Newspaper critics in reviews, journalists in their columns, good professional-middle-class people in their conversation, would casually snap at a book or passage by saying things like 'it unfortunately smacks of Mills and Boon', or, 'in certain parts of the novel it lapses into pure Mills and Boon'. 'Mills and Boon' was a roaming, punitive signifier, a terrier running around and around the boundary that separates serious writing from the low, from sub-literature, para-literature, trash, schlock. 'Mills and Boon' meant embarrassingly 'bad' writing, sentimental, over-explicit, slushy, sloppy, the lush, the unforgivable. (Curthoys & Docker)

Many critics, including Daphne Watson and Kate Ellis, would doubtless have preferred to see the terrier impounded: the former believed that HM&B romance had crossed some literary boundary and was "a kind of subliterary form" (91), while the latter stated that "Harlequin romances [...] are about as far from 'great books' as it is possible to get" (749).

Similarly scathing assessments of this particular publisher's list continue to be expressed:

In the literary world, Mills and Boon has long been the black sheep. Its books—to call them novels would be to raise them far above their station—are lightweight, the plots recycled and the endings predictable and to read them is a waste of precious life. (Freeman)

Having spent a great deal of time reading HM&B romances, I would argue that many are well-written, skilfully crafted works which can and do engage the minds as well as the emotions of their readers, and a few are small masterpieces—as I shall show. I follow in the footsteps of John G. Cawelti who considered "popular formulas to be of more complex artistic and cultural interest than most previous commentators have indicated" (*Adventure* 2) and stated that "it is possible to examine individual works of popular culture as unique artistic creations" ("The Concept" 382).[1] My choice of "individual

---

1   Cawelti himself wrote little about the romance genre; in his *Adventure, Mystery, and Romance* he chose "to deal rather intensively with a few major formulas—

works" has been influenced by availability: most of the HM&Bs to which I refer were published in the UK in recent years. Nevertheless, the corpus of romances on which I draw spans seven decades and includes many novels edited in the US or Canada. I have also been guided by the need to quote from novels that provide clear examples of the topics under discussion.

In analysing literary modes I have drawn heavily on the work of Northrop Frye, who observed that "Value-judgments are subjective [...]. When they are fashionable or generally accepted, they look objective, but that is all" (20). The truth of this is demonstrated by the history of the critical reception of an earlier form of romance literature, *cancionero* love poetry:

> For many years Hispanists have tended to assume that the huge numbers of lyric poems written in the fifteenth century—the so-called *cancionero* poetry, the work of some 700 poets—were nothing more than, as it were, academic exercises ringing the changes on the trivial niceties of courtly love. (Wardropper 182)

Keith Whinnom, however, set out to prove that:

> (1) the technical expertise of the composers of *canciones* is considerable; (2) the poets of the end of the fifteenth century accept in the *canción* a series of technical restrictions which make the *canción* at once a more exacting and a more concise form; (3) simultaneously they restrict their vocabulary to a very limited range of abstract terms; (4) the majority of modern critics who have looked at this verse have either dismissed it as vacuous and insipid or have singled out for enthusiastic approval poems which in form or content are quite untypical, and cannot be taken as representative of the aesthetic ideal of the period. (127)

Despite his work, attitudes to *cancionero* poetry were slow to shift and in 1998 Julian Weiss observed that:

---

various forms of detective and crime stories, the western, and the best-selling social melodrama" (2).

much of the work done on the *cancioneros* is still rooted in largely unexamined assumptions about literary canons, esthetic, social, and political categories and values. This is poetry that since the early nineteenth century has occupied a liminal space in the minds of critics. [...] The history of *cancionero* studies is a measure of our evolving notions of "literature" and "culture," since much of the interpretative criticism has been designed to vindicate or deny its status as "art." (3)

HM&B romances differ in many ways from late medieval *cancionero* poetry but both, despite being hugely popular with their intended audiences, have often been carelessly denigrated by modern scholars.

As for the authors of these works, Ian Macpherson has noted of the *cancionero* poets that "I am personally convinced that many [...] were considerably more enterprising and ambitious [...] than they have generally been given credit for" (62); one could say the same of romance novelists. In addition, both HM&B romances and *cancionero* love poetry are large bodies of work comprised of texts with "concise form[s]". Although the lengths of HM&Bs vary, they are generally "concise" novels and the constraints imposed by their commercial niche prompted Jennifer Crusie, who has written for Harlequin, to compare them to poems: "Category [romance] is an elegant, exacting, exciting form of fiction. It requires precise pacing, tight plotting, and exquisitely brief characterizations. It is truly as fine a form for fiction as the sonnet is for poetry" ("So, Bill"). Dirk de Geest and An Goris have suggested that there are grounds for considering romances to be a type of "constrained writing", a term which "designates a form of literary production in which the writer submits his or her text to specific formal (and to a lesser extent also thematic) constraints" (82).

In the case of HM&B authors, many of the "specific formal (and to a lesser extent also thematic) constraints" are imposed by the publisher. Although Mills & Boon Limited, founded by Gerald Mills (1877–1928) and Charles Boon (1877–1943) in London in 1908, began its existence as a small general publisher, over time it came to specialise in romance novels. In 1957 Harlequin Books Limited, a small Canadian "printer, packager, and book distributor [...] founded in 1949 by Richard Bonnycastle" (McAleer, *Passion's Fortune* 116–17), purchased the Canadian reprint rights for several Mills & Boon romances. Harlequin had also begun by printing works in a variety of genres, but it too came to specialise in romance as the business relationship between the two companies grew ever closer: in "1963 Harlequin published a non-Mills & Boon author for the last time" and, on "1 October 1971, Harlequin acquired Mills & Boon" (McAleer, *Passion's Fortune* 120, 139). The Mills & Boon brand, however, was retained and is used in the Australian, Indian, New Zealand and UK markets, while many of the company's romances continue to be edited at Mills & Boon's UK offices. In July 1984, Harlequin bought Silhouette Books from Simon & Schuster (Thurston 64) and until April 2011 Silhouette continued to exist as one of Harlequin's many imprints:

> Harlequin sells books under several imprints including Harlequin, Silhouette, MIRA, [...] Steeple Hill, LUNA and HQN. [...] In late 2005, Harlequin acquired the assets of BET Books, a leading publisher of African-American women's fiction. These titles will be published by Harlequin under the Kimani Press imprint. (Torstar, *2005 Annual Report* 25)

Despite the fact that HM&B is best known for its 'category' or 'series' romances, some of these imprints publish 'single title' novels and the company therefore:

> publishes books in both series and single title formats. Series titles are published monthly in mass-market paperback format under an imprint that identifies the type of story to the reader. Each series typically has a preset number of titles that will be published each month. The single title publishing program provides a broader spectrum of content in a variety of formats (mass-market paperback, trade paperback, hardcover) and is generally a lengthier book. (Torstar, *2010 Annual Report* 12).[1]

---

1   It should be noted that not all of the books published by HM&B are romances. According to Harlequin's website, the company "publishes over 110 titles a month [...]. These books are written by over 1,200 talented authors worldwide, offering women a broad range of reading from romance to bestseller fiction, from young adult novels to erotic literature, from nonfiction to fantasy" ("About

Each series, or 'line', has its own guidelines which provide details about elements such as settings, levels of explicit sexual reference, and plot, which distinguish it from the other lines. Some lines specialise in particular areas, such as historical romance, medical romance, romantic suspense, and paranormal romance. These guidelines, then, serve as detailed descriptions of the constraints within which authors must work while still producing distinctive and emotionally engaging work.

It may be helpful to compare HM&B authors to the Godmothers in Mercedes Lackey's *The Fairy Godmother* (2004), a romantic fantasy novel published under Harlequin's LUNA imprint. In the lands of the Five Hundred Kingdoms all of life is affected by a magic force known as "The Tradition" (58) which attempts to shape events to make them fit the patterns set by folktales, ballads, and other forms of traditional literature. The role of the Godmothers is to "see to it that the conditions are fulfilled to make things as pleasant as possible for everyone" (68). In order to achieve this they must become conversant with all aspects of "The Tradition" and a significant part of a Godmother's training therefore involves making herself "familiar with every tale that any Godmother has ever been involved with" (90).

Guides to writing romance novels suggest a similar programme of training for romance authors: Daphne Clair and Robyn Donald warn the aspiring author "Don't try to write romances if you've never read one; you need to immerse yourself in them so you can recognise the clichés to avoid" (2), and Catherine Wade similarly suggests "Read as many novels as you can, selecting them from as many of the different types of romances as possible and reading the work of a large variety of authors" (15).[1] Harlequin explicitly advises would-be HM&B authors to read a wide range of their romances:

> we expect you to enjoy reading romance fiction. If you are already a fan, your appreciation for this type of book will be apparent in your writing. If you have not done so already, we encourage you to read many, many books from each series.

Harlequin").

[1]   Catherine Wade writes for the Mills & Boon Modern/Harlequin Presents line of romances under the name 'Kate Walker'.

> The series that emerges as your favorite is probably the one to
> which you should submit your manuscript. ("Writing Guide-
> lines: How to")

Although it might be argued that by packaging the novels into 'lines',
each with its own set of guidelines, HM&B restricts its authors' artistic freedom, this in fact suggests that authors are encouraged to
choose whichever line best suits their particular writing 'voice'.

It should also be noted that HM&B's guidelines have not remained
constant. McAleer describes one period of change, following
Harlequin's acquisition of Mills & Boon, in which:

> some of the authors who started their Mills & Boon careers
> in a more 'chaste' time [...] were faced with the new require-
> ments of the Harlequin era. 'A lot of our authors who could
> not handle sex started to handle it,' Boon said. 'They probably
> read some of the authors who could and imitated it.' Ethel
> Connell ('Katrina Britt') admitted that some of the older au-
> thors did just that: 'A lot of the authors used to read each other,
> like in school. They'd have to copy the frisky bits.' (*Passion's
> Fortune* 287)

Those who begin by imitating, however, may ultimately master the
new techniques and themselves produce innovative novels. McAleer
cites Anne Weale as an example of an author who "made the transition successfully" (*Passion's Fortune* 287) and "demonstrated her
newfound talents in two ground-breaking novels" (288). Although
the casual or infrequent reader is perhaps more apt to perceive the
similarities between HM&B novels, Eva Hemmungs Wirtén suggests
that:

> a very real *experience* of originality and individuality [...] ex-
> ists, not as a result of readers being tricked or duped into con-
> sumption and reading, but as a tangible reality stemming from
> an acquired reading competence that allow[s] texts that are
> written within category romance to be understood as different
> from one another, as having something unique in them. In a
> way, a text should adhere to the requirements of a particular
> line, but also in a sense break out of that frame. (74)

The HM&B romance's format requires from its authors a thorough knowledge of the conventions, yet remains flexible enough to permit them to innovate.

In this it resembles other types of genre fiction. Cawelti, who described popular fictional genres as "literary formulas" (*Adventure* 5), wrote that:

> Each formula has its own sets of limits that determine what kind of new and unique elements are possible without straining the formula to the breaking point. We can point to at least two special artistic skills that all good formulaic writers seem to possess to some degree: the ability to give new vitality to stereotypes and the capacity to invent new touches of plot or setting that are still within formulaic limits. (*Adventure* 10–11)

Writing specifically about romance authors, Anne K. Kaler concurs: "Some writers emerge as great because they 'work' the formula, shaping it to their particular vision" (2). Godmother Elena, the heroine of Lackey's novel, is the equivalent of one of these outstanding authors of romance novels. While "Some Godmothers are only willing to assist in the making of the happy endings" (166), Elena attempts to push "The Tradition" in new directions and is reassured by an older, more experienced Wizard: "What, were you worried because you'd been breaking Traditions? Good lack, girl, that's what the best of us always do! Bend them, anyway. Shape them the way we want them to go" (467). The Wizard's view of "The Tradition" resembles Ralph Cohen's view of genre classifications: "since each genre is composed of texts that accrue, the grouping is a process, not a determinate category. Genres are open categories. Each member alters the genre by adding, contradicting, or changing constituents, especially those of members most closely related to it" (204).

Like a superstitious bride, every romance novel thus combines elements of the old, the new, the borrowed, and the blue.[1] The genre

---

1   The superstition is incorporated into a scene in Paula Marshall's *Lord Hadleigh's Rebellion* (2001) in which the heroine is being dressed for her wedding:

'Now,' said Pandora in her jolly way, 'you must take these four things and bestow them around your person. [...] Something old,' she announced and she handed Mary a small linen pocket-handkerchief.

itself is old: as we have seen it has ancient roots, drawing as it does on centuries of happy and not-so-happy love stories. The borrowing in HM&B romances will include adherence to the guidelines for each line, but in addition may involve the use of elements from other genres or the adoption of a "classic romance plot situation" (Clair and Donald 43), such as a marriage of convenience. The whole must then be given a new twist and "It takes considerable skill to write in a fresh, unforgettable way a story that has been told over and over" (Clair and Donald 4). The novel should also be infused with the 'something blue' of sexual tension because "In romantic fiction the primary tension is essentially an emotional one, with a covert or overt edge of sexual awareness between the couple" (Clair and Donald 29).

Sandra Marton's *The Disobedient Virgin* (2005) can be read as a case study in how all four of the bride's old, blue, borrowed and new items can be combined. Marton borrows imagery from myths and fairytales and makes use of the well-established guardian/ward plot.[1] Germaine Greer, writing about one of the most famous romances containing this type of plot, Georgette Heyer's *Regency Buck* (1935), mentions that the hero's position in the heroine's life transforms him into "that most titillating of all titillating relations, her young guardian" (176). As the use of the word "titillating" suggests, there is 'something blue' inherent in the guardian/ward scenario, and Marton makes good use of the possibilities it provides. As for the 'something new', Cawelti observed that "It is not easy to put into words the rather subtle and even fleeting qualities that make one performance stand out over another" (*Adventure* 10). It is clear, however, that Marton has succeeded in creating 'something new' out of an unusual

---

'Something new,' said Aunt Beauregard, and she decorated the collar of Mary's dress with a small gold pin.
'Something borrowed,' and Serena handed her a garter to hold up one of her stockings.
'Something blue,' murmured Jennie shyly and she handed her mistress a length of blue ribbon to tie around the little finger of her right hand. [...]
'Now you are ready,' said Aunt Beauregard. (283)

1   The novel is the final book in the Ramirez Brides trilogy. Although the trilogy was written as a multi-author series, the initial idea for the series, with its overarching plot of three half-brothers who each have to fulfil a stipulation in their dead father's will in order to learn each other's identities, was Marton's. Each author created the main plot and characters of her own book.

combination of things old, borrowed and blue.

Commentators such as Francesca Segal, who has claimed that HM&B romances are "cherished for their simplicity", might consider the close textual analysis of such a novel to be an exercise in futility. It is true that if one were to read the novel quickly it would be easy to miss all but the most explicit metaphors, but via the use of more subtle word choices Marton makes them permeate the entire novel. A closer reading of the text is in fact invited by the extent to which Jake, the hero, analyses his own words. In one scene the heroine, Catarina, "hadn't expected to find him in the sitting room" (49):

> "I—I didn't realize…"
> Jake bit back a groan. "No," he said, "neither did I."
> He knew they were talking about two different things, but hell, he was lucky he could talk at all—luckier still when a knock at the door signaled the arrival of Room Service.
> "Coming," he called, wincing at his bad choice of response, wincing that he should even be thinking such a thing … (50)

Jake, then, is sexually aware of Catarina and also aware of the inadvertent *doubles entendres* in their conversation. Later in the novel Jake once more questions his choice of words as he looks forward to avoiding Catarina and spending the evening:

> safely ensconced behind the closed door to the master suite.
> And then he'd thought, *Why did I use that word? Safely? Why would I need to feel safe in my own home?* (114)

The answer is that, as Catarina has learned, "Sex was incredibly powerful" (80) and Jake, much against his will, is extremely sexually attracted to Catarina. She, however, is his ward and therefore not available and Jake would prefer to think of her as "a kid. An innocent. A virgin straight out of a convent school" (71).

As I show in Chapters 1 and 2, it is not uncommon for authors of romances to include in their works references to elements of myths, fairytales and chivalric romances. The reader of *The Disobedient Virgin* is introduced to Catarina when she, like Danaë, Rapunzel, or many a damsel in distress, is an imprisoned virgin: she has been shut up in a convent school with Mother Elisabete as her "keeper"

(19) and no possibility of escape until her twenty-first birthday. The reader first encounters her as she pushes open the window of her room and her "long chestnut hair, free of its severely braided coronet [...] tumbled down her back as she raised her eyes to the sky" (19). In keeping with literary tradition, the virgin heroine hopes for rescue and she thinks it may have arrived in the form of Jake:

> She'd stolen a long look at him from beneath her lashes when they were in Mother Elisabete's office. Just for a moment, before they'd told her who he was and what he was going to do with her, she'd conjured up a fantasy about a black-haired, green-eyed knight come to save her from the dragon.
>
> What a shock to find out that the knight *was* the dragon. (42)

He is "the dragon" because he is a "captor" (42) who brings her to his lair: "He'd taken her to Rio. To this hotel, glittering with lights and almost smelling of sin" (42). The use of the word "glitter" recalls the sparkle of the gold and jewels in a dragon's hoard and this particular dragon seems especially attracted to the golden aspects of Catarina herself: he thinks of her "warm golden skin" (48) and her hair which is "the chestnut and gold of an autumn wood" (50), has to fight back "the almost overwhelming desire to touch his hand to the soft, gold-burnished curls" (95), and eventually discovers that elsewhere on her body "the curls that guarded her innocence were a soft whorl of chestnut and gold" (142).[1] This dragon's interest in gold appears to be the result of lust rather than of avarice, and there can be no mistaking the sexual nature of the heat and flames he produces: on their first evening together Catarina "saw Jake watching her with burning eyes. Something happened deep, deep in her belly. Heat, swift and sudden. Heat that spread through her blood, to her breasts" (53); later he kisses her to show her that "she couldn't play with him unless she

---

1   It may simply be a coincidence, but this "dragon" is also a frequent flier. He arrives in Brazil by plane, collects Catarina and then, as she says, "we're flying to your country tomorrow" (57). Although he lacks a mountain-top lair, he does have a predilection for living on the top floors of high buildings. The hotel suite to which he first takes Catarina is on the top floor (43). Back in New York his apartment has "a breathtaking view" (84) and is on the "top two floors" (84) of "a tall building facing the park. Gargoyles peered from the cornices and looked down at the street" (83).

wanted to get burned. But the flame was dangerous for him too" (85).

If Jake is described as being both a handsome man and a terrifying "monster", (36, 60, 71, 72) he is not alone in having two sides to his personality: Catarina is both monstrous and an innocent virgin. Her monstrous aspect takes the form of the Medusa: "The wind had not been kind. It had whipped her hair into a thousand wild strands until she looked like a stand-in for Medusa" (38). The way in which she combines innocent, vulnerable femininity with the powerful, monstrous aspect of her nature is emphasised when "She gave him a look that Medusa might have used to turn men to stone. Except she didn't look like Medusa this morning; she looked more like a woman trying not to show the depth of her terror" (78–9). Her Medusa-like attributes include the ability to speak in a "venomous" (56) tone of voice, her tears, like Medusa's hair, "snaked down her cheeks" (136), and when Jake watches her dancing with another man, he does so "stone-faced" (126). Again, as is the case with Jake, there is a strongly sexual element to her "monstrous" nature: "Even remembering [her touching him] made him hard as stone" (69).

It seems no coincidence that the sexual, monstrous aspects of both Jake and Catarina are reptilian. Medusa, of course, had snakes in place of hair and the dragon takes its name "from the Greek δράκων (a snake), and many of its symbolic qualities are therefore identical with those of the snake": "As an ecclesiastical symbol the dragon remained consistent. It was the Evil Spirit and his works" and "The Tempter in the Garden of Eden was the serpent, and the first thing Adam and Eve did after the Fall was to cover their genitalia: their sin was sexual" (Rowland 66, 68, 142).

As Jake lies beside Catarina, bound to her by a "silk tie" which encircles her wrist and is also "wrapped […] around his" (61) so that she cannot escape from him, Catarina, like Eve, is tempted by the idea of gaining knowledge. She justifies her curiosity on the grounds that "if she touched him she might learn things that would be helpful. Things she should learn about men" (62–3). In the morning she awakens and the silk tie's serpentine nature is revealed: "The only reminder of the night was the brightly colored length of silk he'd used to bind her to him. It lay draped over the headboard like an exotic snake" (66).

Catarina's convent education has taught her to think of sex as sinful and when she and Jake are finally on the verge of having intercourse:

> Her body was on fire. Her breasts tingled. She could feel liquid heat between her thighs, in that place Sister Angelica had once said was the ultimate source of evil.
>
> She wanted to feel Jake's hand there. Between her legs. Was she evil, too, for wanting such a thing? (140)

When Jake says he wants to "taste" (142) her there, "She shook her head. 'No. It's wrong. You mustn't—'" (142). Jake counters by asking "How can it be wrong for me to worship you with my body?" (142). His words echo those of the Anglican marriage ceremony, "with my body I thee worship" (*Book of Common Prayer*), words which assure the couple that sex within marriage, far from being a sin, is a licit and even necessary part of their relationship.

This latter attitude towards sexuality is a feature of many of the novels in the Harlequin Presents/Mills & Boon Modern line. As Patricia Treble noted in 2007, "today's Harlequin authors are increasingly devoting swaths of their books to upfront discussions of [...] serious sexual issues" and she quoted Sandra Marton, who told her that:

> "I think that women who do read our books know damn well that they're going to get something that could be light but could have some meat to it," Marton says. "They are not just perfectly happy getting that—they're interested in getting that."

Marton's heroine, Catarina, has herself learned much of what she knows about sex from romance novels:

> She turned a pale pink. "The girls who went home for weekends, you know, sometimes they brought back books."
>
> *Lady Chatterley's Lover*? *The Story of O*? Jake narrowed his eyes. "And?"
>
> "And in those books..."
>
> "What books, damn it?"

"Romance novels. In some of them kisses were—they were special."

"Ah. Romance novels." He let out a sigh of relief. How revealing could a romance novel be? (87)

Considerably more revealing than Jake would ever expect, and when they are, they encourage readers to come to terms with their own "monstrous" or sexual natures so that henceforth they will feel more at ease with their bodies, like Catarina, who by the end of the novel is persuaded to swim in the nude (177) and rather than thinking of sex as sinful, can jokingly say: "'Wicked man,' […] in such a throaty purr as her body arched to his that Jake grinned and said yeah, and wasn't she glad he was?" (177).

In weaving together the old, new, borrowed and blue *The Disobedient Virgin* serves as proof that:

> genre narratives cannot exist in isolation, but in fact engage, through both adherence to and departure from genre norms, in continual dialogue with the history and pre-existing body of work which constitutes their genre. More than the simple shape of a text, narrative structure becomes a powerful tradition, a set of codes which is continually invoked, rediscovered, and recreated with the telling of every new version, and which thus relies on a self-consciousness about textuality. (Tiffin 3)

One feature of the romance 'Tradition' is the use of metaphors which recur in the novels and can be found in both their texts and, sometimes, their titles, as in the cases of *Built to Last* (L. Evans, 1988), *The Briar Rose* (Dean, 1986) and *Manhunting* (Crusie, 1993). A selection of these metaphors form the subject of Chapter 4. As we shall see, the romance 'Tradition' also includes works of popular culture from other genres as well as texts which form part of the literary canon, and this is discussed in Chapter 3. That the HM&B 'Tradition' also draws on the Bible, classical mythology, fairy tales and chivalric romances is readily apparent from the profusion of novels with titles such as *A Serpent in Eden* (Farnes, 1971), *An Apple From Eve* (Neels, 1981), *Devil's Dare* (Grant, 1996), *Earthbound Angel* (George, 1996), *Hosea's Bride* (Clark, 2004), *Ward of Lucifer* (Burchell, 1976), *Apollo's*

Legend (Ash, 1994), *Handmaid to Midas* (Arbor, 1982), *Moon of Aphrodite* (Craven, 1980), *Neptune's Daughter* (Weale, 1987), *The Garden of Persephone* (Asquith, 1967), *A Groom for Red Riding Hood* (Greene, 1994), *Beauty & The Beasts* (Johnson, 1997), *Fairy-Tale Family* (Montana, 1999), *Rapunzel in New York* (Logan, 2011), *Second-Hand Cinderella* (C. M. Evans, 1937), *Sleeping Beauty Suspect* (Sinclair, 2007), *Bought: Damsel in Distress* (King, 2009), *Her Galahad* (M. James, 2002) and *The Black Knight's Bride* (Mackenzie, 2004).

The HM&B romance's relationship to myths, fairytales and chivalric romances is explored in Chapters 1 and 2. Since it raises questions about the level of realism in HM&Bs, however, I turn first to Northrop Frye's theory of mimetic modes, which provides a way of classifying HM&Bs according to the nature of their protagonists and the social and physical context in which they are placed.

Chapter 1. Mimetic Modes

Two of the major criticisms directed at romances concern their perceived homogeneity and their relationship to reality: "A frequent and
familiar criticism [...] is that 'they are all the same'" (Talbot, "An
Explosion" 106); "It has become popular, even necessary, to note
that, whatever the pros and cons of romance fiction may be, it is
undeniable that the fiction deals in fantasy" (Crusie Smith 81). The
truth, however, is that romances are not "all the same", and can be
classified according to the differing extent to which they 'deal in fantasy'.

Northrop Frye divided all literature into five modes, with each
mode "classified [...] by the hero's power of action, which may be
greater than ours, less, or roughly the same" (33) and by the depiction
of the environment that this hero inhabits. Although some readers
may have a preference for one or more of these modes, Frye does not
ascribe greater or lesser literary value to any of them: "'High' and
'low' have no connotations of comparative value" (34).

Myth

A text in the first of Frye's mimetic modes will feature a protagonist
who is "superior in *kind* both to other men and to the environment of
other men"; in other words, "the story about him will be a *myth* in the
common sense of a story about a god. Such stories have an important
place in literature, but are as a rule found outside the normal literary
categories" (33). Myths are "outside the normal literary categories"
because they were not originally considered to be fiction. For this
reason no HM&B romance could be considered "a *myth* in the common sense" unless it were a retelling of an existing myth in which the
plot, protagonists and settings remained identical to those in the orig-

inal.[1] There are, however, a few HM&B romances that masquerade as myth: although marketed as fiction, within their pages the reality of the gods and goddesses whom they depict remains unquestioned and these divinities both intervene in the lives of humans and are worshipped by them.

P. C. Cast's *Divine by Choice* (2006) is set partly in "twenty-first century America" (16) and partly "in Partholon, a parallel world where mythology and magic lived" (16).[2] Its heroine is "a high school English teacher from Oklahoma" (12) who has become the "Incarnate and Beloved of the ancient Celtic horse goddess Epona" (16). Stephanie Draven's *Poisoned Kisses* (2010) places the gods of ancient Greece in the contemporary "environment" (Frye 33) of her readers and in this modern setting:

> Exhaustion, science and some of the newer gods of peace and goodwill had crowded the old gods off the world's stage. [...] But Ares was different. It had been a long time since anyone had seen him as the Greek god of bloodlust, glowering from beneath his plumed helmet, but men still worshipped him, whether they knew it or not [...]. Warriors no longer called for Ares by name, but they still made bloody sacrifices. And whereas Zeus once ruled the gods of Olympus, Ares meant to rule now. (11)[3]

Although Ares is not the hero of the novel, he plays a major role in it.

---

1   Since I have not read all the novels published by HM&B I am reluctant to say the company has never published such a romance, but I have yet to encounter one.

2   The novel was published under the LUNA imprint whose novels are described by Harlequin as "Powerful, alluring, mythic, elemental—magical". LUNA was launched in January 2004 with the publication of Mercedes Lackey's *The Fairy Godmother*. These novels are not romances according to the strict RWA definition since they do not feature "a central love story" but rather, as stated in the guidelines for the imprint, "contain romantic subplots that enhance the main story but don't become the focus of the novel".

3   The novel was published in the Nocturne line and labelled as "Mythica: Myths that come to life and love".

The Romance Mode

The second of Frye's literary modes is (unfortunately in this context[1]) that of "romance", which Frye uses in the original sense of fictions such as medieval chivalric romances with a hero who is:

> superior in *degree* to other men and to his environment, [...] whose actions are marvellous but who is himself identified as a human being. The hero of romance moves in a world in which the ordinary laws of nature are slightly suspended: prodigies of courage and endurance, unnatural to us, are natural to him, and enchanted weapons, talking animals, terrifying ogres and witches, and talismans of miraculous power violate no rule of probability once the postulates of romance have been established. Here we have moved from myth, properly so called, into legend, folk tale, *märchen*, and their literary affiliates and derivatives. (33)

HM&B has published romances "in which the ordinary laws of nature are slightly suspended" and which have as protagonists creatures such as ghosts, vampires and shapeshifters. These fit into the 'romance' mode. In Rita Clay Estrada's *The Ivory Key* (1987), for example, the "ordinary laws of nature" concerning bolts of lightning are "slightly suspended" in order to ensure that the central couple achieve the required happy ending. The presence of a ghost is also an indication that the novel is set "in a world in which the ordinary laws of nature are slightly suspended".[2] The romantic relationship between the ghost and Hope, a modern woman who has been explor-

---

1   When Frye's mode is meant, 'romance' will have scare quotes to remind readers of its variant meaning.

2   George Paizis suggests that "following Hollywood's foray into love and the supernatural, ghosts suddenly became acceptable; the late 1980s films featuring love and babies opened up a narrative pathway previously thought to be closed" (*Love* 32). The ghost hero in *The Ivory Key* was certainly deemed an innovation when the novel was published. Diane M. Calhoun-French reports that the editors of the 1987 Harlequin edition of the novel "question whether their readers will accept its 'one extraordinary element [...]'" (100) and Mills & Boon's 1992 UK edition included a questionnaire in which it was stated that "The storyline of this book was slightly different from other books in our Temptation series because it featured a ghost as the hero, we would like to know what you think about it".

ing the spot where the ghost is trapped, develops after she is "thrown to the earth by the electrical power of the thunderbolt" (21). Having recovered unharmed, she can see the ghost-hero, who informs her that she resembles Faith, the woman he loved during his lifetime, and also tells her that her "soul was part of Faith's. The part that had to grow as a woman and as a human" (195). As Hope discovers more about the ghost's past, he fades and eventually disappears. Soon afterwards another "bolt of lightning" (219) strikes, this time in the vicinity of a modern man who physically resembles the ghost. Instead of leaving him "fried to a crisp" (219) as Hope feared it would, the electricity seems to effect some kind of merger between the ghost and the man, as evidenced by the fact that the latter begins to whistle "an old French lullaby" (219).

The Nocturne line of paranormal romances was launched in 2006 (Torstar, *2006 Annual Report*, 15) and the guidelines at eHarlequin stated that when writing a novel in this line "The author must be able to set up a unique existence for the characters, with its own set of rules and mythologies. We are looking for stories of vampires, shape-shifters, werewolves, psychic powers, etc. set in contemporary times".[1] Sometimes both protagonists are non-human, as in Lori Devoti's *Wild Hunt* (2008) which features a part-Valkyrie, part-Norn heroine and a hellhound hero, but it is not unusual for at least one of the protagonists to be "identified as a human being", as in Kathleen Korbel's *Dangerous Temptation* (2006) in which Zeke, "a trained and experienced field anthropologist whose specialty was North American Indian tribes" (11), finds himself in Ireland, falling in love with a fairy.[2] Romances of this kind may also occasionally be found in other

---

1   In launching the line Harlequin must have had an eye to the soaring sales figures for paranormal romances: "Nearly 20% of all romance novels sold in 2005 had paranormal story lines, compared with 14% in 2004, according to Romance Writers of America figures" (Memmott). Many paranormal romances were also published in the earlier Silhouette Shadows line, which was in existence from 1993 to 1996.

2   Nuala the fairy would, however, argue that she too is human: "We call you mortals. Not human. We're human ourselves, after all [...] we weren't always faerie" (46), and Zeke learns that thanks to his "great-great-gran who was a witchy woman" (132) he himself is part fairy "no matter how diluted the blood [...] with those bright green eyes of yours, you can't deny us that" (132).
    Devoti describes Norns as "the keepers of the fates, delivering a destiny to

Harlequin imprints. Gena Showalter's *The Nymph King* (2007), for example, was published under the HQN imprint and features a human heroine and a hero who is a male nymph living in Atlantis, "city of the gods' finest creations. Home to nymphs, vampires, demons and many others" (64).

One can also find HM&Bs whose human protagonists have paranormal abilities. Whether or not this aspect of a novel will, on its own, lead readers to conclude that the author has set her tale "in a world in which the ordinary laws of nature are slightly suspended" doubtless depends on each individual's opinion of "psychic phenomena, or psi, as I'm told it's called in studies, […] clairvoyance, parapsychology, ESP, palmistry, telepathy and spiritualism" (Roberts 417). These are the subject matter of the documentary being produced by the hero of Nora Roberts's *Mind over Matter* (1987). One of the contributors explains that even those who believe in such phenomena may differ in the extent to which they consider those who possess such abilities to be "superior in *degree* to other men" (Frye 33):

> "Can anyone do this?"
> "That's something that's still being researched. There are some who feel ESP can be learned. Others believe psychics are born. My own opinion falls in between."
> "Can you explain?"
> "I think every one of us has certain talents or abilities, and the degree to which they're developed and used depends on the individual. It's possible to block these abilities. It's more usual, I think, to simply ignore them so that they never come into question." (Roberts 452)

When assessed in this way, paranormal talent would not be deemed to involve the suspension of "the ordinary laws of nature" (Frye 33) and the novel, which contains a heroine with paranormal abilities, can therefore be assigned to the third of Frye's literary modes.

---

a child at birth" (23) and Valkyries as beings who "were created to attract men fallen in battle, to make their transition from warrior to resident of Valhalla a smooth one" (25). Devoti's hellhounds are shapeshifters who usually look human but not infrequently shift into their "dog form" (33).

The High-Mimetic Mode

This third literary mode is the "high mimetic" (34), in which the hero is:

> superior in degree to other men but not to his natural environment, the hero is a leader. He has authority, passions, and powers of expression far greater than ours, but what he does is subject both to social criticism and to the order of nature. This is the hero of the *high mimetic* mode, of most epic and tragedy. (Frye 33–4)

He has also predominated in HM&B romances thanks to Charles Boon, one of the founders of Mills & Boon, who:

> set down a few ground rules for his authors. Some have survived, and were passed down through the years in the firm [...]. The 'Alphaman' was based on what Alan Boon[1] referred to as a 'law of nature': that the female of any species will be most intensely attracted to the strongest male of the species, or the Alpha. (McAleer, *Passion's Fortune* 149–50)

Today the 'Alpha' can still be found in a great many HM&B romances and a recent set of guidelines for the Harlequin Presents/Mills & Boon Modern line explicitly requested "strong, wealthy, breathtakingly charismatic alpha-heroes".

Given the title of Madeline Ker's *The Alpha Male* (2003), it seems appropriate to take the hero of this novel, Ryan Wolfe, as an example of the high mimetic HM&B alpha male. His surname seems particularly apt given that:

> The popularity of "alpha male" in common parlance suggests that men are seen as sharing the canine genetic imperative for dominance behaviors. "Alpha" was originally used in early twentieth-century studies of animal behavior to refer to the dominant individuals in rigidly hierarchical animal societies, such as some types of insects and, in later work, large mam-

---

1   Alan Boon (1913–2000) was one of Charles Boon's three sons, all of whom followed him into the family firm.

mals like primates and wolves. (Schell 113)

Ker's Mr Wolfe is undoubtedly a dominant male: "Ryan was so certain of everything he did, driving down the rails of life like a locomotive, pulling everything and everyone behind his power and authority" (48). In Frye's terms he is "a leader" (34), and his "larger-than-life presence" (Ker 53), "crackling energy and sense of purpose, his formidable intelligence, his extraordinary way of looking at the world" (80) all combine to make him "superior in degree to other men" (Frye 33). One of his speeches to Penny, the heroine of the novel and "the great love of my life" (70):

> you don't know what it's like to desire another person with such intensity that their body becomes a whole world to you. A world whose landscape you live in, whose tastes and smells you yearn for, every waking minute. A world you can never forget, no matter how much time passes, no matter how much distance comes between, no matter how many sad things happen. (36)

may serve as a demonstration that he also has "passions [...] far greater than ours" (Frye 34).

The alpha male's physical appearance is usually as exceptional as his "authority, passions, and powers of expression" (Frye 34). Daphne Watson, after reading a selection of Mills & Boon novels, observed that they:

> insist on the superiority of these protagonists over mere mortals who exist in a real world. Not one of the heroes and heroines in the texts I have read is anything but extravagantly beautiful and desirable; no place here for the size 16 lady or the chap with the receding hairline and incipient paunch. (83)

Although one can, in fact, find plain heroines in HM&Bs, alpha heroes do tend to be set apart from other men by their "extravagantly beautiful and desirable" bodies. Ryan Wolfe's is "beautiful" (68), "tall and rangy" (15) with "broad shoulders" (22), a "magnificent [...] chest" (37), "strong arms" (27), and "strong yet sensitive hands" (31). The "sheer physical beauty" (Ker 80) of a hero such as Ryan Wolfe is not, however, simply "an ideal of masculine beauty, [...] beauty here is the equivalent of physical strength, and physical strength itself becomes a sign of something more, a definition of authentic virility as a power that is always scarcely contained" (J. Cook 155).[1]

Another common attribute of the alpha male is wealth, although not all alpha males are immensely rich. Jan Cohn argues that this is not "an added-on value; his wealth, his property and economic power, are basic attributes of his masculinity, a principal source of his virile attractiveness" (127) because "the hero's economic power [...] supplies additional energy to his sexual power, as if his houses and cars [...] are metaphors for or manifestations of his sexual allure" (154). Strong support for this reading of the hero's property is provided by Ryan Wolfe's "steel-grey sports car, sleek and obviously very expensive" (12). When it is spotted by Ariadne, one of Penny's female workmates, she exclaims:

> 'Look at that car! My God! Sex on wheels!'
> 'It's just a car, Ariadne,' Penny replied wearily.
> 'I'm not talking about the car, baby.' She watched as the sports car accelerated away, then turned to Penny with bright eyes. 'I never met anyone who was truly magnetic before. But that man is! [...]' (22–3)

The confusion as to whether the phrase "Sex on wheels" describes the hero or his car demonstrates the ease with which the latter can function as a symbol of the former's "sexual allure" (Cohn 154).

The presence of an alpha-male hero such as Ryan Wolfe is more than sufficient grounds on which to classify a romance as high mimetic but his female counterpart may also have high-mimetic attributes. Penny Wellcome, for instance, is "beautiful" (47): in Ryan's opinion she is "lovelier than any movie star, more enchanting than any of them" (96) and when they dine at Claridge's "Even in this exclusive setting, they were a couple handsome enough to attract every eye in the room" (88). She is also an artist whose paintings and sculptures are, in Ryan's opinion, "very good" (31). She has

---

1   For a more detailed reading of the bodies of romance protagonists, see Vivanco and Kramer.

"always had a gift for flowers and décor [...]. Florists, restaurants, agencies were all crying out for work as good as hers" (79–80) and when she got "the job of doing the flowers" (48) for a period film, she soon made herself "essential to every shot, adding the inspired touches that brought the sets to life" (48). In a more domestic setting it "was in her blood to arrange flowers and dinners and parties, and make sure everything was as graceful as she could make it" (95–6). Her surname, Wellcome, seems particularly apt since she has a personality which makes her ideally suited for "the role he [Ryan] had planned for her. Playing gracious hostess to his party, using her beauty and charm to achieve his aims, working in harmony with him to give his friends a happy time" (128). She is, in fact, a high-mimetic "domestic goddess" (180), as superior to other women as Ryan is to other men, and although they do not move "in a world in which the ordinary laws of nature are slightly suspended" (Frye 33), they do end the novel firmly established "at the centre of a glittering world of celebrities and big shots" (48).

The Low-Mimetic Mode

By contrast, the hero of the fourth literary mode, which Frye labels the "low mimetic", is:

> superior neither to other men nor to his environment, the hero is one of us: we respond to a sense of his common humanity, and demand from the poet the same canons of probability that we find in our own experience. This gives us the hero of the *low mimetic* mode, of most comedy and of realistic fiction. (34)

Lynne Hapgood has observed that Sophie Cole's *A Wardour Street Idyll* (1910), *A London Posy* (1917) and *Daffodil Alley* (1926) offer the reader:

> a realistic narrative of the daily and the familiar, enhanced and retextured by the individual's place in her own history and in the wider, older history of London's vast community. By downplaying the drama of events and moments of passion in individual lives but reinterpreting human experience through

the cycle of human fortunes, Cole's perspective points up the enduring nature of women's values and the timelessness and commonality of human feeling. (148)

In Cole's *Mrs. Scarlot's Quaints* (1938) the recently widowed "Audrey Scarlot, aged fifty, and the mother of three children (Cynthia, aged nineteen, William, ten and Amos, six)" (7) opens a clothes shop and forms a romantic relationship with fifty-five-year-old Trafford Storyan.[1] Audrey and Trafford's love story is also a low-mimetic "realistic narrative of the daily and the familiar" which conforms to "the same canons of probability that we find in our own experience" (Frye 34). The couple first meet while Audrey is working in her shop in "The Market" and Cole creates a vivid impression of this bustling shopping area where:

> silk stockings, spring flowers, joints of meat, blouses and jumpers, crockery and ironware, beads and haberdashery, household gadgets, salads, stationery, cosmetics and patent medicines exchanged hands with a zest in the act of buying or selling which was not to be found in the big shops. (7)

and which in summer "smelt of stale cabbage leaves, hot pavements, dust, and the emanations of poor, crowded dwellings" (155).

The lovers are not high mimetic creations with "authority, passions, and powers of expression far greater than ours" (Frye 34). Although Audrey is "a very attractive woman" (153) with a "youthful appearance" (52), her attraction primarily derives from her "charm" (139); she "had no figure to speak of, she was rather pale" (139). Trafford is "rather tall and thin, and dressed in shabby tweeds. The clean-shaven face under the turned-down brim of the felt hat was lined and pallid, and the thin, close-lipped mouth might, she thought, belong to a lawyer" (25). He is, in fact, an actor who is temporarily enlisted in "the great army of the unemployed" (54) and who has become typecast: "A butler I was, a butler I am, and a butler I shall

---

1   Audrey's shop caters to "old ladies who wanted old-fashioned clothes" (13) and although she "was prepared to take them to her heart, to sympathise with their loyalty to old fashions and their readiness to sacrifice style to comfort" (18), she and Trafford refer to them as "Quaints" (60), presumably because of their quaint style of dress.

always be" (57). As Hapgood has observed, Cole has a tendency to downplay "the drama of events and moments of passion in individual lives" (148) and so, despite the fact that Audrey's new-found love for Stafford has created for her "an atmosphere of secret exultation which lent an unreal quality to the prosaic business of living" (124), there is no dramatic crisis when Trafford declares that his uncertain employment prospects make marriage impossible. She merely agrees that his "scruples do you credit. We'll just carry on as we are, and have good times together as pals" (134) and they are soon laughing once more. After the offer of "a job on the films" (230) overcomes Trafford's scruples, the two lovers, neither of whom are "governed by motives of caution and prudence" (7), decide "to have the honeymoon first, and get married by licence as soon as possible after we come back" (230). Cole does not directly relate the events which take place during the honeymoon. Instead the reader is given Audrey's recollections of it:

> These few days in Paris with Trafford were the high-water mark of her life. [...] Well, she had had the experience, and now she would be quite content to settle down, with Trafford, to what, after all, was the real stuff of life, work and the routine of daily duties. Always he would be there to laugh with her, to be cared for, and in his turn, to care for her. They had had their brief apotheosis, and tomorrow they were going home to settle down to the normal conditions of work and middle age. (241–2)

Audrey thus acknowledges that the emotional intensity of these days abroad is a brief aberration, to be followed by a calmer form of happiness.

This is, then, a low-mimetic love story featuring a realistic setting and protagonists to whose "common humanity" (Frye 34) readers can respond. However, much to the dismay of the anonymous reviewer writing for Adelaide's *The Mail*, Audrey and Trafford's is not the only love-story contained in *Mrs. Scarlot's Quaints*:

> Had the author confined herself to this angle and enlarged it, she could have produced a delightful tale [...]. However,

Miss Cole chose to bring in Cynthia Scarlot, a 19-year-old daughter, and her love for a man who had already had a rather sordid affair with a young woman. To cap it all she also introduces a mysterious mansion and an old master which carries with it a curse.

All these things absolutely spoil the book. Miss Cole writes well and her sketches of Mrs. Scarlot, her two younger children, William and Amos, and Albert, the factotum at the mysterious mansion, are brilliant. ("How Writer")

The first objection is the most easily dismissed, from a literary critical perspective: we are concerned here with modes, not morals. The hint of the paranormal, however, is a different matter. Frye has observed that:

In a true myth there can obviously be no consistent distinction between ghosts and living beings. In romance we have real human beings, and consequently ghosts are in a separate category, but in a romance a ghost as a rule is merely one more character: he causes little surprise because his appearance is no more marvellous than many other events. In high mimetic, where we are within the order of nature, a ghost is relatively easy to introduce because the plane of experience is above our own, but when he appears he is an awful and mysterious being from what is perceptibly another world. In low mimetic, ghosts have been [...] almost entirely confined to a separate category of "ghost stories." In ordinary low mimetic fiction they are inadmissible. (50)

The isolated Revenant Manor is located two and a half miles from Revenant's Green and when Gilbert drives Cynthia there he explains that 'revenant' is "the French for one who returns after a long absence—in fact a ghost" (36). It is unclear, however, whether the Manor is really haunted or if the curse associated with the painting of Lady Ursula, namely that "the person who sends her away from it will die a horrible death within three months" (43), is no more than a superstition. Iris, who reads "trashy novels from the local library" (150), certainly gets "it into her head there's a curse on the place. Something she read in one of those mangy novels, I expect. Says there'll never be any luck for any of us so long as that old picture remains" (151). Initially the portrait remains because Totfield, who owns it, has been frightened by the original superstition and is "as afraid to part with it as Iris is anxious to get rid of it" (151). Eventually, however, at Iris's insistence, the portrait is removed from Revenant Manor and Iris, who "has a very poor physique, no stamina to stand any unusual strain" (222), dies shortly after. This could be taken as proof that the original tradition concerning the portrait of Lady Ursula was correct. On the other hand, Gilbert at one point states that "superstition's a rum thing, and coincidence has a nasty way of stepping in to bolster it up" (89) and he later insists that "the idea that getting rid of it brought us bad luck is absurd. We all know the queer part coincidence plays in the affairs of human beings, and coincidence is responsible for the thrill of some of the best ghost stories" (208–09). It is possible, then, that Cole was seeking to combine in one novel an ordinary, low-mimetic love story with the kind of low-mimetic ghost story which creates a "thrill" precisely because the reader becomes unsettled by the various coincidences and begins to wonder whether they could, after all, have been caused by "an awful and mysterious being from what is perceptibly another world" (Frye 50) and another literary mode.

It would appear that certain settings lend themselves more easily to the low-mimetic mode than others: "The Market" is filled with everyday sights, sounds, and smells; romantic Paris is an ideal location for a honeymoon but not for "the real stuff of life, work and the routine of daily duties" (241) and Revenant Manor, which is associated with "a superstition that might have been a relic of the medieval ignorance that burnt witches" (182), is disturbingly uncanny. As the reference to "medieval ignorance" suggests, certain historical periods are closer to "our own experience" (Frye 34) than others, and chronological distance may make it more difficult for us to sense the characters' "common humanity" (Frye 34).

Philippa Gregory has written rather scathingly that:

> a good historical novel includes characters whose basic humanity engages our empathy, and convincing circumstances that remind us that the past is, indeed, another country.

> This is the opposite of romance fiction, which uses historical
> settings [...] because it depends on the imaginary glamour of
> the past. (vii)

Polly Forrester's *Jewel Under Siege* (1990), however, is a historical
romance which features a low-mimetic hero and heroine to whose
"common humanity" (Frye 34) we respond. The back-cover copy of
the novel emphasises the exciting setting of the novel, "Constantino-
ple, 1097—the Crusaders were at the gate—but refused admittance
to the besieged city!", yet the crisis is defused by negotiation, and
without the intervention of either of the protagonists. Similarly, despite the way in which the Byzantine heroine's peaceful existence is
"overtaken by events" (24) of a somewhat dramatic nature when she
is dragged into some bushes by Emil Selest, an injured crusader and
the hero of the novel, she soon realises that far from being a "desper-
ate terrorist", he is "More like a child caught stealing apples [...] with
his downcast face and sudden loss of bravado" (7). Although she is
sure that crusaders "had funny ways" (5), she responds to his "common humanity" (Frye 34) and offers him food, shelter and medical
attention because "In a score of years her own Milo might be in such
a position. Who was this Crusader but some other mother's son?" (9).

Unlike his Alphaman leader, Godfrey, Duke of Lorraine, who is
"a vision of heroism [...]. Tall and fair with eyes of ice, this was
undoubtedly a leader of men" (30), Emil is merely "a tall young man,
painfully thin with features worn by famine and war" (6), albeit with
the "remnants of striking good looks" (15). Elena, the heroine, is
introduced to the reader in a rather prosaic paragraph:

> At least the rain had stopped. There was nothing worse than a
> wet Easter, but now the sky was clearing nicely. Elena swept
> a wrap about her shoulders and slipped out into the garden
> through the dining-room doors. (5)

These very ordinary details and actions which reflect "the same canons of probability that we find in our own experience" (Frye 34) seem
to encourage the reader to identify Elena as "one of us" (Frye 34)
and since Frye has stated that "The organizing low mimetic ideas
seem to be genesis and work" (154), it is evident that Elena's prima-

ry concerns are low-mimetic ones: "Business at the glassworks was good and this evening little Milo was already fast asleep upstairs" (5). Work, or rather the lack of it, was Emil's motive for joining the crusade. His "entire village was starving" (147) and when he and his brothers sought employment elsewhere they "found that you can't get a decent job without being in a guild, and you can't enter a guild without being in a decent job" (148), so "When the priests preached that we should all go East for Christ, I saw an opportunity. […] When I got to the Holy Land I was going to get a good big plot of land, stock it with animals and then send for all my family" (149).

The Ironic Mode

The fifth and last of Frye's literary modes is the ironic, in which the protagonist is:

> inferior in power or intelligence to ourselves, so that we have the sense of looking down on a scene of bondage, frustration, or absurdity […]. This is still true when the reader feels that he is or might be in the same situation, as the situation is being judged by the norms of a greater freedom. (34)

Romance novels written in the ironic mode are rare; according to George Paizis the HM&B 'Tradition' has "allowed humour but no irony—or where there was irony, it was directed towards the heroine by an arrogant hero" ("Category" 143).

Kristan Higgins's *Catch of the Day* (2007), published under HM&B's HQN imprint, is a work in the ironic mode which won the RWA's 2008 RITA award for Best Contemporary Single Title Romance. It could, however, perhaps also be classified as 'chick lit', a sub-genre in which, it has been claimed, "irony is the dominant voice" (Paizis, "Category" 143). Certainly its heroine, Maggie, like the "typical chick-lit protagonist is […] flawed, eliciting readers' compassion and identification simultaneously" (Ferriss and Young 3–4), and as she narrates episodes from "the joke book that makes up my love life" (Higgins 10) she resembles the many chick-lit heroines who "deploy self-deprecating humor that not only entertains but also leads readers to believe they are fallible—like them" (Ferriss and

Young 4). As a result, when Maggie finds herself in embarrassing situations which cause her small home town of "Gideon's Cove, Maine, population 1,407" (Higgins 10) to "have a good laugh over me" (333), the reader of *Catch of the Day* feels she "is or might be in the same situation" (Frye 34), while also having "the sense of looking down on a scene of bondage, frustration, or absurdity" (Frye 34).

Political irony and satire are largely absent from HM&Bs. Some indications of why this is the case are provided by Jennifer Crusie's *Strange Bedpersons* (1994), a romance in the ironic mode. One of its secondary characters, "Norbert Nolan Welch, the great American author" (28), has written a political satire, *After the Ever After*, which reworks the story of Cinderella in order to mock left-wing liberals who believe life is "just a fairy tale where everybody is good and honest and things turn out happily ever after" (106). Welch's *After the Ever After* expresses his "doubts about those happily-ever-afters" (106) and thus poses an implicit challenge to all forms of fiction that conclude in this way. This, of course, includes HM&B romances, which all end on an optimistic note that affirms the possibility of life-long love and happiness. Jennifer Crusie's heroine, Tess Newhart, criticises Welch's novel and implicitly assumes the role of editor: "that book is too biased [...], it's mean [...]. You've got to fix it" (243). *After the Ever After* is clearly a politically partisan novel and in response to Tess's demand that he should "rethink that book and make it balanced" (243) Welch snaps back that "It's satire, damn it. It's not supposed to be balanced" (243). HM&Bs, by contrast, generally eschew political controversy. As Alan Boon wrote in 1949, "we regard ourselves [...] as publishers of entertaining novels [...]. As a minor line of policy, we have sought to avoid 'red-rag' controversial problems—two of which traditionally are politics and religion" (McAleer, *Passion's Fortune* 190).

The advice offered by Leslie Wainger in her *Writing a Romance Novel for Dummies* (2004) suggests that this continues to be HM&B's attitude to politics. In 2004 Wainger was "an executive editor for Harlequin/Silhouette" (Wainger iii) and she urged would-be romance authors:

Don't use your book as a soapbox. Romance novels are popular because they entertain readers and because they offer an escape from real life into a world of romantic fantasy. So don't use your book as a pulpit from which to preach your views on politics, world peace, ecology, the economy, or anything else. (135)

Granting that the "chief distinction between irony and satire is that satire is militant irony: its moral norms are relatively clear, and it assumes standards against which the grotesque and absurd are measured" (Frye 223), it seems likely that editors such as Wainger would consider satire to be a form of "preaching".[1]

Strange Bedpersons itself is a rare example of an HM&B romance which deploys political irony. It does so, however, in a manner that avoids "preaching" on either side of the political spectrum; it is, in fact, so "balanced" that it mocks both and, in the process, strips the

---

1 While Wainger writes that "Your characters are welcome to have opinions of their own" (135), this advice, along with her statements to the effect that both heroes and heroines should be "ethical" (19), must be understood in the context of the company's ethos and history. For many years the protagonists' opinions and ethics have been shaped by what HM&B has believed will be acceptable in its various markets:

> In November 1939 a Mills & Boon novel, *How Strong Is Your Love?* by Barbara Hedworth, made the Irish Government's list of prohibited books, on the grounds that it 'advocate[d] the unnatural prevention of conception', a provision of the 1929 Censorship of Publications Act. [...] Mills & Boon [...] would [...] learn a lesson here, as in later years the fear of offending the Irish—and jeopardizing sales in the lucrative Irish market—would become a cornerstone of editorial policy. (McAleer, *Passion's Fortune* 168)

In more recent decades protagonists' ethics may be influenced by the line in which they are to appear. The guidelines for the Steeple Hill Love Inspired line, for example, state quite clearly that:

> The stories may not include alcohol consumption by Christian characters, card playing, gambling or games of chance (including raffles), explicit scatological terms, hero and heroine remaining overnight together alone, Halloween celebrations, magic, or the mention of intimate body parts. Lying is also problematic in the CBA [Christian Booksellers Association] market and characters who are Christian should avoid lying or deceiving others. (Harlequin)

HM&Bs, then, are not apolitical if one considers the personal to be political. Peter Darbyshire, for example, argues that "Harlequin romances allow their readers to experience the ideal rewards of capitalism, insofar as the novels are usually fantasies of financial empowerment as much as they are romantic fantasies".

protagonists of their dignity. According to Frye, "the low mimetic is one step more heroic than the ironic, and [...] low mimetic reticence has the effect of making its characters, on the average, more heroic, or at least more dignified, than the characters in ironic fiction" (50). Representing left-wing politics, Tess, "a Democrat" (216) and "a feminist" (15), is "involved in all those censorship protests" (31) and has taken "pictures of johns' license plates to stop prostitution" (92). This "bleeding-heart liberal flake" (95) with a resistance to "getting conventional" (179) is "tactless and undignified and spontaneous and out of control" (31) and she rebels against Nick's attempts to make her "all dignified and cold" (170). Nick, the hero, represents right-wing politics as he is "a Republican lawyer" (12). He is also "a power-hungry rat" (9) who not infrequently stoops to insincerity and even sycophancy in the pursuit of his goals. Although Nick is convinced that "ambition [...] was good" (29), he acknowledges a "pathetic, deep-seated, naked ambition, which was bad and which he was riddled with. He knew it was bad because it made him look anxious and vulnerable" (29). His claims to dignity and heroic stature are further undermined by Tess:

> Tess's smile widened. "You have no dignity."
> "Not around you." Nick grinned back at her [...]. "This is why we should be together. You can save me from getting too stuffy."
> "Fine for you," Tess folded her arms and looked at him with mock skepticism. "Who's going to save me?"
> "I am," Nick said. "Hell, woman, can't you recognize a hero when you've got one in your living room?"
> "This would be you?" Tess lifted an eyebrow. (58)

The differences between these "strange [...] bedpersons" (216) ensure that throughout the novel "we have the sense of looking down on a scene of [...] absurdity" (Frye 34). This absurdity culminates in "The dinner party from hell" (216), a farcical event at which Gina, a secondary character who "put her head under the table and threw up" (229), is, in relative terms, "probably the only one of us who wasn't embarrassing" (230).

Determining Mode

Determining whether a romance is written in the high-, low-, or iron-ic mimetic mode can be complex, and decisions reached by readers will inevitably involve subjective as well as objective criteria. The critic's own beliefs, experiences and social context are likely to af-fect what she or he considers to be "authority, passions, and powers of expression far greater than ours", who "is one of us", and who is "inferior in power or intelligence to ourselves" (Frye 34). A lack of realism may be one indication that a work is straying from the low-mimetic mode, from which readers "demand [...] the same canons of probability that we find in our own experience" (34). However, as we have already seen in the context of the discussion of works in the 'romance' mode, readers may have different assessments of what constitutes reality and what indicates a suspension of "the ordinary laws of nature" (33). Similarly, although ghosts are "inadmissible" in "ordinary low mimetic fiction" they can and do appear in the low-mimetic mode in the "separate category of 'ghost stories'"(50).

Some HM&B lines are explicitly described as realistic: in 1991 one letter to readers informed them that "Silhouette Special Editions [...] were the first of their kind and continue to feature realistic stories with heightened romantic tension" (Nicholls 2), and Harlequin's guidelines for its Superromance line begin by stating *"Harlequin Superromance—romance has never felt more real!"*[1] Given that

---

1 Although by 1991 all Silhouette romances had been published by Harlequin for a number of years, Silhouette was not originally an HM&B imprint. Rather, it was "created to compete with Harlequin after the Toronto publisher fired Simon & Schuster's Pocket Books as its U.S. distributor in 1979. [...] The Silhouette Books division was created, [...] and the first Silhouette Romance titles appeared in May 1980" (Guiley 162). Following Silhouette's launch

Reader response [...] clued in the editors that there was a waiting and ready market for more sophisticated romances. Given the changes in society wrought by women's lib and sexual lib, the heroine who was pure as driven snow didn't seem plausible to many readers. [...] "It was important to them to read stories about people they could identify with, so we made some immediate changes. Silhouette heroines were not going to be the eighteen- and nineteen-year-old heroines you found in Harlequins but would be more career-oriented, older and better educated. [...] a lot of changes have taken place in society and in day-to-day living, and we tried to incorporate some of those changes and issues into our next line, Special Edition (launched in

Superromances are expected to feature "today's woman in today's world" and "Secondary characters, situations and subplots should all be [...] believable", the guidelines would appear to "demand [...] the same canons of probability that we find in our own experience" (Frye 34). There are varying degrees of realism, however, and realism in one area of a romance—the issues which form the basis of the plot, the precise nature of the optimistic ending, or details related to the setting—are neither a guarantee of realism in all other areas nor a certain indication that the protagonists will be low-mimetic in nature.

Realism: Settings and Details

When Janice A. Radway interviewed a group of romance readers in the early 1980s:

> All of the [...] women cited the educational value of romances in discussion as other readers apparently have when questioned by researchers for Harlequin, Fawcett, and Silhouette. Romance editors are all very aware of the romance reader's penchant for geographical and historical accuracy. (108)

Romance authors, for their part, often express a commitment to accuracy: when Kate Walker interviewed a number of her fellow HM&B authors for her 2008 guide to romance writing, Nicola Cornick stated that HM&B historical romances must be "set against a richly drawn and historically accurate backdrop" (Walker, *12 Point Guide* 204), Kate Hardy observed that in medical romances "The medical detail must be accurate" (Walker 214), and Anne McAllister, who writes for the Modern/Presents line, revealed that she does "a lot of research. I don't want to get things wrong, and I want my characters to operate out of a realistic world" (Walker 231). Paula Marshall, in an author's note which introduces *The Beckoning Dream* (1997), writes that "This novel, like all of mine, is firmly based on fact" (7). Her claim

---

February 1982). Special Editions [...] touched upon topics previously taboo in contemporary romances, such as women getting out of abusive marriages and making a new life for themselves. [...] Another major change we made in Special Edition was in the characters. The heroine was twenty-eight or thirty, maybe even in her early forties, and there wasn't a big age disparity between her and the hero [...]" Karen [Solem] says. (Guiley 163)

to factual accuracy is bolstered by the details she gives concerning the life of Aphra Behn, to whom the novel is dedicated. Marshall relates that Behn was "mocked [...] for having claimed that, had the Government heeded her report, a major disaster for the British Navy would have been avoided. Three hundred years later, Aphra's claim was vindicated when her letter, giving details of the proposed attack, was discovered in the State Papers" (7).[1] The plot of Marshall's novel is heavily based on this episode in Behn's life: her heroine is a Restoration-period playwright turned spy who sends her superiors "details of the Dutch plan to raid Sheerness and sail up the Medway" (202), which they ignore. One may wonder if Marshall, writing for a publisher whose novels are often believed to lack realism, empathised with Behn, whose claim to truth was "mocked" but later vindicated.[2]

Reality and accuracy in one area can, however, be offset by other elements which distance a work from the low mimetic. Marshall's setting and the details of her plot may be realistic, but her hero and heroine are obviously "superior in degree" (Frye 33) to most readers and it is this which permits the classification of the novel as high mimetic. Similarly, Sandra Marton does:

> lots of research, a combination of travel that features on-the-spot visits during which my husband takes endless photos and I try to speak with as many people as possible; library research; and, increasingly, research that I do online. Not only can I 'see' locations online, I can also contact specialists in whatever fields I need. (Walker, *12 Point Guide* 228)

---

1   According to Mary Ann O'Donnell, "Behn's last document from the Flanders mission preserved in the Public Record Office, dated 26 December 1666, pleads for permission and money to return to London. She had warned the Home Office of the Dutch intention to attack the fleet in the Thames, a warning that was dismissed, and her mission was a failure" (4).

2   Marshall concludes by adding that "In the same way, her right to be seen as the mother of the English novel and as the writer of a number of witty and actable plays was also derided until the Sixties of the present century, when her work was looked at with fresh eyes" (7). In describing Behn as "the mother of the English novel" Marshall appears to be claiming some literary kinship with her, and given that romance novels have also been much "derided" one may wonder whether Marshall had hopes that one day her work would also be "looked at with fresh eyes".

Yet when she was asked to "define the particular features" of the Modern/Presents line, Marton responded "Passion, fantasy and emotion" (Walker 227). The medical line, too, seeks to strike a balance between reality and fantasy. Romances in this line tend to include considerable detail about medical diagnoses and treatments and Gunther Kress suggests that one function of "the appearance of medical discourse" in medical romances is that of "giving 'authenticity'" (139) to these texts. However, these novels' commitment to reality does have its limits. Brendan D. Kelly, for example, observed in the medical journal *The Lancet* that in the romances he sampled from the Medical line "There was a marked preponderance of brilliant, tall, muscular, male doctors with chiselled features, working in emergency medicine" (1482) and Kate Hardy has acknowledged that "The medical side of it does need to be dramatic" (Walker, *12 Point Guide* 215). Thus, as Paul Grescoe was informed by some Mills & Boon editors, a medical romance can be "a 'feet-on-the-ground fantasy,' if you like" (53)

Realism and the Happy Ending

Paizis has suggested that "the romantic novel [...] develops a narrative programme of struggle against those elements of reality that constitute the nightmare of existence" (*Love* 177) and it is true that realism in a romance must always accommodate the requirement that the protagonists achieve an "optimistic ending" (RWA). It should not be assumed, however, that romances "are untrue to psychological reality" (Watson 82) simply because they suggest that romantic love can endure throughout a lifetime. It may be "widely believed that over time romantic love fades and that at best it evolves into a [...] companionate love, a friendship-type love" (Acevedo and Aron 59) but Bianca P. Acevedo and Arthur Aron, from Stony Brook University's Department of Psychology:

> argue that romantic love—with intensity, engagement, and sexual interest—can last. Although it does not usually include the obsessional qualities of early stage love, it does not inevitably die out or at best turn into companionate love—a

warm, less intense love, devoid of attraction and sexual desire. (Acevedo and Aron 59)

In more recent research they, with Fisher and Brown, used functional
magnetic resonance imaging to scan the brains of "a group of long-
term happily married, sexually monogamous individuals reporting
intense romantic love for their partner" and concluded that "Individuals in long-term romantic love showed patterns of neural activity similar to those in early-stage romantic love" but "in line with
behavioral observations suggesting that one key distinction between
romantic love in its early and later stages is greater calm associated
with the latter."

The endings of HM&Bs vary in the levels of "optimism" they
display, and some explicitly acknowledge that the lovers will have
to cope with ongoing difficulties and sorrows. In Jessica Hart's
Promoted: to Wife and Mother (2008), for example, the hero and
heroine are in their forties, with heavy family responsibilities
which include the heroine's mother who is "slithering and sliding
unstoppably into dementia" (177). There can be no quick or painless
resolution to their problems so, as the hero acknowledges, their future
"won't be perfect, Perdita. It will be hard. There aren't going to be
any magic solutions, you were right about that. Your mother isn't
going to get better. The kids aren't going to suddenly become polite
and helpful and bored with partying" (183). Nor are there guarantees
of perfect happiness for the heroine of Maggie Kingsley's *A Wife
Worth Waiting For* (2008). She has been in remission from Hodgkin's
lymphoma for:

'Four years.'
'You do know if you get to five years then the chances of it
never coming back are good?' he said, and she nodded.
'But they're not one hundred per cent certain, Hugh. I might
live to be a little old lady of ninety-seven. I might die next
year.' (114)

A more immediate danger overshadows the war-time wedding of Liza
Deane and Squadron Leader Phil Raymond in Dorothy Critchlow's
Beware of Dreams (1942). It is mentioned at the end of the novel,

after Phil has announced that:

> "I'm afraid our honeymoon will have to go, Liza [...]. I've been recalled. At least, I've got to report to London headquarters to-morrow [...] The King of the Belgians has capitulated. [...] They might fight on for a day or two ... I don't know. After that—"
>
> "But—your men, Phil! Our men—out there!"
>
> "It'll be pretty grim for them—for all of us. It depends on France—" (187)

By the time the novel was published, France had fallen. Critchlow's early readers would have known that, as Phil predicts, "We'll go on fighting, Liza, if we have to do it alone" (188), but with the war still raging they, like Liza and Phil, would have been facing an uncertain future. Readers of Ann Hulme's *The Emperor's Dragoon* (1983) have the benefit of hindsight and therefore know that the army in which this hero serves will eventually be defeated at the Battle of Waterloo. The novel, however, concludes some years prior to that defeat, and Léon faces the future with the words "Only God knows how much time we have. Perhaps it is all written somewhere in some great book which we cannot read" (183). Where fictional characters are concerned, the author takes the place of God, but the ultimate fates of protagonists are rarely revealed to the readers of HM&B books; we can be sure, however, that a true "happily ever after" ending is only possible for the immortal protagonists of some paranormal romances.

Death and taxes may be two certainties in most people's lives, but by the end of a romance the protagonists are highly unlikely to face impending financial ruin or ongoing economic hardship. It has been observed that:

> the novels are usually fantasies of financial empowerment as much as they are romantic fantasies. The standard Harlequin narrative, for instance, usually involves a middle-class woman's relationship with a rich, single male—usually a businessman, wealthy rancher, or male engaged in some similar occupation. The inevitable marriage at the end thus also involves a marriage into wealth, or at least improved financial security. (Darbyshire)

While it is possible to find both heroines who are wealthier than their heroes, and protagonists who are not rich, HM&B romances rarely if ever conclude with the protagonists living together in extreme poverty. Jo Ann Algermissen's *Would You Marry Me Anyway?* (1991) does end with the hero "in debt up to my ears" (250) and the heroine unsure if she is "out of a job" (250), but it seems highly unlikely they will find themselves destitute since both of them are guaranteed employment in her family's construction business. This in itself is no guarantee of financial security given the cyclical nature of the industry: "Construction work is one monstrous roller coaster ride" (175). Nonetheless, a note of optimism is achieved when the heroine's mother, who knows from first-hand experience that "It isn't easy trying to raise a family while the bill collectors are pestering you on the phone" (173), finally admits that "The good times will by far outmeasure the hard times if you truly love each other" (246).

Even though there are romances which strive to be realistic, the constraints of the form ensure that they cannot depict the full range of possible realistic outcomes for their protagonists. Any ending which was realistic but involved the protagonists falling out of love with each other, or facing imminent and permanent separation for other reasons, would immediately propel the novel out of the contemporary commercial niche of the HM&B romance even if it remained within the more broadly defined class of romantic fiction. Thus, although an individual romance may be deemed relatively realistic, a collection of such novels will tend to seem less so. This is perhaps the reason why Kathleen Gilles Seidel, whose romances "offer a level of detail about work hours, grocery shopping, and baby sitters' arrival times that, upon rereading, astonishes even me" (217), would not claim "that my books are realistic. In the universe of my fiction, having professional skills always guarantees professional success, a guarantee that life doesn't offer" (218). Even in that universe, however, the characters act as though they have no awareness of the guarantees the author and HM&B's conventions make to the reader and therefore the existence of such an extra-textual guarantee does not in itself render any individual romance unrealistic.

Realism: Issues

The guarantee of an "optimistic ending" (RWA) would, however, ensure that even if an HM&B author were to attempt to "include a bleak analysis of deprivation, mass cyclical unemployment and the resort to fascism" of the kind to be found in "realist works" (Fowler 139), it could not end on a "bleak" note or foretell a less than optimistic future for the novel's protagonists. Nonetheless, despite this constraint and although it has been argued that "Romances will never become 'problem novels' or 'social criticism' novels because they are read for escape and entertainment" (Jensen 64), HM&Bs do sometimes depict uncomfortable realities. As Paizis has observed, "The romance is not the social novel; nevertheless it has begun the exploration of issues of concern to women of the day: single motherhood, depression, widowhood, wife-beating, infertility, incest, alcoholism" (*Love* 32).

Ida Cook, who wrote for Mills & Boon under the name Mary Burchell, was concerned for refugees and "displaced persons". Before the outbreak of the Second World War she and her sister Louise:

> out of the first profits of the Mary Burchell books [...] financed our own amateur organization for getting people out of Hitler's Germany; from then until ten days before war broke out, we traveled back and forth between England and Germany, getting out what we called our "cases" and starting them on new lives. (Burchell, "Mary" 171)

After the war Ida and Louise:

> joined the Adoption Committee for Aid to Displaced Persons [...]. Our special interest covered the camps for non-German refugees in Germany [...] we did sometimes go out to visit our camp, and so we came to know some of our cases personally [...]. The first time we went [...] we found that our particular camp was housed in a huge barracks. Inevitably, the accommodation consisted of large rooms; and in each of these rooms lived four, six, sometimes eight families [...]. If you wanted a bit of privacy, you put up a blanket or a piece of cardboard. (I. Cook 267–8)

This interest of Ida's found its way into her fiction: as the blurb of her *Love is My Reason* (1957) declares, "Mary Burchell's sympathy for the victims of war, so often shown in a practical way in her life, gives a specially warm interest to this novel" (1). Anya, its heroine, is one of those "non-German refugees in Germany" living with a number of others in "a big room [...] One divides it with blankets or a cupboard or some cardboard" (Burchell, *Love* 9) in "a barracks" (7) which serves as "a camp [...] for displaced persons" (7).

The real displaced persons known to Ida Cook "thought they were the forgotten people, until World Refugee Year came" (I. Cook 268) in 1959–60.[1] It seems reasonable to assume that she hoped *Love is My Reason*, published in 1957, would raise awareness of, and sympathy for, the plight of this "vast number of featureless, rootless, indistinguishable people who shared a common lot" (Burchell, *Love* 69). Although "They were without individuality to those who dwelt in the outside world" (69), Anya is an individual from the very beginning of the novel and through her the reader, albeit via the lens of fiction, comes "to know some of our cases personally" (I. Cook 268).

Charlotte Lamb, who began writing for HM&B in the early 1970s, "produce[d] work that explored taboo areas such as child abuse and rape" (Bloom 211) and Alexandra Sellers's *Season of Storm* (1983) is a:

> SuperRomance [...] strongly critical of racial injustice. The hero of *Season of Storm*, is a Native who is fighting the Canadian government and a logging company for the restoration of his tribe's land rights. The book refers to ruthless corporate policies that place profits before people, to the short life span of Native people, to the police state mentality of the RCMP and to the pervasive racism that even the heroine is forced to acknowledge is part of her and her society. The emphasis that these exploitive relationships receive in this particular book is exceptional. (Jensen 81–2)

---

1   In 1960 Trevor Philpott, "one of the three originators of the idea for a World Refugee Year" (Philpott 17), stated that "There are refugees in Europe. [...] As I write, there are about 20,000 of them still in official camps, mainly in Germany, Austria, Italy, and Greece. About 19,000 have been in refugee camps for ten years or more" (18).

Some HM&Bs explicitly ask the reader to take action in relation to the issues they explore, and may even raise funds for charities which deal with those issues. Janice Kay Johnson, a "volunteer with a no-kill cat shelter, Purrfect Pals" (2), wrote in a letter to the readers of her *Beauty & The Beasts* (1997) that she hoped the plight of the cats in her novel would move them "to tears and smiles" (2) and:

> I hope, too, that you take my message to heart: please, please, neuter and spay your pets. And if you have the time, or just a few dollars, help your local shelters and animal rescue organizations, especially those like Purrfect Pals that don't euthanize unwanted animals. (2)

Sandra Kitt, in a letter to the readers of *For All We Know* (2008), states that "Besides the love story, the secondary subject of my book concerns a serious, life-threatening disease that is decimating African-American lives—HIV/AIDS" and an advertisement included in the book urges readers to donate to St. Jude Children's Research Hospital in order to support "the fight against childhood cancers, sickle cell disease and pediatric HIV/AIDS".

In 2004 Harlequin established Harlequin More Than Words, a "program [...] responsible for the administration of Harlequin Enterprises Ltd.'s philanthropic initiatives dedicated to the well-being of women" (Harlequin More Than Words). It aims to "Raise awareness about worthy causes that are of concern to women", "Provide financial assistance to these important charities", and "Engage employees, authors and readers and the general public in worthy causes and provide opportunities for them to make a difference". These aims are furthered through the sales of novellas (not all of which are romances) inspired by Harlequin More Than Words's chosen charities. One of these novellas is Diana Palmer's 'The Greatest Gift' (2010) which "tells the story of Sue Cobley" (125) who, in:

> 1996, just divorced from an abusive husband, evicted from their rented property and living in a borrowed car with her five children, [...] embarked on a course of action that would literally move mountains of food [...]. She didn't have to know

the statistic—over 35 million Americans, 12.6 million of them children, living with hunger or on the edge of it, according to U.S. Department of Agriculture estimates, and a staggering 96 billion pounds of food wasted each year in the United States—to be aware that there were people going hungry in her own community. (7–8)

Palmer's heroine, Mary Crandall, is a lightly fictionalised version of Sue Cobley and the novella is thus highly realistic both in terms of the central issue it tackles and in the details of its heroine's life. As one would expect in a romance, Palmer gives Mary a "bright" future (124) but this happy outcome is tempered by realism: given her background it is understandable that, rather than leap into marriage, she and her hero, Matt, will remain "best friends for a couple of years" (121). As Matt says, "It's too soon after your divorce […]. You don't really know me yet, or trust me. But I'm going to be around for a long time, and I can wait" (113).

The exploration of a serious issue, combined with the use of realistic details, can incline a novel towards the low mimetic by making it more likely that the work will offer the reader "the same canons of probability that we find in our own experience" (Frye 34). The deciding factor in determining whether or not an HM&B is in the high- or the low-mimetic mode is, however, the nature of the protagonists. The back cover blurb of the volume in which "The Greatest Gift" appears describes Sue and the other "recipients of Harlequin's More Than Words award" as "Everyday women" who have done "exceptional work". Similarly, in the introduction to the novella Sue is positioned as an ordinary woman, "no well-heeled suburbanite or high-placed executive with a mission statement and plenty of backing", although her work with Chefs to the Rescue is deemed "remarkable" (7). Mary, her fictional *alter ego*, is a low-mimetic heroine who is clearly intended to be seen as "one of us" (Frye 34). When she finds herself needing accommodation at a homeless shelter she is told that "There are a lot of nice people who ended up here" (20) because "It's the way the world is today. You can lose everything with a job" (23).[1] She is, then, just one of many

---

1   The same sentiment is repeated later in the novella by another minor character:

"nice people" who happen to have been unlucky. Similarly, she is not presented as being unique in her response to adversity, despite the fact that she is described as "an amazing person" (67) and "an inspiration to all of us" (106) who has:

> taken charge of your own life, and the lives of your children. You've organized a food rescue program to benefit needy people, you've kept the children in school and up with their homework, you've found a decent place to live and you're on your way to financial independence. (65)

Many characters in the novella engage in charity work and Bev, the manager of a homeless shelter, has followed a similar trajectory to Mary's: "I was homeless myself [...] and I ended up in a women's mission. [...] I got involved trying to better the situation of other people in trouble" (57). In addition, it becomes clear that although Mary's spirit is extremely willing, her flesh does not have powers greater than those of other mortals: she eventually collapses as a result of "palpitations [...] induced by stress" (110) and has to "give up some work" (120). Firmly low mimetic, Mary's story is that of an Everywoman figure. In both her troubles and her successes "we respond to a sense of [her] common humanity" (Frye 34).

Realism in issues explored, settings, and outcomes can, however, be found in high- as well as in low-mimetic romances. *Sea Lightning* (1979), a:

> Harlequin Romance by Linda Harrel, a Greenpeace supporter, is basically a "save the whales" romance. The heroine, an illustrator, is called to the coast of Argentina to work with the hero, a marine biologist, who is on a one-man crusade to save a whale breeding ground from heedless offshore oil drilling companies. (Jensen 64)

The novel's detailed and sympathetic descriptions of whales suggest that Harrel's attitude towards her novel is expressed in the hero's words about his own writing: "most people still seem to think of whales as monsters—vicious creatures swimming about smashing

---

"Anybody can end up homeless [...] through no fault of his or her own. It's the times we live in" (59).

boats and swallowing up latter-day Jonahs. If nothing else, I hope my book will help destroy these misconceptions which have contributed to their slaughter" (23). *Sea Lightning*, first published in 1979, certainly counters misconceptions with abundant facts about the southern right whale that Harrel appears to have drawn from Roger Payne's 'At Home with Right Whales', one of three articles in the March 1976 issue of *National Geographic* to focus on Patagonia.[1] The end-

---

1   From his research station on the coast of Patagonia's Península Valdés, Payne studied "southern right whale anatomy, acoustics, and population changes, as well as behavior" (329) and Harrel's fictional Dr Adam Ryder has been studying the "behaviour, population changes, [and] anatomy" (23) of the same species of whale from a fictional research station further down the coast of Patagonia, from which it is "a rough drive up to Peninsula Valdes" (77). There are many other indications that Harrel drew on the three *National Geographic* articles for information about Patagonia and its wildlife. Payne begins his article with an anecdote:

> I glanced out the window at the porch roof. With ominous sounds it began to part company from the house, threatening to fly off across the Patagonian desert. Shouting for help to my two colleagues [...] I dashed outside and grabbed a loosened rafter. Chris and Bernd joined me and for 20 minutes we hung on for dear life, alternately being lifted off our feet and set back on the ground as we struggled to lash the roof fast.
>   Finally we managed to run a rope from the roof to our truck and secure it. The storm abated, and we all trooped back inside. (327)

In the novel, "At one point, the roof boards groaned ominously and seemed doomed to lift off entirely. Jensa watched anxiously as the two men, resorting to crawling on their hands and knees, struggled to secure ropes to the eaves" (66). On another day Adam observes that "right whales have one advantage, in terms of study, over any other species. They have very distinct markings on their heads. We call them callosities" (24); Payne explained that "One of the things that convinced me right whales were ideal for study is that, alone among all whales, they are adorned with series of peculiar growths called callosities" (329). The "cramped, plywood interior" (35) of Adam's "observation post" (34), which has a "hard wooden seat set up before a large telescope" (35), resembles that shown in a photograph of the inside of Payne's "clifftop hut" (327). Beneath this photograph is another in which Payne lies on a beach at night beside a small fire, using "a dish antenna and battery-powered recorder to investigate whale noises" (327). When Jensa meets Adam on the beach at night he too has a "campfire. Beside it, a dish-shaped receiver pointed towards the Atlantic. A battery of complex recording devices lay around it" (95). When Adam and Jensa visit Península Valdés "Small brown Patagonian ducks darted over the surface of the pond while rare Darwin rheas—ostrich-like birds—calmly strutted at the edge of the water" (80). These are species photographed together by Des and Jen Bartlett for the *National Geographic* (298–9). Adam's comment that "Only the tough, conservative forms make it here [...] They don't go in for the elabo-

ing of the novel also seems to draw on Payne's article. In response to Jensa's worries about how they will combine parenthood with their conservation work, Adam states that "a child would be lucky to have the entire world for a nursery" (189). Payne was of the opinion that "One of the most rewarding aspects of our work [...] is the rare opportunity it has afforded our children" (333), and his practice of taking "Katy [his wife] and our four children with me on major expeditions" (329) demonstrates that Adam's solution is not an unrealistic one. There is a realistically optimistic outcome for the right whales, too: in Harrel's novel the long-term future of their breeding ground is secured when "The land around the bay had been acquired for a sanctuary" (177) and in the real world "the provincial legislature of the Province of Chubut [...] set aside forever all of Golfo San José [...] as a permanent sanctuary for right whales" (Payne 339).

The manner in which the fictional whale sanctuary is established is, however, indicative of Adam Ryder's high-mimetic nature. Whereas in the real world it was an "interest in tourism" which led "the provincial Department of Tourism and Wildlife" to "set up a system of wildlife reserves and parks" (Conway 297), in Harrel's novel the land surrounding the whales' breeding ground belongs to a "businessman by the name of Felipe Mendez" (25). Adam is a key figure in the negotiations to purchase it from Mendez and while the funding comes "half from the government, half from our international organisation" (183), a "larger buffer zone was a gift from my mother" (183), who "is loaded—through birth, divorce, remarriage" (184). Adam himself is "not without means. My father inherited money—a great deal, really—and like me, he didn't squander it. So it all came down to me" (188). This extreme wealth is far from the only aspect of Adam's life which sets him apart from most readers but if we do not "respond to a sense of his common humanity" (Frye 34) as we would to a low-mimetic hero it is probably because, as stated quite

---

rate plumage and pelts you see in other parts of the world. But while the colours may be dull, the actual life forms are just fantastic" (79) echoes William G. Conway's statement that in Patagonia "Ancient, conservative life forms are the rule, clothed in the brown, gray, and tan colors familiar to all who study desert fauna. [...] It is the strangeness of these creatures [...] that give[s] Patagonia's wildlife unique interest" (294).

explicitly in the novel itself, he seems "not quite human" (45). As far as his physique is concerned, he is literally "superior in degree to other men" (Frye 33) as he is "an unusually tall man, and well built" (7–8), with "arms like bands of steel" (19). As "a brilliant scientist" (8) he is also exceptional intellectually and the intensity of his emotions are indicated by the way "he tackled everything—people and work—fiercely" (24). Realistic elements can, then, be found in varying degrees even in high-mimetic works, but Frye suggests that "as the modes of fiction move from the mythical to the low mimetic and ironic, they approach a point of extreme 'realism' or representative likeness to life" (134).

Variations Within a Single Mode

Frye argues that "Our five modes evidently go around in a circle" (42), and if each mode is considered to be part of a circle, variation must be expected as we gradually progress from the beginning of one segment to its end. The existence of a gradient, from high to low, within each mode, can be demonstrated by a brief analysis of two high-mimetic HM&Bs: Charlotte Lamb's *Dark Fate* (1994), which is at the upper edge of the high mimetic, bordering the 'romance' mode, and Fay Robinson's *A Man Like Mac* (2000), which is at the lower edge of the high mimetic, where it borders the low-mimetic mode.

Keely, the heroine of *A Man Like Mac*, has talents, "passions" (Frye 34) and actions which clearly proclaim her to be a high mimetic heroine who is "superior in degree" (Frye 33) to other people. She is an Olympic silver medallist, a woman with an "iron will" (19) of whom it is said that she "is ninety percent guts [...] And the rest is heart" (226). After finally accepting that her sporting career has been destroyed by an accident that almost killed her, she becomes a success in a new arena: "Her ability to see a problem and find a solution continued to astound Mac. Her company produced a range of equipment used by able-bodied and disabled athletes and held several patents for medical equipment" (294).

Mac also has a personality and achievements which clearly place him in the high mimetic mode. Fay Robinson, in a letter to the reader, describes him as "an extraordinary man" (2). He is certainly "a leader" (Frye 34), having quickly been promoted to "athletic director" (15) of the university at which he works and "As a coach, he was as gifted as anyone in the business" (21). Indeed, his success is such that he is subject to "social criticism" (Frye 34) from the envious Doug Crocker. As an athlete "People have started calling him the Terminator because, when he races, he dresses all in black and he wipes out the competition. He's unbeatable in the shorter distances" (46) and at the end of the novel he wins a gold medal in the 2000 Sydney Paralympics. If this "special guy" (92) has a flaw it is that "He's too nice sometimes" (92) and gets "into [...] self-sacrificing mode" (52). Two major incidents which demonstrate this tendency towards self-sacrifice are his intervention to save a woman whose boyfriend "was trying to bash her skull in with the butt of a gun. If Mac hadn't jumped in, he probably would have killed her" (95), and his decision to care for his siblings:

> he had rearranged his life for them; Keely was certain of it. When his parents had died and he'd brought his sisters and brother to live with him, it must have caused an immense change in his life. Twenty-two, responsible for himself and four children ...
>
> How many men would have done what he had? None she could think of. (67)

He is, then, clearly "superior in degree to other men" (Frye 33).

Keely and Mac are high-mimetic protagonists because of their exceptional personalities and abilities but the hero and heroine of Charlotte Lamb's *Dark Fate* push at the very upper edge of the high mimetic, where it borders the 'romance' mode. In part this is because "Saskia is telepathic, genuinely telepathic" (134) and "During the two years they had been apart, Domenico had been trying to reach her, anyhow, any way he could, and he had somehow tuned into her wave-length" (128) and gained the ability to communicate telepathically with her. These paranormal abilities would certainly seem to set them apart from most other people and Domenico, if less telepathically gifted, also seems larger than life because of his possession, in greater than normal quantities, of wealth, breeding, intelligence, and power. He "must be one of the richest men" (46) in Italy and is the acting head of a family which is:

> incredibly wealthy; they headed a conglomerate which owned various companies: food-manufacturing, paper-milling, a drug company, a hotel chain. They were hard-working, ambitious, clever men, the men of the Alessandros clan, but they had not got rich suddenly—the family was a very old one; you could trace the name back to the fifteenth century and beyond. (35)

He also has "a clear, diamond-hard, ice-cold mind" (16), a "powerful body" (21), and is "a possessive and demanding lover" (10). He is, indeed, so "superior in degree to other men" (Frye 33) that for Saskia this high-mimetic hero "had ruined her for any other man. They were all tame, dull, predictable compared to him" (180). As for Saskia herself, although she may believe she is a low-mimetic "little nobody without either money or family connections" (88), she does not appear this way to others:

> They were jealous of you! [...] Of course they were. If you weren't so wrapped up in your own insecurity you'd know that. You [...] were everything they had forgotten how to be—young, gentle, untouched, beautiful. You were a living reproach to them all. You radiated the very spirit of youth. (182)

In her own way, Saskia is as high mimetic as Domenico.

The modal differences between the personalities of Lamb's and Robinson's protagonists are matched by their surroundings. In Lamb's novel the hero's milieu is that of the rich and famous, which is described as "a crazy world" (Lamb 51) very different from "the ordinary world" (58). While his world is not the magical world of the 'romance' mode, most readers will feel that a glamorous lifestyle which includes servants, bodyguards, mansions, and expensive clothes is one in which the financial constraints under which they themselves labour have been rather more than "slightly suspended".[1]

---

1   I have used the word "glamorous" because the original meaning of 'glamour', referring to an enchantment or spell, indicates the proximity of a 'glamorous'

By contrast, one aspect of Keely and Mac's lives which brings them closer to being "one of us" (Frye 34) are their unostentatious living arrangements:

> Keely looked [...] at the small lots and plain but charming houses of Mac's subdivision. People were walking or working in their yards, and the kids were playing up and down the quiet street the way they probably did in her older more upscale neighborhood on a Sunday afternoon. [...] Mac's place was [...] a small house with white vinyl siding and green shutters. (56)

Their world is imbued with realism: in an acknowledgement Robinson thanks "Paralympics gold-medal winner Shawn Meredith, respiratory therapist Steve Patton and rehabilitation specialist Lynn Carpenter-Harrington for their help with research. [...] Thanks also to the many disabled people and their spouses who were willing to answer questions" (6).[1] The novel includes less than glamorous details about the physical effect that running a marathon has on Keely's body and the practicalities of being in a sexual relationship with Mac who, in a rare moment of bitterness, describes himself as "a paraplegic in a wheelchair. A guy who can't get it up and can't hold his bladder half the time" (54). Such matters may not be part of the daily experience of most readers, but they are presented in an unsensationalised manner alongside other mundane details of Mac and Keely's lives, such as a description of part of "their weekly grocery-shopping trip" (170):

> The green peppers were out of season and outrageously expensive, but full of vitamin C. Keely picked over them, found some she liked and put them in the cart. She checked them off the grocery list.
> "You're insane," Mac said at her elbow.
> "I know. A dollar a pepper is highway robbery, but I've got a taste for them." (168)

---

lifestyle to the magical settings of the 'romance' mode.

1   As mentioned above, realism is one of the defining features of the Superromance line, the line in which *A Man Like Mac* was published.

Readers of *A Man Like Mac* will therefore probably respond "to a sense of his common humanity, and demand [...] the same canons of probability that we find in our own experience" (Frye 34), just as they would of a low-mimetic hero. The novel, then, while remaining high mimetic because of the talents, "passions" (Frye 34) and actions of its protagonists, nonetheless tends towards the lower edge of the mode, where it borders the low mimetic.

By contrast, Lamb's characters and their environment are at the upper edge of the high mimetic and her use of hyperbolic metaphors helps to push her novel away from low-mimetic realism and towards the 'romance' and mythic modes. Although her characters are not actually "superior [...] to the environment of other men" (Frye 33), her use of metaphors and similes suggests that the intensity of their passions can unleash the forces of nature: "Domenico's anger returned in a surge like the sea on a stormy day; she felt it beating inside him with all the violence of the elements let loose, and her terror rose to meet it" (54); "Domenico had an ice-cold manner, very controlled, and yet under that ran burning lava which could erupt without warning and devastate those it touched" (13); "she felt the surge of his rage and it was like being hit by lightening. Her whole body reacted with a jerk of terrible shock" (5); "she felt the heat of his [...] desire, like flames leaping out when you opened a furnace door" (22); "they had always been able to forget everything else in bed, [...] their bodies melting in a desire so hot it consumed them both" (71).

Such hyperbolic metaphors are not, as some assume, common in all HM&Bs, but can often be found in those written at the upper edge of the high-mimetic mode. Romance authors Linda Barlow and Jayne Ann Krentz have argued that this "effusive imagery has a purpose. [...] Lush use of symbols, metaphors, and allusion is emotionally powerful as well as mythologically evocative" (24). Jan Cohn has observed that Violet Winspear's high-mimetic *A Girl Possessed* (1980), which uses "mythologically evocative" (Barlow and Krentz 24) language, "plays on themes from Arthurian romance, enhancing the sense of an alien world, a medieval world of old romance into which the heroine has entered. The materials of such a story are highly provocative of fantasy" (Cohn 45).[1] Despite being "provocative of fantasy" the novel remains high mimetic because it eschews settings "in which the ordinary laws of nature are slightly suspended" and protagonists who are actually "superior in kind both to other men and to the environment of other men" (Frye 33). Nonetheless, by hinting at the proximity of the mythic and 'romance' modes, "effusive imagery" tends to take a novel to the very upper limit of the high mimetic mode.

Modal Counterpoint

In addition to the broad distinctions which have been drawn between romances on the basis of their modes, and the finer ones which can be made about an individual novel's placement within a particular mode, it is also important to be aware that HM&Bs vary in their use of "modal counterpoint":

> Once we have learned to distinguish the modes [...] we must then learn to recombine them. For while one mode constitutes the underlying tonality of a work of fiction, any or all of the other four may be simultaneously present. Much of our sense of the subtlety of great literature comes from this modal coun-terpoint. (Frye 50–1)

Briefly juxtaposing elements from more than one mode, as happens when extreme realism or hints of fantasy appear in a high mimetic work, does present certain risks: if done badly it will create incon-gruous shifts of tone. In the hands of a skilled author, however, such combinations can enrich the reading experience and may therefore serve as an indicator of the author's mastery of the form. Kate Walk-er, in her guide to romance writing, stresses the need to include some scenes in which the protagonists "talk about more ordinary things"

---

1   The Arthurian references begin when the heroine is forced to abandon her car and walk, at night, through the Cornish countryside:

> Janie was aware of being a stranger in a strange land where a lot of time had stood still. The gothic land of Arthur where the Knights of the Round Table had sworn to fight for glory and the Grail. Merlin's country where he had cast his spells and runes, and where the tall stones stood in memory of mystic rites carried out by moonlight. (Winspear, *A Girl* 8)

(*12 Point Guide* 30) and "reminisce, discuss, joke and tease" (30).
She argues that these lower mimetic moments "add to the reader's
identification with your characters" (30) and "are important as a balance to the heated arguments, dramatic confrontations, conflicts and
tensions" (30) which create the impression that the protagonists have
"authority, passions, and powers of expression far greater than ours"
(Frye 34).

Perhaps because authors are often urged to ensure that readers are
able "to identify with the heroine" (Walker, *12 Point Guide* 19), it is
not infrequently the case that the heroines of romances written in the
high-mimetic mode provide some modal counterpoint to their heroes.
Bridget Monroe, the heroine of Mary Burchell's *On The Air* (1956),
is a case in point. Her hero, Jerome Callender, is a television producer
who:

> is more brilliant and knowledgeable, more serious and, if you
> like, more dedicated to his art than anyone else at Tele House.
> He has everything that makes the lone genius. But ... that's all
> right in writing, I guess, or painting or something like that. In
> anything like our job you must also have that human link with
> the poor ordinary mortal. I'm not sure that he has that link,
> Bridget. Maybe [...] it's you who will supply it. (76)

Bridget, though she is hardly a nonentity, is no genius and she does
indeed supply that link for both the readers of the novel and the viewers of a series of television interviews "in which big personalities
have time to put over themselves and their contribution to the art of
drama" (73). Jerome chooses Bridget to be the interviewer because:

> There are [...] two common reactions of the ordinary person
> to the extraordinary person. Either an exaggerated admira-
> tion and awe, or else—more usual nowadays—an instinctive,
> though perhaps vague, resentment and a desire to debunk.
> Both are fatal, of course, to a knowledge and enjoyment of the
> particular contribution to life that the extraordinary person has
> to give. [...] But there is also [...] a third reaction. An appre-
> ciation of—a genuine delight in—all that makes an outstand-
> ing person remarkable and different. Coupled with this, how-

> ever, is a basic, human sense of oneness that makes contact
> between the ordinary and the extraordinary person perfectly
> easy and natural. (96)

In this situation Bridget acts like the romance author who is able to transmit "a genuine delight" in protagonists written in the high-mimetic mode while also encouraging the reader to feel a low-mimetic "basic, human sense of oneness" with them.

Some modal counterpoint may derive from the author's attempts to convey the impact of love itself. Bridget's emotions in the final scene of *On The Air*, for example, suggest that a setting can be partially transformed if described from the point of view of someone who is in love: "In her newfound happiness, it seemed to her that everything looked brighter and more beautiful and significant than ever before" (191). Similarly, when Cynthia has an unexpected encounter with Gilbert in Sophie Cole's *Mrs. Scarlot's Quaints* (1938):

> the sight of him filled her with an intoxicating sensation of
> happiness. It was just as if a clock which had stopped was
> suddenly set going again, or as if she had been blind and had
> regained her sight. The sounds of the streets made music in
> her ears, and an air of gaiety irradiated their vivid life. (148)

Conversely, some settings may give the impression that they are part of "a world in which the ordinary laws of nature are slightly suspended" (Frye 33) and create an atmosphere which encourages the protagonists to fall in love. In the initial pages of Nina Bradshaw's *Knight in Armour* (1935) Rosamonde's surroundings resemble those of the 'romance' mode: "The whole world seemed new-washed and glittering and golden, radiant and young as Rosamonde herself" (7–8) and "she made an enchanting picture sitting there dreaming beneath the cherry-tree" (7). It is perhaps unsurprising that Peter responds to this "enchanting picture" by "staring up at Rosamonde as if he could not tear his eyes away. Looking up from the lane, he saw her [...], a vision all green and white and gold [...]. His eyes and thoughts were full of the entrancing picture of her" (9). The use of the words "enchanting", "vision", and "entrancing" hint at the magic of both love and the 'romance' mode.

It is the Greek landscape near the Temple of Apollo at Delphi which has a profound effect on the heroine of Anne Hampson's *Wife for a Penny* (1972):

> Behind Nigel rose the perpendicular walls of the Phaedriades in all their harsh, convulsed splendour. The vast unreal silence of this sacred place affected Liz's senses and in spite of her thorough dislike of the man she found her imagination stimulated in a way that could only be described as flattering to him. A figure out of place in this mundane world, he seemed [...]. No doubt about it, there was a certain peerless nobility about him which Liz had never before encountered in a man. He would look more at home on Olympus—among the gods, she thought. (62)

The setting creates a modal counterpoint "in a way that could only be described as flattering" to Nigel because it suggests that he is, if not actually a god, at least "superior in degree to other men" (Frye 33).

According to psychologists, "Romantic love begins as an individual comes to regard another as special, even unique" (Fisher 88) and, "Swept up in the experience of love, trusting, satisfied individuals embellish their partners' virtues" (Murray, Holmes and Griffin 1155). Romance authors often seem to replicate this process of idealisation when they highlight similarities between their own protagonists and well-known figures from myths, fairy tales and chivalric romances.[1] When Nuala, the heroine of Pamela Browning's *The Flutterby Princess* (1987), reveals that her "parents named me after the Nuala in Irish mythology [...] The original Nuala was the wife of the king of the western fairies" (110), Will takes this as an opportunity to "embellish" her virtues: he claims that the original Nuala cannot have been "nearly as beautiful as you. You are well named, Nuala Kemp. Because I think of fairies as joyful beings, and

---

1   In more recent research Murray, Griffin, Derrick, Harris, Aloni and Leder found that:

> Rather than setting couples up for disappointment, unrealistic idealization predicted resilience against the corrosive effects of time. Idealizing one's partner and being idealized by one's partner predicted sustained relationship satisfaction. Rather than tempting fate, seeing one's partner as a close reflection of one's ideals seems to invite happiness. (625)

I find great joy in you" (110).

Comparisons with gods and goddesses may indicate both physical perfection and, appropriately enough given the frequent sexual liaisons of many of the members of the classical pantheon, the intensity of the sexual attraction felt by an observer. In Leslie LaFoy's *The Money Man's Seduction* (2008), for example:

> There were no half-naked nymphets scattering flower petals and the red Porsche wasn't exactly a classic chariot, but the man getting out of it was a certified Greek god. [...] Tall, broad shoulders, narrow hips and dark hair just long enough to blow in the light breeze. [...] Emily smiled appreciatively [...] if he was here in Augsburg, Kansas, taking nymphet applications, she just might be tempted to fill one out." (LaFoy 10)

Moving down from the mythic to the 'romance' mode for a source of comparisons, we encounter the figure of the chivalrous knight. Pat, the low-mimetic heroine of Hilary Neal's *Nurse Off Camera* (1964), acknowledges mundane reality but seems to yearn for the trappings of the 'romance' mode:

> It's odd how casual the important things often seem at the time, the unobtrusive way upheavals can begin. Like the way I met Chris. He ought to have come thundering into my life astride a great plunging horse with steamy nostrils, to a clash of bright accoutrements. Instead we met—or more accurately I picked him up—in the studio canteen one Thursday evening. (9)

Although Chris is not a knight in shining armour, and the setting of their first meeting is prosaic in the extreme, this brief allusion to the heroes of chivalric romances indicates that the love he will arouse in Pat is just as intense as that experienced by any damsel in distress.

In some romances, however, comparisons with characters from the modes of myth and 'romance' are explicitly rejected. This is perhaps particularly likely to occur in low-mimetic or ironic romances since the protagonists of these novels are not even "superior in degree to other men" (Frye 33). When such a comparison is assessed, found unrealistic, and rejected, it does not necessarily imply that the protagonists love each other any less than protagonists who embrace such comparisons. According to Lisa A. Neff and Benjamin R. Karney, who developed "a model characterizing love as a cognitive network that combines global evaluations of a partner with specific perceptions of that partner's traits and abilities" (481), "global perceptions might include evaluations of the partner's general worth, whereas specific perceptions refer to the particular traits and behaviors that make up the foundation on which global evaluations are based" (481). A disinclination to express a positive "global evaluation" in terms derived from the mythic and 'romance' modes may simply indicate a desire to describe the beloved in words which reflect accurately the "specific perceptions" on which the "global evaluation" is based.

In Karen Templeton's *Everybody's Hero* (2004), Taylor McIntyre clearly has an extremely high estimation of Joe Salazar's general worth: she states that, with one possible exception, he is "the most generous, selfless, noble man I have ever met in my entire life" (211). Nonetheless, because she has truly "*got* him. Understood him" (198), she sees through his "brave I'm-da-man-I-fix-everything front" (137) and tells him that "You're already everybody else's hero. You don't have to be mine" (240). Taylor's rejection of the word "hero" arises from her awareness that Joe is neither a mythic hero with "superhuman strength, courage, or ability, favoured by the gods" (*OED*) nor even a high-mimetic hero who "exhibits extraordinary bravery, firmness, fortitude, or greatness of soul [...]; a man admired and venerated for his achievements and noble qualities" (*OED*). She knows he is "Just human" (232) and therefore worries that in attempting to be a high-mimetic hero he is "overdoing it. Yeah, yeah, the guy was young and healthy, he could probably weather the stress okay. But for how long?" (123). She would much rather he behaved like "one of us" (Frye 34) and allowed himself to have what he really wants: "something resembling a normal life" (23).

The eponymous protagonist of Emilie Richards's *Billy Ray Wainwright* (1998) is another admirable man who is nonetheless still "one of us" (Frye 34). Initially, however, he appears to be cast in the ironic mode:

Billy Ray Wainwright, defender of dognappers, bar-room

brawlers and alligator poachers. Billy Ray Wainwright, who had served as editor in chief for the *University of Miami Law Review*, ranked first in his law school class and turned down an associate position in that city's most prestigious law firm so that he could come back to the Florida Panhandle and take over his father's defunct law office.

Don Quixote had nothing on Billy Ray Wainwright. (162)

Although Billy is clearly not "inferior in [...] intelligence to ourselves" (Frye 34), his quixotic nature places him in River County, a "scene of bondage, frustration, or absurdity" (Frye 34) where "folks [...] liked to tweak the truth. It was easier than trying to change things" (163). In keeping with his quixotic nature, however, Billy sets out on a quest to defend widowed Carolina Grayson against her father-in-law. He succeeds not because he is a hero of myth, legend, or chivalric romance who can defeat an enemy in single combat, but because his bravery and integrity encourage others to stand up to Judge Grayson, "the most powerful man in River County" (181). This is a collective victory:

> It's a new day in Moss Bend, Billy Ray. A day when maybe we'll get on with being more of a town and less of a kingdom. Judge Grayson announced his retirement from the bench this afternoon. Rumor has it a delegation of the town's leading citizens forced him into it. (367)

Thus although Billy "wished that he had single-handedly slain all of Carolina's dragons [...] he had only carried the standard" (363). He is convinced that he and Carolina move in "different worlds" (361): she is a "beautiful woman [...] blessed with beauty, poise, wit and wealth" (172) whose husband initially "treated me like a princess" (222) and he is no "knight in shining armor" (363). Put in Frye's terms, it would appear that Billy sees Carolina as a high-mimetic heroine and himself as a protagonist in the ironic mode who is "nobody's idea of a knight, nobody's hero. He was a backwoods lawyer, in debt up to his eyeballs" (363). Carolina therefore has to show Billy that she is a low-mimetic "full-grown woman" (374) who wants and esteems Billy for who he is. She tells him that there are lots of reasons to love a man. Because he's smart, or good-looking, or knows how to kiss a girl silly. You're all those things, so you've got that part down pat. But the best reason is because he stands beside you when you need him most. I was raised to believe in Southern gentlemen. I know the real thing when he's right in front of me. (376)

By designating Billy a "Southern gentleman", Carolina challenges Billy's assessment of himself as a quixotic failure in the ironic mode and also expresses her high level of global esteem for him in terminology which is compatible with the low-mimetic world they inhabit. She succeeds in making him accept that:

He was nobody's knight, nobody's hero. But for the first time he was completely satisfied that Carolina […] knew exactly who he was.
    He was the man she wanted beside her. Forever. (377)

The novel ends as Billy rejects the standards of the 'romance' and high-mimetic modes and accepts her love.

All these examples of references to or comparisons with protagonists from the mythic and 'romance' modes give the reader insight into the protagonists' feelings about each other. Such allusions may also foreshadow aspects of the plot. In Nina Bradshaw's *Knight in Armour* (1935), for example, Rosamonde compares Sir Peter to "a picture hanging up in the schoolroom of a knight in armour. I'm not quite sure who he's meant to be—Sir Galahad, I think. But he's awfully like you" (43). She hopes that he will also act the part of "a knight in armour" and Sir Peter considers this to be an indication of her youthful idealism:

At her age, of course, life must appear a good deal like a story-book romance. She saw her sister as a beautiful heroine about to be offered up to the villain of the piece […] and felt convinced that there must be a hero somewhere at hand to save her. And he had happened to drop into her life just at the right moment. (41–2)

While the comparison to the "knight in armour" reveals much about

Rosamonde's personality and her view of Sir Peter, it also hints at the eventual outcome of the novel because she has chosen him to be:

> her modern knight, whom she had summoned to Isobel's aid, as in the days of the Knights of the Round Table Lynette sought the help of Sir Gareth to save her sister. The end of that adventure had been a bit doubtful, and had often worried Rosamonde, for the historian had seemed uncertain whether in the end Sir Gareth married Lyonors or Lynette. (56)

The similarities between Sir Peter and Sir Gareth do indeed prefigure later developments: it is Rosamonde, and not her sister Isobel, who will marry Sir Peter.

The next chapter examines more plots from the mythic and 'romance' modes which have made their way into romance novels in the high, low, and ironic modes. The presence of elements of these plots is more overt in some novels than others and so some of the consequences of including overt references to the source of the plot will also be explored.

Chapter 2. Mythoi

A mythos is defined as "a traditional or recurrent narrative theme or plot structure" (*Oxford Dictionaries Online*) and many romance plots are based on mythoi derived from myths and fairytales. Although "The vast majority of romance novels do not consciously invoke specific fairy tales, [...] many still implicitly draw on the tradition, its conflicts and quests, and occasionally its motifs" (Lee 57). HM&B authors Clair and Donald describe some "classic romance plot situations" (43) derived from myths and fairy tales: the basis of a romance in which a "working woman meets [a] millionaire" (43) is Cinderella; when the heroine "is unawakened or has withdrawn after being emotionally injured, and only he [the hero] can awaken or heal her" (43), it is a Sleeping Beauty plot; when a heroine is "kidnapped, downed in the jungle, caught in a no-man's land with a dangerous male" (44) there are echoes of the myth of Pluto and Persephone. Jayne Ann Krentz, another author who has written for HM&B, also acknowledges the influence of these mythoi:

> Some of the basic myths and legends that animate the romance genre include the tale of Persephone (echoed in a thousand stories involving a woman being carried off by a mysterious, powerful male who is in turn enthralled and brought to his knees by her). Another popular one is the story of Beauty and the Beast [...]. ("Trying" 113)

The editor of the 'Lovers & Legends' mini-series of romances, published in the Temptation line, also recognised the importance of mythoi, stating that "Fairy tales and legends are basic human stories, retold in every age, in their own way" (Editor) and presenting this series as an attempt to retell them "in sizzling Temptation style!"[1]

---

1   Other mini-series of this kind include the 'In Her Shoes' romances (the first was published in 2009) in which "Modern-day Cinderellas get their grooms" (Hart,

In addition to mythoi drawn from myths and fairy tales, romances also employ mythoi derived from chivalric romances. Although the "knight in shining armor" (Krentz, *Too Wild* 24) may at first glance seem to be a character type rather than the protagonist of a clearly defined mythos, he is in fact associated with a simple "plot-formula": in the HM&B "knight-fantasy [...] Knights were heroic. Knights were romantic. Knights took charge" (McClone 31), or, as the heroine of Carol Townend's *An Honourable Rogue* (2008) explains, "A young maiden meets a handsome young knight and falls in love with him. He falls in love with her and comes to carry her off on the back of his white charger. He takes her to his castle and ..." (274).[1] According to this mythos, then, the knight demonstrates his love for his lady by risking discomfort, and perhaps even danger, in order to please her. In return, he receives her hand in marriage.[2]

Few HM&B heroes are actually knights on white chargers but a hero may be deemed to resemble a knight when he performs a rescue or other service for his heroine. In *Gifford's Lady* (2002) Abigail explains this to Gifford after he tells her that

> 'Earlier tonight I went to look in the library for a book on courtly love—King Arthur and his knights and so forth [...]

Cinderella back cover), the 'Once Upon a Kiss' fairytale-based series which ran from 1997–8 in the Harlequin American Romance line, and the four-book series 'The Greek Tycoons', published in 2010 in the Mills & Boon Modern (Harlequin Presents) line. In the first book in this latter series, *The Greek Tycoon's Achilles Heel* (2010), it was announced that:

> Legends are made of men like these!
> [...] As gorgeous and god-like as their mythological ancestors, they put the 'man' into Romance! (Gordon 2)

In a note to the reader, Lucy Gordon stated that she had "really enjoyed the chance to write about Achilles, because of all the charismatic Greek heroes he's the one whose story still speaks to us down the centuries" (5).

1   This type of knight is primarily a literary creation. As the medievalist heroine of Jayne Ann Krentz's *Too Wild to Wed?* (1991) recognises, "The real thing was a tough, arrogant warrior who would have done all sorts of horrid things" (45).

2   It should be noted that authors may deliberately play with readers' expectations. In *Blueprint for a Wedding* (2005) the heroine repeatedly dreams of a knight who follows the expected script but she eventually realises there is an alternative: "She could wait for her knight to find her, or, Faith smiled, she could rescue him herself" (McClone 180). She chooses the latter option, proposes to Gabe, and then elopes with him in her jet.

To teach me how to romance you properly. But I couldn't find one.'

'Gifford!' Abigail was amazed at his admission. 'You don't need a *book*. You're already the perfect knight—'

'Baronet,' Gifford corrected, but he looked more than pleased by Abigail's praise.

'Don't quibble,' she told him severely. 'Every lady needs a champion, and you are my perfect champion. [...].' (Thornton 294)

In Anne Gracie's *Tallie's Knight* (2000) the chivalric mythos is initially separated from the rest of the narrative: it appears in italics, as the stuff of Tallie's "foolish dreams" (15). The register of the language in which these dreams are written also signals their difference from the surrounding text. In the first example the speech of Tallie's knight, a fiction within a fiction, is pseudo-medieval and unlike that of the other characters—"*Begone you vicious curs!*" (14)—and later the knight's words are directly contrasted with those of Tallie's husband, Magnus:

> *It is getting very late and she wishes her Knight would return from his latest Quest soon. And when he does he will stride up to her on his long, handsome legs and bend over her and kiss her, saying, 'Oh, my beloved one, I have returned to you. Tallie, my dearest love...'*
>
> 'Tallie, we're back, sweetheart,' said Magnus. 'Were you asleep?' (280)

Magnus may not be a 'romance' hero, but he is a high-mimetic one, albeit in a particularly family-orientated, HM&B way, and this is made clear by his temporary transformation into the Knight of Tallie's daydreams. He may not slay dragons or defeat magical opponents, but:

> he had risked his life a hundred times over, so that she could be united with her brother. [...] *And* he'd given a childless widow five needy children to care for. He'd even removed Maguire from his life of crime and given him a position of respect in his homeland.

The very contemplation of his noble deeds threatened to overwhelm her. (269)

Here the language of the romances of chivalry inserts itself into Tallie's reality via her "contemplation of his noble deeds" and the process can therefore occur in reverse with very little difficulty when she sits with her baby, daydreaming of her Knight:

> *do you know what my Brave and Gallant Knight brought back from the wilds of the terrible Alps? He brought our own little knight, your uncle Ricardo, rescued him from Durance Vile. Wasn't that a wonderful Quest to make—better than finding a silly old Grail, don't you agree?* (280)

Magnus, then, is "everything I've ever dreamed of" (276) and a true knight in shining armour, albeit in the high-mimetic, rather than the 'romance' mode.

Mythoi and Modes

Frye stated that "we may think of our romantic, high mimetic and low mimetic modes as a series of *displaced* myths, *mythoi* or plot-formulas progressively moving over towards the opposite pole of verisimilitude, and then, with irony, beginning to move back" (52). The progress of one mythos from the high-mimetic to the ironic mode is visible in the following analysis of Anne Weale's high-mimetic *If This Is Love* (1963), Marcia King-Gamble's low-mimetic *All About Me* (2007) and Jane Sullivan's ironic *The Matchmaker's Mistake* (2001), all of which draw on the myth of Pygmalion, "king of Cyprus, who fell in love with a beautiful statue (according to Ovid made by himself). He prayed to Aphrodite to give him a wife resembling the statue; and she did more than this, for she gave the statue life, and Pygmalion married the woman so created" (Howatson 475). The precise route by which a mythos reached a particular authors is rarely clear but, as we shall see, in at least two of these HM&Bs the mythos has been filtered through Shaw's *Pygmalion* (1912) and its musical adaptation, *My Fair Lady* (1956).

High Mimetic

Although Anne Weale's *If This Is Love* does not explicitly refer to the Pygmalion myth, it can nonetheless be read as a high-mimetic version of it with David Ransome, "an attractive, successful, worldly man" (20) who is "absolutely *the* best of our fashion photographers" (12), taking the place of the Cypriot sculptor-king. Jan Cohn has observed that when a "heroine-as-child" receives "her education at the hands of the hero, can be shaped into the perfect object of his desire [...] romance reenacts the Pygmalion myth, now told from the point of view of Galatea" (159). Galatea is the name now associated with Pygmalion's statue and in Weale's novel her part is played by Jane Baron.[1] Since the novel is in the high-mimetic rather than the mythic mode, Jane is not literally a piece of ivory or marble to be sculpted by her Pygmalion. Instead, she is "a thin, tangle-haired, rather shabby young girl" (6) with "Straight mid-brown hair; a wide, slightly lop-sided mouth; a passable bosom, but no other curves to speak of—how could such unpromising material be fashioned into a semblance of glamour?" (42). The answer is by sending the "unpromising material" on "a three-week training course at a very good model school" (42) and then effecting a "final transformation" (49). After David Ransome has "selected a complete basic wardrobe for her" (51), purchased all the necessary accessories and put her "into the hands of a famous hair-stylist to whom David gave precise instructions about what was to be done with her" (54), "she looked at herself in the glass and saw ... a stranger, a girl who was Jane and yet not Jane" (54). David sometimes treats this new Jane "as an animated doll, a fashionable dummy" (84).

Weale adapts the Pygmalion mythos by making the transformation an obstacle to David's love. It is eventually revealed that he fell in love with Jane before she became his "creation" (55):

---

1   In Greek mythology a Nereid named Galatea was the object of the Cyclops Polyphemus's affections but "the name Galatea does not appear in any Greek or Roman version of the [Pygmalion] myth and is apparently introduced comparatively late into modern literature" (Law 337). Meyer Reinhold states that there were in fact "three names which the statue acquired in modern times—Agalméris, Galatea, Elise" but that "only Galatea has survived until today" (317).

> "The first time I ever fell in love was in a shelter on the pier
> at Starmouth."
>
> "Oh, David, I don't believe you. I looked like nothing on
> earth then. Besides, it was the first time we met."
>
> "It's true all the same," he assured her. "You were the first
> natural girl I'd met in about five years. [...] Then I brought you
> to London and made you a fashionable beauty, and everything
> changed. You weren't my Starmouth Jane any more. [...]" (156)

David admits to Jane that having "forced you into one mould" he "re-
gretted it" (157) because the mould transformed her from "Starmouth
Jane" into one of many "successors" (91) to Margot, "David's first
discovery" (88). Margot decided to "sell herself" (88) by marrying
"a Bermudian millionaire who was old enough to be her grandfa-
ther" (88) and when Jane herself temporarily becomes engaged to
an extremely rich man the newspapers "made her sound like a cheap
adventuress, a dumb or designing blonde" (142). In this novel, then,
modelling is a profession which offers women opportunities to sell
their beauty in return for wealth. The original Pygmalion had witnessed the behaviour of:

> the first
> Strumpets to prostitute their bodies' charms.
> [...]
> and horrified
> At all the countless vices nature gives
> To womankind lived celibate and long
> Lacked the companionship of married love.
> (Ovid, trans. Melville, 232)

Similarly David, after his experience with Margot, remained unmar-
ried and is not prepared to have a model as a spouse because then he
would have "to share my wife with the world" (157). It is therefore
only after a second metamorphosis has occurred, rendering Jane un-
recognisable "as the fashion model who had been in the headlines
recently" (154), that David finally declares his love for her.

Despite its brevity, the "spectacular" (157) nature of Jane's career
is one indication that although she may think of herself as "a very

ordinary girl" (20), she is not really "one of us" (Frye 34). As David says, "To be a successful fashion model, you have to have a whole lot more than an appealing face and figure. You need a distinctive quality" (25). There is also something rather high mimetic about the circumstances in which she acquired her original job as a "receptionist and clerk" (18) at a seaside hotel. Jane worked there because she is an orphan who was "offered a home by her mother's younger sister and brother-in-law. They ran a commercial hotel" (10) and had:

> virtually forced her into working for them at the Crown. She would have been glad to be of use to them if they had ever shown her the least affection or kindness. [...] Jane had known from the first that she lived with them on sufferance, and that they grudged every penny they had to spend on her. (16–17)

Her orphaned status, her exploitation at the hands of her relatives, their dislike of her, and the resultant poverty which compels her to wear a garment that her more favoured cousin describes as "a rag" (10) combine to suggest that the description of Jane's early life owes a considerable debt to the "*Cinderella Story*" (141) and should not be read as a realistic depiction of the actual living conditions of the average English hotel receptionist in the 1960s.

Low Mimetic

Whereas Jane's high-mimetic metamorphosis into a model in *If This Is Love* is outside most readers' experience, in Marcia King-Gamble's low-mimetic *All About Me* the reader enters "a world that we may call the *analogy of experience*" (Frye 154). Chere Adams has "planned on losing weight, getting my man and starting a new career" (27) but her progress towards those goals is attended by a host of realistic con-straints and difficulties. Chere has two jobs and therefore has to slot her elocution classes and sessions with her physical trainer into gaps in a busy schedule.[1] When she exercises, "sweating, quivering flesh"

---

1   Elocution classes may be less common than exercise classes and therefore more likely to be outwith the readers' experience, but "This kind of training—called 'accent modification' or 'accent reduction'—has become very popular. In fact, the *US News & World Report* (11 December 2008) listed 'accent reduction specialist' as one of the 'best-kept-secret careers' for 2009" (Siegel 193).

(9) is in evidence. In addition, she is obliged to monitor "how much all this reinventing was going to cost" (25). By the end of the novel she has lost some weight, is "doing okay as a Realtor" (287), and has made Quen Abrahams admit that he loves her, but she is neither as thin as she wished to be, nor has she received the proposal of marriage she wants from Quen.

Further support for the conclusion that Chere is a low-mimetic heroine is provided by the confiding, colloquial manner in which she addresses the reader directly, drawing us into her world and giving the impression that she is chatting to us as she might to a close friend. The mere fact that a novel is written in the first person is not, of course, sufficient to ensure that readers will feel that the narrator is "one of us" (Frye 34). However, Chere's determination and successes are such that she does not convey the impression that she is "inferior in power or intelligence to ourselves", and her honest account of her failings ensures that readers are unlikely to feel she "has authority, passions, and powers of expression far greater than ours" (Frye 34).

The presence of the Pygmalion myth is felt only very distantly in this novel about a heroine who chooses to transform herself: Chere believes that only "a miracle" (134) will gain her the hero's love; she attends a "'Step and *Sculpt*' class" (11, emphasis added); her elocution teacher eventually exclaims "Bravo, Ms. Adams, bravo. You're finally getting it" (190), much as in *My Fair Lady*, "A musical play in two acts based on *Pygmalion* by Bernard Shaw" (Lerner and Loewe 3), Henry Higgins, who has promised to teach Eliza "how to speak beautifully" (36), responds to her progress with "I think she's got it! I think she's got it!" (Lerner and Loewe 56).[1]

---

1   While it is not uncommon for the words "miracle" and "sculpt" to be used, respec-
tively, in the context of relationships and aerobics and they may therefore not
have been chosen consciously by King-Gamble in order to recall the Pygmalion
myth, there is a firmer connection between the myth and the elocution teacher's
exclamation. King-Gamble has previously acknowledged *My Fair Lady's* influence on one of her earlier novels: the UK Amazon webpage selling her *Under
Your Spell* (Kensington 1999) includes a statement from the author to the effect
that this novel was "supposed to be a sweet modern day version of *My Fair
Lady*". The impression that *All About Me* was also influenced by the musical
is strengthened by the fact that Chere, who wishes to "improve myself" (25),
pleads for help to "become a lady" (188), much as Eliza asks for assistance to

Unlike the original myth, *My Fair Lady*, or Shaw's *Pygmalion*, all of which portray the metamorphosis as a unique process, *All About Me*, in common with all "low mimetic treatment of human society reflects [...] Wordsworth's doctrine that the essential human situations [...] are the common and typical ones" (Frye 154). Chere's obesity is far from unusual, a fact emphasised in the novel itself when she turns on a television and sees "some skinny woman [...] talking about the importance of good nutrition, and that America had a huge obesity problem" (81). Chere also learns how obesity has affected others in her own social circle. Quen:

> used to be very heavy [...]. I come from an overweight family with a myriad of health problems. [...] Diabetes, heart problems, high blood pressure. I lost an overweight sister at a fairly young age. Trust me that wakes you up. [...] Vaughn was only twenty-five when she died. [...] Anyway, that was my wake-up call. I was the youngest and weighed probably more than she did. I was determined not to go like that. (162–3)

Despite this stark warning about the dangers of obesity, the issue is treated in a nuanced manner which supports Susie Orbach's theory that for many women "Fat is a response to the many oppressive manifestations of a sexist culture" (Orbach 33). She suggests that "many women first become fat in an attempt to avoid being made into sexual objects at the beginning of their adult lives" (Orbach 25) and Chere states that:

> My weight had always been my best friend. I trusted those folds and dimples more than any man. I'd been heavy for most of my life and truthfully it felt comfortable.
>
> As a teenager I'd begun piling on the pounds, hoping that my appearance would protect me, especially when I started getting unwelcomed male attention [...]. And so I wallowed in my fat and pretended to be this happy, jolly woman with more confidence than most. (82–3)

Given that there is "something positive to be gained from being fat"

---

become "a lady in a flower shop" (Lerner and Loewe 31).

(Orbach 42), one might expect there to be some negative consequences of losing fat.

In Chere's case her use of diet pills with "enough caffeine in
them to hot-wire a horse" leaves her hospitalised, "dehydrated,
undernourished" and with "blood pressure [...] way above normal"
(269). Her obsession with her weight also has a negative psychological
impact:

> I'd turned into this whole other person constantly worried
> about what I put into my mouth, concerned about what I
> looked like, and worried about what others thought of me. In-
> stead of me feeling better about me, I was agonizing and push-
> ing myself to be thin. Because I thought thin meant happy and
> would get me the guy I wanted. (270)

Mary E. Connors and Sue A. Melcher, writing about obesity for fellow psychologists, caution that:

> Professionals tend to overestimate the harmful effects of
> obesity and underestimate the negative impact of dieting on
> physical and psychological functioning. We propose that psy-
> chologists accept diversity of body size as a manifestation of
> human differences, promote overall health over thinness, and
> help clients become self-accepting instead of self-depriving.
> (404)

All About Me leads its readers to draw a similar conclusion by demonstrating that obesity exists in a complex social and psychological
context.

Ironic

Jane Sullivan's *The Matchmaker's Mistake* also places its protagonists in a complex social context since it is a work in the ironic mode
and "Irony descends from the low mimetic: it begins in realism and
dispassionate observation" (Frye 42). Sullivan's "realism and dispassionate observation" focus on American attitudes towards social
class. Liz, the heroine, has come "from nothing" (48) and she knows
that some would label her a "low-class, drink-slinging barmaid" (21).

She is contrasted with Gwen, who "manages a high-class art gallery on Ashworth Avenue. She went to Vassar, and she speaks three languages" (17). Mark, the hero, is now a "Tax Accounting Manager" (20) at a firm which "cater[s] to a very-high class clientele" (*sic*, 174) but his social background has proved a barrier to advancing further in his career. As he tells Liz:

> "I grew up in a trailer park three miles outside Waldon Springs that was so shabby I was ashamed that people knew I lived there. My mother was a maid at a motel in a nearby town. [...] I never knew my father. He took off before I was even born. We were the local charity case. [...]" [...]
>
> [...] He hadn't told her about working odd jobs from the time he was ten years old just to help put food on the table. He hadn't told her about kids laughing at his tattered clothes, his rusted-out secondhand bicycle, his shoes with holes in the soles. (49–50)

Sullivan does not provide a similar level of detail about Jared Sloan, an "ex-frat boy" (7) who is Mark's main rival at Nichols, Marbury & White, but we do learn that Jared's wife, Tiffany, is a immense asset to him professionally because she is so well-connected socially:

> Tiffany was the daughter of one of Dallas's most prominent neurosurgeons. She had a master's degree in anthropology. She belonged to the Junior League, and she was on the board of the Dallas Symphony. She was acquainted with movers and shakers all over the state of Texas, and she'd used that influence more than once to snag her husband a client. (6)

With Tiffany's assistance, Sloan brings "clients to the firm in droves" (9).

Sullivan's focus on class may be due, at least in part, to two of her sources of inspiration. In a letter to the reader she writes that "I've always loved transformation stories: [...] Eliza Dolittle blossoming into My Fair Lady, Cinderella rising from the oppressed stepsister to the object of Prince Charming's affection" (2). Cinderella's story charts her demotion to the working class and subsequent ascent into the royal family, while in *My Fair Lady* Eliza is a "draggle-tailed guttersnipe" (Lerner and Loewe 33) whom Henry Higgins transforms into a lady. Eliza's father, Alfred Doolittle, is "a common dustman" from London who inherits "four thousand pounds a year" from "an old American blighter named Wallingford" (Lerner and Loewe 100). In Shaw's original version of the story Doolittle explains that the bequest gave the American "the chance he wanted to shew that Americans is not like us: that they reckonize and respect merit in every class of life, however humble. Them words is in his blooming will" (120). This is just one example of the way in which "America is invariably characterised as a classless society while Britain is frequently portrayed as a class-bound society" (Devine ix). Fiona Devine, however, has demonstrated that "In America and Britain, social class remains an important form of structured social inequality in the late twentieth-century" (x). Sullivan perhaps tacitly acknowledges the parallels between British and American social inequality when Mark, who wishes to discourage Liz from attending his firm's dinner dance, mentions that "Everybody dresses up like they're going to a ball at Buckingham Palace. You'd hate it" (151–2). Liz decodes the message and retorts that Gwen would "fit in real good at Buckingham Palace […] I'd fit in better in the servants' quarter" (153).

bell hooks, an American, has suggested that:

> The closest most folks can come to talking about class in this nation is to talk about money. For so long everyone has wanted to hold on to the belief that the United States is a class-free society—that anyone who works hard enough can make it to the top. […] While it has always been obvious that some folks have more money than other folks, class difference and classism are rarely overtly apparent, or they are not acknowledged when present. (5)

Mark's career does provide some support for the belief that "anyone who works hard enough can make it to the top":

> As one of the "poor folks" in town, he'd spent most of his early years ducking his head in shame, but as he grew older, he turned that shame into a motivating force that drove him to graduate near the top of his class. That had helped land

him a college scholarship that paid part of his tuition. [...]
When he'd graduated and gone to work for Nichols, Marbury
& White, he'd naturally assumed that hard work would have
its reward. (9)

However, having amassed a considerable amount of wealth it becomes increasingly clear to him that class is not just about the fact
that "some folks have more money than other folks". Paul Fussell
observed of the various classes in the US that:

At the bottom, people tend to believe that class is defined by
the amount of money you have. In the middle, people grant
that money has something to do with it, but think education
and the kind of work you do almost equally important. Nearer
the top, people perceive that taste, values, ideas, style, and behavior are indispensable criteria of class, regardless of money
or occupation or education. (16)

Mark has money, a good degree and a professional job but "regardless
of money or occupation or education" he lacks many of the markers
which would bring him acceptance from people at "the top". At his
firm it takes "The right look. The right attitude" (166) to become a
partner because "professional excellence meant more than being a
good accountant. It meant poise and polish, wining and dining" (9).
    Poise and polish are qualities that Mark lacks because:

In Waldon Springs, you were considered a social success if
you drank wine that didn't have a screw top and didn't pick
your teeth at the dinner table. Mark's knowledge of the social
graces had ascended a step or two above that over the years,
but he still got queasy at the very thought of approaching a
poised, confident, cultured woman. (10)

Gwen is one such woman and she is extremely aware of the more subtle markers of class. When she sees a label revealing that Mark had
bought his suit from Zoltan, a firm which "sells [..] designer seconds
or last year's overstock" (47), she tells him that "her maid's husband
looked really spiffy in his Zoltan suit at his grandson's christening,
and the gardener at her condo complex got a bargain there when he

had to have a suit for his grandmother's funeral" (47). In other words, the label on Mark's suit reveals his low class status.

Mark goes home from that encounter with "a sick feeling [...] in his stomach—a feeling of utter and complete defeat" (41) which is consonant with the ironic mode's ability to evoke in the reader a "sense of looking down on a scene of bondage, frustration or absurdity" (Frye 34). Nor is it the only such encounter which Mark has to endure: Jared Sloan leaves him experiencing "insecurity" (8), "Anger and resentment" (7), and an earlier meeting with Gwen had sent him to "the Humiliation Zone" (23). In addition, Mark makes himself appear absurd when he is so vociferously outraged at the cost of a stylish haircut that he looks as "if his eyeballs were going to pop right out of his head. The receptionist sat paralyzed on her stool, staring at Mark as if he were only one healthy brain cell away from being totally deranged" (56).

Even in these early chapters, however, the reader's sympathies are with Mark, who is "a nice guy" (8) "worth ten women" (45) like Gwen, and *The Matchmaker's Mistake* can be classified as a:

> comedy of manners, the portrayal of a chattering-monkey society devoted to snobbery and slander. In this kind of irony the characters who are opposed to or excluded from the fictional society have the sympathy of the audience [...] we may have a character who, with the sympathy of the author or audience, repudiates such a society to the point of deliberately walking out of it. (Frye 48)

This is precisely what Mark does. He resigns from his job rather than "treat a sweet, wonderful woman like Liz as if she didn't even exist, just because she didn't meet the expectations of people he thought he wanted to emulate, but had just discovered he didn't give a damn about" (175). Mark then marries Liz, sets up his "own accounting firm" (181), and his first client chooses him because he too wishes to repudiate the upper-class society represented by Nichols, Marbury & White:

> Look, Mark. I grew up in a lower-middle class family, where my dad worked two jobs just to make ends meet. If I hadn't

been such a computer geek, I never would have made all this
money, and it makes me uncomfortable to give my business
to people who are used to dealing with the rich folks. (180)

Together they form what might be considered an alternative society.

One final aspect of the ironic mode which has not been mentioned
so far is the way in which it moves "steadily towards myth" (Frye
42). *The Matchmaker's Mistake* is the only one of the three novels
in this section which includes explicit references to *My Fair Lady*,
a musical based on the Pygmalion myth: as noted above, Sullivan's
letter to the reader mentions "Eliza Dolittle blossoming into My
Fair Lady" (2) and in the novel itself Eddie stares at Mark "with the
tight, narrow-eyed expression of a very short, very intense Henry
Higgins" (62) before giving him a wardrobe makeover. Higgins is
the Pygmalion figure in both *My Fair Lady* and Shaw's *Pygmalion*
and since Eddie does his work at Liz's request, the transformation he
effects could be ascribed to her. In addition it is stated quite explicitly
that Liz, like Pygmalion, has fallen in love with her creation: "the
man she'd created was the man she wanted" (116). These allusions
to the Pygmalion myth have Liz playing the role of Pygmalion/
Henry Higgins to Mark's Galatea/Eliza Dolittle but the role of Henry
Higgins is not one which seems entirely appropriate for Liz: as we
have seen, her lack of social connections is stressed in the novel.
It may therefore be more satisfactory to reconsider the casting of
Pygmalion and Galatea while recalling that in the original version of
the myth Aphrodite also had an important role to play.

If Gwen, "The Most Perfect Woman on Earth" (119), who smiles
with "a cutesy, Barbie doll expression" (16), is Galatea, then Mark
must be Pygmalion. Certainly Mark, like Pygmalion, has fallen in
love with a woman he believes is "perfect for me" even though he
hasn't "actually spoken to her" (17). Given that Mark wants Gwen,
and Liz does "everything in her power to get him a shot at his dream
woman" (95), there are certainly parallels between Liz's role and
that of Aphrodite. The hypothesis that Liz is the goddess of love,
transposed into the ironic mode, is strengthened by the fact that
she intends "to specialize in couples therapy. She couldn't imagine
anything more satisfying than being an interim matchmaker, spending

her days repairing broken relationships and bringing people back together again" (20). There is also something slightly superhuman about Liz, to whom one secondary character offers "complete and total adoration" (131): she has "a kind of glow about her that warmed a room the moment she stepped into it" (74), so much insight into other people that Mark wonders "What was this woman, anyway? A human lie detector?" (51), "a pair of long, shapely legs that had stopped more than a few men in their tracks" (17) and "a thousand-watt smile, one that would send even the most experienced ladies' man to his knees" (184).

Gwen is not, of course, either a doll or a statue, but she does appear to be lacking in human warmth. She has "ice-blue eyes" (35), is "icy-perfect" (76), and even after she has been awakened to Mark's possibilities there are aspects of her behaviour which suggest that she retains some of the traits of an inanimate object: when he looks into those "icy-blue eyes [...] he felt as if he were looking into ... well, *nothing*" (131) and "She prattled on as if she were a talking doll" (132). Early in the novel Mark's obsession with the beautiful but arrogant Gwen prompts Liz to wonder "Were men really that blind? Or did they truly not care what was inside the package as long as the wrapping was pretty?" (17). *The Matchmaker's Mistake* appears to be an ironic reworking of the Pygmalion myth which addresses these questions by having the modern Pygmalion realise that he had been attracted by his Galatea's "veneer of beauty and refinement" (133) but had failed to give "a single thought to whether they'd even *like* each other or not" (134). He therefore rejects her in favour of his Aphrodite, who has transformed him into a fitting consort for her: "With her in his life, he'd sprout wings and fly" (182).

I'd like to suggest that those wings are unlikely to be those of a bird, or a plane, and might actually be a cape, since Sullivan's depiction of Mark's transformation was inspired by what Umberto Eco termed the "Myth of Superman" (14). In her letter to the reader Sullivan mentions "the superhero hiding behind the horn-rimmed glasses" (2) and in the novel itself Liz observes that Mark is wearing "A pair of utilitarian horn-rimmed glasses" (18) which "made him look like Clark Kent, but she was pretty sure there was a superhero in there somewhere" (58). When Eddie removes Mark's glasses and dresses him in a new outfit, it is blue, like Superman's, and reveals Mark's impressive physique:

> He wore a dark navy double-breasted suit, a cornflower-blue shirt, and a tie in brilliant jewel tones. The cut of the suit showed off his body in a way his other suits never had, making him appear taller, trimmer in the waist and even broader in the shoulders. (66)

One can, then, read *The Matchmaker's Mistake* as a very American reworking of the Pygmalion myth: Pygmalion is transformed into Superman and flies away with his working-class Aphrodite to an Olympus, the appropriately named "Morrison *Heights*" (183, emphasis added), where they can feast on a plentiful supply of ambrosia-alternatives from the "deli next door", which makes "the best sub sandwiches in town" (183).

Adapting Mythoi

As a mythos moves from the mythic or 'romance' mode it will, as we have seen, have to be adapted in order to form the basis of a novel written in the high-mimetic, low-mimetic, or ironic modes. The extent to which a mythos is adapted can vary greatly. Sophie Weston's high-mimetic *More Than a Millionaire* (2001), for example, draws heavily on the tale of Cinderella and explicitly acknowledges its use of the mythos. Its hero calls the heroine Cinderella (81); she wears a borrowed dress and uncomfortable shoes to go to an important social event at which there is dancing; at the dance she meets the rich and eligible hero who then "found [...] and kept" (186) her lost shoe; the heroine has an evil "stepmother who openly disliked" (45) her and therefore took actions which led the heroine to accept a job in which she "worked hard and did her fair share of the dull stuff" (40). By contrast, in other romances the Cinderella mythos may be boiled down to a common "ingredient of modern romance fiction", namely the "fantasy of upward mobility through marriage" (Talbot, *Fictions* 7). In such novels explicit allusions to the Cinderella tale may therefore serve as little more than a quick means of indicating that the novel includes a woman who is poor, perhaps working in a menial job, and who then meets a rich and handsome man. This type of explicit but shorthand use of a fairy-tale reference to acknowledge the presence of a mythos can be found in Catherine George's *City Cinderella* (2003), which is devoid of balls, lost shoes, evil stepmothers and ugly sisters but is just as high mimetic as *More Than a Millionaire*. The heroine, who has "soot-black curling hair" (6), is working as a cleaner because the job "paid enough to provide financial backing while she tried her hand at writing a novel" (14). When her employer comes home early and catches her in his kitchen, writing on her laptop, "She'd felt like Goldilocks caught by the bear. Emily chuckled. Wrong hair, wrong fairy tale. There were no fireplaces in Lucas Tennent's flat, but her role was Cinderella just the same" (12).

Another shorthand allusion, this time to a different fairy tale, can be found in Weston's *More Than a Millionaire*:

> '[...] I was going to give you until eight, then do the Sleeping Beauty routine,' he told her blandly.
> Their eyes met.
> Abby had a vision [...] of Emilio coming into that huge bedroom, bending over the huge bed, kissing her awake as she lay among the tumbled pillows. (98)

Yet another mythos makes a similarly fleeting appearance in *City Cinderella* when, "bag of shopping in hand" (20), the heroine goes off to visit the hero when he is in bed with flu: in these circumstances she feels "like Red Riding Hood off to visit the wolf" (20).

Some variations in the use made of a mythos may arise because the mythos itself exists in significantly different versions. Margaret Malcolm's *Leave Me No More* (1963) and Jessica Hart's *Business Arrangement Bride* (2006), for example, both recall the mythos of 'Sir Gawain and the loathly lady' which was:

> one of the most popular stories of late medieval England. The transformation of the loathly lady [...] occurs in a popular ballad [...] and in more polished literary renditions from the late fourteenth century by Geoffrey Chaucer and John Gower. The story also served for the plot of an interlude performed at one

of Edward I's Round Tables in 1299. (Hahn)

Whereas Malcolm's novel brings to mind the mythos as it appears in both *The Marriage of Sir Gawain* and *The Wedding of Sir Gawain and Dame Ragnelle*, Hart's novel more closely resembles Chaucer's version in 'The Wife of Bath's Tale'.

As the tale is told in *The Marriage of Sir Gawain*, King Arthur's life and kingdom may be forfeit to "A bold Barron" unless he can discover "what thing it is / That a woman most desire". Gawain is "a curteous knight" who, out of loyalty to his King, marries a fearsomely ugly lady in return for the correct answer, namely that "A woman will have her will". On the wedding night the lady is transformed into a beauty but she tells Gawain that he must choose "Wether thou wilt have me in this liknesse / In the night or else in the day". He answers that "because thou art my owne lady / Thou shalt have all thy will" and in granting her the thing women most desire he completes the breaking of the enchantment and she declares that "as thou see me att this time, / From hencforth I wil be".

Leave Me No More can be read as a novel which reworks only the elements of the mythos which directly concern Ragnelle, the enchanted lady who is in conflict with her brother, named as "Sir Gromer Somer Joure" in *The Wedding of Sir Gawain and Dame Ragnelle*, and whose release from the spell is secured in two stages by the choices of a chivalrous knight. Unlike Ragnelle, Katherine is "Lovely" (8) but Dexter, who will adopt the role of Gawain, sees:

> in her wide grey eyes something that made his flesh chill.
> Dumb suffering, utter hopelessness. It was the face of a wom-
> an in torment from which she knows there is no escape. (10)

He wishes he could speak to her and say "Madam, you appear to be in some distress. I ask nothing better than to be your knight errant" (11) but since "One did not say things like that these days, even translated into modern language [...] he must wait" (11). The part of the menacing Sir Gromer is played by Katherine's husband, Paul Kavorna, who, like the Gromer in Ethel Johnston Phelps's modern and feminist retelling of the tale in *The Maid of the North* (1981), is responsible for casting the evil spell on Ragnelle.[1] Paul is "Jealous of her having any life of her own" (26) and so "He's crushing the life out of her, robbing her of any identity apart from his" (27).

The question at the core of the mythos also appears, albeit fleetingly and obliquely, when Katherine implies that her young cousin needs a man who is:

> "Strong and reliable—better able to judge what's good for Sally than she herself can—"
>
> She broke off, conscious of the wistful note in her voice. Perhaps that was what every woman wanted. What she herself wanted. (37)

Dexter is certainly "Strong and reliable" but if he, with his "strong, masterful nature" (62), were to set himself up as "better able to judge what's good for [Katherine] than she herself can", he would come uncomfortably close to repeating Paul's abusive control over her. Instead, he breaks the enchantment in two stages by letting Katherine "have her will" ("Marriage"). On the first occasion:

> He had cherished her when she was ill. More than that, he had given her perfect freedom. Freedom to slip into the sane, sweet life of the Ancasters' home and to recover her own sanity. Freedom to wait until she was well again before she made any decision. (134)

Later, after Paul's death, he again leaves her "free to make her own choice" (119):

> He who had always had his own way, who had ridden rough-shod over the wishes of others, now found the greatest happiness of all in deferring to the needs of the woman he loved. [...] And immediately he had his reward.
>
> Before his eyes, Katherine seemed to blossom like a rose in the sunshine. (189–90)

With the spell finally broken Katherine, like Ragnelle, regains her

---

1   Although the change from brother to husband is a significant one, "In the earlier nature myth, Sir Gromer may have been married to the mysterious lady" (Aguirre 279).

full beauty.

In comparison to the modern Gawain we have already encountered, Tyler Watts, the hero of Jessica Hart's *Business Arrangement Bride*, makes "an unlikely knight, it had to be admitted. He was irascible rather than chivalrous" (176). This may be because he bears a much closer resemblance to the knight in Chaucer's version of the mythos, which differs from *The Marriage of Sir Gawain* and *The Wedding of Sir Gawain and Dame Ragnelle* in a number of ways. Most significantly, the male protagonist of Chaucer's 'The Wife of Bath's Tale' is not the courteous Gawain, but an unnamed knight who rapes a young woman. As punishment:

> a curiously feminized Arthurian court [...] commissions the knight to solve the riddle of what women most desire or else lose his head, and it is his vulnerability in this dilemma that enables the loathly lady to get him in her grasp; after the hubris of his act of rape, he must hunt more abjectly for the answer to the riddle of womanly want. (Carter 336)

The answer the rapist knight learns from the loathly lady is that:

> A woman wants the self-same sovereignty
> Over her husband as over her lover,
> And master him; he must not be above her.
> (Chaucer 304)

He then applies this knowledge to his own relationship: having married the loathly lady he grants her "the mastery" (309) and she declares that, as a result, she will be "both fair and faithful as a wife" (309).

Although Tyler Watts is no rapist, he has been chastised by his best friend's wife on account of his behaviour towards women:

> He had recently spent a weekend with his best friend and his wife, and Julia had spent her whole time banging on about 'relationships' and making free with her advice.
>
> 'For someone so clever at business, you're extraordinarily stupid when it comes to women,' she had told him bluntly. 'You've got no idea how to have a relationship.'

Tyler had been outraged. 'Of course I do! I've had loads of girlfriends.'

'Yes, and how many of them have lasted more than a few weeks? Those are encounters, Ty, not relationships!' (27)

While Tyler's lack of understanding of what women want in a relationship does not threaten his life, it does put in question his success, as he discovers at a:

reunion he had gone to […] where all his peers seemed to be measuring their success suddenly in terms of wives and children rather than share value or racehorses or fast cars.

'That's what being really successful is nowadays,' Mike had said, amused by Tyler's bafflement. 'You're going to have to get yourself a wife and family, Tyler, if you want to be the man who really does have it all!'

'And you won't be that until you learn how to have a relationship,' Julia added. 'If you want to be the best, Ty, you're going to have to get yourself a relationship coach. (27–8)

Tyler chooses Mary to be the coach who will tell him "what women really want from a man" (72) and while she is not precisely loathly, he gives her the impression that he thinks she is: "She knew that she wasn't beautiful and, OK, she was a bit overweight at the moment, but she wasn't *that* bad […]. He had no call to look as if he would rather pick up slugs than touch her" (32).[1]

Unlike either Ragnelle or the Chaucerian loathly lady, both of whom demand marriage in return for their assistance, Mary expects only a financial reward. The question of marriage is, however, raised early in the novel: Tyler tells Mary that "I don't want to marry *you*" (32) and she observes that "that's what the princess in the fairy tale always says to the frog, and you know what happens to them!" (32). According to Jack Zipes:

It is obvious that "The Frog Prince" is related to all the ancient and modern tales of the beast/bridegroom variety. In an article titled "The Story of 'The Frog Prince': Breton Variant, and

---

1   Mary's answer differs from that of the loathly lady: she believes that "Most women just want to feel loved and desired and appreciated" (162).

Some Analogues" (1890), the erudite British folklorist William Alexander Clouston refers to numerous oral and literary
versions of the medieval tale "The Knight and the Loathly
Lady" that may have contributed to the ultimate formation
of the Grimms' "Frog Prince." These include [...] Chaucer's
"The Wife of Bath's Tale," and Gower's "Tale of Florent" in
the first book of the *Confessio Amantis*. (119)

Since Mary's terms for agreeing to teach Tyler include the stipulation
that she "move in" (74) with him, she finds herself in a similar position to that of the frog prince: she eats from Tyler's plates and sleeps
in one "of his ten bedrooms" (74). However, as this is neither a fairy
tale nor a chivalric romance, by the end of the novel Mary looks
"just the same" (238). Tyler nonetheless finds it "difficult to believe
that he had ever thought her ordinary. When had he realised just how
beautiful she really was?" (238). He gives her the freedom of choice
so necessary to both Ragnelle and Chaucer's lady, although in this
case it takes the form of the opportunity to go back to the father of
her child and "choose him" (245). Mary, however, chooses Tyler, her
knight who has at last learned "what women really want from a man,
and [...] put it all into practice" (72).

Tania Modleski believes that "To commit ourselves to a search for
the utopian promises of mass art for women [...] is to put ourselves
in the way of answering the great vexed question of psychoanalysis
first posed by Freud: 'What do women want?'" (30–1). If she is
correct, then romance novels, like the loathly lady, may answer the
question "What is the thing that women most desire?" (Chaucer 301).
Many, though certainly not all, romances include a dangerous hero
who, like Chaucer's knight, "plays two roles: he is both hero and
villain" (Krentz, "Introduction" 8) and feature a struggle between
the protagonists "for what used to be called mastery" (Clair 68). As
in Chaucer's tale, in such romances "The ultimate outcome is the
powerful, successful man's recognition that his life and happiness
depend on the love of a powerful and very special woman" (Clair 67).

However, even if Modleski is right in believing that romances can
provide an answer to the question of what women want, researchers
may, like Anthony Gawain, the hero of Tiffany White's *Naughty Talk*

(1993), "find no definitive answer. The reason is that each woman is an individual—unique and special. Every woman has her own wants, her own desires" (220). This is the lesson learned by Cole Raven in Claire Thornton's *Raven's Honour* (2002). He too asks the question at the centre of the tale of Sir Gawain and Lady Ragnelle: "What did women want? he wondered. He'd always assumed it was obvious—a husband and children. But his experience with Honor was teaching him not to take the obvious for granted" (180). In this novel the presence of the mythos is not made explicit, but Honor does fleetingly think of herself as being "like a heroine in an Arthurian romance" (136). Once she is given the opportunity to choose, Honor does in fact want the "obvious" but only in the context of what, in the early nineteenth century, when the novel is set, would be rather less "obvious", namely an equal relationship in which "you'd take care of me ... and—and I'd take care of you" (182).[1] The choices that heroines make vary, but the presence of the mythos of Gawain and Ragnelle can perhaps always be detected when, as in Helen Kirkman's *Embers* (2004), a heroine is given "power over my own life" (359) by a hero who "valued me for what I was" (358).

The use of the Gawain and Ragnell mythos generally remains implicit in romances. Tiffany White's *Naughty Talk* is a rare exception: the hero is named Anthony Gawain. White stated that she chose to "write about the legend of Sir Gawain's marriage because of its contemporary message" (220). Explicit references to a mythos can create a variety of effects on the mode and tone of the novels in which they occur. I have already observed that modal counterpoint can be created by the likening of a low- or high-mimetic protagonist to a character from a myth or a tale in the 'romance' mode. The impact of

---

1   As she expresses this wish "There was a hint of defensiveness in her voice, as if she expected him to argue the point with her" (182) which suggests that Honor does not envisage the "care" being provided strictly according to traditional gender roles. Honor is a woman whose badly wounded first husband was able to say before his death that there were "No wagons—so she carried me. I was meant ... to take care ... of her" (35). Cole may hope that "he would never need Honor to protect him—because he would be protecting her. Still ... 'Would you carry me—if I was wounded?' he asked" (187). Honor replies: "I don't think I could carry you, Cole [...] Patrick was shorter than me, and you're so much taller— and heavier. But I'm sure I could drag you" (187).

such a comparison is likely to be greater if it is accompanied by the use of the mythos associated with the mythic or 'romance' character.

The first third of Louise Allen's *The Earl's Intended Wife* (2004) draws on the mythos of Odysseus and Circe. The earliest explicit reference to the mythos is made by Major Alex Beresford, who suggests to Hebe Carlton that "perhaps Circe would be more appropriate" (35) as a name for her. Since she has "rather sketchy memories of Greek myths" (35) she has to carry out some research in order to discover that Circe was the:

> 'Daughter of Helios, the sun god, and Perse, a sea nymph ... An enchantress, mistress of the island of Aeaea, who had the power to turn men into wolves, lions or swine.' She broke off, frowning at the book. That did not sound a very desirable comparison: Circe appeared to be more of a witch than any-thing else. 'She turned all of Odysseus's crew into swine, but he forced her to turn them back and he stayed on her island with her for one year before continuing his voyage.'
>
> So, Alex compared her to an enchantress and one who had had such power over the great hero that he had remained on her island for an entire year. (44–5)

It is a comparison which makes Hebe reassess her self-image.

Hebe has hitherto thought of herself as a low-mimetic, "plain, very ordinary young lady" (47) and to her the island of Malta has appeared equally low mimetic: it is a place where the social life is "no more restricted than that experienced by the residents of a resort such as Brighton or Harrogate" (14) and where a "respectable young woman" (29), who finds it "enjoyable to hunt for bargains in the markets, barter over purchases and keep the household supplied at a cost that no servant would have bothered to achieve" (27), can "walk unattended in perfect safety" (29). The arrival of Alex Beresford, however, moves her existence into the high-mimetic mode. Before she met him, "life had seemed to consist mainly of ordinary days: after it, looking back, she could recall few that were" (7). Indeed, Alex's references to the mythos give Hebe the confidence to believe that "*I am enchanting* [...]. *I remind men of the daughter of a Greek nymph...* She felt better already" (50) and, in so doing, metamorphose a plain, low-mimetic "mouse" (50) into a high-mimetic "enchantress" (51).

If the sole points of comparison between the mythos and Hebe and Alex's love story had been that Alex, like Odysseus, is a soldier who arrives on an island inhabited by an enchanting woman and falls under her spell, Hebe's transformation would have been followed by unalloyed happiness. However, both Hebe and the reader are warned that "someone like Alex Beresford will have a long history of, shall we say, entanglements, behind him" (70), and it is indeed the case that Alex, like Odysseus, has an "entanglement" which means that he is not free to enter into a permanent relationship with his Circe.[1] Alex's use of the mythos therefore deepens the novel's emotional impact by creating a sense of poignancy: it prefigures the lovers' parting and so, even as we watch Hebe embrace the role of Circe and find happiness with Alex, we fear that she, like Circe, may soon be abandoned because of her hero's prior relationship with another woman. Clair and Donald argue that "Emotional impact is what readers want from a romance" (76) and they observe that it will be lacking if the only obstacles facing the lovers are "a series of coincidences, random happenings or foolish misunderstandings" (81). From the outset Alex is aware of a potential obstacle to his relationship with Hebe and by having him refer to a mythos which acts as a portent of their separation, Louise Allen subtly gives her readers advance warning of the nature of the obstacle and thus ensures that it will not seem either coincidental or random when it is finally revealed.

According to Pamela Regis all romance novels present the protagonists with a:

> barrier and point of ritual death [...]. The "barrier" is the con-
> flict in a romance novel; it is anything that keeps the union of
> heroine and hero from taking place. The "point of ritual death"
> is that moment in a romance novel when the union of heroine

---

1   Odysseus was a married man and his wife, Penelope, was patiently awaiting his return. Alex's "entanglement" is due to the fact that:

> before I left England [...] I proposed marriage to Lady Clarissa Duncan. I had no real expectation that she would accept me. [...] I doubted that Clarissa even took it seriously. It is so long ago since I saw her, since I proposed. She writes to say she accepts my proposal. (98)

and hero seems completely impossible. It is marked by death or its simulacrum (for example fainting or illness); by the risk of death; or by any number of images or events that suggest death, however metaphorically (for example, darkness, sadness, despair, or winter). (14)

The inclusion of these elements ensures that HM&Bs incorporate at least some of the tragically romantic atmosphere valued by Ursula Heathcote, an HM&B heroine from the 1950s, who states that "Happy love isn't very romantic [...] you can't write a book about it. There's no *story* in happy love" (Wyndham 60). She could have been describing HM&Bs when she adds that "every story finishes on the happy note [...] 'The prince and princess lived happily ever afterwards.' There's no more to be said about them after that" (60).

Lucian Marlow, the hero of Mary Burchell's *Always Yours* (1941), seems to have a similar appreciation of the tragic. When he first meets his heroine he is only nineteen and she is a nine-year-old who plays a game in which she imagines he is "a prince" (10). He considers her:

'[...] a dear little thing. Like something in one of Hans Andersen's fairy stories. [...] The Little Mermaid.'

'I haven't got a tail,' Resi objected.

'Nor had she when she came to earth. Don't you remember? She had it cut off so that she could be near the prince she loved.'

'I don't know the story,' Resi explained. And then, rather shyly, 'Had she got a prince too?' [...]

'Yes, she had a prince too.'

'And did she marry him?'

'No, Resi. He was silly enough to love someone else.'

'Oh.' Resi looked solemn. 'It sounds a sad story.'

'I suppose so. It is one of the most beautiful love stories ever written, though.' (15)

The mythos of the Little Mermaid forms a template for Resi's life: she loves her "prince" from afar, and once she is able to approach him on his own ground has a disability which places a barrier between them; then he, not realising that she loves him, becomes engaged to another woman. However, although the prince only ever loves the mermaid "as he would love a little child" (Andersen 226), Lucian eventually realises that Resi is "everything" (187) to him and so the novel concludes with his statement that "we have not been reading fairy stories. We have been living one—happy ending and all" (191).

Lucian believes it is "a profound human truth" that "to appreciate real happiness you must be unhappy first" (11) and if he is correct, this may explain why the "barrier" and the "point of ritual death" are essential elements of every romance novel. Each concludes with a "happy ending" but it would appear to be the case that the emotional impact of the novels increases as the barrier to the happy ending is rendered more formidable. Romances thus mix the tragic and the joyful, and:

> we confront the ultimate excitements of love and death [...] in such a way that our basic sense of security and order is intensified rather than disrupted, because, first of all, we know that this is an imaginary [...] experience, and, second, because the excitement and uncertainty are ultimately controlled and limited by the familiar world of the formulaic structure. (Cawelti, *Adventure* 16)

Even when a romance makes use of a tragic mythos, the reader's "excitement and uncertainty are ultimately controlled and limited" by the knowledge that the author will somehow ensure that the novel concludes with an "optimistic ending" (RWA). The reader's sense of security may be increased still further when the author of a romance makes explicit use of a mythos which also ends on an optimistic note. In Fiona Harper's *Invitation to the Boss's Ball* (2009) this high level of security is evoked by an author's note in which Harper explains that:

> This book is my modern-day take on the classic Cinderella story. It has a downtrodden heroine, a suitably remote and regal prince, and it even has versions of the ugly sisters and the fairy godmother—who actually waves a wand at one point. See if you can spot it! (3)

This last sentence in particular appears to encourages a highly playful interaction between reader and text.

Betty Neels's *A Christmas Proposal* (1996) also makes use of the Cinderella mythos. Its heroine, Bertha, is described by a secondary character as being "Like Cinderella" (68), and poor Bertha does indeed resemble Cinderella for she has an absent father and her "mother died when I was five, and I suppose he was lonely, so he married my stepmother" (14).[1] The "vulgar, scheming" (94), "ghastly" (18), and "dreadful" (85) stepmother favours her own daughter, Clare, whose "cast-offs" (25) Bertha is obliged to wear, and while Clare "goes out a great deal and has lots of friends" (13), Bertha is told to "make yourself useful" (15). The plot of the novel develops as one might expect from a romance so closely based on the tale of Cinderella: Bertha's hero falls in love with her "the moment I clapped eyes on you" (102) at a party which "will go on until midnight" (15); some shoes, in this case "a pair of Italian shoes—white kid with high heels and very intricate straps" (44), play an important role in the story; Bertha's paternal aunt takes on the role of fairy godmother by buying her new "skirts and blouses and dresses which fitted her slender person and were made of fine material in soft colours" (96); and the hero has to search far and wide for his missing beloved before he finds her and the novel ends happily.

In addition to reworking the Cinderella mythos, Neels seems subtly to suggest that there is a kinship between fairy tales and romance novels. Bertha reads both in the course of her charitable activities: Mrs Duke, "an old lady" (19) who "likes a nice bit of romance" (19), asks Bertha to read aloud from "*Love's Undying Purpose*" (27), a "colourful saga of misunderstood heroine and swashbuckling hero" (28), and later Bertha shares stories from "an out-of-date book— an old fairy tale collection" (41) with a group of children. The juxtaposition of romances and fairy tales may encourage the reader to ponder whether they possess any shared characteristics. It is certainly a question which Bridget Fowler would answer in the affirmative. She believes that "Modern romances are fairy-tales sieved through a net of

---

1   The father is "a lawyer [who] does a lot of work for international companies" (12) and Bertha wishes "that her father were at home. He so seldom was ..." (16). He remains absent throughout the novel.

realism" (12). For her part Linda J. Lee has observed that "Romance novels have much in common with traditional fairy tales" (52), and Sara Craven, an HM&B author, has stated quite explicitly that her romances are "fairy stories for grown-ups" (Black). In reaching this conclusion Craven focused on two very specific elements of fairy tales: "'once upon a time' and 'they all lived happily ever after'" (Black).[1]

Another characteristic shared by many fairy tales and romance novels is their didacticism. The Freudian psychologist and critic Bruno Bettelheim observed that:

> the message that fairy tales get across to the child in manifold form [is] that a struggle against severe difficulties in life is unavoidable, is an intrinsic part of human existence—but that if one does not shy away, but steadfastly meets unexpected and often unjust hardships, one masters all obstacles and at the end emerges victorious. (8)[2]

As for romance novels, the RWA has stated that they:

> are based on the idea of an innate emotional justice—the notion that good people in the world are rewarded and evil people are punished. In a romance, the lovers who risk and struggle for each other and their relationship are rewarded with emotional justice and unconditional love.[3]

---

1   It should be noted, however, that although all romances conclude with some form of "happily ever after", not all fairy tales do so:
   When the wonderful happens, when [...] an unlikely romance ends happily, we commonly exclaim it was 'just like a fairy tale', overlooking that most events in fairy tales are remarkable for their unpleasantness, and that in some of the tales there is no happy ending, not even the hero or heroine escaping with their life. (Opie and Opie 11)

2   Maria Tatar, however, points out that
   Defenders of fairy tales often fall into the trap of elevating these stories into repositories of higher truths and moralities. Fairy tales, we have been taught to believe, offer comfort to children, for in them we find a moral corrective to everyday life, a world in which the good are consistently rewarded and the evil are just as consistently punished. In reality, the picture is quite different. Although fairy tales often celebrate such virtues as compassion and humility and show the rewards of good behavior, they also openly advocate lying, cheating, and stealing. (11)

3   The RWA subsequently streamlined their definition and by early 2011 the phrase

Deborah Lutz observes that many of these novels fall "under Bal-laster's category of didactic love fiction—romance that has a didactic project, is future-directed, and attempts to represent a moral way of living, a 'just' kind of love (depending on what constitutes the 'mor-als' of the particular time period in question)" (*The Dangerous* 2).[1]

In Neels's *A Christmas Proposal* Bertha is one of the "good people in the world", but, unlike Cinderella, she is physically "a plain girl" (18), and her stepsister is a "pretty girl" (10); it would appear that in this novel true beauty is judged according to moral rather than physical criteria. Bertha proves she is not "one of them la-de-da ladies" (19) when she visits old Mrs Duke and "The doctor, watching her, saw with relief that she had neither wrinkled her small nose at the strong smell of cabbage and cats, nor had she let her face register anything other than friendly interest" (27). He then sets a test for her by omitting to tell her in advance that the children to whom she will be reading have "special needs" (41):

> The doctor was watching Bertha's face. It showed surprise, compassion and a serene acceptance. Perhaps it had been un-kind of him not to have told her, but he had wanted to see how she would react and she had reacted just as he had felt sure she would—with kindness, concern and not a trace of repug-nance. (41)

A third test occurs after Clare buys herself a new pair of shoes and Bertha reflects that the "shoes were on the wrong feet" (44). Al-though Bertha never has the opportunity to wear them, they fit her in a moral sense, because she uses them to do good: on seeing an old lady being mugged she "ran across the street and swiped at one of the youths with the plastic bag containing Clare's new shoes. [...] She swung the bag again, intent on hitting the other youth. The bag split

---

defining "emotional justice" as "the notion that good people in the world are re-warded and evil people are punished" had been removed.

1   Lutz is referring to Ros Ballaster who, "In her study of early romance genres (from 1674 to 1740), [...] creates two categories of use here: didactic love fiction and amatory fiction" (*The Dangerous* 2). It should be noted that Lutz also places some modern romance novels "under the rubric of amatory fiction" which "can-not be, generally speaking, recuperated morally, nor does it play out in a socially sanctioned realm" (2).

this time and the shoes flew into the gutter" (44). Instead of physically demonstrating which of the sisters has the smallest feet and is therefore the prince's chosen bride, these shoes give Neels's sisters a chance to prove their moral worth. The episode with the shoes demonstrates conclusively that Bertha's stepsister is indeed the ugly sister: she lacks Bertha's courage, her concern is for the shoes, not the old lady and she tells lies in an attempt to take credit for Bertha's act of bravery. The novel as a whole can therefore be read as a statement to the effect that, in the words of Samuel Richardson's explicitly didactic *Pamela* (1740), "It is Virtue and Goodness only, that make the true Beauty" (20).

In Sara Seale's *The Gentle Prisoner* (1949) the heroine herself draws out the moral of the mythos on which the novel is based and, consequently, of the novel itself. The back cover copy of the 1977 edition notes the:

> curious similarity between the fairy tale of "Beauty and the Beast" and Shelley Wynthorpe's relationship with Nicholas Penryn. The Beast lived in a remote house, surrounded by high walls; so did Nicholas. Beauty's father brought her a white rose from the Beast's garden; so did Shelley's father [...]. The Beast was hideously ugly—and Nicholas, badly scarred, was convinced that no woman could ever feel anything but revulsion for him.

Nicholas implies that real life is not like fairy tales: "It's so simple in fairy-tales, isn't it?" [...] You make the right spells, say the right words, and lo! the enchantment is ended" (97). Nonetheless Shelley discovers that they can contain lessons which are applicable to her own situation. As she stares at a portrait of Nicholas which was painted before he was scarred she is:

> reminded of the princess in *Riquet of the Tuft* who had been given the gift of making whoever she loved as handsome as she pleased: *"Could you love me enough to do that?" "I think I could," said the princess, and her heart being softened towards him, she wished that he might become the handsomest prince in all the world ...*

Could love do that? she wondered, startled. Were all fairy-
tales which ended in the disenchantment of the beast only an
exposition of the loving heart? (120)

Later, when Nicholas asks her if "there's a moral in fairy-tales", she
replies that they "point out that if you love enough, there is no such
thing as ugliness" (133).

By making explicit their use of fairy tale mythoi, novels such as
Invitation to the Boss's Ball, *A Christmas Proposal*, and *The Gentle
Prisoner* draw attention to their relationship with other fictions. This
is particularly true of *Invitation to the Boss's Ball*, in which the reader
is explicitly invited to draw comparisons between the novel and the
mythos on which it is based, and *The Gentle Prisoner*, in which
the characters frequently consider the parallels between their own
experiences and events which occur in fairy tales. In addition, *The
Gentle Prisoner* can be read as a longer prose version of, or gloss
on, the lines of poetry Shelley finds in an "anthology of seventeenth-
century verse" (60):

> *Yes I could love if I could find*
> *A mistress fitting to my mind,*
> *Whom neither pride nor gold could move*
> *To buy her beauty, sell her love [...]*
> *Were neat, yet cared not to be fine,*
> *And loved me for myself, not mine ...* (60)[1]

Given that these lines encapsulate Nicholas Penryn's feelings about
love and that Shelley eventually fulfils the criteria they set, one can
read the novel as a prose exploration of the circumstances in which a
man might demand these qualities from his beloved, and might win
the love of his ideal woman.

In addition to the inspiration provided by this poem and the fairy
tale of Beauty and the Beast, Seale's depiction of Nicholas's house
may have been influenced by the initial description of Manderley in
Daphne du Maurier's *Rebecca* (1938): Clive Bloom has identified

---

1 Seale quotes only these lines. A. H. Bullen, who included the poem in *Speculum
Amantis: Love-poems from Rare Song-books and Miscellanies of the Seventeenth Century*, found it in "*Malone MS. 16*" (57), in the Bodleian Library, Oxford.

a similarity between "the opening paragraph of Sara Seale's *The Gentle Prisoner*" (148) and the beginning of du Maurier's novel. One may also detect echoes of Frances Hodgson Burnett's *A Secret Garden* (1911) which, like both *Rebecca* and *The Gentle Prisoner*, takes as its setting a large country house haunted by the memory of a dead woman who was once loved by its owner. Seale's young heroine does not become quite as interested in gardening as Burnett's but does take "a little plot for herself in the garden" (Seale 132) and both heroines, having walked through the big house at night, discover a boy crying in his bed and befriend him. Burnett's novel was written about children and these similarities may therefore subtly emphasise Shelley's childlike nature and pair her with the young boy, Martin, making him "an unconscious barrier" (104) between Nicholas and Shelley.[1]

It is, however, another male secondary character, with the same name as Burnett's boy, who poses a far greater threat to Shelley and Nicholas's relationship. Colin is a young man in whom Shelley "recognized her own kind and was happy, for was he not the playmate she had never had, the friend with whom she could share her own most secret thoughts?" (87). He may well be that playmate and friend, but he is also a man whom Shelley's father believes will make "a cuckold of" (125) Nicholas, for unlike Burnett's Colin, Seale's Colin is closely identified with Pierrot in *Prunella* (1904), "[Laurence] Housman's little play" (89).[2] Colin, like Pierrot, is an actor who "is always in and out of love" (171) and he is engaged in "Pierrot's old game" (90) of dalliance. He himself tells Shelley that she is "rather like Prunella" (89), a young woman who abandons her home and guardians in order to elope with Pierrot. When Nicholas wrongly accuses Shelley of having taken Colin as her lover she is literally transformed into Prunella: she runs to Colin who finds her a temporary job playing the part of Prunella. Although Shelley is only an amateur, she succeeds in the role because "She's just playing herself, running away from security and a sheltered life" (163). When

---

1   There is also a similarity in the names of the housekeepers: in Seale's novel the post is held by a Mrs Medlar, in Burnett's a Mrs Medlock.

2   The full title of the play is *Prunella or Love in a Dutch Garden* and it was co-authored by Laurence Housman and Harley Granville Barker.

the play's short run is over, however, Shelley reverts to being Beauty. She reads in a newspaper that:

> 'Mr. Nicholas Penryn [...] was found unconscious yesterday in the grounds of his home. [...] The extent of Mr. Penryn's injury is not, as yet known.' [...]
>
> Foolishly, maddeningly, a passage from the old story which she had read only that morning, ran through her dazed thoughts. *The beast lay dying in the rose-garden ... forgetting all his ugliness she threw herself upon his body, weeping and sobbing the while ...* [...]
>
> "I must go to him." (181)

She does go to him and the ending of the novel, in which Shelley and Nicholas declare their love for each other, represents a "triumph of faith in the fairy-tales" (187).

It is possible that Seale's abundant use of quotations from, or allusions to, poetry, other novels, drama and fairy tales, contributed to the book's success; "*The Gentle Prisoner* (which Alan Boon called 'one of the great classic books we published') was awarded 'Romantic Novel of the Year' by *Woman and Home* magazine in 1949" (McAleer, "Scenes" 281). The next chapter takes a closer look at romances which acknowledge or explore their own fictionality, their relationship to other fictions, or their place in popular culture.

Chapter 3. Metafiction

Dana Polan has observed that "one recurrent aspect of popular culture is its self-reflexive dimension—its pointed commentary on, and even pastiche or parody of, its own status as cultural item" (175). Many HM&Bs have this type of "self-reflexive dimension", which can range from a brief moment of self-awareness to a comprehensive exposition of HM&B conventions. An example of the former can be found in Eleanor Farnes's *Secret Heiress* (1956), the dénouement of which is engineered by the heroine's father: Farnes wryly refers to him as "the *deus ex machina*" (184). Liz Fielding's *Secret Wedding* (2000) is a prime example of the latter: the heroine is "bestselling romance novelist Mollie Blake" (179) and the text of each chapter puts into practice the advice contained in its epigraph, excerpted from "Mollie Blake's Writing Workshop Notes" (179). Hope Tarr's *It's a Wonderfully Sexy Life* (2006), her first novel for the Blaze line, falls somewhere between the two. According to Harlequin's guidelines:

> The Blaze line of red-hot reads is changing the face of Harlequin and creating a continual buzz with readers. The series features sensuous, highly romantic, innovative stories that are sexy in premise and execution. [...] We want to see an emphasis on the physical relationship developing between the couple: fully described love scenes along with a high level of fantasy, playfulness and eroticism are needed.

It seems likely that Tarr had this in mind when she wrote the following description of Mandy, the heroine, applying her lipstick:

> *Why I bother I don't know*, she thought, and then rolled the lipstick on anyway. She didn't usually wear bright colors, let alone red, but somehow the name, Blaze, seemed to promise all sorts of wonderful, sexy fantasies come true. (11–12)

Further evidence of Tarr's awareness of the type of novel she is writing can be found in Mandy's statement that until she met Josh "she'd
thought guys like that only existed between the covers of paperback
romance novels" (141). Josh himself comments on the outcome of
the suspense plot that "The whole scenario seemed straight out of
an overplotted fiction novel rather than something that would occur
in real life" (220). A similarly blatant but brief comparison between
reality and fiction is included in Mary Burchell's *It's Rumoured in
the Village* (1946), which opens as Naomi Fulder learns that she has
become the guardian of a twelve-year-old girl. Her friend Sidney responds by musing that:

> I can't see you as a guardian, somehow. You're not the right
> weight, age or sex. Guardians should be male, middle-aged
> and impressively solid. Unless, of course, they are the main-
> stay of a romantic novel, in which case they are younger than
> they look, wear shabby but well-cut tweeds, and are addicted
> to pipe-smoking, philosophizing and long country walks ac-
> companied by a devoted dog. (11)[1]

The reader is thus reminded that Sydney is a character in "a romantic novel", and alerted to the fact that she herself is in the process of
reading a romantic novel in which at least one of the romance conventions has been subverted.

Jayne Ann Krentz, in her 'Ladies and Legends' trilogy (1990),
rather than subverting the conventions, draws attention to the ways
in which she is adhering to them. Each novel features a heroine who
is a romance author, contains a short embedded excerpt from one
of her works, and highlights the similarities between each heroine's
husband-to-be and the type of hero she writes about. *The Pirate*, for
example:

> is self-referential. This novel points explicitly to its own gen-
> re. Krentz uses the romance novels that her character has writ-
> ten to create a perspective—an echo, a mirror, a doubling, an

1   The attributes of guardians who are "the mainstay of a romantic novel" have
    undoubtedly changed somewhat since the 1940s when this romance was writ-
    ten but, as is apparent from Sandra Marton's *The Disobedient Virgin* (2005),
    discussed in the Introduction, hero-guardians can still be found in HM&Bs.

ironic contrast—for the essential romance elements of the actual novel, *The Pirate*, that we, the readers, are holding in our hands. Through mirroring or echoing an element of the core romance novel, Krentz adds a set of meanings to the actual romance novel, intensifying them, commenting ironically on them, but never actually undercutting them. (Regis 171)

Nora Roberts, another prolific and high-profile romance author, not content with the possibility of including an excerpt of an author-heroine's romance, has actually written an entire novel, *Lawless* (1989), which:

n'est autre que le roman prétendument écrit par l'héroïne de "Loving Jack" [...]. En outre, l'histoire de *Lawless* est, dans le monde de la fiction, adaptée au cinéma et son personnage féminin principal incarné dans le film par la protagoniste du troisième tome de la série des O'Hurleys, "Skin Deep" (Olivier)[1]

More recently Harlequin published Victoria Dahl's *The Wicked West* (2009), "the story that Molly Jennings was writing during *Talk Me Down!*" (Dahl). Dear Author reviewer 'Janet' states that it was "a clever promotion to actually publish this story under the pen name Holly Summers [Molly's pseudonym], because for those who have read *Talk Me Down* the tie ins are fun and illuminating".

The more self-aware romances can be said to meet at least one, if not both, of the criteria for designation as 'metafiction'. This "is a term given to fictional writing which self-consciously and systematically draws attention to its status as an artefact in order to pose questions about the relationship between fiction and reality" (Waugh 2). HM&Bs with a "self-reflexive dimension" all "self-consciously" remind the reader of their fictionality and some, including Trish Wylie's *Her Real-Life Hero* (2004), also "pose questions about the relationship between fiction and reality". In this novel Tara, another romance-writing heroine, is quite literally posed some questions

---

1   This translates as: "is the novel supposedly written by the heroine of *Loving Jack*. Furthermore, in the fictional world the story of *Lawless* is adapted into a screen-play and in the movie the principal female protagonist is played by the heroine of the third book in the O'Hurley series, *Skin Deep*".

"about the relationship between fiction and reality" (Waugh 2) at the "South East Writers' Workshop" (Wylie 175):

> 'Do you still believe in happily ever after?'
>
> Her eyes narrowed. 'I believe it's possible. For *some* people.' [....]
>
> 'I was wondering if you think that the hero types in your stories exist in real life?' [...]
>
> [...] 'I think they're out there *somewhere*. [...] Everywhere, I think. If we just look for them. [...] I guess I mean the ones we overlook—your everyday hero. [...] A man whose strength lies in knowing his own weaknesses. The kind of man who can open himself to his feelings and not see that as a failing. Someone who's brave enough to take a few chances. I think that's pretty heroic.' (177–9)

Questions "about the relationship between fiction and reality" are also raised by the second novel in Krentz's trilogy, in which the heroine asserts that she knows "the difference between fantasy and reality" (*Adventurer* 329) but only later comes to recognise "the raw truth [...] that she could not make real life turn out as neatly as a novel of romantic suspense" (381–2). Krentz's readers, however, are aware of the presence of the extra-textual romance novelist, Krentz herself, whom they know will ensure that the novel "turn[s] out [...] neatly". While not every romance which "self-consciously [...] draws attention to its status as an artefact" explicitly raises questions about "the relationship between fiction and reality", it could perhaps be argued that every such HM&B is, at least implicitly, engaging with one of the major criticisms which has been made of romances.

Defending Romance and its Readers

Daphne Watson has noted that:

> As readers we are forced to become aware of the reading process only if the writer draws our attention to it, by foregrounding the text as a construct [...]. Like the fairytales we listened to in childhood, popular novels are popular because they make no such demands upon us. (12)

HM&Bs, she concludes, "can at best be described as escapist" (94). Tania Modleski considers them to be indicative of "women's long-ing to 'disappear,' their desire to obliterate the consciousness of the self as a physical presence" (37), and Bridget Fowler suggests that in consuming romances "readers initiate a tacit contract to enter these mythic worlds in return for the pleasures of temporary oblivion" (35). However, an element in a romance which "draws attention to its status as an artefact" is surely "foregrounding the text as a construct" and, in so doing, will tend to interrupt any escape, or "oblivion", by reminding the reader of her "physical presence" located outside the "mythic world" depicted by the artefact.

While it certainly should not be assumed that all HM&Bs which draw attention to their status as artefacts were written this way in order to engage with their critics, there are some which quite explicitly challenge negative assessments of romance novels, their authors, and their readers. One pervasive stereotype of those readers is that of the "200-pound lady with a bad complexion, a husband who philanders, and kids who never shut up. She didn't graduate from high school, had to get married, and can't afford a psychiatrist" (Bold 1138). Romance authors have sometimes sought to show romance readers in a rather different light. Jayne Ann Krentz, for example, includes an acknowledgement of her readers' perceptiveness in the final novel of her 'Ladies and Legends' trilogy: "Margaret [...] had long ago learned to appreciate some of the insights her readers had into her books" (*Cowboy* 464). Robyn Donald includes a secondary character in her *A Reluctant Mistress* (1999) who thoroughly challenges the idea that all romance readers are relatively uneducated:

> '[...] You've been reading Regency books again,' Natalia accused, laughing. 'I'll bet your supervisor didn't know you devoured popular fiction when she steered you into first-class honours with your MA.'
>
> 'I *like* Regencies,' Liz told her unrepentantly. 'I have this thing for tall, dark, handsome, very rich aristocrats.' (14)

Although it is suggested that Liz's supervisor believes a love of Re-gency romances is incompatible with the academic study of literature, it is clear that Liz, who is "heading off to Oxford to bury myself in mediaeval English texts" (13), has no intention of abandoning either type of literature.

Another exchange between a heroine and her romance-reading friend can be found in Nicola Marsh's *Contract to Marry* (2005). Here Liv, the romance reader, is mocked by Fleur:

> 'Let me guess. The tall, dark and handsome hero is about to rip off the heroine's bodice and thrust his—"
>
> 'No! Romance novels aren't bodice-rippers. They're contemporary fiction. How many times have I told you that?' Liv stared at Fleur over her rimless spectacles, a faint blush staining her cheeks.
>
> Fleur grinned. 'All those books seem the same to me. Lots of hot action, with the main protagonist being men with broad, naked chests and big—'
>
> 'OK, you've made your point. Liv snapped the book shut and held up her hand to silence her. 'Enough of your literary critiquing. […]' (7)

While it is undeniable that a large number of romances do indeed include a "tall, dark and handsome hero" and "Lots of hot action", Liv's objection to any mention of ripped bodices is shared by many romance readers and writers, including Daphne Clair and Robyn Donald, who in their glossary of romantic fiction's jargon state that "this term is offensive to writers in every subgenre" (12). Nicola Marsh ensures that Liv is avenged, for only pages later Fleur is punished (in a suitably romantic fashion) for her cynicism about romance novels when she literally bumps into a stranger and "experienced that strange, fluttery feeling that Liv's romance novels raved about, that once-in-a-lifetime gut-churning, toe-curling reaction that signalled *the one*" (12).

Sandra Marton's *Naked in His Arms* (2006) appears to include a subtle defence of romance authors' literary talent. Cara, the heroine of the novel, is a librarian whose:

> major concentration had been in English. Creative Writing, to be exact. That meant that using lots of adjectives was a no-no.

> So said the intelligentsia ... but then, perhaps the intelli-
> gentsia had never known Alexander Knight.
> He was strong. Smart. Protective. He was beautiful. (123)

Cara remembers the rules she's been taught about creative writing
but proceeds to break them because of her feelings for Alexander,
who earlier in the novel had challenged another of her assumptions
about literature:

> "Iron bars do not a prison make," she said coldly.
> "It's stone walls. 'Stone walls do not a prison make, nor iron
> bars a cage.'" His smile thinned. "Gotta get it right, if you re-
> ally want to impress the peasants."
> She knew her mouth had dropped open. She couldn't help
> it. Alexander Knight, quoting an obscure seventeenth-century
> poet?
> "Unpleasant, isn't it?" [...]
> "What's unpleasant?"
> "Being labeled. [...] You've written me off as something a
> lady like you wouldn't want anywhere near her." (86–7)

Clearly Cara has underestimated Alexander's knowledge of English
literature, but this passage can also be read as a response to those
who would be astonished to discover a quotation from Richard Love-
lace in one of the novels they consider to be "factory-produced hack-
work" (Bold 1139).

Together, these two passages perhaps subtly suggest that many
authors of romances are conversant with "high" culture but, like Cara,
may deliberately choose not to follow the current rules governing
literary fiction because they wish instead to employ other techniques
which they believe better convey the emotions experienced by their
characters. As Linda Barlow and Jayne Ann Krentz have written, "we
are talented professionals. We're quite capable of choosing other,
more subtle, less effusive forms of narrative and discourse. [...] We
write this way because we know that this is the language which best
serves our purposes as romance authors" (21). There is, nonetheless,
a great deal of variation between HM&B romances and while these
authors defend the artistic integrity of their decision to use scorned

techniques or phrases, this does not necessarily mean that at other times they, or other romance authors, cannot be found using "more subtle, less effusive forms of narrative and discourse".

Almost all of them, however, would probably concur with Elizabeth, the author-heroine of Essie Summers's *No Orchids by Request* (1965), who says of the process of writing her "potboilers" (66) that:

> Despite what people said who didn't know, writing couldn't be just done in spasms or when the mood or inspiration took you—it was like every other job, it needed regular hours, much self-discipline—and, as in other gifts, practice made perfect. It wasn't something that "just came". (83)

This evaluation of the work of the writer of popular fiction prefigures some of the attitudes to be found in the recent handbooks for romance writers studied by de Geest and Goris: in them "Literary creation is treated as a specific kind of craft, an activity based on expertise and hard work rather than on innate talent alone" (92).

The work involved in creating art is also stressed by Marcus Searle, a successful scene-painter and the hero of Sophie Cole's *Secret Joy* (1934), who states that he achieves his effects "by putting on dabs of colour, dear lady, as novels are written by adding line upon line of words. Art in the making is a toilsome business; you can't escape drudgery whichever way you turn" (39). Cole's novel is another "self-reflexive" HM&B and despite this acknowledgement of the "drudgery" involved in creating literature, the act of writing fiction nonetheless evokes the "secret joy" (32) which gives the book its title. Its heroine:

> Celia Halstead is married with three children. Her novel, *Anna Croone*, is published anonymously by the firm of Spender & Trant, whose imprint 'is a guarantee the novel's worth taking seriously'. The same could be said by this time of the Mills & Boon imprint. (McAleer, *Passion's Fortune* 148)

M&B implicitly offered a similar guarantee: in an advertisement placed at the end of *Secret Joy* the reader is advised to avoid disappointment by limiting "your reading to those publishers whose lists

are very carefully selected, and whose Fiction imprint is a sure guarantee of good reading", and it is then stated that with M&B's fiction
list readers can "rest assured that each novel has been carefully chosen, and is worth reading".[1]

Opinions about what makes a novel "worth reading" vary widely,
however, and *Secret Joy* was published in the midst of, and can be read
as a contribution to, "a heated public discussion taking place not only
on the BBC, but in numerous newspapers, periodicals, and books"
(Cuddy-Keane 16) about literary tastes and standards. Virginia Woolf
named this "heated public discussion" "the Battle of the Brows" (113)
because its key terms were the words "highbrow", "middlebrow"
and "lowbrow". In the 1930s M&B's fiction was moving inexorably
towards the lowbrow end of the market as the company targeted "the
'pay-as-you-read' or 'tuppenny' lending libraries, which, unlike the
free public libraries, catered to the 'low-brow' reading tastes of the
lower middle and working classes" (McAleer, "Scenes" 267), and
by 1936 "the publications of a defiantly 'popular' firm like Mills
& Boon" (Kenyon 785) were offered up by Max Kenyon, writing

---

1   Another clue that Spender and Trant may have been based on Mills & Boon can
also be found in this advertisement, which mentions that M&B "make a point
of reading every MS. that is sent them, whether it is by a known or unknown
author". Cole gives no indication that such a policy is in effect at Spender and
Trant: Marcus Searle recommends that Celia send her manuscript to them because "I've an idea your novel would appeal to them. They published 'Spring
Twilight.'" (37). Nonetheless, if Cole was taking M&B as her model, this policy
would have made Spender and Trant seem like a good choice for an author
such as Celia, albeit that, according to McAleer, "Most publishers endorsed such
a policy, but Mills and Boon were the only ones to place it in print" ("Scenes"
270). Another aspect of M&B's publishing model which might have made them
seem a good choice for a first-time author such as Celia was that "First novels
by new authors were given prominence in publication lists" (McAleer, "Scenes"
270). The derogatory nature of Spender and Trant's name may reflect some of
Cole's negative feelings towards her publisher: 'Spender' speaks for itself, while
'tranter' is a Middle English word for an itinerant pedlar or hawker. At the time of
Secret Joy's publication Charles Boon's sister, Margaret Boon, who also worked
at Mills & Boon, had for many years been engaged in an affair "with a married
man, Frederick Maule, who happened to be the brother-in-law of Sophie Cole.
[...] Betty Richards, Cole's grand-niece [...] noted that clues to the affair are
scattered throughout Cole's books. In one, for example, a character is called
'Madge'. In another, the hero sports a red Jaeger dressing gown, similar to one
that Margaret gave Maule" (McAleer, *Passion's Fortune* 39).

about "The gap between 'highbrow' and 'lowbrow'" (785), as a clear example of the latter.

If Spender and Trant is based on Mills & Boon, it seems fair to assume that it too is a firm associated with the lowbrow. For her part Celia, who moved "to London to earn her living as typist in a City office" (12) at the age of seventeen, has had an early working life in conformity with one of the stereotypes of the lowbrow reader. Max Kenyon referred to a generic Mills & Boon reader as "the typist" (285) and Q. D. Leavis, whose *Fiction and the Reading Public* (1932) was "probably the first to undertake a serious categorization of brow levels" (Cuddy-Keane 21), observed of the most famous of the "desert romances" (Teo, "Orientalism" 244) that "*The Sheik* [...] in the year of its publication was to be seen in the hands of every typist and may be taken as embodying the typist's day-dream" (Leavis 138).[1] As for Celia's novel, *Anna Croone*, it becomes "The most talked-of novel of the year" (253) and would presumably have been classified by Leavis as one of the many lowbrow "Absolute bestsellers" (45).[2]

One of Leavis's objection to such novels was that:

> In the bestseller [...] the author has poured his own day-dreams, hot and hot, into dramatic form, without bringing them to any such touchstone as the 'good sense, but not com-mon-sense' of a cultivated society: the author is himself—or more usually herself—identified with the leading character, and the reader is invited to share the debauch. Once the pos-sibilities of fiction as a compensation for personal disabilities and disappointments were discovered, hosts who would never otherwise have thought of writing produced novels. (236)

This could serve as an uncharitable description of Celia Halstead and her writing process: her novel is "the ship of her dreams" (33), "eve-rything she had ever felt or dreamed had gone to the making of that book" (42) and the act of creating fiction provides her with both "a

---

1 Leavis classifies *The Sheik* as a "bestseller" most of which is "nonsense" (259).
2 Celia spots this description of her novel as she walks with Searle "down the nar-row High Street, where the low-browed shops were reluctantly lighting up" (253). Cole's use of the word "low-browed" may not have been intended to hint at the status of the novel, but it certainly seems rather apt.

refuge from the prosaic, which no longer threatened to engulf her" (10) and a space in which "she could let herself go—could give the reins to sentiment" (13). In addition, although Celia denies that she is Anna Croone, they certainly resemble each other to such an extent that Marcus Searle, having spent a day with Celia in her hometown, observes that "I [...] have spent hours with a companion who is half ghost, and half real woman. Sometimes it was Anna Croone to whom I was talking, and sometimes the little lady who created her" (97).

Cole, however, instead of indicating that these are problematic aspects of Celia's writing, seems to suggest that the free flow of the author's emotions and the lack of distance between the author and her subject matter in fact make it more likely that *Anna Croone* will have literary merit: having heard only "the story of the manuscript" (36) Marcus Searle asserts that "it'll be a good book" because "truth always provides the shock that real art gives" (36).[1] This can perhaps be read as a response to highbrow critics such as Leavis who, while in agreement about the shock value of good novels, would not have considered authors of Celia's type capable of creating them:

> The peculiar property of a good novel [...] is the series of shocks it gives to the reader's preconceptions—preconceptions, usually unconscious, of how people behave and why, what is admirable and what reprehensible; it provides a configuration of special instances which serve as a test for our mental habits and show us the necessity for revising them. (Leavis 256)[2]

In this context it is easy to see *Secret Joy* as a novel which attempts to shock readers by presenting them with a number of such "special instances". The increasing poverty and misery of the hitherto unsuccessful highbrow playwright, Geoffrey Farrent, provide an "extreme provocation" (109) which compels Celia's daughter, Rosalie, who is

---

1   Cole has earlier mentioned *Anna Croone*'s essential truthfulness: "It might be a mock world, but it was fashioned out of the deepest experiences of her life, and had the dignity that characterises truth" (33).

2   Allison Pease has noted that "In *A Survey of Modernist Poetry* (1927) Robert Graves and Laura Riding similarly advocated shock, or mental excitement, to their so-called 'plain reader,' or middle- and low-brow consumer, as a way of approaching modernist poetry" (177).

"in her unsentimental way, more than half in love with him" (23) to overcome her "deep-seated and instinctive repugnance for the easy-going morality of [...] others" (76) and agree to barter her sexual favours in return for her boss's agreement to stage Geoff's play. The suicide of George, Celia's husband, is presented as an act of heroism which, while it shortens his own physical suffering, is also intended to benefit his wife and her beloved:

> he was in pain [...] but he could bear it with equanimity be-
> cause it was soon to end in the long, long, sleep.
>   "It's the right thing to do," he told himself as he watched
> those two—so happy in each other's company—"and they'll
> never know."
>   In this moment George Halstead, a commonplace, unimagi-
> native man, rose, all unconsciously, to heights of heroism. It
> was not a coward's part he was going to play, but, according
> to his lights, a well-reasoned act of humanity. (219)

Secret Joy will also give a shock to any reader with "preconceptions" of women like Celia. She may be a lowbrow, relatively uneducated housewife who, as her husband alleges, is "addicted to sentiment and the reading of silly novels" (214), and she may listen in "a mood of frank enjoyment" to "the rhythmic drone of Henry Hall's slick orchestra" with "its sentimental appeal" (57–8), but she has eclectic tastes and can also appreciate "a picture of Corot's, or the music of 'Tristan,' [...] 'The Doll's House' [...], [...] the tragedy of Omar Khayyám's verse, and the beauty of Coventry Patmore's poetry" (8).[1] Most shocking of all, perhaps, would be the critical success of her novel, *Anna Croone*: "an article in a literary journal" describes it as "the book [...] of the season" (153) and it receives an extremely positive review from "the author of several highbrow novels which had brought him fame" (93).

---

1   Celia hears Henry Hall's orchestra after Searle has "switched on a portable wire-
    less-set" (57). We can therefore assume that the action of the novel takes place
    at the earliest in the 1920s, but more probably in the early 1930s, since "when
    the Gleneagles Hotel opened in 1924 Hall persuaded the BBC to broadcast his
    band on the opening night" but it was not until 1932 that "Hall succeeded Jack
    Payne as musical director of the BBC dance orchestra" (Wallace).

It is not entirely implausible that Celia's writing should make "a strong appeal" (93) to a highbrow author: Virginia Woolf, addressing lowbrows, once asked:

> how can you let the middlebrows teach *you* how to write?—you, who write so beautifully when you write naturally, that I would give both my hands to write as you do—for which reason I never attempt it, but do my best to learn the art of writing as a highbrow should. (117)[1]

Much more qualified praise, however, was offered by an unnamed highbrow author who acknowledged the "power" of one lowbrow work but did so with what Leavis described as "the fascinated envy of an ever-intellectual novelist for the lower organism that exudes vital energy as richly as a manure heap" (63). In general, then, in the "Battle of the Brows":

> For those engaged in "middle or low culture," the compelling issue was exclusion from cultural prestige—or cultural capital—especially since threatened highbrows frequently responded by disparaging the quality of non-highbrow work. (Cuddy-Keane 21)

As we have seen, Cole's depiction of Celia Halstead and *Anna Croone* incorporates many aspects of the stereotypes about lowbrow literature and its authors. It does so, however, in a way which casts the author and her work in a positive light, granting "cultural prestige" to a Spender and Trant novel and thus perhaps indirectly to some of its real-world Mills & Boon counterparts. It should be noted, however, that *Anna Croone* is not a romance of the HM&B type, although it contains romantic elements, and therefore its "cultural prestige" does not reflect directly on romances. It is a novel focused firmly on its eponymous heroine, describing her life from her childhood onwards, and when Marcus Searle suggests that "Anna never loved, *really*" (98), Celia agrees that "her story is incomplete from that point of

---

1   According to Cuddy-Keane (22–3) this essay, published in 1942, was composed in 1932 as a letter to the Editor of *The New Statesman*. It was therefore roughly contemporary with *Secret Joy*, but could not have influenced Sophie Cole's depiction of a lowbrow author.

view" (98). Nonetheless, by giving Celia and Marcus's love story a happy ending, Cole may have been very subtly attempting to lay claim to *Anna Croone*'s accolades by virtue of writing what is, in a sense, the sequel which Marcus Searle hopes Celia will produce:

> "Yes, it demands a sequel," he suggested.
> "I shall never write it," she stated with conviction.
> "Why not?"
> "I don't know," she answered, but in her heart she thought she did know. There was no need—now—to seek in dreams that which she had missed in life because, now she had the reality. (98)

The story of that "reality", the relationship with Marcus Searle which fulfils Celia's dreams of romance, is told in *Secret Joy* and since Celia Halstead is Anna Croone's *alter ego*, Cole's own novel can, in a sense, be considered both the continuation of the fictional text created by her protagonist and, perhaps, deserving of at least some of *Anna Croone*'s popular and critical success.

While Cole may have attempted to claim "cultural capital" for some lowbrow authors and their works, a significant subplot in *Secret Joy*, concerning the highbrow playwright Geoffrey Farrent, suggests that Cole also wished to assuage some of the fears of highbrows.[1] According to Cuddy-Keane:

> The hostilities that arose when people wrote and talked about the brows were [...] fueled by perceived or feared injustices in the distribution of power. For the defenders of "high culture," the issue was the threatened loss of economic and communicative resources, since they were concerned that small volume publication was becoming less financially viable and that intellectual influence on general culture was rapidly diminishing in its effect. (21)

In *Secret Joy* these fears are shown to be groundless, at least as far as Geoffrey is concerned because, despite the suggestion that his first

---

1   Unlike Celia, Geoffrey is an educated author who "had been to Oxford and taken a degree" (23) and he is prone to the highbrow pastime of expounding "his views on such subjects as modern art in its relation to life" (23).

play is "too highbrow" (86), it is "a flaming success" (140); although his second ends tragically because "he would not truckle to a public who wanted cheap sentiment. He would take the risk of failure rather than prostitute his art" (231), it too is extremely well received by the audience, while "The unanimous opinion of the Press representatives [...] was that "Carlotta" was the finest thing that had been staged for the last ten years" (241).

This reference to "a public who wanted cheap sentiment" is not the only one which appears to express some hostility towards lowbrows. When asked if his *Carlotta* "ends happily", Geoffrey states "defiantly" that it does not, because "I'm not going to pander to a lot of empty-headed fools with no more feeling for art than a cow has for music" (233). Lowbrows were thought to have a preference for happy endings, as J. B. Priestley made clear in 1927: "Low will have nothing but happy endings in his fiction, and High will have nothing but unhappy ones" (164).[1] However, despite being a highbrow, Geoff has no intrinsic objection to happy endings. He had in fact begun "the play with the intention of making it end happily, but the farther I got into it the more certain I was it couldn't be done without deliberate insincerity" (233). We may therefore conclude that he objects only to audiences who would demand a happy ending regardless of whether or not it is artistically appropriate, and to works which conclude with such an ending.[2]

---

1   This observation, while it may have reflected general preferences of highbrows and lowbrows, is expressed in absolutist terms which have to be treated with some caution; Priestley openly declared that he wished to ensure that the words "Highbrow" and "Lowbrow" (he considered himself a "Broadbrow") were "loaded with the worst possible meanings" (162).

2   H. M. Walbrook expresses this view in his 1909 essay on "Happy Endings to Plays": "The first and last condition with regard to the ending of a play that is presented as a serious work of art is that it shall be logical. Be it happy or unhappy, let it ring true!" (482). Actors and theatre managers whom he interviewed held similar opinions: Lady Bancroft had "no sympathy with pandering to the desire for happy endings at all costs. There should only be such an ending when there is a good intrinsic reason for it in the play itself. In serious drama let the story be told right to its proper end!" (483); W. H. Kendal admitted that "from the commercial point of view the happy ending is always the best. The majority of playgoers are easily amused, and are a good deal more anxious to laugh than to cry. If, however, the happy ending of a play is not in unity with what has led up to it, but is dragged in arbitrarily, it is preposterous" (483); J. Forbes Robertson

In addition to contributing to the debate about the literary merit of various types of literature, *Secret Joy* also appears to address concerns about the psychological effects of lowbrow reading. Q. D. Leavis felt that some novels constituted a "detrimental diet" for their readers because "a habit of fantasying will lead to maladjustment in actual life" (54) and the consequences of such "maladjustment" had already been amply illustrated in Gustave Flaubert's *Madame Bovary*. By the 1930s Emma Bovary was well established as a figure who:

> typifies all those whom romantic literature has spoiled for living. She is a martyr to the ideal, a victim of The Book, unable to fight reality in the borrowed armour of poetry. *Madame Bovary* [...] is the indictment of life against a large part of our fiction. (Shanks 137)[1]

Madame Bovary is mentioned on only one page of *Secret Joy* but it plays an important role in bringing Celia into conversation with Marcus Searle for the first time: she inadvertently drops the novel and he returns it to her, asking "Is this yours, madame?" (18). Throughout *Secret Joy* Emma Bovary's personality and actions seem to provide an implicit point of comparison with Celia's.[2]

Henry James, in an essay included in one of the editions of

---

observed that "From the box-office point of view the happy ending is undoubtedly the thing. But if, as the play marches along, the audience feel that a death or some other catastrophe is inevitable, then it should be forthcoming" (484); Robert Loraine was of the opinion that "in simple, elementary melodrama, [...] the happy ending is a necessity" (484) but that in what Walbrook referred to as a "Thesis play", "the happiness or unhappiness of the ending does not matter. The only consideration is its suitability, its inevitability" (485). That these views were expressed in 1909, rather than closer to the publication of *Secret Joy*, does not make them irrelevant to analysis of the novel. Cole was born in 1862 and the authorial attitudes towards literature expressed in *Secret Joy* are likely to reflect opinions formed over the course of her lifetime. While she may not have read this particular essay, it clearly expresses attitudes held by influential individuals in the artistic community when Cole was in her forties.

1   Shanks's article dates from 1922. Further examples of this interpretation of Emma Bovary's character can be found in the *OED* entry for "bovarism", meaning "(Domination by) a romantic or unreal conception of oneself", including quotations from Aldous Huxley (1929) and T. S. Eliot (1934).

2   Interestingly Marcus Searle is also compared, albeit very briefly, to another literary figure deeply affected by his reading material—Don Quixote: "you're a quixotic old fool" (59).

Madame Bovary which would have been available to readers like Celia, describes Emma as "a victim of the imaginative habit" (xiv) and "an embodiment of helpless romanticism" (xv).[1] Celia, too, is a "romantic" (13) who was once an "imaginative child" (11) and is still imaginative in adulthood. Both are less than happily married, and much as Emma:

> questioned whether, indeed, there might not have been some means, through other combinations of chance, of encountering some other man; and she sought to fancy what might have been those events that had never happened, that different life, that husband whom she did not know. (Flaubert, trans. Blaydes, 57)

Celia would often "lie awake beside her sleeping husband, picturing herself in romantic situations in company with a lover who wouldn't go to sleep when he went to a symphony concert, a man who would understand what she felt" (8). No wonder, then, that when Marcus Searle observes of Emma Bovary that "You'd find many a romantic of her type under the skin of the British housewife busy with her pots and pans" (18):

> Celia felt as if the probe had been applied to a sensitive nerve.
> "I wouldn't be surprised," she agreed, and told herself perhaps that was why she had found the story so absorbing. (18)

However, in many very important respects Celia is shown to be unlike Emma. In a "Study of the Modern Mind", published in 1933, C. Delisle Burns states that:

> Madame Bovary, a commonplace woman, by reading romances built up a fantastic world of passion around her, in which she played the part of the poetic beloved. Her life was a tragedy of the failure to reconcile this world of poetry with the sordid reality. The poetic world proved to be just real enough to destroy the power of the reader to live in the actual world of breakfast and dinner. (230)

---

1   Since Celia "can't read French" (18), her copy of *Madame Bovary* must have been an English translation. The edition quoted here was published in 1923.

Celia, although "she had aspirations for which no outlet was found in the daily sordid round—making beds, cooking food, washing and ironing, mending stockings, and all those varied preoccupations incidental to the care of a husband and three children" (7), nonetheless manages to continue steadfastly providing breakfasts and dinners while literally and metaphorically concealing her "world of poetry": she hides her manuscript in "the bottom drawer of an old brass-handled bureau" (10) and then goes:

> about her duties as cook with a mechanical precision born of long practice. To-morrow there would be marmalade to make and the curtains to wash; every day brought its tasks, but there was now that secret room in the house of her thoughts wherein she could take refuge, shutting the door against the tyranny of such things. (11)

This competence continues after she has met Marcus Searle: she changes only just sufficiently for her daughter to notice she "had not been *quite* the perfect housewife she used to be" (118) and she continues to care for her husband and children because:

> George had not been her husband and the father of her children for nothing. There were ties existing between them that were interwoven with the homespun of her life, ties formed of the mutual fight to provide for the well-being of the children. They had never been lovers, they had never been even pals, but the affection which grows out of habit is a force to be reckoned with. (177)

Celia may be "a sentimental woman" but she is, "moreover, [...] an idealist" (122) and her secret relationship never leads her to commit adultery. Sophie Cole rewards her heroine's romanticism, and demonstrates the innocuousness of her reading habits, by giving her both literary success and a new and happy marriage.

Claiming Kinship with Classics

References to works of 'high' culture such as *Madame Bovary* can serve a variety of functions in HM&B romances but all implicitly suggest that their readership has some knowledge of the texts cited. Certainly the HM&B editors who accepted for publication novels such as Anne Vinton's *Dr Pilgrim's Progress* (1963), which contains references to John Bunyan's *The Pilgrim's Progress*, and Nicola Cornick's *Kidnapped: His Innocent Mistress* (2009), "a homage" to "Robert Louis Stevenson's classic novel *Kidnapped*" (2), seem to have decided that literary allusions would not spoil, and might even enhance, the pleasure readers derive from these texts.

Many of the allusions to, quotations from, or discussions of, works accepted as part of the literary canon involve texts that can be considered precursors of HM&B romances, such as Shakespeare's comedies or the novels of Jane Austen. One HM&B author, Karen Templeton, quite explicitly pays homage to "Jane Austen, for inspiring me (and every other romance writer who's ever trod the globe!)" in the dedication of her *Pride and Pregnancy* (2007), which clearly alludes to Austen's work of a similar title.[1] Kate Walker's *No Gentleman* (1992) also contains a brief reference to *Pride and Prejudice*. The heroine attends a fancy-dress ball wearing a "dress that might have been worn by a Jane Austen heroine, and indeed the costume hire shop owner had said that it was one of a pair: the costumes for Elizabeth Bennett and Mr Darcy in a recent production of *Pride and Prejudice*" (22). Naturally the hero also attends the ball, and he appears "taking on the role of Mr Darcy that his costume suggested" (32).

As Mary M. Talbot has observed:

> It is worth noting here that this episode is intertextual in two ways. It alludes to an actual prior text, Jane Austen's *Pride and prejudice* [*sic* ...], probably assumed to be known by

---

1   Although the titles of some HM&B novels are selected by their editors rather than by their authors, that was not the case in this instance. Templeton wrote on her blog that "the hero has to pull off an intervention that echoes *Pride and Prejudice* enough that at least some readers will get that I deliberately chose PRIDE AND PREGNANCY as the title for this book".

the reader [...]. Through the literary allusion, it intertextu-
ally connects the current romance with thousands of others as
well. *Pride and prejudice* is well known as the source of many
of the generic conventions of romance fiction. (*Fictions* 94)[1]

One can even occasionally find examples of HM&B romances in
which characters come into direct contact with Austen's novels. In
Paula Marshall's *Lord Hadleigh's Rebellion* (2001), for example, the
heroine, Mary, is found "seated in the garden, trying to decide whether to read Miss Jane Austen's *Persuasion*" (155). This may perhaps
be a subtle acknowledgement of the fact that both novels depict the
rekindling of a relationship between a formerly betrothed couple.[2] In
Claire Thornton's *Gifford's Lady* (2002) the hero's reading of *Sense
and Sensibility* gives him greater insight into some of the social constraints placed upon the heroine:

> 'It was ... educational,' Gifford replied. [...] 'It was,' he said,
> remembering the mixture of claustrophobia and frustration
> he'd felt when he read it. 'I'd never considered such a mode
> of living before,' he continued slowly. [...] 'It was a woman's
> world [...] we were shown the world through a woman's eyes.
> [...] You have no choice. No genuine freedom of action. You
> must wait modestly to see if a man favours you. And if his
> conduct confuses you, you must appear unconscious and pre-
> tend indifference. [...]' (49–50)[3]

---

1   The episode also directly "connects the current romance with thousands of oth-
    ers" via a reference to the rakish heroes often found in the modern Regency
    romance. When Walker's heroine sees her hero, "It was as if the rake in every
    Regency romance novel she had ever read had suddenly stepped off the page
    to appear, alive and infinitely disturbing, before her" (29). It is important to note
    that the Darcy of Austen's novel is no rake; that role is Wickham's. In modern
    romances, as in Walker's text, heroes not infrequently combine aspects of the
    personality of "the romantic Mr Darcy" (32) with the dangerous, "disturbing",
    sexuality of the rake.

2   Marshall's wish to acknowledge similarities between her novel and *Persuasion*
    would explain her reference to the latter despite the slight anachronism of *Lord
    Hadleigh's Rebellion* taking place in the spring, summer and autumn of 1817
    while *Persuasion* was first published "in December 1817 (though 1818 appears
    on the title-page); *Northanger Abbey* and *Persuasion* were issued together in
    four volumes" (Davie).

3   He recalls this conversation some time later, which leads him to ask: "Seen from

Although HM&B romances are often set in contexts very different from those which appear in Austen's novels, "It is a truth universally acknowledged" (Austen, *Pride and Prejudice* 51) that they tend to show the reader "the world through a woman's eyes". As a result it has been suggested that, much like Gifford's experience of reading Austen's *Sense and Sensibility*, reading romances "can tell us much about how women have managed not only to live in oppressive circumstances but to invest their situations with some degree of dignity" (Modleski 14–15).[1]

Romance authors have not, however, limited their literary references to works created by women. Marina, the heroine of Paula Marshall's *The Lost Princess* (1996), which is set in Tuscany in 1460, turns to Boccaccio's *Decameron* to make sense of her own circumstances. Describing the many adventures she has experienced in the course of the novel she says that "It was like one of Messer Boccaccio's tales, where a lady of high degree is disguised and performs tasks and duties which she has never dreamed of—and finds herself to be quite another person" (264).[2] In addition, various characters make frequent use of the metaphor of the nightingale singing, from tale V.4, which, the hero explains, "echoes what Messer Boccaccio hath hinted" and provides "polite words for the act of love itself" (78).[3] It is significant

---

Abigail's perspective, had his conduct been confusing?" (285).

1   Modleski also states that the literary lineage of "Harlequins can be traced back through the work of Charlotte Brontë and Jane Austen" (15).

2   She may perhaps be recalling the *Decameron*'s tales V.2, in which:

> Gostanza, in love with Martuccio Gomito, hears that he has died, and in her despair she puts to sea alone in a small boat, which is carried by the wind to Susa; she finds him, alive and well, in Tunis, and makes herself known to him, whereupon Martuccio, who stands high in the King's esteem [...] marries her and brings her back with a rich fortune to Lipari. (378)

and II.9, in which:

> Bernabò of Genoa is tricked by Ambrogiuolo [into believing that his wife has been unfaithful to him, after they made a bet about it], loses his money, and orders his innocent wife to be killed. She escapes, however, and, disguising herself as a man, enters the service of the Sultan. Having traced the swindler, she lures her husband to Alexandria, where Ambrogiuolo is punished and she abandons her disguise, after which she and Bernabò return to Genoa, laden with riches. (165)

3   The hero's explanation is required because although Marina has read the *Decameron* she had previously been unaware of tale V.4: "It was not in the

that the tale most often alluded to in Marshall's novel is from the fifth day of the *Decameron*: the tales told on that day all concern "the adventures of lovers who survived calamities or misfortunes and attained a state of happiness" (363), and thus contain the essential "central love story" and "optimistic ending" (RWA) which define the HM&B romance novel.

The male canonical author to whom writers of HM&Bs have most frequently turned, however, is almost certainly Shakespeare. Laurie E. Osborne has demonstrated that, in Jane Donnelly's *Dear Caliban* (1977) and Kay Thorpe's *Curtain Call* (1971), Shakespearean plays provide a starting point from which to "meditate on the genre's features and conventions" (136):

> These popular Harlequin writers used Shakespeare to ratify their generic model—impossibly naive heroines, rapacious female losers, manipulative, powerful fathers and father figures, and transcendent true love are features that Shakespeare apparently shares with Harlequin romance novels. However, neither Harlequin conventions nor Shakespeare's plots and characters emerge in these novels without critique. (136–7)

Shakespeare's *Antony and Cleopatra*, as played by the characters in Thorpe's novel, contains an instance of "transcendent true love" (Osborne 137), "Not an ordinary, everyday love, but something wondrous and intoxicating and totally irresistible" (Thorpe 182), yet it certainly does not conclude with the "optimistic ending" (RWA) required of romance novels. Shakespeare's comedies, however, provide many examples of love stories that end happily. Elizabeth Beacon's

---

manuscript of the *Decameron* which she had read, being one which the scribe who had copied it out had considered to be too improper to be repeated" (192). Boccaccio's tale is indeed somewhat bawdy, for its lovers "After exchanging many kisses [...] lay down together and for virtually the entire night they had delight and joy of one another, causing the nightingale to sing at frequent intervals" (396). After the lovers fall asleep "Caterina had tucked her right arm beneath Ricciardo's neck, whilst with her left hand she was holding that part of his person which in mixed company you ladies are too embarrassed to mention" (396), and her father, who finds them thus, tells his wife that "your daughter was so fascinated by the nightingale that she has succeeded in waylaying it, and is holding it in her hand" (397). The identity of the body-part referred to as a "nightingale", and the type of "singing" it makes, are therefore very clear.

An Innocent Courtesan (2007) makes brief mention of one of them:

> '*All's Well That Ends Well*, Caro, you must remember it. The one where that stuffy Count Rousillon rejects poor Helena after he's been forced to marry her against his will.'
>
> Seeing all too many parallels to her own situation, Caro shot out of her comfortable seat by the fire as if she had been stung. (33)

Although the plot of Beacon's novel differs in a great many particulars from that of Shakespeare's play, there are, as Caro, an unwanted and abandoned wife, is all too acutely aware, a great many "parallels" between them. Unfortunate though this may be for her at the start of the novel, by its end she is able to decide:

> to let all the pain and misery of unrequited love go, and savour the glorious promise of the future instead. If she had to go through that to get to where they were now, she would do it twice over, however much pain it took to reach the wonderful destination at the end of it all. (295)

It would appear that she has adopted the philosophy that 'all's well that ends well', thus securing for herself and her husband a happy outcome to a story with a most unpromising beginning.

Sir Edmund Fitzhugh, the hero of Deborah Hale's *My Lord Protector* (1999), demonstrates a similar preference for Shakespearian happy endings. Rejecting the tragic *Romeo and Juliet* on the grounds that "On so cold and gray a day, who needs their spirits depressed with further tragedy?" (91), he chooses to read a play more in keeping with the conventions of the HM&B romance: "Something to lighten the gloom—*A Midsummer Night's Dream*, to my mind Shakespeare's finest comedy" (91).[1] Tragedy is also rejected by both the hero and

---

1   The characters quote from a variety of other sources but *A Midsummer Night's Dream* takes on a special significance for Edmund and Julianna. When Edmund discovers Julianna sleeping outdoors on a "'bank whereon the wild thyme blows.' [...] Edmund spoke King Oberon's words" (134) and Julianna, in memory of that occasion, later chooses to attend a masked ball dressed as "Titania, queen of the fairies, gowned in leaves and crowned with roses" (242). The tangled web of misunderstandings between lovers is almost as complicated in Hale's novel as in Shakespeare's play: Crispin loves Julianna, but in his absence she is obliged

heroine of Claire Thornton's *Raven's Honour* (2002):

> 'You would have preferred a morally uplifting tragedy?' she
> enquired, unable to resist teasing him a little.
> 'There is nothing uplifting about tragedy,' Raven said
> trenchantly.
> 'I never thought so,' Honor agreed. (99)

By championing comedy over tragedy, these novels perhaps indirectly assert their own worth, for "Romance novels are a subgenre of
comedy" (Regis 16).

Romance as Part of Popular Culture

While some HM&B authors have referred to works of 'high' art in
ways which implicitly refute criticisms of romances, it is also the
case that "The attack on romances from all perspectives has been
so pervasive that Harlequin writers have felt compelled to address
the issue of stigmatized popular culture in their fiction" (Jensen 26).[1]
In Cindy Myers's *The Daddy Audition* (2009), for example, Tanya,
the heroine, declares that "Soap operas are the romance novels of
the television world—popular with viewers, but they don't get much
respect" (153). Here the comparison between romances and another
popular genre is made explicit but even when such parallels remain
implicit, romance authors can "voice the common criticisms [of ro-
mances] and take a strong position in favour of them through their
characters' debates about the worth of popular fiction" (Jensen 26)
in a variety of media. In Valerie Parv's *The Love Artist* (1986), for

---

to marry Edmund to avoid the lustful attentions of Jerome, her step-brother and
guardian. Julianna loves Crispin until she literally awakens to the attractions
of his uncle, Edmund, and "Queen Titania, waking in the embrace of the yeo-
man ass, Nick Bottom, could have experienced no less intense instant of shock
and bafflement" (133). Julianna, however, comes to believe that Edmund loves
Vanessa, while Edmund, who considers Julianna to be "a thousandfold more alluring than the fairy queen of his imagination" (139), is convinced that she loves
either Crispin or Laurence. In the end Vanessa marries Clive Farraday, who has
"worshipped her for as long as I can remember" (280), Julianna reveals her true
feelings to Edmund, who reciprocates her love, and Crispin and Laurence set off
for a long voyage to the South Seas.

1   Jensen (26–8) gives some examples of HM&B romances that address this issue, and an additional example can be found in Thomas (74–6).

example, the heroine's father is a cartoonist who has more than once been asked "when I'm going to do some real work, like oils, instead of this childish black and white scribble" (127–8). It seems no coincidence that one of "the standard and inevitable questions that interviewers and 'just plain folk' alike find themselves unable *not* to ask a romance writer" is "When are you going to write a real book?" (Tetel Andresen 174). The hero of the novel is also a cartoonist and he "has been fighting this kind of prejudice all his life" (181); his happy future with the heroine is assured when she tells him that although other forms of art are more prestigious, "what you do is so much more important. You make people happy, teach them a thing or two" (186).

In Hilary Neal's *Nurse Off Camera* (1964) a few of the more "common criticisms" are directed at a hospital drama named *Casualty Bell*. One director, on learning that he may have to direct a number of its episodes, declares that it is "Not my cup of tea, but it might be restful to be non-creative for a bit" (36), thus impugning the show's artistic value. Another not only describes the scripts as "inane" (57) but also states that he cannot remember reading the one he is about to direct because "I try to forget the thing again as quickly as possible. One doesn't want all that sticky escapism littering up one's brain, surely?" (57). Neal demonstrates, however, that this second director makes an effort to ensure that the drama is both factually and emotionally realistic, and for Pat Kenyon, the heroine of the novel, the plot of *Casualty Bell* is not escapist at all: "It was all too near home. A car smash, and the victims being brought in from the ambulance, wasn't exactly an escape from my own problems" (60).[1]

Pat is an experienced nurse and the "professional adviser on *Casualty Bell*" (37), a job which involves "sitting in on rehearsals and spotting flaws in nursing technique" (37). She also comments on the actors' general demeanour, as when she notes that Sylvia, who is new to the show, "gives [a] hard, impatient, impression. She needs to move more calmly and speak more gently. A nurse would be infinitely more deliberate" (60). Pat takes her role as adviser

---

1   Accuracy with respect to the details of hospital life is apparently demanded by *Casualty Bell*'s audience: in the early days of the programme's history a lack of attention to detail led to the station receiving "many terrible diatribes from the dear viewers" (59).

seriously and she is fully prepared to insist on "another change in the cast list" (61) should Sylvia be unable or unwilling "to project a respectable image of the profession" (61). Hilary Neal had herself been a nurse (Meldrum 523) and according to McAleer was one of the M&B authors who "fought for a greater degree of realism in their hospital stories" (*Passion's Fortune* 271).[1] He gives as an example her *Casualty Speaking* (1971), published under the pseudonym 'Kate Norway', in which she "offered a graphic account of an inner-city hospital, not unlike the medical drama programmes currently in vogue on television" (271). Thus, in their respective roles as an author of medical romances and an advisor on the set of a hospital drama, both Hilary Neal and Pat Kenyon insist that medical fictions must be set in an accurately rendered context. They may also be said to share a similar attitude towards the depiction of medical personnel: Pat is adamant that the actors must be "prepared to project a respectable image of the profession" (61) while Neal's medical romances "usually revolve around a young female nurse (occasionally doctor) who is dedicated, competent, and attractive" (Meldrum 525).[2]

Such parallels between an author and a heroine may not be immediately apparent to a reader unaware of Neal's personal history, but the centrality and role of *Casualty Bell* within *Nurse Off Camera* ensure that even without that extra-textual context it poses "questions about the relationship between fiction and reality" (Waugh 2). It is intimated as early as the first chapter that the distinction between the two is not as clear as Pat expects: although she "hadn't imagined I could be mistaken for anything else" (10), Christopher Starling, the hero, initially assumes she is not a real nurse but "one of the cast" (10) of *Casualty Bell*. Later in the novel it is precisely because she is a real nurse that she is inveigled into showing Sylvia "how a *real* Casualty Sister would behave" (76) and ends up replacing her in the role:

---

1   'Hilary Neal' was one pseudonym employed by Olive Norton (Meldrum 523).
2   According to Julia Hallam, M&B medical romances of this period were united in their positive depiction of the National Health Service: "the one thing that they unequivocally share is support for the NHS. [...] Dedication to medicine for the sake of suffering humanity is given positive value, practising medicine as a way of making money or conferring social status viewed negatively" (71).

It didn't seem like acting. It was simply a case of doing what I'd do anyway. It came naturally. I had only to play up to the others.

That, at any rate, was what I said to Simon when we broke for lunch. "Well of *course*, dear girl, it was pure Method. You *were* Sister Whatsaname. [...]" (77)

The plot of *Casualty Bell* further parallels Pat's own life, and thus the plot of *Nurse Off Camera*, when the script-writer introduces "a bit of sub-plot romance for you" (114). Her character is supposed to remain stoic upon learning that the man she loves has been injured, and for all that the production assistant thinks such a reaction is "corny [...] I bet real nurses flap like crazy when their dear ones are brought in all mashed up, whatever script writers think" (114), the reader may recall that when Pat was told her boyfriend had sustained a "concussion and head injuries" (45) in a car accident, she certainly did not "flap like crazy". Pat herself has some doubts about the verisimilitude of another aspect of the plot:

> Roddy Cashmore's idea of sub-plot romance struck me as a little naïve. Harry, the old flame, was to arrive among several casualties from a train-crash. [...] It seemed to me contrived, to say the least, that this Harry should return from darkest Africa to search for his long-lost love and manage to land instantly in the right hospital as a casualty. However, if the viewers liked that kind of thing—and they obviously did to judge from the audience-ratings—it was not my worry. My job was to make it look convincing. (126–7)

She does so by thinking of Christopher, her own estranged beloved, and her final scene in *Casualty Bell*, in which the Casualty Sister is reconciled with Harry, merges Pat's reality with the plot of the drama: Pat sees that Christopher has returned to her, races "towards the camera, and what I said can't have been in the script because it was: 'Chris! Oh, *Chris!*'" (155). This conclusion to Pat's time on the show seems to suggest that although certain aspects of *Casualty Bell*'s plot may be "contrived, to say the least", there is nonetheless a basis of emotional truth to it; Pat retains "a cutting from my last script" as one of three mementoes which remind her "that anything that can be imagined is possible" (158).

These, the final words of the novel, recall Pat's earlier musing that "Hadn't somebody once said that anything a man can imagine is possible? Or was that just another way of saying that man's imagination was limited to rearranging the possible, the known?" (55). Neal's own novel, and the hospital dramas that Neal implicitly defends against the accusation that they are mindless and unrealistic escapism, may limit themselves to "rearranging the possible", but Hope Tarr's *It's a Wonderfully Sexy Life* (2006), which also explores the similarities between real life and popular culture fictions, does not. It is a novel which, as suggested by its title, takes its premise from the heroine's:

> hands-down favorite Christmas flick [...] It's a Wonderful Life. When Jimmy Stewart's George Bailey stands ready to jump off that bridge on Christmas Eve, who can't help getting a tear in their eye? For me, the scene stealer in that film is the guardian angel sent down to earth to earn his wings by helping poor, down-on-his-luck George see how terrible life would turn out for his loved ones if he'd never been born. (8)

Although at one point the hero, Josh, distinguishes between "real life" and "reel life" (39), the back-cover copy reveals that Tarr's novel is also the story of a Christmas miracle:

> Mandy Delinski isn't expecting any miracles this Christmas. She's thirty, a touch too round, still very single and she lives with her parents. So who could have guessed that her whole life would change before New Year's Eve? That a simple job policing a Christmas party would find her in the arms of sexy-as-sin bartender Josh Thornton? [...] That Mandy would find her perfect man in the morgue the next day? Or that she'd be given a magical chance to go back a week, save Josh ... and have the best sex of her life.

Mandy writes in her diary that "Like George Bailey standing on that bridge or Dorothy clicking the heels of those ruby slippers, sometimes you have to close your eyes and just believe" (10). These references to *It's a Wonderful Life* and *The Wizard of Oz* align Tarr's novel with other works of popular culture which include the fantastic, the miraculous, and the magical. Tarr does not apologise for this. Instead she states in her letter to the reader that "sometimes the very best gift we can give ourselves [...] is the permission to close our eyes and dare to believe" (2). Tarr does not specify what it is that her readers should "dare to believe" but it perhaps includes belief in "happy endings, make that Happy Beginnings" (233) of the sort she and other romance writers give their characters. Certainly when Mandy makes a wish because "she desperately needed to believe in something—in the possibility of happy endings and magic and make-believe; in the power of wishing" (69), it comes true, giving her a chance at finding her "happy ending". Neal's and Tarr's differing attitudes towards realism and fantasy seem to reflect the differing mimetic modes in which their novels are written: Neal's is a low-mimetic romance, whereas the miracle in Tarr's moves it into the 'romance' mode.

Their shared preoccupation with popular culture productions for the screen (whether it be the TV screen, as in Neal's novel, or the big screen, as in Tarr's) is evinced by many other HM&Bs. In Casey Douglas's *Edge of Illusion* (1984), for example, the heroine is "an unqualified success in her writing career. A popular romance novelist, Cam already had a half-dozen books published under her pseudonym, Camille de la Croix" (5). In addition, "The movie rights to her last novel [...] had been sold to a Hollywood studio, and her agent [...] had negotiated for Cam herself to write the screenplay" (7). Cam's success in having her novel made into a movie may represent something of a professional fantasy for some HM&B authors: although "Several Harlequins have been adapted for the screen" (Grescoe 282), they represent only a tiny proportion of the total number of novels published. It is far more usual for film and television to inspire HM&B authors and even, very occasionally, their fictional counterparts: Mary Wibberley has admitted that

> One day I was watching television and an episode of a series called *Heartland* came on. [...] I knew immediately that the girl in the play was my heroine for my next book. Her name is Arwen Holm [...]. I watched the entire play in total fascina-

tion, and then played it back and made comprehensive notes of every mannerism of the actress, a detailed description of her physical appearance, clothes, voice, personality. Two days later I began writing the book, called it *Fire and Steel* and named my heroine Arwenna. (52–3)

Tara, the romance-writing heroine of Trish Wylie's *Her Real Life Hero* (2004), sometimes has "ideas for stories" that come from "a film I don't like the ending of" (176).

Movies may also serve as a point of reference when an author is describing the context in which her characters find themselves. In Jeanne Allan's *No Angel* (1990), for example, a post-coital situation evokes thoughts of movies: "It was a pity that they didn't smoke. In films that always seemed to take care of this awkward moment" (154). It is similarities, rather than differences, between romantic comedies and the emotional background of his own life that are identified by Seth, a young secondary character in Karen Templeton's *Everybody's Hero* (2004). He deduces that his half-brother and the heroine of the novel are "in love with each other but didn't know what to do about it" (178) because he:

> had watched lots of those stupid romance movies with his mom, where people were all the time acting dumb because they actually liked each other, so he figured he pretty much knew the signs. However, Seth also figured nobody would be much interested in hearing a kid's take on the issue [...] so he kept quiet about that [...]. After all, in most of those movies, everybody eventually stopped acting dumb and just went ahead and admitted they loved each other, so everything turned out okay in the end. (178)

Seth's assessment of the situation is entirely correct and everything does indeed turn "out okay in the end" for precisely the reasons he has identified.

Romantic comedies inspired the plots of Liz Fielding's *Eloping with Emmy* (1998) and Nancy Warren's *Hot Off The Press* (2003). The former sees the hero "chasing around the South of France with a runaway heiress" (Fielding 90) and, as he himself acknowledges,

"The whole thing was like some 1940s romantic comedy with Cary Grant. Except there was nothing funny about the situation, at least not from his point of view" (Fielding 90). *Hot Off the Press* is even more self-reflexive in its treatment of romantic comedies. In a letter to the reader Warren writes that:

> I love movies. My favourites are still the old black-and-white romantic comedies. *It Happened One Night, His Girl Friday* and *Roman Holiday* are just three that spring to mind where the hero is a newspaper reporter. [...] I thought it would be fun to write my own romantic comedy about a pair of competitive newspaper reporters after the same big story. [...] Tess Elliot and Mike Grundel [...] share a love of the movies and a keen nose for news. (2)

Excerpts from Tess and Mike's film reviews provide epigraphs for each of the chapters. The penultimate chapter opens with an except from a review in which Mike admits that sometimes even he "buys into a happy ending" (201); in the chapter itself he works to ensure his own. Another excerpt asks "Have you ever noticed the so-called 'chick flicks' are about love, strong women and family? 'Guy movies' are about war, bloodshed and big machines. Think about it" (24). Romance novels, like 'chick flicks', are certainly "about love" and many are also "about [...] strong women and family".

Popular culture references such as those in Fielding and Warren's novels can be read as acknowledgements that, as Camille de la Croix's agent argues, "Movies, paperbacks, TV—they're all part of the same entertainment package" (Douglas 104). All references to specific actors or works of popular culture will, however, fail to achieve their intended effects if readers do not possess the requisite knowledge of the actors, authors, or works mentioned. Authors may therefore allude to works of popular culture which have international appeal in preference to ones which will be intelligible to only a small proportion of HM&B's global readership. For example, in the UK in "the seventies editors were warning authors, 'Don't talk about *The Archers* if you want to sell abroad.'" (Haddon and Pearson 232): the M&B editors clearly felt that this BBC radio soap opera would be unknown to most overseas readers, despite being extremely popular in the UK.

Other references may quickly cease to have the intended impact on readers if the contemporary actors or works to which they refer achieve only an ephemeral success. In her guide to writing romances Leslie Wainger, an editor at Harlequin, advises that authors should:

> **Be careful about pop-culture references**. Today's hit is to-morrow's trivia question. So when it comes to pop culture references—music, movies, television, best-selling books, and even computer games—you're better off having your characters rent a DVD (videos are already passé) of a classic like *Casablanca* or *M*A*S*H* [...] rather than something that's current (and will probably be forgotten by the time the book comes out). Or, just as good, mention that they rent a *just-released hit* [...], which lets you avoid mentioning any specifics. (24)

Since HM&Bs are themselves often considered to be ephemeral, it might be thought that it would not be a matter of concern to HM&B authors if their books quickly became dated. However, as Wainger observes, there is inevitably a delay between the day on which the author completes the novel and "the time the book comes out". In addition, translations and reprints may appear years after a work was first published. Mary Burchell's *Dearly Beloved*, for example, first appeared in 1944 and in one scene in the original edition the heroine shows her new engagement ring to a co-worker, Kathleen, who responds ecstatically:

> Oh, Miss Saldyn, isn't it a beauty? [...] Oh, and fancy it being Mr. Trander. It's just like a film. Did you see that one where Ginger Rogers married her boss? He was awfully stern too, but he loved her like anything in the end. Oh, Miss Saldyn, I do think it's romantic. (124)

Mills & Boon appear to have decided that the reference to Ginger Rogers would badly date the novel: in the 1968 edition of the novel Kathleen now asks "Did you see that one where Julie Andrews married her boss?" (124).

Discussions of, and allusions to, older films do not, however, date a novel if they are included in a way which either implicitly or explicitly acknowledges that the works are not recent releases. In Elizabeth Ashton's *Moonlight on the Nile* (1979), for example, both the hero and heroine of the novel are temporarily involved in the production of "one of your good old-fashioned desert melodramas" (22) with a plot that the heroine, Lorna Travers, describes as "rather old hat" (49). Its director admits that "the theme's dated, of course, but it's due for a revival and it always appeals to females" (49).

Moonlight on the Nile in fact invokes elements to be found in both sheikh movies and romance novels. The first wave of HM&B sheikh romances included Louise Gerard's *A Sultan's Slave* (1921), which "portrays a hero obviously based on E. M. Hull's *The Sheik* (1919)" (Dixon 52), and "Although the subgenre of the British-authored 'sheik novel' had run out of steam by the late 1930s, the 1970s saw its revival" (Teo, "Historicizing"). In HM&B romances "sheik-heroes return with Violet Winspear's *Blue Jasmine* (1969), her tribute to E. M. Hull's *The Sheik*" (Dixon 7) and they remain popular to this day. Although *Moonlight on the Nile* is not a sheikh romance, Lorna first encounters her hero, Miles, in the Egyptian desert:

> He had seen her, he was galloping towards her, his cloak, burnous or whatever it was streaming behind him like a cloud. An Arab? It was unlikely to be a European. She had always enjoyed novels about the desert, the handsome sheik who carried the lovely heroine to his tent and promptly fell in love with her, but she knew that only happened in romances. The nomads she had seen in the vicinity of Cairo were far from prepossessing. [...] The horse came nearer, its pace reduced to a steady trot [...]. Its rider was enveloped in a white burnous and wore the usual headdress of white cloth, held on by triple cords. They could be bought from street vendors throughout the land for the price of one dollar upwards. (Ashton 8–9)

This passage evokes the romantic associations of both film and prose sheikh romances yet also slightly distances itself from them through the prosaic description of the ubiquity and low cost of the headdress, and via the irony of the statement that "she knew that only happened in romances".[1] Since Lorna *is* the heroine of a romance, the remainder of the novel relates what happens after her rescuer carried this "lovely heroine to his tent and promptly fell in love with her".[2]

The ambivalence is maintained, and the lines between reality and fiction are blurred yet further, when Lorna and Miles act as stunt doubles:

> 'You don't have to act,' Bob told her. 'Just let yourself be mauled a bit when you get collared. You see you've run away from the Sheik, but he recaptures you. That's the bit we're going to do. Much what happened yesterday, I imagine.' (48).

The scene, as Bob says, bears some resemblance to Miles's real rescue of Lorna and later, during the shooting of it, when Miles provokes her into struggling, Lorna finds it difficult to distinguish between fiction and reality:

> His mouth came down on hers, hard and compelling. Lorna's heart seemed to stop and then began to race [...] her soft mouth parted under the pressure of his lips, then she remembered he was only acting and out there Mario and Bob were watching. She felt outraged that he dared to so exploit her, and a wave of fury overwhelmed her. (52)

Lorna initially responds as though the kiss were real, then assumes it

---

1   The rider, though not a sheikh, does turn out to be the hero, and throughout the novel continues alternately to confound and conform to expectations raised by romantic fiction. His features, for example, "would not have disgraced a romantic hero, a clear-cut, aquiline profile [...] a brown face, but the eyes which looked at her enquiringly were of a piercing, brilliant blue" (9). Lorna, well versed in how a romance sheikh should look, instantly responds: "They ought to be black" (9). Later, in the tent to which he carries her, he comments that "'You must find my quarters a bit of a let-down.' With a sweep of his hand he indicated the bare little tent. 'No Bokhara rugs, or Oriental hangings, no silken divan and leopardskins, the scent of insecticide instead of jasmine, and no passionate lover to fall at your feet.'" (28). He does, however, remove Lorna's sandals and "bent his head swiftly as if moved by an uncontrollable impulse and pressed his lips on her foot" (29), only to add " 'A bit sandy,' he remarked prosaically" (29).
2   Much later in the novel Miles reveals that "The damage to me was done when I saw you lying on that miserable camp bed in my tent. Such a lovely delicate-looking being, crying out for love and protection" (147).

is part of an act. At this point she and Miles are fictional characters in a romance novel, pretending to be the film-stars Mario and Rosina, who in turn are acting in a movie (a fiction within a fiction) that can trace its ancestry back to another novel and film. E. M. Hull's 1919 novel *The Sheik* "reached its pinnacle of fame and influence when it was filmed in 1921 with Rudolph Valentino playing Ahmed" (Cadogan 130) and "firmly established the convention of a desert passion and sparked off a whole train of sandy romances" (R. Anderson 189).[1] In the movie being shot in Ashton's novel, the role of hero is played by "an Italian who by virtue of his sexy good looks was famous in two hemispheres" (24), just as it was in the Hollywood version of *The Sheik*, but in *Moonlight on the Nile* it is Miles, temporarily working as the actor's double, who is described as a man who could "go

---

1   Unfortunately *Moonlight on the Nile* also contains questionable instances of intertextuality. Evelyn Bach has observed that "the settings [...] of [...] desert romances, [are] carefully researched and endorsed as authentic by both readers and publishers" (14) and this desire for authenticity perhaps led Ashton to cling too closely to the text of certain passages from the *Encyclopaedia Britannica* entry on Thebes. She describes the temple of Amon-re thus: "The hypostyle hall had at one time been converted into a Christian church. The great court is surrounded on three sides by a double row of graceful columns carved to represent papyrus clusters, their capitals the umbels of the papyrus plant in bud" (100–01). The *Encyclopaedia* states that "the hypostyle hall was at one time converted into a Christian church [...]. The great court is surrounded on three sides by a double row of graceful papyrus-cluster columns, their capitals imitating the umbels of papyrus in bud" (978–9). Ashton also relates that at a nearby site there are:

> two great statues which had originally flanked the gateway in front of the temple pylon. Temple and pylon had gone, and they were left like lonely sentinels in the midst of fields. They both represented the Pharaoh himself and with their crowns on had been nearly seventy feet high; each was hewn from a single block of stone. [...]. The northern one had been celebrated in classical times as the 'Singing Memnon' because on certain days shortly after sunrise it emitted a curious high note, until during Roman times it was patched up with masonry and never sang again. (102)

This is extremely close to the wording in the *Encyclopaedia*:

> the two great statues known as the Colossi of Memnon [...] once flanked the gateway in front of the temple pylon but now sit like lonely sentinels in the middle of cultivated fields. The statues represent Amenhotep III; with their crowns they were nearly 70ft. high and each was hewn from a single block of stone. The northern one was the "singing Memnon" celebrated in classical times because on certain days, shortly after sunrise, it emitted a curious high note; [...] in the reign of Septimius Severus the statue was patched with masonry and never sang again. (980)

far once he got a start, another Valentino over whose celluloid image hysterical women raved" (36).

Another popular genre to which some HM&Bs make metafictional reference is the Gothic, both in various older forms and in the version which emerged as a result of "The latest [subgeneric] Gothic revival [which] began in 1960, with the publication of Victoria Holt's *Mistress of Mellyn*" (Williams 101). It has been argued that "in a number of ways, the Gothic romance never did fully die out: many Gothic themes could be found in other popular romance lines, particularly 'romantic suspense,' 'paranormal romance,' and various types of historical romances" (Lutz, "The Haunted" 82). Anne Stuart's *A Dark & Stormy Night* (1997), which repeatedly alludes to Gothic romances, is both a paranormal and a romantic suspense novel, and although it is a contemporary rather than a historical romance, its heroine does briefly think that "It would have been nice if she'd been a Victorian heroine […] it would have been lovely to sink to the floor in a graceful faint" (21).[1] Due to a storm, Katie finds herself in a large house "perched out on a spit of land with the sea all around it" (31) and "wasn't sure who she found more unsettling, the brooding master of this gothic mansion or his faintly sinister servant" (103). In addition, the house resembled:

> something out of a gothic novel. All she needed was a flowing

---

1   The novel abounds with intertextual references, beginning with its title, which alludes to the first line of Bulwer-Lytton's *Paul Clifford*; the phrase is repeated early in the text (15). O'Neal, the hero, is reading "the latest *Star Trek* novel" (89) while Katie, the heroine, has lost "her stash of murder mysteries and romance novels" (83), "loved Jane Austen" (173), is less than keen on Dickens (83, 103), and mentions *Wuthering Heights* and *Jane Eyre* (36–7, 159). Although O'Neal states that he's neither "a gothic hero" (159) nor "a romantic hero" (38), Katie persists in thinking of him as "a second-string version of Mr. Rochester" (67). One villain has a "long, jagged scar across the top of his forehead, beneath his shaggy hair [that] gave him the eerie look of Frankenstein's monster" (80) and his equally villainous mother, who appears "comfortable, elderly, warm and sensible" (25), has a voice that can make her sound "bizarrely like Mrs. Doubtfire" (41). As that last description indicates, Stuart does not limit her intertextuality to novels: on a number of occasions Katie compares her current circumstances and surroundings to those in films (73, 137, 139, 149, 153) and on television, as when she wonders if "Maybe she was living in some old 'Twilight Zone' episode" (86) and concludes that "the old stone mansion was like something out of a thirties' horror movie" (104).

white nightgown and a candlestick to fit the bill.

Of course, that was exactly what she'd had the night before, as she'd gone in search of the brooding master of the house. (83)

Eventually Katie becomes so aware of resemblances between fiction and her own existence that she briefly questions the reality of her surroundings: "Led here by ghosts, watched over by a caretaker and her silent son, lured by a brooding master of the house worthy of a gothic romance, it was almost as if this place didn't really exist" (175).

The Gothic also plays a significant role in Deborah Simmons's *The Last Rogue* (1998), a historical romance which takes as its hero Deverell Fairfax, Viscount Raleigh, who has unexpectedly inherited an estate from a deceased relative. Raleigh observes that "this whole wretched place looks like something out of Lady Ravenscar's books [...] Prudence [...] writes Gothic novels and married a friend of mine, Sebastian, earl of Ravenscar" (106).[1] Raleigh's "copy of the Ravenscars' new book" (155) goes missing and it becomes apparent that "Someone had endeavored to enact for their benefit, one of the ghostly happenings from the gothic novel" (182). Part of a fiction within a fiction is thus transformed into reality within the pages of *The Last Rogue*. Two scenes from Horace Walpole's *The Castle of Otranto* (1765) are also recreated (190, 212), which leads Raleigh to deduce that "Our mischief-makers are not well-read at all. It appears that they are limited to but two gothic novels" (212).

The heroine of Carola Dunn's *A Lord for Miss Larkin* (1991) has read rather more than two Gothic romances and the novel begins as:

> With a sigh of satisfaction, Alison closed the marbled covers of Mrs. Kitty Cuthbertson's latest novel. Curled in the corner of the shabby sofa [...] for a few moments she let her imagination drift through marble palaces and dark, sinister, ruined abbeys. How romantic it would be to have a handsome young lord swooning at one's feet! (5)

Alison "is a slave to Minerva Press novels" (50). The Minerva Press:

---

1   Prudence and Sebastian were the protagonists of an earlier novel by Simmons, *The Devil Earl* (1996).

in the years between the death of Smollett and the rise of Scott was the chief purveyor of the circulating-library novel. So closely identified with cheap fiction was the famous publishing house in Leadenhall Street that to nineteenth-century critics the name Minerva meant little more than a convenient epithet of contempt. 'Minerva Press every grain of it', the *Athenaeum* called the happy ending of the Begum's story in *Pendennis*. (Blakey 1)

The parallels with Mills & Boon are obvious, since it too was once known as a "library house" and it is now a publisher of "cheap fiction".[1] In addition, the company's name is also used as "a convenient epithet of contempt". Mary Cadogan reports that:

In the autumn of 1993, for example, Dr John Habgood, the Archbishop of York, when discussing the soaring divorce rate, informed a Mothers' Union conference that 'those with too many hopes are going into something with quite unrealistic expectations, supported by media hype, Mills & Boon romantic novels, pop songs and screen images of highly romantic and highly sexual love ...' (310)

In Dunn's novel Alison has "unrealistic expectations" because, in the words of her aunt, Mrs Zenobia Winkle, she has been "addling [her] noddle with too many novels" (33). Dunn encourages the reader to ponder the relationship between life and romantic fiction by contrasting Alison's own love story with those contained within the Minerva romances.

As a result of her reading, Alison thinks it would be "the most romantic thing in the world" (44) "to have a lord at one's feet professing undying love" (117), and "used to suppose that all lords were alike.

---

1   Relatively early in Mills & Boon's history, when there were "commercial libraries opening across the country, particularly during the early 1930s, there was money to be made as a 'library house'" (McAleer, *Passion's Fortune* 59). Later:

During the years from 1958 until 1964, the commercial libraries were winding down, and the transition to paperbacks was under way, but not yet complete. In 1964 Mills & Boon started printing paperback novels in Britain (as opposed to importing a limited number of novels printed in Canada), allowing a fuller saturation of the home market. Readers responded—and profits rose annually. (McAleer 114)

At least Mrs. Meeke and Mrs. Cuthbertson would have it so" (142).[1]
After a series of disillusionments, however, she comes to "think that
everything Mrs. Meeke and Mrs. Cuthbertson ever wrote is all a hum"
(242–3). Yet although Alison does not marry an aristocratic and titled
"hero of a gothick romance" (250), she eventually discovers that
"nothing in the whole world could possibly be half as romantic as
being Mrs. Philip Trevelyan" (286).[2] This discovery of romance in a

---

1   Mrs Meeke, who wrote for the Minerva Press, "was a prolific writer. Besides
     some two dozen romances under her own name, she published four others
     under the pseudonym 'Gabrielli', as well as various translations from German
     and French" (Blakey 60). Roberta Magnani's calculation of Mrs Meeke's out-
     put differs slightly: "her overall production consists of 26 novels in 95 volumes
     published between 1795 and 1823, exceeding Scott, who wrote 22 novels in 71
     volumes during the first two decades of the nineteenth century" (116). What is
     clear, however, is that she was extremely prolific. The fourth edition of Catherine
     Cuthbertson's *Santo Sebastiano* was published by the Minerva Press in 1820
     (Blakey 329).

2   It seems probable that Dunn gave Philip this surname after reading G. O. Trev-
     elyan's *The Life and Letters of Lord Macaulay*. Mrs Meeke and Mrs Cuthbertson,
     who are mentioned so often in *A Lord for Miss Larkin*, were both favourites with
     Macaulay:

     "There was a certain prolific author," says Lady Trevelyan, "named Mrs.
     Meeke, whose romances he all but knew by heart; though he quite agreed
     in my criticism that they were one just like another, turning on the fortunes of
     some young man in a very low rank of life who eventually proves to be the
     son of a Duke. Then there was a set of books by a Mrs. Kitty Cuthbertson,
     most silly though readable productions, the nature of which may be guessed
     from their titles:— 'Santo Sebastiano, or the Young Protector,' 'The Forest of
     Montalbano,' 'The Romance of the Pyrenees,' and 'Adelaide, or the Counter-
     charm.' [...]" (Trevelyan 1: 132)

     In Dunn's novel Alison appears to have analysed one aspect of *Santo Sebas-
     tiano* in particular detail:

     "I see. Then you are perfectly free to have any number of peers swooning
     at your feet."
     "Have you read Mrs. Cuthbertson's novels?" asked Alison eagerly. "Letty
     has lent me most of them. I do think, though, that her heroes and heroines
     waste a lot of time in fainting fits. We counted them in one book, *Santo Se-
     bastiano* I think it was, and there were twenty-seven swoons altogether. (46)

     Dunn's source for this information is likely to have been *The Life and Letters of
     Lord Macaulay*. Trevelyan notes of Macaulay's copy of *Santo Sebastiano* that:

     As an indication of the thoroughness with which this literary treasure has
     been studied, there appears on the last page an elaborate computation of the
     number of fainting-fits that occur in the course of the five volumes. [...] A sin-
     gle passage, selected for no other reason than because it is the shortest, will

more realistic, attainable form is paralleled by the lesson that Alison teaches Philip. He too has to learn to "look beyond the label", in his case the labels of "'urchin' or 'eccentric old maid' to see them as individuals" (227). Read as metafiction, Dunn's novel would appear to ask the reader to "look beyond the label", to judge each romance on its own merits, and to find the kernel of reality that lies at the heart of even the most extravagantly unrealistic romantic tales.

HM&Bs, then, can and do use references to other works of fiction in order to "pose questions about the relationship between fiction and reality" (Waugh 2). At other times however, as Dixon has noted, quotations may simply be incorporated into the authors' shared stock of common allusions, words and metaphors:

> the typist [...] had queried my use of the word "bereft". I left it in, as it was one of the key Mills & Boon words at the time, used to express the heroine's feelings of despair and desolation at her separation from the hero. It is no longer part of the language of Mills & Boon books. That is to say, it is not a "code" word carrying a symbolic resonance over and beyond its usual meaning [...].
>
> As head copyeditor I experienced a similar event in the mid-1980s. A new freelance editor queried the phrase, "I have been faithful to thee, Cynara! in my fashion," a quote from Ernest Dowson's poem *Non sum qualis eram sub regno cynarae*. [...] I left it, aware that it had been used before in Mills & Boon books and was then, for a short time, part of the vocabulary of the readers, *as readers of Mills & Boon books*. (37–8)

The repeated use of "code" words, phrases, and metaphors is a characteristic which the HM&B romance shares with older forms of literature such as the courtly love poetry mentioned in the Introduction. Indeed, the vocabulary employed by the *cancionero* love poets was even more restricted than that of HM&Bs: it was "remarkably limited both in quantity and in type (nearly all of the words are ab-

---

serve as a specimen of these catastrophes: "One of the sweetest smiles that ever animated the face of mortal now diffused itself over the countenance of Lord St. Orville, as he fell at the feet of Julia in a death-like swoon." (1: 132)
The "elaborate computation" produces a total of twenty-seven swoons.

stract)" (Deyermond 198). In addition, "the number of stanzas, the number of rhymes, and the arrangements of the rhyme-scheme" were "closely delimited" and "This restriction is a sign of ingenuity: to operate successfully within the very narrow limits allowed by the [...] convention is a supreme test of a poet's skill" (Deyermond 198). By comparison, the page limits imposed by HM&B, and their authors' shared pool of allusions, key words and metaphors, seem expansive. Barlow and Krentz argue that the test of the romance author's skill is not to demonstrate linguistic originality (although given the fact that HM&Bs are less restricted than the *cancionero* poems there is considerably more room for such originality) but to succeed in using "stock phrases and literary figures [...] to evoke emotion" (21). The next chapter explores just a few of the common metaphors employed in HM&Bs. As we shall see, there can be considerable variation in the way a metaphor is expressed; some authors are more skilled than others and a metaphor's meaning can alter subtly depending on the context and the underlying attitudes and beliefs of the author.

Chapter 4. Metaphors

> Metaphors are everywhere. They come naturally and no high-
> er education is required to be able to use them. In fact many
> people apply them without even noticing. On the other hand,
> to use metaphors to some effect, to hit the right note, to im-
> press the audience, is a matter of natural talent and cannot, at
> least not entirely, be acquired from another. (Leidl 32)

The fact that the authors of romances employ metaphors is hardly
surprising and cannot in itself constitute proof of any literary merit in
HM&Bs. Nonetheless, as I hope to demonstrate in this chapter, some
extended metaphors to be found in individual novels may "impress
the audience" and thus demonstrate their authors' "natural talent".
Even the most common of metaphors, however, perhaps used without the author "even noticing", may reveal much to the literary critic.

George Lakoff and Mark Johnson have suggested that metaphors
"can have the power to define reality" (157) and this can very literally
be the case in fiction. Diana Holmes, writing about the popular
romantic fiction of Belle Époque France, has observed that:

> The transparency of signs is another very evident mark of
> the popular [...]. Moral or emotional events always produce
> physical effects: thus in volume ii of Lesueur's *Calvaire de
> femme*, the innocent young Bérengère, denied the right to
> marry the man she loves, almost dies of an unnamed illness;
> in *Le Masque d'amour*, the pretty but mean-spirited Françoise
> is physically altered by jealousy of her more beautiful cousin
> [...] 'Her dimples lengthened into wrinkles.' (26)

Thus an emotion which might metaphorically be described as a sick-
ness actually causes a physical illness, and an emotion which might
metaphorically be described as ugly appears to cause Françoise to

lose some of her beauty.[1] It has been argued that "Cultures are dis-
ciplines that provide codes and social scripts for the domestication
of the individual body in conformity to the needs of the social and
political order" (Scheper-Hughes and Lock 26) and in fiction this
process can be intensified, with individual bodies also adapted "in
conformity to the needs of" HM&B authors and readers. Romance
heroes, for example, tend to be taller and more muscular than the
average real man:

> The body of the romantic hero may represent an ideal of mas-
> culine beauty, but beauty here is the equivalent of physical
> strength, and physical strength itself becomes a sign of some-
> thing more, a definition of authentic virility as a power that is
> always scarcely contained. (J. Cook 155)[2]

The mental images of the heroes' bodies created by these texts can
therefore be thought of as visual metaphors for, or symbols of, masculinity. This tendency towards idealisation and intensification with
regards to the bodies and emotions of the heroes and heroines is, of
course, a characteristic of the high-mimetic mode, in which the protagonists have "passions, and powers of expression far greater than
ours" (Frye 34).

---

1   These metaphors may, however, have some basis in medical science. As
Salovey *et al.* have observed:

> That the arousal of emotion might have consequences for physical health is
> not a new idea. [...] Although Hippocrates no doubt had the details wrong, he
> provided prescient guidance regarding possible connections between emo-
> tion and health.
>   Psychotherapists and practicing physicians similarly have recognized the
> comorbidity of psychological and physical disorders. (110)

For many centuries lovesickness was considered a serious medical condition,
and its history has been briefly summarised by Nancy Dzaja, who concludes
that "Many of the symptoms and signs remained constant regardless of what
point in time or in what culture you examine them; this adds to the authenticity of
the disease. Many aspects of the disease can be explained by elements of modern psychiatric disorders, which makes it likely that there are still many patients
suffering from lovesickness even today" (69). As for Françoise, since frowns
and other facial gestures associated with negative emotions can contribute to
the formation of wrinkles, their appearance here could perhaps be considered to
have been accelerated in order to serve as an indicator of her ugly feelings.

2   For a more detailed analysis of the representations of the bodies of the heroes
and heroines of romance novels, see Vivanco and Kramer.

Holmes also found that in late nineteenth-century French romantic fiction, "the pathetic fallacy is a commonplace, so that the reader is secure in their translation of a storm as the harbinger of violent events, and blue skies as signifiers of at least a temporary happiness" (26). Paizis similarly suggests that in modern romances, "by a simple substitution of the term 'feeling' for the notion 'weather' where it features prominently [...] we obtain a reflection of the heroine's affective state" (*Love* 62). Readers, like the hero of Nan Asquith's *The Certain Spring* (1956), are undoubtedly aware that, as "Binyon wrote [...] 'Earth cares for her own ruins, naught for ours. Nothing is certain, only the certain spring.'" (186) but, like the heroine of the novel, this is unlikely to prevent them responding emotionally to weather which mirrors the protagonists' mood:

> Penny looked through the window at the bright blue sky be-yond, at the cherry tree in the inn yard opposite, snow-white against the sky, shedding its petal confetti over the cobble-stones. She said:
> "Isn't it a beautiful day, Steve? I'm so happy. I feel as if eve-rything's just beginning for us. I can't believe now that it was ever wintertime and that I was ever sad." (185)

That the weather in romances reflects or contrasts with the emotions of heroines and heroes is perhaps not surprising given that although romances are generally written in the high- and low-mimetic modes, they often borrow from both the mythic mode, in which gods may directly affect the weather, and the 'romance' mode, in which "the ordinary laws of nature are slightly suspended" (Frye 33).

Unfortunately romances' use of symbolism and metaphor have not always been recognised or appreciated by their critics. Radway, for example, noted "the genre's careful attention to the style, color, and detail of women's fashions" (193) but concluded that "The details [...] are part of an essential shorthand that establishes that, like ordinary readers, fictional heroines are 'naturally' preoccupied with fashion" (193). Radway, it seems, failed to consider the possibility that:

> Clothes have a privileged role as a narrative sign in romantic fiction because the readers can be assumed to have a finely

honed sense of what is being indicated. The garment signifies so effectively because it possesses all of the qualities of matter (natural/man-made, shade, texture etc.) and is therefore economical and rich in nuance. It is also central to the definition of personality. (Paizis, *Love* 83)

Objects, then, may become visual metaphors or symbols and a close examination of clothing and accessories in romances can enrich one's understanding of the texts.[1] At other times, verbal metaphors may be used to describe the protagonists' feelings. This chapter will focus on a few of the more prominent metaphors which have been used in HM&Bs to describe love.

Lakoff and Johnson have observed that, "For the most part, our comprehension of love is metaphorical, and we understand it primarily in terms of concepts for other natural kinds of experience: JOURNEYS, MADNESS, WAR, HEALTH, etc" (119). Although psychologist Robert J. Sternberg has not explored the impact of such metaphors on non-fictional romantic relationships, he has argued that "a clean separation of fact from fiction simply isn't possible in the context of personal relationships, because we shape the facts of a relationship to conform to our personal fictions" (5), and that these personal fictions are likely to have been affected by literary fictions since "All our lives we have heard stories of various kinds, many with love as a leitmotif. We thus have an array of stories we can draw on when composing our own" (26).[2] Sternberg noticed that certain story types about romantic relationships "came up over and over again in our interviews" (26)

---

1   See, for example, my essays on ring symbolism in the genre ("One"), and on the uses of underwear in the novels of Jennifer Crusie ("Jennifer").

2   The "array of stories we can draw on" may include, but is certainly not limited to, romance novels. Sternberg, Hojjat and Barnes observe that:

   Almost all of us are exposed to large numbers of diverse stories that convey different conceptions of how love can be understood. Some of these stories may be explicitly intended as love stories; others may have love stories embedded in the context of larger stories. Either way, we are provided with varied opportunities to observe multiple conceptions of what love can be. These stories may be observed by watching people in relationships, by watching television or movies, or by reading fiction. It seems plausible that, as a result of our exposure to such stories, we form over time our own stories of what love is or should be. (199)

and, while these stories are complex and certainly not identical to the love metaphors identified by Lakoff and Johnson, Sternberg does summarise many of the stories through the use of similes and metaphors: someone in a "house and home story" may feel that "An ideal relationship is like a well-tended home—beautiful, immaculate, well ordered, something to be proud of" (109); "In a war story, a couple views love as a series of battles in a war" (193); "In a garden story, the relationship is viewed as a garden that needs continually to be nurtured and otherwise cared for" (147). A similar gardening metaphor appears in Lucy Monroe's *The Playboy's Seduction* (2004):

> "Deep, abiding love between two people must grow." [...]
> "Yes," she stressed. "Like a plant. It takes lots of water, sunshine and healthy soil to make a flower bloom. Real love can't just happen in an instant."
> "But there are plants that grow in a day. They are unique, extremely rare, but no less real than their more conventional counterparts." (16)

In Monroe's story the focus of the metaphor is a plant, rather than a garden, and it is used to describe the growth of love, rather than the maintenance of a healthy relationship. The differences between Sternberg and Monroe's versions of the gardening metaphor demonstrate that even apparently similar metaphors can differ significantly in their meanings. I will examine metaphors of building, flowering, and hunting, as well as some of the similes and symbolisms which cluster around them. The chapter concludes with an extended case study of Marion Lennox's *Princess of Convenience* (2005) in which the author has woven together a number of complementary verbal and visual metaphors.

Building a Relationship

Janice Radway observed that "descriptive detail [...] characterizes the mention of domestic architecture and home furnishings in romantic fiction" (194), and it is certainly the case that many HM&Bs include detailed descriptions of homes and their décor. According to Radway these "descriptions assert tacitly that the imaginary world of the novel is as real as the reader's world" (194), and she gives as an example a "characteristic passage" (from a non-HM&B romance) in which "The emphatic massing of detail […] reveals little about character or mood" (194). An analysis of some equally characteristic passages in Caroline Anderson's *The Impetuous Bride* (2001), however, reveal a great deal about both "character" and "mood". Lydia Benton ran away from Jake Delaney "just forty-eight hours" (6) before their wedding because she wasn't sure he loved her. When she returns a year later, Jake is in the process of selling the home they would have shared but he suggests that she "ought to come and see the house before it goes […] I've done a lot more since you left" (33):

> 'This is my room,' he said finally, pushing open a door, and a huge lump wedged in her throat, because this was what she'd said she wanted—the walls, carpet, curtains, all soft creamy white, with a huge four-poster in the middle, its massive barley-twist posts and heavily carved head and foot boards gleaming with the patina of age. […]
> 'Did you do the bathroom?' she asked in a choked voice, and he nodded. […]
> It was lovely—antique fittings with brass taps, the bath a monster with huge ball and claw feet […].
> 'I got all the stuff from that reclamation yard you told me about.' (40–1)

Jake believes that the implications of the room being "what she'd said she wanted" are obvious:

> He was mad. Certifiably, stark raving mad. Why on *earth* had he taken her into his bedroom? Now she'd know he'd hung on her every word and built her dream for her, in the vain hope that she'd come back and share it with him. (41)

In other words, his bedroom demonstrates that he is, and was, hopelessly in love with Lydia, and that he wished to reclaim his former beloved as well as the "antique fittings".

The description of Jake's bedroom is repeated, with only minor variations, later in the novel. While one could take this as indicative of romance authors' and readers' irresistible urge to wallow in such minutiae, Anderson built the novel around a series of repetitions and revisions. Lydia jilted Jake and when she returns home a year later it is in order to attend another wedding. The new couple closely resemble the old: they are Mel, the non-bride's sister, and Tom, the non-groom's best man whom he has known "from birth, practically" (13). The arrangements for the new wedding also echo, or repeat, those of the old, since Mel has chosen to use "last year's plan, last year's caterers and florists, last year's marquee, last year's dressmaker" (55). As Mel says to Lydia:

> 'It'll all be horribly familiar,' […].
> Of course. Mel had thrown herself into planning Lydia's wedding last year […]. And now, like some kind of awful joke, it was all going to be re-enacted, but this time the cast would change places and the curtain wouldn't come down until after the final act. (13–14)

Lydia wishes "she could turn back time and change the course of the last year" (19) and in a sense she can, because having revisited their memories, and returned to the locations where much of their courtship took place, she and Jake eventually succeed in revising the "final act" of the novel so that it includes not one, but two, weddings.

In repeating the description of Jake's bedroom, Anderson strengthens the feeling of *déjà vu* which pervades the novel. This time the description of the room appears in a context which encourages the reader to understand what Lydia's plan for the décor of the room revealed about her. That it does have an underlying symbolism had been strongly hinted at earlier in the novel when it was revealed that she had put "so much love into the planning" (36) of various parts of what to her will "Never" be "just a house" (36). When Jake first showed Lydia the room he had asked her to:

> 'Tell me what you'd do in here.'
> Love you, she thought […], and she imagined lying in a great high bed and looking out across the garden towards the river.
> 'It needs a four-poster,' she said slowly. 'A huge mahogany one, with slender, barley-twist posts with carved bases, and a

> great carved headboard, and I'd do it all cream [...], and then
> he took her into the dressing room off it and said he was think-
> ing of creating an *en suite* bathroom.
>   'Oh, fantastic—it's huge! You could have one of those fabu-
> lous Victorian showers [...]. And a roll-top bath with ball and
> claw feet. (81–2)

Lydia's ideas for the bedroom seem to reflect her desire for Jake, and
the emotional context in which she wished that desire to be fulfilled.
She had refused to have sex "until I'm married. I know it's old-fashioned, but I always said I'd be a virgin on my wedding night" (84).
Her plans for the bedroom are also "old-fashioned" since they incorporate Victorian bathroom fittings and a four-poster bed; the creamy
white colour-scheme perhaps indicates that this is the room in which
she wishes to make the transition from virginity (often symbolised by
a pure white) to wifehood.

   While it would be foolish to claim that all descriptions of
buildings and their interiors in HM&Bs possess symbolism or
function as metaphors, a great many do. Jan Cohn has suggested that
"in contemporary romance, [...] the hero's economic power [...]
supplies additional energy to his sexual power, as if his houses and
cars, won in the competition of the marketplace, are metaphors for
or manifestations of his sexual allure" (154); for HM&B author Kate
Hewitt houses represent "safety, security, comfort, love—the very
essence of a home". Jake Delaney's London apartment "in a highly
exclusive neighbourhood near Butler's Wharf" (C. Anderson 70)
fulfils both functions: it certainly demonstrates his economic power
since "it was prestigious, but it was more than that. It was a home,
his home, filled with his things [...]. It was, in a way, the real Jake
Delaney" (103) and Lydia finds it a "welcoming" (103) place where
she feels "comfortable" (104).

   The house at the centre of Jennifer Crusie's *Getting Rid of Bradley*
(1994) also reveals a great deal "about character" (Radway 194). For
Lucy, the novel's heroine, her house represents "the dream of her
heart" (56) and she had "wanted that house with a passion that she'd
never in her life felt for a man" (55). The novel opens as Lucy is
waiting for her divorce from Bradley to be finalised and she later

admits that:

> I think I married Bradley to get my house. [...] I think I just
> convinced myself I loved him because it was so sensible that I
> should, and then when he offered me the house, it was just too
> much. [...] I love the house more than I ever loved Bradley.
> (14)

Lucy's house may, however, symbolise not only her dreams, but also
Lucy herself. Crusie has stated of her work that:

> I'm big on houses. I've been criticized for that ("Why are there
> always houses?") which I don't get [...] because I think the
> places people live say a lot about them, the places they choose
> to live (if they can afford to choose) and the things they put
> in the places they choose. Plus houses are a huge metaphor.
> The house in *Crazy for You* is very consciously a metaphor for
> Quinn; when her ex-boyfriend breaks in, it's a symbolic rape.
> ("Vince's Place")

In *Getting Rid of Bradley* Lucy is quite explicitly compared to her
house:

> Anthony came by the house late in the afternoon. He stood
> in the middle of Lucy's soft, flowered living room and said,
> "This is a wonderful room. It feels good just to be here." He
> smiled down at Lucy. "It's like you."
> Lucy beamed back. "That's the nicest thing you could have
> said to me." (106)

In addition to being "soft", Lucy's home is repeatedly described as
being warm: "the warmth and color of her beautiful old house" (33);
"A big, safe, *warm* house" (55); "warm with the glow of the stained-
glass windows" (33). Zack, the hero, associates both of these qualities with Lucy herself. To him she seems "soft and warm and the best
place he'd ever been" (114) and "whenever he looked at her, he felt
like he was home" (121–2).

The contents of a character's home may also convey much about
their personality and value-system. Laura Barclay, the heroine of
Marilynne Rudick's *Fixing to Stay* (1986), rapidly concludes on the

basis of Chris Johnson's response to her furniture that "Their differing tastes in decor [...] symbolized all that would be wrong between them. Their incompatibility would extend to food, clothes, politics, philosophy of life" (68). She is wrong about their incompatibility, but only because she gradually adapts to small-town life; this change is, of course, accompanied by alterations to the furnishings of her apartment. By contrast Lucy, in *Getting Rid of Bradley*, prefers to change her man rather than her décor. After her divorce her sister urges her to remove all of Bradley's belongings from what used to be the marital home: "Psychologically, this is a very big deal. Get rid of his things and you'll get rid of him" (Crusie 25). The final item to be disposed of is his chair: "It was ugly—a recliner upholstered in synthetic olive-green flecked with red. If Bradley had been born a piece of furniture, he would have looked like that chair. Practical, boring, and irritating" (58). Lucy throws it into her basement and "Halfway down, it hit the stair rail and broke through it, tumbling over the side of the steps to smash on the concrete below" (58). When Bradley himself returns, intent on committing murder, Lucy deals with him in the same place, and in much the same way, as she dealt with the chair that symbolised his presence in her house: "she swung the bat solidly into the back of his head. His head jerked forward, and he flung his arms wide as he fell through the broken rail to the floor" (216).

Although the functions of homes and their contents discussed so far are perhaps more properly described as symbolic rather than metaphorical, the symbolism inherent in real homes gives power and meaning to metaphors of home-building. It is often said that "Home is where the heart is" (Lennox 186) and the phrase is elaborated on in Olive Standley's *My Heart's Your Home*. Set during the Second World War and published by Mills & Boon in 1946, the novel's original readers, many of whom would have lived through the Blitz, would have been aware that although some buildings may represent "safety, security", in fact no house, however sturdily built of stone, brick, or concrete, is an impregnable refuge. Arnold and his large home on the "little island of Limerick, British West Indies" (10) are, however, both safe from German bombs. By contrast Dick, the hero of Standley's novel and Arnold's rival for Avril's love, is:

a rescued merchant seaman. One of that band of men, who, their ship having been torpedoed from under them, have escaped death by a miracle, but who forthwith set out once more—the bravest of the brave, the men who go back, and do it all over again. (191)

He is also a man who has "never had a real home [...] Unless you call an orphanage a home" (33–4). When he sees Arnold's house, Dick recognises that it is "solid and secure, builded on a rock. That was what Arnold Camberwell had to offer Avril, and in his mind's eye he saw what he had to offer her, a narrow, comfortless cabin on a dangerous ocean, and afterwards—what?" (167). Avril, however, embraces Dick and the uncertainty of life on the home front, reassuring him that:

> You'll have a home now. I'll build it for you in my heart, stronger and more indestructible than any made of bricks and mortar. And wherever you are, whatever you're doing, it'll be waiting for you, warm and bright, for our love will have lighted a fire there that will never grow cold, never go out. Oh, Dick, don't you see? My heart's your home! (192)

Given that Avril had previously asked her step-mother whether "it's wrong, cowardly, of us, to be living so safe and untouched here, not helping, while those nearer in England and Europe have so much to put up with" (11), her choice of homeless but heroic Dick over the security represented by Arnold and his large house represents the triumph not only of romantic love but also of patriotism.

Although few HM&B heroines face a future as uncertain as Avril's, she is far from unique in her use of building metaphors. In "Building Love" (2007), a short story by Shirley Jump, building metaphors and similes abound as Jessie and Tag explore the reasons for Tag's string of romantic disasters. Jessie may describe him as a "hopeless romantic" because of his ability to see the potential in "the old hotel they were rehabbing" (71), but in his personal life she considers him to be "like a relationship wrecking ball" (71). Tag eventually suggests that his relationships have failed because:

> 'I keep looking at the wrong properties. The fancy ones. Their

foundations are never good. What I really want is one that's not so worried about the cosmetics, about its façade. One with a good, solid base.'

'Are we talking hotels or—'

'*Or.*' His lips were a breath away. 'I'm looking for an investment property. A long-term commitment. Know anyone available?'

'Well,' she said, taking a huge chance, '*this* address is vacant [...].' (73)

Hank, in Jo Ann Algermissen's *Would You Marry Me Anyway?* (1991), is another hero whose job inspires his choice of metaphors: "I use my energies to build apartment projects rather than building a relationship with a woman" (18).

Building imagery and metaphors are also plentiful in Michelle Styles's *A Christmas Wedding Wager* (2007). Jack Stanton asks Emma Harrison if she will "*cement* our new-found friendship with a trip to the pantomime" (451, emphasis added) and then, having married her, thinks that "a protracted wedding trip [...] would give them a chance to get to know each other better, to *build on their foundation*" (573, emphasis added). The relationship-as-building metaphor is central to Styles's novel since Jack and Emma's progress in designing and overseeing the construction of Newcastle's High Level Bridge runs in parallel with the emotional bridge-building in which they engage.[1]

Emma is insistent that the creation of the bridge must not lead to the demolition of the old "castle. The keep and the royal apartments are to be retained if possible" (313) because the keep is the "symbol of Newcastle" (318) and "symbols matter" (443). It may also be a symbol of Emma herself because in comparison with Jack who, like the railway, has been "constantly on the move, going from one project to the next" (323–4), Emma has remained static: "I have rarely been out of the North East these past seven years" (324). According to Jack, both the castle and Emma are reminders of distant history: "The

---

1   In a letter to the reader Styles states that the bridge "in the story does exist, and is a Grade 1 listed building [...] trains still trundle across it on their way into the Central Station from London. I trust you will forgive the few alterations I made to the actual history. I am a novelist writing historical romance, rather than a historian writing non-fiction" (308).

castle belongs to the city's past" (387) and "Emma Harrison and all she had once stood for belonged to a former life. One he had hoped to blot out for ever" (319). He is equally determined to abide by the original plan for the bridge, which will necessitate the destruction of the castle (321). In this frame of mind, he marginalises Emma and takes over the responsibility for "overseeing the bridge-building" (350).

Figuratively, bridge building signifies "the promotion of friendly relations" (*New Sh. OED*, *s.v.* 'bridge', n[1] *Comb.*) and Emma and Jack's progress in this form of bridge-building is symbolised by the joining of their hands, an action which literally bridges the gap between them. When they first meet, however:

> She extended her hand, forced her heart to forget what he had been like seven years ago. The pain he had caused was a distant memory.
> 'Mr Stanton. It has been a long time.'
> 'Miss Harrison.'
> He gave a nod but ignored her hand. (316)

Later, after they have become reacquainted:

> He held out his hand, a strong hand, with tapering fingers.
> 'Shall we start again, Miss Harrison? Shall we be friends? Work together instead of against each other?'
> 'Start again?' She put her fingertips against his, felt his fingers curl around hers for a brief instant before she withdrew. Friends. That was all, and she would have to remember that.
> 'I think I can agree to that. I welcome your friendship.' (440)

The final stage of their relationship is reached after their marriage when Jack, who has just told Emma that he is "holding [her], and [...] never intend[s] letting [her] go again" (600), gives her a ring "On the gold band [of which] two hands were clasped" (600) in what appears to be a symbol of the permanent joining of their hands in both friendship and marriage. Appropriately, the future of the construction of the High Level Bridge reflects this new and lasting accord between them: it will be sited "so the keep is saved. [...] The bridge will be built to our design—yours and mine. And it will last" (602). Having come to terms with their past, and cooperated to secure their future, they can now move on in the certainty that their marriage, like the bridge, "will last".

The Flowering of Romance

Whereas bridges and houses are generally wholly human construction, gardens are often places in which "man expresses [...] his perception of his relationship with nature" (Meisami, "Allegorical Gardens" 229).

Woman as Garden

As "women have traditionally been perceived as closer to nature and men as closer to culture" (Roach 50), in art and literature gardens and garden metaphors can express a man's "perception of his relationship" with a woman. In Violet Winspear's *The Girl at Goldenhawk* (1974), for example, Pedro Almanzor de Ros Zanto tells Jaine Dare that "There is something curiously enticing about "*A garden enclosed ... a spring shut up, a fountain sealed.*" Are you acquainted with the Song of Solomon?" (63). He is quoting from Chapter 4, which contains an extended version of the metaphor of woman as garden. As Elizabeth A. Augspach has observed, "The Song of Solomon played a pivotal role in the development of the *hortus conclusus* [enclosed garden] topos as female space" (23) and in the context of the European Middle Ages:

> The rise in the cult of the Virgin Mary, with its identification of the Virgin as the *hortus conclusus* of the Song of Solomon[,] endowed the literary garden with rich metaphoric language that easily passed from the language of religion into the language of courtly love. The beauty of the beloved was naturally patterned after the beauty of the Virgin, as were their respective gardens. (Augspach 160)

The association between women, love, and gardens persisted down the centuries and:

> love was firmly fixed in the Victorian consciousness as tran-

spiring in the sovereign domain of the earthly paradise, and more precisely, in the middle-class garden or its perimeters in nature. Tableaus [*sic*] of girlish innocence, or, more specifically, of ladies awaiting seen or unseen admirers at appointed trysting places or flowery nooks were extremely common [...]. Such depictions owed part of their iconographic debt to the visual tradition of the Virgin Mary, whose wall-bounded *hortus conclusus* served as a general prototype for the secularization of circumscribed feminine chastity. (Casteras 71)

The depiction of Lady Desire Godwin, heroine of Claire Thornton's *The Abducted Heiress* (2005), may also owe something to this tradition. She is introduced to the reader as she stands "in the middle of her rooftop garden" (10). It is both "her sanctuary" and "her sole creation" (10) and as a woman's space so clearly associated with Lady Desire herself and untouched by others, it may symbolise her chastity. Certainly the unexpected arrival of three male strangers in this space provokes in her menservants "the need to avenge the violation of the house" (22), a response which suggests that they feel it to be the symbolic equivalent of an attempted rape or sexual assault on the lady herself.

Certain aspects of the arrival of the first of these strangers may, however, recall the Annunciation, for although Lady Desire is not "the handmaid of the Lord" (Luke 1:38), her humble clothing ensures that she may be mistaken for "a maidservant" (13), and she is greeted by a seemingly angelic being:

> An angel who had taken mortal form. [...] He looked just like the archangel Desire had seen once in a stained-glass window. All the colours in the picture had been given heavenly radiance by the sunlight streaming through the glass. This man reminded her of that shining, golden image. (11)

Despite these parallels, Desire's name, temperament, and the events which are set in motion in her "small Eden" (10) will ultimately align her more closely with Eve, the Virgin's sinful analogue. The conceptualisation of the Virgin as a:

> second Eve, through whom the sin of the first was ransomed,

> was imported to the west, where it inspired the ingenious im-
> agination of the medieval Christian to pun and riddle with a
> characteristic sense of delight and love of symmetry. For the
> greeting of the angel—Ave—neatly reversed the curse of Eve.
> (Warner 60)

In *The Abducted Heiress* it is almost as though Desire experiences the
process in reverse, for the arrival of the angel in Lady Desire's "personal Eden" (14) announces death and danger rather than a virgin
birth, and Desire, like the post-lapsarian Eve in the presence of the
divine, becomes ashamed and attempts to hide herself: "Shame and
distress thundered through her. She half-raised her hands to cover her
face, then turned her back on him instead" (12). It is not long before
she begins to wonder if he is not God's messenger but "a *fallen* angel" (14); she then addresses him as "You *serpent*" (16) and it is later
stated that "the angel who'd invaded her garden at sunset had turned
into a devil at twilight" (23). Fallen angels are, of course, devils, and
although "there is no devil or Satan figure in the Genesis account
of the temptation of Eve, [...] Jewish as well as Christian tradition
came to associate such a figure with the serpent" (H. A. Kelly 302).
Shortly after her meeting with the "serpent" Lady Desire, like the
first Eve, is "forced out. However difficult life became, she could
never retreat to the peaceful sanctuary of her [...] garden" (249). She
is kept away not by "Cherubims,[1] and a flaming sword" (Genesis 3:
24) but by the man she had earlier described as "a *fallen* angel" (14),
the encroachment of the Great Fire of London, and the flames of a
second, more localised, blaze which completely destroy the sheltered
hortus conclusus.

Another *hortus conclusus* is depicted in Liz Fielding's *The Sheikh's
Guarded Heart* (2006), in which Hanif bin Jamal gives Lucy Forrester
a book containing "Some of the translated poems of the Persian poet,
Hafiz [...] He uses the imagery of the garden to express love in all its
forms" (124).[2] Fielding sets the main action of her novel within an

---

1   The erroneous plural is in the Authorised Version.
2   Hafiz was a: "fourteenth-century Persian court poet [...], the acknowledged
    master of the brief lyric form known as *ghazal*. [...] Hafiz, however, is unique
    among the court poets of his time in emphasizing the allegorical nature of the
    garden within the context of the courtly *ghazal* dealing primarily with erotic and

enclosed garden known as "The Garden of the Bride" (71) because it was created by one of Hanif's "ancestors for his Persian bride, homesick for the garden she'd left behind" (71). Its main pavilion:

> '[...] was built as a setting for a princess. The only man allowed within its walls would have been her husband. [...] This was a citadel. A place apart where no one could come unless she permitted it.'
>
> 'Not even her husband?'
>
> 'Not even her husband.'
>
> [...] 'So where did he stay?'
>
> 'There is a lodge, out of sight of the pavilion, where he stayed with his men, as I did myself until Noor became ill and I took a suite of rooms for myself to be near her.'
>
> Something knotted in Lucy's stomach, a feeling she could not describe. But in her head she saw the beautiful Noor summoning her husband to her. [...] She would have offered him food, made him laugh, made him wait as she drove him wild with desire. (109–10).

The "Garden of the Bride" is thus an erotic *locus amoenus* ('pleasant place') which expresses a woman's control of both the physical space around her and, implicitly, her own body.[1] Nonetheless her freedom, like her garden, is a gift granted to her by her husband and it has strictly demarcated boundaries: she may refuse him entry but she may not give another man access to either her garden or her body.

Since this garden was "laid out centuries earlier as an earthly reflection of heaven" (54), it also possesses some of the attributes of the heavenly Paradise. In the aftermath of a near-fatal car accident this is apparent to Lucy: "Maybe she was dead, she thought

---

panegyric topics; he thus finds a closer kinship than his contemporaries with medieval European lyric poets who found in the garden a rich store of symbolic imagery." (Meisami, "The World" 153)

1   Ernst Robert Curtius translates *locus amoenus* as "pleasance" and states that "from the Empire to the sixteenth century, it forms the principal motif of all nature description. It is [...] a beautiful, shaded natural site. Its minimum ingredients comprise a tree (or several trees), a meadow, and a spring or brook. Birdsong and flowers may be added. The most elaborate examples also add a breeze" (195).

dispassionately. Heaven would be green. And quiet" (10). Later, however, this garden which "had seemed to promise heaven on earth" (191) more closely recalls the earthly Paradise, the Garden of Eden, for the novel concludes with Hanif and Lucy, like Adam and Eve, leaving the garden to seek employment and bring forth offspring.

Although the sacred and secular have long been intermingled in depictions of literary and artistic gardens, it is possible to find examples which appear to lack any spiritual overtones. In Kate Hardy's *In the Gardener's Bed* (2007), for example, gardening is literally and metaphorically an earthy activity, and one which produces a rich crop of innuendo. The very title, *In the Gardener's Bed*, plays on the double meaning of "bed" as a place where flowers grow in a garden and the piece of furniture "indoors" to which the hero, as "He punctuated each word with a kiss. To. My. Bed" (121), wishes to take the heroine.[1] This hero and heroine have been brought together in order to create a reality TV programme "About two people with opposite lifestyles spending a week with each other and learning from each other's lives" (9); gardening is supposed to give Amanda the opportunity to take a break from her high-powered job as a London accountant and "take time to smell the roses" (9). What she quickly begins to wonder, however, is whether gardening hones skills which can be transferred from the flower bed to the bedroom. During a lesson in "seed-planting" (47), for example:

> 'Shouldn't we be wearing gloves?' she asked.
> 'No. They decrease sensitivity.'
> Was he deliberately making *double entendres*? (48)

And having prepared the compost:

> He took two pots from the stack next to him. 'Don't squash the compost into it. Just let it fall in and end up in a mound.

---

1   This title was not used for the North American edition of the novel, nor was it Kate Hardy's original title, which also involved wordplay, but of a different nature:

There's a TV series in the UK called 'Wifeswap' where two women with completely opposite lives swap families for two weeks and try to improve each other's lives. And I had this mad idea of doing the same sort of thing with my hero and heroine. . . Luckily, my editor loved the idea—though I didn't get to keep my original title, 'Lifeswap'. (Hardy, "In the Gardener's Bed")

Then brush your hand lightly over the top.' He demonstrated
with his pot. 'Your turn.'
    Brush your hand lightly over the top...
    Oh, lord. She really had to get her mind out of the gutter.
    (49)

Her thoughts, however, seem destined to remain firmly rooted in
the compost: "he demonstrated actually sowing the seed. She really
shouldn't be having these kinds of thoughts. Watching his finger slide
into the compost and wondering how it would feel sliding into her
body instead …" (49), and:

> 'Label it so you know what it is—the plant's name, the date
> sown, and your initials.' He handed her a pencil and a piece of
> plastic that reminded her of an ice-lolly stick with a pointed
> end. 'If you rub the top half between your finger and thumb,
> you'll feel that one side's rougher than the other. That's the
> side that's easier to write on.'
> All she had to do was slide the plastic between her fingers. It
> was a perfectly innocent act. And yet it felt somehow … sex-
> ual. A come-hither kind of gesture. As if she were suggesting
> to Will that her fingers could stroke him in the same way. (50)

In this novel, then, gardening is not solely an activity carried out by
men and directed towards a feminised garden.

Woman as Flower

Although an entire garden can symbolise a woman, Augspach has
observed that as early as:

> the 13th century there was less emphasis on the enclosure of the
> garden as signifying woman's virginity and consequently the
> woman herself. The contents of the garden, the flowers in par-
> ticular because they stood for virtues and virginity, had become
> sufficiently important to be singled out and described.(71)

The Virgin Mary is often compared "conspicuously to roses, rosaries,
and flowers in enclosed gardens. The reason for this is clear once you
recall that the popular expression 'defloration' supposes that virgins

possess flowers" (Vaz da Silva 248). In the Middle Ages "the flower which above all others symbolises the female sex is, of course, the rose" and, in a secular context, "The metaphor of plucking a flower or, specifically, a rose, is a commonplace of erotic diction" (M. Jones 263).[1] The literary and linguistic connection between women and flowers has been strongly reinforced by visual representations of flowers:

> Central to the visual arts throughout its iconographic development, the flower is now the most recognizable symbol of so-called vaginal iconography. Via a relatively simple path, the flower motif came not only to allude to the feminine but to signify it directly. The metaphorical structure of language has fostered the association of woman and flower through visual correspondence with the female genitalia. The association of woman/flower became flower/vulva. (Mangini 2)

In HM&B romances we find that flower metaphors can provide "labial imagery, a la Georgia O'Keefe [*sic*] [...] Two of JoAnn Ross's [...] heroes use rose petal similes" (Johnson-Kurek 118). The heroine of *In the Gardener's Bed* also finds herself thinking about "the sort of plant Georgia O'Keeffe had painted, all sexy unfurling petals just waiting for a man's touch" (Hardy 50), and when the hero:

> stooped down to show her a pale lilac flower [...] The way his fingers gently caressed the petals made desire flicker down her spine. Would he touch her skin in the same way, treat her as if she were as delicate and rare and special? (41)

In a sex scene written by Jo Ann Algermissen, the hero watches the heroine "as his fingers parted the petals of flesh protecting her womanhood" (128), and one of Sandra Marton's heroes, during foreplay with his heroine, "Saw how beautiful she was. The petals of her labia. The pink bud of her clitoris" (*Naked* 95). Floral metaphors are not always so explicitly sexual. The hero of *In the Gardener's Bed*, for ex-

---

1   In the 1950s the spines of Mills & Boon's romantic novels were adorned with a small Cupid and the letter 'R' but the rose was later adopted as the symbol of the company and has been retained to the present day, although over the decades the rose logo has taken many different forms.

ample, thinks the heroine has "a beautiful mouth. A perfect rosebud" (Hardy 87). A veritable bouquet of comparisons between flowers and a heroine's physical features can be found in Pamela Kent's *City of Palms* (1957), in which Susan is described as having "slightly ruffled hair—pale, like a primrose" with a "flower-like mouth" (9), blue eyes which remind a secondary character "of gentians" (23), and "slim, white, and rather flower-like fingers" (132).

In addition to emphasising similarities between flowers and parts of a woman's body, HM&B authors may also include comparisons between a single flower and a whole woman. At the end of *City of Palms*, for example, the hero reveals to Susan that "You have always been my little English moonflower of a girl" (Kent 174). Flowers have been strongly associated with women and femininity for centuries:

> Floral names were [...] a popular choice for girls throughout the nineteenth century and into the twentieth. [...] Baby books gave every name a specific meaning, but floral names, which were reserved for girls, tended to be assigned traits that were perceived to be feminine. Violet meant modesty, Jasmine suggested amiability, Mimosa signified sensitivity, Petunia indicated a soothing presence, Rose meant perfection, and Dahlia connoted instability. (Stott 71–2)

Although "flowers have sometimes been personified as men, they are far more frequently associated with women. This has been true throughout the history of Western culture, in varying degrees" (Seaton 680). *In the Gardener's Bed* contains a rare counter-example of a male character described as a flower: Amanda observes that "Will Daynes [...] was a bit like a wild flower. Sturdy, strong, and secure in his environment, but put him in the city and he'd droop" (Hardy 99).[1]

Evidence of the strength of the general association between women and flowers is provided by Jan Tempest's *Ask Me Again* (1955): when the heroine tells her hero that "My name is Willow. Like the tree" (49) he immediately responds "Impossible! Why should any girl be named after a tree" (49), and later says that she reminds him "of

---

1   Readers primed by the earlier sexual innuendoes will perhaps be relieved to discover that crucial parts of Will certainly do not droop at crucial moments during his visit to Amanda in London.

lilies, even if sometimes you're a tiger lily" (192). In this novel floral and colour symbolism are inextricably linked since the heroine and her three sisters Rose, Anchusa and Saffron:

> all have different tastes and different lines. Father vows that's because he named us after different colours and dressed us in different colours, when we were children. [...] Certainly, Rose has a rose-tinted outlook on life in general, and, if blue is really the colour most attractive to men, that may account for Anchusa's many admirers. (144)

Howard, the man Rose loves, "had been disposed to ridicule Professor Madderley's notion of naming his daughters after colours" (76) but he changes his mind one evening. Tempest allows the reader access to Howard's increasingly infatuated thought processes:

> She was nicely curved in the right places. She was deliciously feminine. Above her sheer stockings he caught a glimpse of something rose-pink and frilly, as he followed her upstairs. [...] Even her name was feminine and romantic. "Rose Madderley." It sounded like a colour in an artist's paintbox, or a very special variety of rose in a rose garden. [...] Now, it seemed to him that "Rose" was the perfect name, and "rose" the most attractive colour in the world. Rose, the colour, was heartening and warming and essentially kind. So was this Rose. [...] She was sweet all through; sweet and fragrant and naïvely, unconsciously alluring. (75–6)[1]

The importance of colour symbolism in the choice of flower is also evident in Winspear's *The Girl at Goldenhawk*, in which Jaine Dare, who was previously compared to a garden, "droop[s] like an English flower which has been exposed to a little too much tropic sunlight. It is a white flower I am thinking of, Virgin's Ladder, or some such name, with dense green leaves which likes the shade of trees" (83). Pedro, the hero of the novel, may be thinking of a white flower not only because he has "Never [...] seen a face so devoid of colour" (28)

---

[1]   Howard's view of Rose is not entirely inaccurate, but in his ignorance of her "practical side" he is thinking of her as "a delectable luxury" rather than as someone who could be "a reliable partner" (89).

as hers, but also because "the cleanliness of white fits the purity of ideal motherhood, ultimately impersonated by the Madonna. Moreover, whiteness is a fitting symbol for milk and, thus, the nurturing aspect of motherliness" (Vaz da Silva 249): Jaine Dare is "obviously virgin" (12) and Pedro employs her as a companion for Tristao, a boy who has "never known a mother, [...] in place of the mother the boy had expected" (75).

Despite its obviously floral title, Rosemary Pollock's *White Hibiscus* (1979) withholds any explicit woman-as-flower metaphors until the final chapter when, in "a tiny arbour, filled with hibiscus bushes" (171), Paul, the hero, declares that "I have never known a girl like you. You are a perfect flower that opens at the touch of the sun—a white hibiscus blossom" (172–3). In the course of the novel Emma, who believes that "One has to wait for the right man" (41), has indeed demonstrated herself to be a white (chaste) flower who opened neither in response to one man's "amorous fumblings" (86) nor to another's man's "loathsome violence" (86), but only to Paul, in whose embrace, "as if obeying some irresistible compulsion, she moved, tilting her head to look up at him" (87) as though she were indeed a flower opening only to the sun above her. Paul has "never known a girl like" Emma because she is "unusual. For an English girl [...] often they are very sophisticated. Very—liberated" (124). Paul does not "approve of liberated women" (124) but it has already been established that Emma is "not a supporter of the Women's Liberation movement" (114) because she sees no reason "why one should deny one's femininity" (114–15). Emma's floral femininity is thus upheld as the ideal, in defiance of 1970s British feminism.

As Annette Stott has demonstrated, flower imagery was used in much the same way in the late nineteenth-century genre of "floral-female painting", in which:

> the artist placed one woman or more in a flower garden setting and manipulated composition, color, texture, and form to make the women look as much like flowers as possible. [...] Floral-female paintings encoded a traditional Victorian definition of femininity that large numbers of American women were just then vociferously challenging in word and deed.

This type of painting can best be understood as a conservative response to the "New Woman" of the 1890s, the flapper of the 1920s, and all their liberal sisters in between. (61)

It is perhaps no coincidence, then, that in Roberta Leigh's *Give a Man a Bad Name* (1993) the woman-as-flower metaphor makes an appearance when the hero describes his attitude towards marriage:

> 'I *have* avoided marriage until now. No matter how beautiful, charming or intelligent my girlfriends were, I saw no reason to tie myself to one when there was always another who was ready, willing, and able. I'm not saying my behaviour was laudable. I'm merely stating how it was for me. And incidentally, how it is for many men these days. Why have one flower in a vase when an entire bouquet is there for the picking?'
>
> Why indeed? Marly agreed cynically, and thought that women had embraced liberation without weighing up all the pros and cons.
>
> 'Then I met *you*,' Alex continued [...] 'and suddenly one flower was all I desired.' (137)

And yet, even as Marly seems to agree that female sexual liberation makes marriage less attractive to men, she also appears to believe that a marriage proposal made primarily for the "Rawly sexual" reason that the man cannot have a particular flower without it, is "no recipe for a lasting relationship" (136). Leigh is perhaps ambivalent about, rather than hostile to, feminism for although Marly has "old-fashioned views" (15) about sexuality, she is also a computer programmer who is "more interested in her career than cooking, in climbing the corporate ladder than catering to a husband's whims" (5), and "definitely not the submissive type" (184). The novel may thus demonstrate what Ann Rosalind Jones, writing about HM&Bs from the previous decade, had described as a "multi-leveled incoherence in dealing with" (204) feminism.[1]

---

1   It should be noted that in this area, as in many others, there is considerable variation among HM&B romances. Some HM&B authors, for example, describe themselves as feminists, as do some HM&B heroines (see Vivanco, "Feminism").

A more recent example of the use of the metaphor of woman as flower, however, demonstrates no such "incoherence". Liz Fielding, in her *The Sheikh's Guarded Heart*, makes it clear that the flower metaphor, while seeming to compliment a woman, may also imply a desire to limit her autonomy: "Dependence and passivity are concepts easily expressed through flowers, whose principal function is decorative" (Stott 62), and Fielding's heroine rejects the opportunity to become one. When Hanif describes Lucy as "Too good for the world, maybe. I do not think I should let you go back to the world. I should keep you in my garden with the other flowers, where you will be safe. [...] You have all the attributes of the rose, including the thorns" (221–2), Lucy states that "I'm not a flower" (222) and insists on proving "to them both that the only person she *needed* was herself" (231) so that her later choice to be with Hanif is clearly one made out of love and not because of a need for masculine protection or support.

The Hunt of Love

The metaphor of love as a battle has equal, if not greater, potential for expressing power imbalances than that of woman as flower. As Denis de Rougemont has observed, "Already in Antiquity poets used war-like metaphors in order to describe the effects of natural love" (244). Sometimes it is Love itself (either personified, or identified as a god) which fights against an unsuspecting mortal: "Stealthily, on silent feet, unsought and unwanted, love had crept up on" the heroine of Anne O'Brien's *Chosen for the Marriage Bed* (2009) "and ambushed her" (218). At other times the lovers appear to be engaged in combat with each other, as in the contemporary (non-HM&B) examples provided by Lakoff and Johnson:

> He is known for his many rapid *conquests*. She *fought for* him, but his mistress *won out*. He *fled from* her *advances*. She *pursued* him *relentlessly*. He is slowly *gaining ground* with her. He *won* her hand in marriage. He *overpowered* her. She is *besieged* by suitors. He has to *fend* them *off*. He *enlisted the aid* of her friends. He *made an ally* of her mother. Theirs is a

misalliance if I've ever seen one. (49)[1]

Since war and hunting are both aggressive and dangerous activities, the addition of animal imagery can easily transform the metaphor of love as war, particularly as it relates to flight and pursuit, into a metaphor of the hunt. This too has a long literary history:

> Medieval poets writing narratives of love seemed to be almost effortlessly receptive to any suggestion of a chase, even of the briefest sort, figurative or otherwise, in which to involve their heroes. Hunting lovers and amatory hunters begin to abound in vernacular literature late in the twelfth century and thereafter. (Thiébaux 104)

While immensely popular in the Middle Ages, the metaphor of "The hunt of love had been developed earlier by Greek and Latin authors" (Thiébaux 12) and although "The pursuit of a girl [...] described in the terminology of hunting [was] originally a learned conceit", it was "assimilated by the traditional poetry of many European countries" (Rogers 15) and can also be found in works written in prose. In Fernando de Rojas's fifteenth-century *Celestina*, for example:

> avian imagery is [...] used to represent the "hunt of love." Even where the predator is a human hunter, the foolish lover, either male or female, who is the prey, may still be represented as a bird. In addition, the shifts between hunter and hunted, predator and prey which exist in the text underscore the sudden changes of fortune, which can occur just when the characters least expect them. (Vivanco, "Birds" 18)

Given the flexibility and extremely long history of the motif, it is not surprising that it should have remained in use into the present day even in societies in which real hunting is rare.

In HM&B romances the hunt of love always reaches a happy conclusion, but that it is, nonetheless, a hunt, is suggested by the many comparisons which are made between the heroes of romance

---

1   Some additional examples can be found on Tatar's list of "warlike metaphors" (143) used to describe "passionate erotic actions" (142): "Men *pursue* women, deliver *assaults* on their virtue, and *conquer* them. Women are *besieged* by their admirers, put up *resistance*, and *surrender* to men" (143).

and dangerous predators. Sarah Wendell and Candy Tan, in their humorous guide to romance novels, have observed that the "Perfect Title" for a "Lordly Hero" includes the name of a "Predatory Animal" such as a hawk, lion or wolf (90). This naming technique may also be used on non-aristocratic heroes, and examples include Heraklion Mavrakis in Violet Winspear's *The Child of Judas* (1976), who is usually referred to as "Lion", and Benjamin Wolfe, hero of Paula Marshall's *The Wolfe's Mate* (1999). Other heroes, although not named after dangerous birds or beasts, share some of their attributes: Jack Stanton "stalked in, moving with the grace of an untamed predator" (Styles 316), the Duque Pedro Almanzor de Ros Zanto has eyes which "seemed to glitter and gleam like those of a puma on the prowl" (Winspear, *The Girl* 26), and it is not just the year of his birth according to "the Chinese astrological zodiac" which makes Anton Zell, hero of Madeleine Ker's *The Millionaire Boss's Mistress* (2004), "A dragon" (50, 51). He is "a hunter […]. Of success. Of women" (110) who buys Amy, his heroine, a jade bangle "carved with a dragon, whose sinuous and muscular body writhed all around the band, his fire-breathing jaws meeting his fiery tail" (53):

> 'Ah, yes,' she said wryly. 'Don't think I didn't get the sym-
> bolism of that particular perk.'
> 'Symbolism?'
> 'Oh yes. […] You wanted to put a bangle carved with a
> dragon around my wrist.'
> 'Correct.'
> 'Giving everybody the message that I belonged to the big
> dragon himself.'
> 'Or maybe that the big dragon belonged to you.' (74)

He later clarifies that with the bangle "I was trying to say […] that you had conquered me, and could wear me on your arm, your own tame dragon" (187).

That it is generally heroes, not heroines, who are cast as the predators in the hunt of love may be due to the influence of opinions such as those of Salvatore in Sharon Kendrick's *Bought for the Sicilian Billionaire's Bed* (2008). He is a hero who subscribes to "fiercely traditional values about the roles of the sexes" (12) and believes that "men should do the chasing" (12). Hunting is an activity strongly associated with male sexuality:

> In the U.S. cultural landscape, the language of hunting is a discourse of patriarchy. Hunters' attitudes and actions toward social and natural objects (weapons or hunted prey) are constructed by a combination of experiences and absorbed cultural messages that validate and exacerbate white male dominance and power [...]. Further, the cultural construction of hunting as rooted in a symbolic system that values predation and dominance conjoins hunting and sex with women and animals. (Kalof, Fitzgerald and Baralt 239)

Brian Luke's

> sampling of North American hunters' literature indicates the validity of a sexual interpretation of hunting. The pattern is that of a buildup and release of tension organized around the pursuit, phallic penetration, and erotic touching of a creature whom the hunter finds seductively appealing. (Luke 635)

Of course this does not mean that there are no women hunters or that women are never described metaphorically as hunters but, as anthropologist Eleanor Burke Leacock has observed, "Female sexual 'aggression'" has tended to be "covertly recognized in our culture by the Shavian saw, he chased her until she caught him" (286). Individuals such as Salvatore take a dim view of women who openly chase men. Indeed, he prefers to classify them as scavengers, eaters of carrion, rather than as predators: "they behaved like vultures when they saw a virile man with a seemingly bottomless bank account" (Kendrick 12). In general, then, a heroine's "success in marrying well [...] must seem almost an accident [...] she is a negation of the purposeful, self-interested, mercenary woman" (Cohn 127).

In romance novels a hero-predator will therefore succeed in his chase but, in the words of HM&B author Daphne Clair, he will then be "tamed and domesticated by a woman's gentle strength" (70). Mary, a secondary character in Mary Burchell's *The Brave in Heart* (1948), argues that "Every woman would rather tame a dragon than drive a sheep any day" (45); HM&Bs in which the hero is, metaphorically, a dangerous beast tamed by the love of a good woman, adopt a model of romantic relationship dynamics which "has been present in the genre for centuries" (Vivanco and Kramer) and is also one of the most common. Nonetheless, a statement made by Candice, a secondary character in Penny Jordan's *Past Loving* (1992), suggests that this metaphor may be best suited to the high-mimetic, 'romance', and mythic modes: "Perhaps in fairy-tales it's always the man who makes the moves, while the woman waits demurely for him to do so, but men aren't gods, they're only human" (181). Metaphors which cast the hero as a dangerous animal certainly allow authors to draw on tales from the modes of myth and 'romance' such as the one mentioned in Sara Seale's *To Catch a Unicorn* (1964):

> In olden times when knights were bold and fabulous beasts as common as cows or sheep, it was the great thing to hunt uni-corn, for they were fierce and untameable and not to be caught by usual methods of the chase, so what do you think they did? [...] Well, when they wanted to catch a unicorn they put out a young virgin as bait [...] and the first unicorn that came along just trotted up and trustfully lay down at the maiden's feet, and so he was caught. (63–4)

If the hero is like a "fabulous beast" (Seale, *To Catch* 66) this can help to raise a relatively ordinary contemporary heroine from the low- to the high-mimetic mode: she is cast as a high-mimetic version of a fair damsel whose purity has attracted the unicorn, a princess who has tamed rather than been eaten by a dragon, or Beauty who won the love of the Beast.

In a low-mimetic context, however, where men are "only human", the concept of taming a man can have rather different implications. Rachel, the heroine of Cindi Myers's *The Man Tamer* (2007), advocates "Man Taming" (7), but when Moira applies these techniques to her boyfriend, who is "so absentminded. He'll get to working on his car or watching a game and the next thing you know, he's forgotten all about me" (9), she eventually reaches the conclusion that:

> Your man-taming techniques were part of the problem, [...] if

> you hadn't convinced me man taming would work I wouldn't
> have wasted so much time with him. [....] I know you mean
> well, but maybe those techniques of yours do more harm than
> good. (224)

Moira's experience suggests that, in a low-mimetic, everyday context, attempts to tame, or train, a partner are unlikely to work and may prevent the formation of equitable, truly loving relationships:

> who says it's a woman's job to remake a man? Don't we all
> want to be loved for who we are already? [...] Maybe training a man like a dog isn't the most loving thing to do. Maybe
> the loving thing is to accept him, flaws and all. And hope that
> he'll accept us that way, too. (224)

If one moves to the ironic mode, however, where scenes of "frustration, or absurdity" (Frye 34) are to be expected, animal metaphors may once more come into their own.

Steve Nakamoto, author of *Men are like Fish: What Every Woman Needs to Know About Catching a Man*, notes the profusion of angling metaphors in common usage:

> Have you ever noticed how people commonly use relationship words and fishing words together? Here are some of the
> many examples that I noticed in our everyday language: he's
> a nice catch, she landed a husband, she'd like to hook up with
> the right guy, there are more fish in the sea, he was the big one
> that got away, and he's definitely a keeper. (32)

These fish metaphors are perhaps particularly well suited to the ironic mode because they describe creatures that generally lack the aggressive connotations of the predators discussed above.[1] Certainly

---

1　Of course, not all fish lack aggression. There is a "barracuda named Valerie"
(123) in Jennifer Crusie's *Manhunting* (1993) who does not get her man. Another
exception can be found in Sarah Morgan's *Doukakis's Apprentice* (2011). An
employee of a company recently acquired by the hero of this novel humorously
yet nervously suggests that 'Damon Doukakis is probably just going to feast on
the staff. He's like a great white shark.' The narrative continues:
　Adding to the aura of menace, Debbie made a fin with her hands and
　hummed the theme from *Jaws*. 'He glides through the smooth waters of commerce, eating everything that gets in his way. He's at the top of the food

in Jo Ann Algermissen's *Would You Marry Me Anyway?* (1991) the fishy secondary character whom Cat McGillis's mother considers "the prize catch of the day" (23) provides some modal counterpoint to Hank, the low mimetic hero: "Compared to Hank, the insurance agent she occasionally dated looked positively puny" (10) and:

> In an uncharitable mood, Cat had to admit Bradley did resem-
> ble a fish—red-eyed, from reading the fine print in his com-
> petitors' contracts, and cold-blooded, from the feel of his lips
> when they grazed across her forehead later that same evening.
> (Algermissen 23)

Another scorned suitor, this time in Lori Wilde's *Eager, Eligible and Alaskan* (2002), is also considered by some to be a "catch" (198) but the "mere idea of kissing" Harvey, who makes "fish lips" at Sarah, has her wanting "to scrub her mouth with a scouring pad" (199).

In Jennifer Crusie's *Manhunting* (1993) there is something rather fishy about most of the men Kate Svenson meets. Her friend Jessie points her in the direction of a resort where finding Mr. Right should be "Like shooting fish in a barrel" (13). Unfortunately Kate is less than impressed by most of her dates and she isn't content with "just throw[ing] back the men [...] without maiming them" (113); the scenes in which Kate "almost drowned Lance, [...] scared Peter into heart palpitations, [...] stabbed Donald with a fork, and [...] hit Brad over the head with a bottle" (113) are written to generate laughs.

The irony inherent in Kate's relationship with Jake Templeton is somewhat more subtle and derives from the length of time it takes for them to recognise their attraction to each other. For much of the book Kate is convinced that Jake is "not my type" (44) and he thinks that Kate is "absolutely safe because she was interested only in Yuppies, and he wasn't going to fall for her" (47). Eventually Kate has the truth explained to her by a secondary character:

> Kate carefully didn't look back at Jake for fear her knees
> would go. God, she'd been stupid. "Am I the last to know?"

---

chain, whereas we're right at the bottom of the ocean. We're nothing more than plankton. Let's just hope we're too small to be a tasty snack.

Uncomfortable with the analogy, Polly glanced protectively towards the fish tank that she kept on her desk (13–14).

"Pretty much, although Jake ran you a close second. […] I
can't tell you how we've enjoyed it."
"We who?" (145)

Those entertained by the spectacle include Crusie's readers who,
judging the situation "by the norms of a greater freedom" (Frye 34),
can feel superior to both Kate and Jake. The irony is strengthened by
the fish symbolism which makes the situation an example of the para-
dox of "the angler angled" (Cunnar 80). On a literal level it can be
stated of Kate and Jake's relationship that "Some of [their] best moments were in front of the fish" (215); symbolically, although Crusie
does not, like John Donne (1572–1631) in his parodic poem 'The
Baite', call to her "reader's attention two traditions of fishing, one
sacred and the other profane" (Cunnar 78), she does follow Donne
in using fishing imagery "to defend ironically reciprocity and mutual
sexuality in human love" (Cunnar 78).

Kate and Jake are dissatisfied with their lives; they are "both, so
to speak, in the same boat" (82). They also spend a considerable
amount of time together in a very real "rowboat" (42) and their lack
of predatory intent towards each other is symbolised by the lack of
bait on their hooks. As Jake explains, "If you bait your hook […] you
will catch a fish" (43). Despite this lack of bait, however, Kate does
catch a fish (44). Later, feeling the heat of the sun, she strips down to
her underwear and "dabbling her hand in the water" (48), calls "Here,
fish" (48). The 'fish' she attracts this time is Jake, who notices that
"There was a lot of woman under that blouse" (49). Nonetheless, he is
still wary, because he feels sure "You eat guys like me for breakfast"
(80). On another day on the lake Jake also inadvertently catches a
"fish. It was a big one, and it broke the water battling, flapping water
all over him" (112). Its struggles perhaps match Jake's; it is he who
demonstrates resistance to "commitment of any kind" (202) after he
is 'hooked' by Kate and enters into a sexual relationship with her.

The next time Jake is drenched in lakewater both he and Kate
join the fishes as their boat breaks apart in the aftermath of sexual
intercourse. Kate recognises the symbolism of the moment but
misinterprets it:

By the time they swam to shore, the boat was gone.

She wondered if that was symbolic of their relationship, and shivered. The timing was definitely right. Because great sex notwithstanding, she could feel a sense of impending doom [...] they still hadn't talked about the future.

Maybe because they didn't have one. (186–7)

They certainly do have a future but a sunken boat is no less effective than a burnt one at symbolising a relationship which has reached a point of no return. Jake can no longer "Float on the lake" (189), detached from both commitment and the emotional waters which surround him. As anglers who have hooked a fish, each must decide what to do with the catch. Jake's quandary is that he "can't let her go [...] but [...] can't see any way to keep her, either" (188); Kate resolves his dilemma by returning to the city, an action which cuts their lines of communication and sets them both free. Some time apart, however, helps them realise that Kate could be happy as a big fish in a small pond, helping "little businesses" (205) and swimming through life with Jake in "an old cottage on the lake" (213), so when she returns to him he doesn't "let her go again" (209) but instead catches her forever with "two carved wedding bands and a solitaire" (213) with "carvings. On the band" (215) of the fish which witnessed their courtship and symbolise their transformation from anglers to angled.[1]

Love is a Journey: Marion Lennox's *Princess of Convenience* (2005)

Marion Lennox's award-winning *Princess of Convenience* explores a very different set of metaphors: life as a journey, death as a journey, and love as a journey.[2] George Lakoff and Mark Turner have observed that "When we think of life as purposeful, we think of it

---

1   This is another example of the phenomenon I have described elsewhere whereby rings in romance novels can indicate "that the hero and heroine have found their 'One' and may also symbolise the sexual attraction between them, commemorate their triumph over 'the barrier,' recall a moment of particular importance to their relationship, or reflect aspects of the personality and appearance of the heroine, the hero, or both" (Vivanco "One").

2   The RWA gave the novel the 2006 RITA Award for Best Traditional Romance.

as having destinations and paths toward those destinations, which makes life a journey" (3); Marcel, a secondary character in Lennox's *Princess of Convenience* says that in life we "face the future" (25) and "move on" (25). This metaphor of "moving on" (184) through life is one which is repeated throughout the novel, particularly by the protagonists: Raoul, for example, states that "we move on" (15), while Jess tells herself to "Move on" (20) and observes that a secondary character "could move on" (167).

Death can perhaps be seen as a continuation of the journey begun during life. The metaphor of death as a journey is a common one:

> we say things like "He's gone," "He's left us," "He's no longer with us," "He's passed on [...]." All of these are [...] instances of a general metaphorical way we have of conceiving of birth, life, and death in which BIRTH IS ARRIVAL, LIFE IS BEING PRESENT HERE, and DEATH IS DEPARTURE. (Lakoff and Turner 1)

Life's "stopping point is death's departure point. Consequently, death too can involve a journey with a destination" (Lakoff and Turner 4). In the New Testament, for example, it is stated that "strait is the gate, and narrow is the way, which leadeth unto life" (Matthew 7:14) and in medieval vision literature one can find accounts of good souls passing over a narrow bridge, whereas others fall off.[1] In *Princess of Convenience* there are no explicit religious allusions but Sarah, a minor character interested in "Money and power and prestige" (8), dies because her "drunken speeding on her way to meet a lover" (8) leads

---

1   Among such visions are the *Vision of Sunniulf* in which there is "a bridge so narrow that there was scarcely room for one foot on it. [...] Sunniulf asks the meaning of all this and is told that those religious who are careless of the discipline of their flock fall from the bridge and those who are strict pass over in safety to the house" (Patch 98), and the *Vision of the Monk of Wenlock*, in which is seen:
   a pitchy river boiling and flaming, over which was placed a piece of timber for a bridge. Over this the holy and glorious souls strove to pass. Some went securely, others slipped and fell into the Tartarean stream. [...] Beyond the river were walls shining with splendor great in length and height—the heavenly Jerusalem. (Patch 101)
   In the twelfth-century *Vision of Alberic*, Alberic saw "a river of burning pitch, over which is an iron bridge. This the righteous find broad enough for easy passage; but for sinners it becomes as narrow as a thread in the middle and they fall from it" (Patch 111).

to her literal fall: her car "slewed off the cliff and into the sea" (12).
Jess's near-death experience caused by the collision with Sarah's car
constitutes what Regis has described as a:

> "point of ritual death" [...] that moment in a romance novel
> when the union of heroine and hero seems completely impossi-
> ble. It is marked by death or its simulacrum (for example faint-
> ing or illness); by the risk of death; or by any number of images
> or events that suggest death, however metaphorically. (14)

In the aftermath of this crash Jess spends "six days" (15) "awake
but not awake. In some dream world" (11). Many medieval visions
of the other world were experienced when the visionary was in a
similar state.[1] In the "dream world" (11) Jess "simply accepted [...]
the astounding view through her casement windows" (11) and even
when full consciousness has returned she feels as if she has been
transported to another world: "Made of glistening white stone, with
turrets, towers and battlements and set high on the crags overlooking
the sea, the castle looked as if it had been taken straight out of a fairy
tale" (5).

The similarities that exist between *Princess of Convenience* and
the texts describing dream visions and journeys to the other world
may be coincidental, and as Howard Rollin Patch has observed, even
in the older literature:

> When scenes like these appear, [...] it is not always obvious
> that ultimately they derive from a mythological origin [...].
> Parts of an earlier idea may be borrowed, certain elements in
> several descriptions taken over, until the precise channel of
> transmission is thoroughly obscured. Perhaps it is never quite
> safe to draw a definite conclusion about sources immediate or
> remote. (1)

Nonetheless, the explicit references to fairy tales which occur

---

1   Alberic had his vision while he lay for "nine nights and nine days [...] as if dead"
(Patch 110) and the *Vision of Gunthelm* relates the experience of "a novice lying
on his pallet (in 1161), apparently more dead than alive" (Patch 117). Also in the
twelfth-century, "A youth in the monastery at Eynsham (near Oxford), who had
been ill a long time, and was found as if dead, had a vision of which he told on
his return to consciousness" (Patch 118).

throughout the novel demonstrate the heroine's awareness that the
changes in her life have been so significant that at times it seems as
though she has moved out of her quotidian reality and into a world
like those experienced by the visionaries, "a world in which the ordinary laws of nature are slightly suspended" (Frye 33). Inside that
"castle [which] looked as if it had been taken straight out of a fairy
tale" (5) there is a "fairy-tale bedroom" (11) and Henri, the "elderly butler" (20) "was definitely a fairy godfather" (21). There are,
however, frequent returns to the low-mimetic mode: the castle has "a
fairy-tale setting, but the toast and the marmalade made it real" (45)
and although as "a little girl" Jess had "read the tale of Cinderella
[…] and […] dreamed of princes […] Reality was very different […].
Real princes weren't riding white chargers ready to whisk a woman
away from the troubles of the world. Real princes came with trag-
edies of their own" (19). Despite these reminders of reality, however,
the presence of the fairy-tale 'dream' lingers. After all, as Raoul tells
Jess, "Magically it's happened, my love" (179): she has married her
prince in what one newspaper headline declares to be a "FAIRY-TALE
WEDDING" (172), she will live in the castle which "looked straight out
of a fairy tale" (176) and she accepts that she and Raoul can "have a
happy ending" (179) together. As is the case with both fairy tales and
journeys to another world, the setting offers the reader some distance
from her own reality and this perhaps softens the emotional impact of
the novel's exploration of how the protagonists deal with, and "move
on" (69) from, multiple bereavements.

In *Princess of Convenience* the linear view of life and death, in
which the dead are considered to have "gone" or "passed on" seems
to have been espoused by "everyone" (68) who sought to console
Raoul after his sister's death and "said I should get away and forget"
(68), and also by Jess's cousin Cordelia, who urged her to travel to
the principality of 'Alp'Azuri' after the death of her son because "It'll
take your mind off things best forgotten" (12). Raoul and Jess have,
in effect, been urged to leave the past behind and continue on their
own life journeys. A similar view of the past informed the actions of
both Raoul's brother and father who, following the latter's separation
from his wife Louise, "just dismissed her. She was forgotten the

moment she walked out of the palace and she was never permitted back" (67). Although Louise was forced to abandon her older child when she took Raoul and his twin sister away with her, she tried to maintain contact with him:

> No one answered our phone calls to the palace but we wrote to Jean-Paul every week. Every one of us did. But he never answered. Mama thought for a long while that my father was keeping the letters from him, but no. The servants confirmed for us ... Jean-Paul, like my father, had simply moved on. (67–8)

The linear view of time implicit in the belief that one can "move on" and forget the past is not, however, one shared by all cultures.

Gideon C. Goosen suggests that the work of "Eugene Stockton, a Catholic priest, biblical scholar, and archeologist" who has "knowledge of Aboriginal communities and [...] awareness of the huge difference between the world-views of Aborigines and Westerners" (85), may be useful in bridging the gap between the different cultural conceptions of time:

> His solution is to think of a three-dimensional image with time as a spiral. It is forward-moving if viewed from the side, cyclic if viewed from above, and spiraling outwards if viewed from inside. Thus there do seem to be points of coincidence between Aboriginal time and Western time. (87–8)[1]

As Eva Rask Knudsen has noted, the linear and the cyclic coexist:

---

1   The spiral is not alien to European literature, science and theology. For Samuel Taylor Coleridge, for example, the ascending spiral "represented the laws of nature" and "also represented the laws governing the human understanding and described the natural growth of knowledge" (Jackson 852). According to H. J. Jackson he:

> must have encountered it in the equiangular spiral of Descartes as well as in the scientific writings of Goethe and Steffens and Erasmus Darwin [...]. The spiral also appears in eighteenth-century aesthetics, in the writings of the mystics [...], and in scholastic theology [...]. Its most memorable literary use is Dante's, for the diminishing and descending circles of Hell have their counterpart in the circular ascent of the mountain of Purgatory. (852)

More recently it has been discovered that DNA, which the individual inherits from his or her ancestors, is arranged in pairs of intertwined helices.

> in Aboriginal Western-Desert paintings. [...] The concentric
> circles of Western-Desert art represent sacred Dreaming sites
> or 'home-centres' (camps or places of significance to the life
> of the individual artist) and the semi-circles represent ances-
> tors resting or people celebrating Dreamings in their travels
> from site to site. The notion of travelling itself is represented
> by the connecting lines between these sites. Thus, a painting is
> characterized by a double movement—the circular and the lin-
> ear—but the overall composition is cyclic, as, on Aboriginal
> land, travelling inevitably results in a return. Beginnings and
> endings are therefore ambiguous in this overlapping structure,
> where linearity is constantly halted by circularity. (24)

While Marion Lennox may not have drawn on this precise iconographic tradition, it is possible that, as an Australian author, she had
some knowledge of the Aboriginal conception of time and journey-
ing and the ways in which they have been expressed symbolically via
circles and spirals.[1]

Such a reading of the depiction of time in *Princess of Convenience*
may also be suggested by the fact that Lennox's characters often rest,
or are encouraged to rest, during their journey. Louise, for example,
urges Jess to stay at the castle a little longer after her accident—"Let
us give you just a little time out" (17)—and after Jess and Raoul have
had an informal dinner in the castle kitchen:

> 'Thank you,' she told him. 'This was a great ... time out.'
> 'Time out from what, Jess?' he asked softly [...].
> 'I mean, time out for you,' she tried. 'Time out from
> worrying.'
> 'You were just as in need of time out as I was,' he told her.
> (41)

---

1   Lennox's heroine is also Australian and in the text of the novel itself we learn
    that her weaving, like Western-Desert art, depicts the Australian environment
    of its maker although in her case rather than representing the land, the cloth's
    "colours [are] mingling in the shimmering waves that were Jess's trademark—
    the colours of the sea" (22). Also like that art, Jess's weaving appears to have
    a spiritual dimension: "The skirt combined three tones of aquamarine, blended
    in soft waves. The colours were almost identical but not quite, and when spun
    together they *were somehow magical*" (19, emphasis added).

On one occasion this "time out" is actually described as a time of dreaming: after her accident Jess had "been awake but not awake. In some dream world. Taking the time out she so desperately needed" (11). In what might be described as another "time out", during which, "For this moment—right now—this was her man" (157), Jess finds herself "curving against" (157) Raoul, and thus creating a curve or semi-circle within "a looping curve with carpet in the centre" (157).

Heather Harris has noted that although the "concept of a spiral conveys the idea of regular movement in one direction, […] in the Indigenous view one can move through time in any direction if one is powerful enough. The dead seem to be able to do this, maintaining ongoing contact between themselves and the living" (36). Marion Lennox herself has dedicated considerable time and effort to maintaining some of the links between the dead and the living. Writing under her real name of Linda Brumley, she was the lead author of *Fading Links to China: Ballarat's Chinese Gravestones and Associated Records 1854–1955*. Brumley and her co-authors mention the ways in which the Chinese community remained linked to its dead, with their cemeteries providing "a ritual focus for those who remained" and they state that their research itself "turns history into people".

In *Princess of Convenience* both Jess and Raoul feel compelled to act in accordance with the perceived wishes of their dead loved ones. Jess's son Dominic "died three months ago. […] He was four" (65); during the novel she meets the orphaned three-year-old Edouard and gives him the same teddy bear she had once handed down to Dominic (59). When Jess offers the bear to Edouard, she wonders "What made her think so strongly that it was the right thing to do? That Dom would have wanted this …?" (59). Similarly, when Jess wants to buy some baby alpacas for Edouard, Raoul is hesitant because the animals remind him of his dead sister who "had loved alpacas […]. She'd had a pet one" (100) but then he tells Jess that:

> 'Maybe I need to be reminded of Lisle.' He caught himself, tried to rethink—but he knew that he was right. 'Maybe Lisle would tell me to get over it.'
> She looked up at him, uncertain. 'Lisle would want you to

take these home?'

'I guess she would.' He managed a smile, albeit a lopsided one. 'OK, I know she would. [...].' (107–08)

The dead, then, are not confined to the past but continue to exert an influence in the present.

The spiral of time thus combines repetition and change. When Jess marries Raoul, for example, she recalls that "she'd made these vows once before. [...] It might just work this time, she thought as Raoul made his own vows, strong and sure" (89). Similarly, Raoul, "From the time his mother had taken him and Lisle away from this palace when he was aged six, [...] hadn't looked back" (73), but now he is "back here [...]. And your mother is facing losing again" (68), although this time Alp'Azuri's politics could ensure she is parted from her grandson rather than from her eldest child. The words with which the novel opens are repeated, almost verbatim, towards its close when Jess finds herself "back where this had all started" (176), with the road still spiralling "around snow-capped mountains" (5, 176). Once more Jess asks herself whether she "should be driving on this side of the road" (5, 176) and catches "a glimpse" of a car, "coming fast" (5, 176) towards her. There are several significant differences between the two scenes, however, the most notable of which are that this time Jess is not injured and the driver of the other vehicle does not die.

At the heart of the novel is a third scene in which a pair of fast cars race around a road. This time, however, the road is to be found inside the royal palace itself, and both the track and the cars are toys:

> the road they made was amazing; tunnels, bridges, sweep-
> ing curves that looped round and round the room. It made
> the racing excellent. Once the road was finished they raced in
> earnest. They pushed their cars to the limit, the curves mak-
> ing them overturn, sweep off the sides, fly off into the carpet,
> crash against each other. (154)

This road with "sweeping curves that looped round and round" can be considered a miniature version of the road which "spiralled" (5), "looping above and below" (5) in the first and last chapters. After "twenty-three wins apiece, the tiny cars were starting to smell of burned rubber and their little engines were starting to fade" (154). The cars, then, show signs of wear as a result of their repeated laps of the circuit, much as Jess herself bears "signs on your body that tell me you've had a child" (10). The toy racing track thus allows for the passing of time and change but does so within a context of physical and imaginative repetition. It permits Raoul to revisit his childhood:

'[…] It's my slot-car set, […] I turned six the day before my father kicked us out of the palace,' he told her. 'But on my sixth birthday I was given the sort of slot-car set any small boy dreams of. It's sat here untouched for nearly thirty years and you can't imagine how many times I thought of it with regret. (151–2)

Like Jess's teddy bear, the slot-cars represent a lost past, and neither protagonist can "move on" emotionally until they have revisited that past and learned to take risks. As Raoul says:

'I don't think any real marriage is possible until we both move on from the past. I'm starting to think that maybe I'm prepared to take a risk, but you … maybe you're not ready to do that. Are you?'
    'N … no.' (151)

Their ability to "move on from the past" and "take a risk" is prefigured by their play with the slot-cars, which ends when Jess's:

tiny red Porsche did a double back somersault and flew into the air.
    And hit Raoul beneath the eye.
    'Ouch!' He fell back against the bed, laughing so hard he could hardly hold his hand to his face. […] 'You've even drawn blood. […] I think it's mortal.'
    She couldn't stop laughing. (155)

The risk of possible accidents, injury, and even death is, in this context, rendered unthreatening and, as is the case with the novel as a whole, the scene optimistically suggests that joy can eventually follow tragedy.

Taken together, the three road scenes create a metaphor of life as a journey in which the road along which we all travel is a spiral which circles around, repeating itself, but also incorporating change since each circuit of the track leaves permanent marks on the individual. This spiralling depiction of time challenges "the Western view. In the Western view, we can only live in the present, the past is over and the future does not yet exist" (Harris 36). By the end of the novel both protagonists have rejected the concept of time as a straight line; that would entail putting the past, and the dead, wholly behind them. Whereas in the first scene Jess is "concentrating on not thinking about the empty passenger seat" (5) once occupied by Dominic, later in the novel she angrily questions the cultural belief that forgetting the dead is both necessary and possible:

> 'You don't recuperate from a child's death,' she whispered, and she couldn't stop the sudden flash of anger. 'But that's what they all said. You go overseas and forget, they told me. Start again. How can I start again? Why would I want to?'
>
> 'Like me,' he said softly and her eyes flew to his. 'Only harder. [...] I believed them,' he told her, his voice gentling. 'Or maybe, like you, they just wore me down by repeating their mantra and I hoped like hell they were right.' [...]
>
> 'You've lost someone, too?' she whispered, though she already knew the answer.
>
> 'My twin. My sister. Lisle.' [...]
>
> 'How long ago?'
>
> 'Three years.' He shrugged. 'I know. I should be over it.'
>
> 'Of course you shouldn't be over it,' she snapped. (66)

She then says that "We both need to move on. We need to remember Lisle and Dominic—but we also need to get on with our lives" (69). The novel closes with both protagonists having found a way to "move on" in their lives not simply by "remembering" the dead but by considering them to be a part of their family. The sense they previously felt, of having "an emptiness, a hole" (66) has been replaced by the conviction that the dead can remain with the living: Raoul tells Jess that "I still love my twin [..] She's part of my life forever.

[…] Because of you, my darling Jess, Dominic will live on, with us, with those we love now and with those who come after" (180–1) and in the final paragraphs of the novel they scatter Lisle and Dominic's ashes and:

> this time there was no desolation.
>   This was right.
>   Lisle and Dominic had come home.
>   With their families. (187)

Instead of 'passing on', the dead travel with the living.

Life and death are not the only metaphorical journeys to be found in *Princess of Convenience*. Lakoff and Johnson give the following sentences as illustrations of the presence in popular speech and thought of the metaphor of love as a journey:

> Look *how far we've come*.
> We're *at a crossroads*.
> We'll just have to *go our separate ways*.
> We can't *turn back now*.
> I don't think this relationship is *going anywhere*.
> *Where* are we?
> We're *stuck*.
> It's been a *long, bumpy road*.
> This relationship is a *dead-end street*.
> We're just *spinning our wheels*.
> Our marriage is *on the rocks*.
> We've gotten *off the track*.
> This relationship is *foundering*.
>
> Here the basic metaphor is that of a JOURNEY, and there are various types of journeys that one can make: a car trip, a train trip, or a sea voyage. (44–5).

In *Princess of Convenience* the dangerous possibilities inherent in the kind of travelling suggested by the metaphor of being 'on the verge of falling in love' are given new intensity by Lennox's rephrasing of it: Jess feels "as if there was an edge somewhere really close, and she was about to go into free-fall" (124). Jess and Raoul try to avoid love because they fear it will hurt them and this fear is conveyed through the use of metaphors. Thus Raoul is described as having "a killer smile. It made Jess stare up at him and feel something inside twist" (37) and when she thinks about his admirable qualities, "Once again there was that twisting inside that she scarcely understood. She had to find some safe ground" (44). Jess also perceives the "gut-twisting sensation" (61) as something which is "threatening to spiral out of control" (61). The use of the words "twisting" and "spiral", and Jess's search for "safe ground" recall the dangerous road along which Jess travelled in the first chapter of the novel, and from which she almost fell to her death:

> The road spiralled around snow-capped mountains, with the sea crashing hundreds of feet below. Every twist in the road seemed to reveal postcard magic. [...]
> The twist she'd just taken had given her a fleeting glimpse of the home of the Alp'Azuri royal family. [...]
> She braked hard, turning her car onto a slight verge. (5)

Raoul is the acting head of "the Alp'Azuri royal family", and he too experiences love in terms which recall the dangers of that road: "His world was being tilted and he'd spent his life desperately trying to keep his world right way up [...] he'd sworn never to get that emotionally involved again [...] but now ..." (75). What he has to deal with "now" is a woman whose conversation has him "trying desperately to get back on track. The world seemed to be spinning and he felt dangerously close to falling off" (108) and soon he has to admit that he is "falling so hard for you" (159). If Jess's journey of love is prefigured at the start of the novel by her travel along the road spiralling up to the royal palace, for Raoul the metaphor assumes an almost fatal degree of reality at the end of the romance as he speeds down the same road, "flicked a glance sideways" (177), spots Jess, and "came really, really close to driving straight off a cliff" (177). He avoids disaster, however, and states that "if you let me love you, [...] we'll be taking our love for each other and we'll be moving forward" (181). Jess decides that although it "needed courage to take this leap, [...] he was right here to catch her, forever and ever and ever" (184) and so, instead of falling to her death, she can jump safely, and the two of them can then "move forward ... together" (181) on their journey of love and life.

Death in this novel threatens not just the protagonists but, metaphorically, the entire principality of Alp'Azuri because:

> this country has been known as one of the most corrupt places in Europe [...] When Jean-Paul died I had a visit from no less than three heads of state of neighbouring countries. The ordinary citizens here have been bled dry. They've been taxed to the hilt and given nothing in return, so much so that there's the threat of real revolt. The country has become a hotbed of illicit activity with corruption undermining neighbouring stability as well as ours. Change has to occur and it can only change through the constitution—through the ruling prince or regent. (43)

As the term "heads of state" suggests, it is common in political theory to think of countries as a body politic, with the prince in this case taking the role of the head, and the people that of the rest of the body. This body is clearly feverish, its sickbed also a "hotbed", both because it has contracted the contagious disease of corruption (which might spread to its neighbours) and because a bladed weapon is embedded in it up "to the hilt", with the result that the body has been "bled dry". A cure can only be applied by the "ruling prince or regent", and appropriately Raoul, the new prince regent, is "a doctor" (35) who has been working for "Médecins Sans Frontières [...] Doctors Without Borders ... They go to the most desperately needy places in the world" (43). In order to have the authorisation to treat this patient, however, Raoul needs to find himself a wife because the "constitution says that the role of regent can only be held by a married man" (25–6). It is for this reason that his marriage to Jess is described in one newspaper headline as "JUST WHAT THE DOCTOR ORDERED" (172).

The marriage was, however, suggested by Jess (70–1) and it is she who, when the media's questions about it were "getting nastier" (115), "twisted them around your little finger" (120). This metaphor is entirely fitting given that Jess is literally "a master weaver"(63) and metaphorically "A wonder weaver" (63). On a literal level, Jess "started designing at school" (22) and now owns Waves, a clothing company "known throughout the world" (23). Since Alp'Azuri "was famous [...] for its fabulous weavers [...] she'd come here because [...] of fabric and yarns" (11). When she offers to make clothing for Sebastian (a toy bear) her comment that she will do so by "Magic" (60) could be seen as merely a figure of speech but it may also hint that there is a deeper symbolic subtext to the act of weaving, particularly as the balls of yarn are also described as "Magic. She'd produced only the coarser of her selection—there was no time for fine weaving now—but the coarser ones were magic enough" (61).

As Maria C. Pantelia has observed, "the art of weaving produces a fabric which often bears a design and has the potential for conveying a concrete message" (494). Although the cloth Jess weaves for Edouard's bear is much smaller and less complex than those woven by "Helen, Andromache, and Penelope [...] Circe and Calypso" (Pantelia 497) or by "Philomel and Arachne" (Hackett 13), it can nonetheless be seen to be both "conveying a concrete message" and, through its "Magic", helping that "concrete message" to become reality. Earlier Jess had found the idea of

> Time out [...] almost incredibly appealing. And it was the only thing she could think of to do. What else? Pick up the threads?
>   What threads? (18)

The implication appeared to be that Jess was unsure which threads she had left to "pick up" following her divorce and Dominic's death. As Raoul observes, "Back in Australia she had no one [...]. She had no family and she'd lost her child" (143). The metaphor of "the fabric of the family" is one in common use and if it is present here, and if threads symbolise family members, it is unsurprising that Jess is not shown weaving until she becomes involved with the royal family of Alp'Azuri.[1] Certainly the colours of the threads she uses appear to

---

1   Among the many available examples of this metaphor, Denise Côté-Arsenault's "Weaving Babies Lost in Pregnancy Into the Fabric of the Family" provides a particularly extended version in which babies are described as threads in the fabric of the family:

   A family's fabric is woven over time and often includes new babies whose

have some symbolic meaning. Jess begins her work on "a tiny loom already threaded with black warp thread" (60), and the threads in this funereal colour perhaps represent Jess's, Raoul's, and Edouard's many dead family members. The new fabric takes shape around them while Raoul and Edouard "looked on in wonder" (62) much as, in Somalia, Raoul had "watched [...] over and over, with awe" (180) as he saw that:

> no matter how dreadful the circumstances, no matter how many deaths there are in families, families seem to reform. Regroup. Two families become one. Two teenage girls, friends, get together to raise siblings. Grandmas and uncles and second cousins once removed are stepping in to pick up the pieces. (180)

It seems appropriate that the creation of a family from disparate elements should be symbolised by the weaving of a new fabric since "weaving unites what must be united. To weave is to unite, to interlace, to bind" (Scheid and Svenbro 10). The fabric that forms around the black warp threads on Jess's loom is also a composite, woven with "skeins of brightly coloured yarn [...]. The balls were unique, vibrant colours and amazing textures" (60–1). Jess asks Edouard "to choose four skeins for the cross thread—the weft" (61) and he picks out balls of "red, gold, a deep blue and a soft lemon that made her smile" (62). Red represents Jess, for as she later tells Raoul, "Red's my colour" (153). Blue is declared by Raoul to be "royal" (153), and having previously dressed in blue he plays with a "tiny blue Lamborghini" (155).[1] The "soft lemon" seems suitable for young Edouard because its pallor matches his paler complexion: he is "as fair as his

---

birth is anticipated. Pregnancy is the time when this baby's thread is added, and how it is incorporated depends on the timing of the pregnancy, whether there are other children, the effort that has gone into achieving the pregnancy, and particular characteristics of this baby. When the baby dies, she or he has already been woven into the family story and cannot be simply ripped out. (30)

1   On one occasion he wears a "jet-black suit and [...] blue-black silk tie" (21) and his "dress suit" is "of a fabric so blue it was almost black" (137). The connection between royalty and blue is reinforced by the fact that, as the novel opens, Raoul's fiancée and "distant cousin" (7) Sarah, who was "brought up to royalty" (7), is driving "a blue, open-topped sports car" (5).

big uncle was dark, with wispy white-blond curls, skin that was almost translucent and huge brown eyes" (53). The gold skein is the
most difficult to interpret but could symbolise Edouard's grandmother, Louise, who "for state occasions" (140) wore a dress "heavily em-
broidered with crimson and gold" and "sweeping to a glorious train
of gold and silver at the back" (141). As "unique" as the individual it
represents, each of the skeins is "vibrant", full of movement and life
as it is woven through the warp threads.

Another weaving metaphor, already alluded to, is that of weaving
stories. As we have seen, Jess can twist the press around her
"little finger" (120) and she can do so because, both literally and
metaphorically, she has "true weaver's fingers" (62). When she began
her weaving she "considered for a little, and then she set to work. The
shuttles flew in her hands, back, forth, pressing each thread into place
in her chosen pattern " (62), and she shows similar dexterity when
dealing with the media: she has "learned to manipulate the media for
her own ends. Now she chose to answer exactly what she wanted to
answer. Any other questions she ignored with the deftness born of
practice" (142).

Traditionally "The activity of narration is [...] closely identified
with the archetypal feminine activities of spinning and weaving [...].
In fact the word 'text' derives from the Latin word for weaving,
texere" (Hackett 12–13).[1] Romance authors, writing what might be
thought of as an "archetypal feminine" type of fiction, create their
texts around the warp threads of the central romance.

---

1   Scheid and Svenbro note that "the Latin word *textus* in the sense of 'text' is
not attested before Quintilian (who died in about 100). But the verb *texere*, 'to
weave', is already common in the sense of 'composing a written work' in Cicero
(106–43 B.C.)" (106).

Conclusion

This book, far from being comprehensive, is merely an introduction to the literary art of the HM&B romance. This art can perhaps usefully be compared to that of the 'Peepshow with Views of the Interior of a Dutch House' by Samuel van Hoogstraten that Jo, the heroine of Julie Cohen's *Married in a Rush* (2006), encounters almost immediately after planning to "go home and read a good sexy novel" (24).[1] HM&B romances have always been "sexy" novels because "Sexual tension is not just about getting naked. It's about wanting something and knowing it's out of reach. It can be a look instead of a touch" (Fielding, *Secret* 198). In the aftermath of what may, therefore, be a metafictional reference to HM&Bs, Cohen introduces readers to an object in the National Gallery which is significantly different from the oil paintings that surround it:

> a large box on a wooden pedestal. The outside was painted and lacquered wood. She walked around the box and saw that the front of it was open and glassed over. (24)

Like the peepshow, HM&Bs are packaged in a way which sets them apart from the oil paintings of literary fiction.

In addition, although they share many characteristics with other types of fiction, their contents are shaped by their 'Tradition' and the guidelines provided by their publisher:

> The inside of the box was painted with the interior of a room, but the perspectives were skewed, irregular, and yet eerily realistic, like a small slice of Alice's Wonderland. (24)

Daphne Watson, a critic of HM&Bs, has argued that they too present

---

1   In a letter to the reader Cohen mentions that "the artwork I've described really is in the National Gallery" (2) and on her website she names the peepshow as "the Van Hoogstraten peep show" ("Married").

us with "rooms, beautifully furnished rooms, described to the last rug and ornament" (91–2) and "offer a distorted picture of the world" (94). According to Janice Radway, even the more sexually explicit romances "refuse finally to unravel the connection between female sexual desire and monogamous heterosexuality. The stories therefore close off the vista they open up by virtue of their greater willingness to foreground the sexual fantasy at the heart of the genre" (16).[1] The spatial and sexual perspectives of many HM&B romances may indeed be as limited as these scholars have suggested, but such constraints do not preclude literary merit. Jane Austen is, at least according to romance author Jennifer Crusie, "the mother of the romance novel [...] Because she set the standard for the genre" ("Jennifer" 240) and despite the "traditional rejection of Austen's small world, her 'little bit (two inches wide) of Ivory'" (Newman 704), her talent is rarely questioned. HM&Bs authors are not, of course, all latter-day Austens, and in some ways the "box" within which they paint their worlds is more constraining than Austen's "little bit [...] of Ivory": although their characters may travel further and engage in a wider range of activities than Austen's, HM&Bs tend to be considerably shorter in length and much more tightly focused on the relationship between the protagonists.

If, unlike Ann Barr Snitow, one is "concerned here with developing an admiration for their buried poetics" (Snitow 247), it will not do simply to dismiss HM&Bs as "unrealistic, distorted, and flat" (Snitow 247). Instead, like Jo, one must take a closer look:

> She began to walk around it again and noticed that there was a peephole in the side of the box. Jo stooped and looked through it. (24)

Both Margaret Ann Jensen and David Margolies have suggested that

---

1   It should be noted that Radway's statement was made in 1991. In the twenty-first century HM&B has published "erotic fiction" under its Spice imprint: "Spice Books are not traditional romances, nor do they require a happily-ever-after ending" (Harlequin, "Spice"). Carina Press, "a digital-first imprint from Harlequin" (Carina, "About") launched in 2010, also publishes some erotic fiction and in addition its romance novels range "from the very sweet to the incredibly sexy, featuring couples (or multiples) from all walks of life and sexual orientation, including same- sex romances" (Carina, "Submission").

critics of HM&Bs must adopt a similar posture: "In order to understand the appeal of romances we must [...] examine romances *within
their own framework*" (Jensen 24), and:

> To gain the entertainment, the reader must accept, even if
> 'temporarily', the consciousness of the romance. [...] Once
> the conventions of the form become familiar to her, the ro-
> mance reader knows she must understand the world through
> the eyes and feelings of the heroine. She wishes to enter the
> world of the heroine, the story, but there is only one door in,
> and she must assume a particular posture to go through it.
> (Margolies 12)

Having peered through the peephole:

> As if by magic, the small, limited perspective made the whole
> picture make sense. What had been skewed became straight.
> What had seemed flat suddenly appeared three-dimensional.
> Jo was looking into a real house, with a tiled floor and red
> velvet chairs and paintings on the wall and a small black-and-
> white dog. (24)

Janice Radway observed that "descriptive detail [...] characterizes
the mention of domestic architecture and home furnishings in romantic fiction" (194) but as we have seen, these literal interiors often
reflect emotional interiors, so the peepshow can also be considered
a representation of the emotional scope of most HM&Bs, which are
very much focused on the emotional interiors of one or both of the
protagonists.

To some, the scene depicted within the peepshow will never
appeal. To them it may seem that "A potentially vast landscape
is confined to a claustrophobic inner vision. There are very few
characters in the romance" (Margolies 9). It may be, however, that this
claustrophobically narrowed vision mirrors, or seeks to reproduce,
the effects of falling in love. The behaviour of Mallory Hawthorne,
heroine of Jessica Marchant's *A Part of Heaven* (1993), would
certainly support this theory: "She knew [...] why she had pretended
to forget everything about her past life. From the moment she'd met
him it had all ceased to matter. None of it had any significance, except

as the track she had needed to take through the world to find him" (95). Similarly, when Laura Jamieson first meets Gideon Maitland in Carole Mortimer's *Passion from the Past* (1982),

> she couldn't have looked away if her life had depended upon it [...]. Laura couldn't ever remember noticing so much about one person on sight before [...]. It was as if time suddenly stood still, allowing her to look her fill of this man she felt captivated by. And she didn't ever want to stop looking at him. (11)

Voluntarily or involuntarily, these heroines reshape their worlds in response to romantic love.

HM&Bs, too, are often shaped so that they recreate the effect of falling in love. According to Kate Walker's guide to writing romance, "Reading the book should send her [the reader] on the same emotional roller-coaster ride that the characters experience" (19). Like roller-coasters, HM&Bs are designed so that the plot quickly carries the reader through the pages and, as Julie Cohen has observed, their purpose and format impose certain constraints on the authors:

> For me, writing category romance is a bit like building a roller coaster. You know where it's going to begin, and you know where it's going to end, and within those two extremes you have to construct something beautiful and exciting. The pace is fast, the space is limited, and the rules are strict—but within those rules, you have artistic freedom. ("From a Roller Coaster")

Cohen's *Married in a Rush* features a hero, Bruno Deluca, who creates roller coasters. He states that "When you design a roller coaster you think of two things: the thrill and the safety. The rolls and the speed make you know you're alive. The safety bars keep you from dying" (149). HM&Bs also provide excitement within a safe context: "The reader knows when she picks up a romance that the happy ending is guaranteed. She isn't reading the book to find out *what* happens—she wants to know and enjoy *how* it happens" (Walker, *12 Point Guide* 19).

A good HM&B, like a good roller coaster, will not just be

exciting but will also have a solid, reliable framework: consistent characterisation, a plot with no holes and, at the nuts and bolts level, a correct use of language. Bruno's roller coaster, however, is not just a *good* roller coaster which provides a safe but exciting ride:

> It was a beautiful shape, all curves and arches and filigree supports, made out of gleaming silver metal. Twining around the green trees, higher than all of them, it looked like a graceful dragon, or a solidified eddy of steam: half air, half water. (175)

HM&Bs vary greatly but the very best of them, like Bruno's roller coaster, are far more than a type of entertainment which provides quick thrills; they are outstanding and beautiful examples of what can be achieved within the constraints of a very specialised literary art-form. Like a fairground roller coaster, HM&Bs are designed to be attractive to a mass audience yet they are not merely a commercial product: many of the mythoi, intertextual references and metaphors they use draw on literary tradition. Perhaps, indeed, their very debt to past works of literature contributes to their dismissal by some critics: to many modern scholars their conventions, like those of *cancionero* love poetry, may seem archaic and limiting. Theirs is, however, a living tradition which constantly changes, reflecting on and responding to social change, and often incorporating references to the newest of popular cultural phenomena. Written for both love and money, with care and knowledge as well as passion, the literary art of the Harlequin Mills & Boon romance deserves far more careful consideration than it is usually afforded.

Bibliography

Harlequin Mills & Boon Romances

Algermissen, Jo Ann. *Would You Marry Me Anyway?* Richmond, Surrey: Silhouette, 1991.

Allan, Jeanne. *No Angel*. Richmond, Surrey: Mills & Boon, 1990.

Allen, Louise. *The Earl's Intended Wife*. 2004. Don Mills, Ontario: Harlequin, 2006.

Anderson, Caroline. *The Impetuous Bride*. Richmond, Surrey: Harlequin Mills & Boon, 2001.

Arbor, Jane. *Handmaid to Midas*. London: Mills & Boon, 1982.

Ash, Rosalie. *Apollo's Legend*. Richmond, Surrey: Mills & Boon, 1994.

Ashton, Elizabeth. *Moonlight on the Nile*. London: Mills & Boon, 1979.

Asquith, Nan. *The Certain Spring*. London: Mills & Boon, 1956.

Asquith, Nan. *The Garden of Persephone*. 1967. London: Mills & Boon, 1976.

Beacon, Elizabeth. *An Innocent Courtesan*. Richmond, Surrey: Harlequin Mills & Boon, 2007.

Bradshaw, Nina. *Knight in Armour*. London: Mills & Boon, 1935.

Browning, Pamela. *The Flutterby Princess*. 1987. Richmond, Surrey: Harlequin, 1988.

Burchell, Mary. *Always Yours*. 1941. London: Mills & Boon, 1972.

Burchell, Mary. *Dearly Beloved*. London: Mills & Boon, 1944.

Burchell, Mary. *Dearly Beloved*. 1944. London: Mills & Boon, 1968.

Burchell, Mary. *It's Rumoured in the Village*. 1946. *The fourth anthology of 3 Harlequin Romances by Mary Burchell*. Don Mills,

Ontario: Harlequin, 1983. 7–189.

Burchell, Mary. *Love Is My Reason*. London: Mills & Boon, 1957.

Burchell, Mary. *On The Air*. 1956. Toronto: Harlequin, 1980.

Burchell, Mary. *The Brave in Heart*. 1948. Toronto: Harlequin, 1975.

Burchell, Mary. *Ward of Lucifer*. London: Mills & Boon, 1976.

Cast, P. C. *Divine by Choice*. New York: LUNA, 2006.

Clark, Dorothy. *Hosea's Bride*. New York: Steeple Hill, 2004.

Cohen, Julie. *Married in a Rush*. Richmond, Surrey: Harlequin Mills & Boon, 2006.

Cole, Sophie. *Mrs. Scarlot's Quaints*. London: Mills & Boon, 1938.

Cole, Sophie. *Secret Joy*. London: Mills & Boon, 1934.

Cornick, Nicola. *Kidnapped: His Innocent Mistress*. Don Mills, Ontario: Harlequin, 2009.

Craven, Sara. *Moon of Aphrodite*. 1980. London: Mills & Boon, 1981.

Critchlow, Dorothy. *Beware of Dreams*. London: Mills & Boon, 1942.

Crusie, Jennifer. *Getting Rid of Bradley*. Don Mills, Ontario: Harlequin, 1994.

Crusie, Jennifer. *Manhunting*. Don Mills, Ontario: Harlequin, 1993.

Crusie, Jennifer. *Strange Bedpersons*. 1994. Richmond, Surrey: MIRA, 2004.

Dean, Dinah. *The Briar Rose*. 1986. London: Mills & Boon, 1987.

Devoti, Lori. *Wild Hunt*. New York: Silhouette, 2008.

Donald, Robyn. *A Reluctant Mistress*. Richmond, Surrey: Harlequin Mills & Boon, 1999.

Douglas, Casey. *Edge of Illusion*. London: Harlequin, 1984.

Draven, Stephanie. *Poisoned Kisses*. Don Mills, Ontario: Harlequin, 2010.

Dunn, Carola. *A Lord for Miss Larkin*. 1991. Richmond, Surrey: Harlequin Mills & Boon, 1997.

Estrada, Rita Clay. *The Ivory Key*. 1987. Richmond, Surrey: Mills &

Boon, 1992.

Evans, Constance M. *Second-Hand Cinderella*. London: Mills & Boon, 1937.

Evans, Laurel. *Built to Last*. Richmond, Surrey: Silhouette, 1988.

Farnes, Eleanor. *A Serpent in Eden*. London: Mills & Boon, 1971.

Farnes, Eleanor. *Secret Heiress*. 1956. London: Mills & Boon, 1968.

Fielding, Liz. *Eloping With Emmy*. Richmond, Surrey: Harlequin Mills & Boon, 1998.

Fielding, Liz. *Secret Wedding*. 2000. Richmond, Surrey: Harlequin Mills & Boon, 2005.

Fielding, Liz. *The Sheikh's Guarded Heart*. Richmond, Surrey: Harlequin Mills & Boon, 2006.

Forrester, Polly. *Jewel Under Siege*. Richmond, Surrey: Mills & Boon, 1990.

George, Catherine. *City Cinderella*. Richmond, Surrey: Harlequin Mills & Boon, 2003.

George, Catherine. *Earthbound Angel*. Richmond, Surrey: Harlequin Mills & Boon, 1996.

Gordon, Lucy. *The Greek Tycoon's Achilles Heel*. Richmond, Surrey: Harlequin Mills & Boon, 2010.

Gracie, Anne. *Tallie's Knight*. 2000. *The Regency Rakes: Volume 1*. Richmond, Surrey: Harlequin Mills & Boon, 2003. 3–282.

Grant, Laurie. *Devil's Dare*. 1996. Richmond, Surrey: Harlequin Mills & Boon, 2001.

Greene, Jennifer. *A Groom for Red Riding Hood*. 1994. Richmond, Surrey: Silhouette, 1995.

Hale, Deborah. *My Lord Protector*. 1999. Richmond, Surrey: Harlequin Mills & Boon, 2003.

Hampson, Anne. *Wife for a Penny*. 1972. Don Mills, Ontario: Harlequin, 1982.

Hardy, Kate. *In the Gardener's Bed*. Richmond, Surrey: Harlequin Mills & Boon, 2007.

Harper, Fiona. *Invitation to the Boss's Ball*. Richmond, Surrey:

Harlequin Mills & Boon, 2009.

Harrel, Linda. *Sea Lightning*. 1979. London: Mills & Boon, 1983.

Hart, Jessica. *Business Arrangement Bride*. Richmond, Surrey: Harlequin Mills & Boon, 2006.

Hart, Jessica. *Cinderella's Wedding Wish*. Don Mills, Ontario: Harlequin, 2009.

Hart, Jessica. *Promoted: to Wife and Mother*. Don Mills, Ontario: Harlequin, 2008.

Higgins, Kristan. *Catch of the Day*. Don Mills, Ontario: HQN, 2007.

Hulme, Ann. *The Emperor's Dragoon*. London: Mills & Boon, 1983.

James, Melissa. *Her Galahad*. 2002. Richmond, Surrey: Silhouette, 2003.

James, Sophia. *One Unashamed Night*. Richmond, Surrey: Harlequin Mills & Boon, 2010.

Johnson, Janice Kay. *Beauty & the Beasts*. Harlequin: Don Mills, Ontario, 1997.

Jordan, Penny. *Past Loving*. Richmond, Surrey: Mills & Boon, 1992.

Jump, Shirley. "Building Love". *Mills & Boon Annual 2008*. Richmond, Surrey: Harlequin Mills & Boon, 2007. 70–73.

Kendrick, Sharon. *Bought for the Sicilian Billionaire's Bed*. 2008. Richmond, Surrey: Harlequin Mills & Boon, 2009.

Kent, Pamela. *City of Palms*. 1957. London: Mills & Boon, 1973.

Ker, Madeleine. *The Alpha Male*. Richmond, Surrey: Harlequin Mills & Boon, 2003.

Ker, Madeleine. *The Millionaire Boss's Mistress*. 2004. Richmond, Surrey: Harlequin Mills & Boon, 2005.

King, Lucy. *Bought: Damsel in Distress*. Richmond, Surrey: Harlequin Mills & Boon, 2009.

King-Gamble, Marcia. *All About Me*. New York: Kimani, 2007.

Kingsley, Maggie. *A Wife Worth Waiting For*. Richmond, Surrey: Harlequin Mills & Boon, 2008.

Kirkman, Helen. *Embers*. 2004. Richmond, Surrey: Harlequin Mills

& Boon, 2006.

Kitt, Sandra. *For All We Know*. New York: Arabesque, 2008.

Korbel, Kathleen. *Dangerous Temptation*. New York: Silhouette, 2006.

Krentz, Jayne Ann. *The Adventurer*. 1990. *The Pirate, The Adventurer & The Cowboy*. Don Mills, Ontario: HQN, 2006. 217–425.

Krentz, Jayne Ann. *The Cowboy*. 1990. *The Pirate, The Adventurer & The Cowboy*. Don Mills, Ontario: HQN, 2006. 427–632.

Krentz, Jayne Ann. *Too Wild to Wed?* Richmond, Surrey: Mills & Boon, 1991.

Lackey, Mercedes. *The Fairy Godmother*. New York: LUNA, 2004.

LaFoy, Leslie. *The Money Man's Seduction*. New York: Silhouette, 2008.

Lamb, Charlotte. *Dark Fate*. Richmond, Surrey: Mills & Boon, 1994.

Leigh, Roberta. *Give a Man a Bad Name*. Richmond, Surrey: Mills & Boon, 1993.

Lennox, Marion. *Princess of Convenience*. Richmond, Surrey: Harlequin Mills & Boon, 2005.

Logan, Nikki. *Rapunzel in New York*. Richmond, Surrey: Mills & Boon, 2011.

Mackenzie, Myrna. *The Black Knight's Bride*. 2004. Richmond, Surrey: Harlequin Mills & Boon, 2005.

Malcolm, Margaret. *Leave Me No More*. London: Mills & Boon, 1963.

Marchant, Jessica. *A Part of Heaven*. Richmond, Surrey: Mills & Boon, 1993.

Marsh, Nicola. *Contract to Marry*. Richmond, Surrey: Harlequin Mills & Boon, 2005.

Marshall, Paula. *Lord Hadleigh's Rebellion*. Richmond, Surrey: Harlequin Mills & Boon, 2001.

Marshall, Paula. *The Beckoning Dream*. 1997. *Rogues and Rakes*. Richmond, Surrey: Harlequin Mills & Boon, 2008. 3–299.

Marshall, Paula. *The Lost Princess*. Richmond, Surrey: Harlequin

Mills & Boon, 1996.

Marshall, Paula. *The Wolfe's Mate*. Richmond, Surrey: Harlequin Mills & Boon, 1999.

Marton, Sandra. *Naked in His Arms*. Richmond, Surrey: Harlequin Mills & Boon, 2006.

Marton, Sandra. *The Disobedient Virgin*. Richmond, Surrey: Harlequin Mills & Boon, 2005.

McClone, Melissa. *Blueprint for a Wedding*. New York: Silhouette, 2005.

Monroe, Lucy. "The Playboy's Seduction". 2004. *Mills & Boon Christmas Treasury of Romance*. Richmond, Surrey: Harlequin Mills & Boon, 2009. 3–35.

Montana, Pat. *Fairy-Tale Family*. 1999. Richmond, Surrey: Harlequin Mills & Boon, 2000.

Morgan, Sarah. *Doukakis's Apprentice*. Richmond, Surrey: Mills & Boon, 2011.

Mortimer, Carole. *Passion from the Past*. London: Mills & Boon, 1982.

Myers, Cindi. *The Daddy Audition*. Don Mills, Ontario: Harlequin, 2009.

Myers, Cindi. *The Man Tamer*. Don Mills, Ontario: Harlequin, 2007.

Neal, Hilary. *Nurse Off Camera*. London: Mills & Boon, 1964.

Neels, Betty. *A Christmas Proposal*. *Christmas Miracles*. Richmond, Surrey: Harlequin Mills & Boon, 1996.

Neels, Betty. *An Apple From Eve*. London: Mills & Boon, 1981.

O'Brien, Anne. *Chosen for the Marriage Bed*. Richmond, Surrey: Harlequin Mills & Boon, 2009.

Palmer, Diana. "The Greatest Gift". *More Than Words: Stories of Hope*. Don Mills, Ontario: Harlequin, 2010. 7–125.

Parv, Valerie. *The Love Artist*. 1986. London: Mills & Boon, 1987.

Pollock, Rosemary. *White Hibiscus*. 1979. Toronto: Harlequin, 1980.

Richards, Emilie. *Billy Ray Wainwright*. *Southern Gentlemen*. Don

Mills, Ontario: MIRA, 1998. 159–377.

Roberts, Nora. *Mind over Matter*. 1987. *Going Home*. Richmond, Surrey: Silhouette, 2004. 401–649.

Robinson, Fay. *A Man Like Mac*. Don Mills, Ontario: Harlequin, 2000.

Rudick, Marilynne. *Fixing to Stay*. 1986. Richmond, Surrey: Mills & Boon, 1987.

Seale, Sara. *The Gentle Prisoner*. 1949. London: Mills & Boon, 1977.

Seale, Sara. *To Catch a Unicorn*. 1964. London: Mills & Boon, 1975.

Showalter, Gena. *The Nymph King*. Don Mills, Ontario: HQN, 2007.

Simmons, Deborah. *The Devil Earl*. Don Mills, Ontario: Harlequin, 1996.

Simmons, Deborah. *The Last Rogue*. 1998. Richmond, Surrey: Harlequin Mills & Boon, 2003.

Sinclair, Dani. *Sleeping Beauty Suspect*. 2007. Richmond, Surrey: Harlequin Mills & Boon, 2008.

Standley, Olive. *My Heart's Your Home*. London: Mills & Boon, 1946.

Stuart, Anne. *A Dark & Stormy Night*. 1997. Richmond, Surrey: Silhouette, 1998.

Styles, Michelle. *A Christmas Wedding Wager*. *Christmas by Candlelight*. Richmond, Surrey: Harlequin Mills & Boon, 2007. 307–603.

Sullivan, Jane. *The Matchmaker's Mistake*. 2001. Richmond, Surrey: Harlequin Mills & Boon, 2002.

Summers, Essie. *No Orchids by Request*. 1965. London: Mills & Boon, 1966.

Tarr, Hope. *It's a Wonderfully Sexy Life*. 2006. Richmond, Surrey: Harlequin Mills & Boon, 2007.

Tempest, Jan. *Ask Me Again*. London: Mills & Boon, 1955.

Templeton, Karen. *Everybody's Hero*. 2004. Richmond, Surrey: Silhouette, 2005.

Templeton, Karen. *Pride and Pregnancy*. 2007. Richmond, Surrey:

Harlequin Mills & Boon, 2008.

Thornton, Claire. *Gifford's Lady*. Richmond, Surrey: Harlequin Mills & Boon, 2002.

Thornton, Claire. *Raven's Honour*. Richmond, Surrey: Harlequin Mills & Boon, 2002.

Thornton, Claire. *The Abducted Heiress*. Richmond, Surrey: Harlequin Mills & Boon, 2005.

Thorpe, Kay. *Curtain Call*. London: Mills & Boon, 1971.

Townend, Carol. *An Honourable Rogue*. Richmond, Surrey: Harlequin Mills & Boon, 2008.

Vinton, Anne. *Dr Pilgrim's Progress*. 1963. London: Mills & Boon, 1984.

Walker, Kate. *No Gentleman*. Richmond, Surrey: Mills & Boon, 1992.

Warren, Nancy. *Hot Off the Press*. Richmond, Surrey: Harlequin Mills & Boon, 2003.

Weale, Anne. *If This Is Love*. 1963. London: Mills & Boon, 1971.

Weale, Anne. *Neptune's Daughter*. 1987. Richmond, Surrey: Mills & Boon, 1988.

Weston, Sophie. *More Than a Millionaire*. Richmond, Surrey: Harlequin Mills & Boon, 2001.

White, Tiffany. *Naughty Talk*. 1993. Richmond, Surrey: Mills & Boon, 1994.

Wilde, Lori. *Eager, Eligible and Alaskan. The Bachelors of Bear Creek*. Don Mills, Ontario: Harlequin, 2002. 193–377.

Winspear, Violet. *A Girl Possessed*. 1980. London: Mills & Boon, 1981.

Winspear, Violet. *The Child of Judas*. 1976. London: Mills & Boon, 1981.

Winspear, Violet. *The Girl at Goldenhawk*. 1974. London: Mills & Boon, 1981.

Wylie, Trish. *Her Real-Life Hero*. 2004. Richmond, Surrey: Harlequin Mills & Boon, 2005.

Wyndham, Esther. *Tiger Hall.* 1954. London: Mills & Boon, 1966.

Other Texts Cited

Acevedo, Bianca P., and Arthur Aron. "Does a Long-Term Relationship Kill Romantic Love?" *Review of General Psychology* 13.1 (2009): 59–65.

Acevedo, Bianca P., Arthur Aron, Helen E. Fisher and Lucy L. Brown. "Neural Correlates of Long-Term Intense Romantic Love". *Social Cognitive and Affective Neuroscience.* Advance Access.

Aguirre, Manuel. "The Riddle of Sovereignty". *Modern Language Review* 88.2 (1993): 273–82.

Andersen, Hans Christian. *Hans Andersen's Fairy Tales.* Trans. Mrs. Paull. London: Frederick Warne & Co, 1867.

Anderson, Rachel. *The Purple Heart Throbs: The Sub-literature of Love.* London: Hodder and Stoughton, 1974.

Augspach, Elizabeth A. *The Garden as Woman's Space in Twelfth- and Thirteenth-Century Literature.* Studies in Mediaeval Literature 27. Lewiston, NY: Edwin Mellen, 2004.

Austen, Jane. *Pride and Prejudice.* Ed. Tony Tanner. London: Penguin, 1972.

Bach, Evelyn. "Sheik Fantasies: Orientalism and Feminine Desire in the Desert Romance". *Hecate* 23.1 (1997): 9–40.

Barlow, Linda, and Jayne Ann Krentz. "Beneath the Surface: The Hidden Codes of Romance". *Dangerous Men and Adventurous Women: Romance Writers on the Appeal of the Romance.* Ed. Jayne Ann Krentz. Philadelphia: U of Philadelphia P, 1992. 15–29.

Bartlett, Des and Jen Bartlett. "Patagonia's Wild Shore Where Two Worlds Meet". *National Geographic* 149.3 (1976): 298–321.

Beer, Gillian. *The Romance.* The Critical Idiom 10. 1970. London: Methuen, 1977.

Bettelheim, Bruno. *The Uses of Enchantment: The Meaning and Importance of Fairy Tales.* 1976. London: Penguin, 1991.

Black, Claire. "Mills and Boom". *Scotsman* 4 Nov. 2008. 5 Nov.

2008   <http://thescotsman.scotsman.com/features/Mills-and-Boom.4656074.jp>.

Blakey, Dorothy. *The Minerva Press 1790–1820*. London: Bibliographical Society, 1939.

Bloom, Clive. *Bestsellers: Popular Fiction Since 1900*. Houndmills, Basingstoke: Palgrave Macmillan, 2002.

Boccaccio, Giovanni. *The Decameron*. Trans. G. H. McWilliam. 2nd ed. London: Penguin, 2003.

Bold, Rudolph. "Trash in the Library". *Library Journal* 105.10 (1980): 1138–9.

The Book of Common Prayer. London: Oxford UP, n.d.

Bowring, Joanna and Margaret O'Brien. *The Art of Romance: Mills & Boon and Harlequin Cover Designs*. Munich: Prestel, 2008.

Brumley, Linda, Lu Bingqun and Zhao Xueru. *Fading Links to China: Ballarat's Chinese Gravestones and Associated Records 1854–1955*. 1992. Melbourne: History Department of the University of Melbourne, 2001. 1 Jan. 2010 <http://www.chaf.lib.latrobe.edu.au/brumley/brumley.htm>.

Bullen, A. H. *Speculum Amantis: Love-poems from Rare Song-books and Miscellanies of the Seventeenth Century*. London: Privately Printed, 1889. <http://www.archive.org/details/speculumamantis01bullgoog>.

Burchell, Mary. "Mary Burchell". *Harlequin 30th Anniversary 1949–1979: The First 30 Years of the World's Best Romance Fiction*. Toronto: Harlequin, 1979. 169–72.

Burke Leacock, Eleanor. "Social Behavior, Biology, and the Double Standard". *Myths of Male Dominance: Collected Articles on Women Cross-Culturally*. New York: Monthly Review Press, 1981. 280–301.

Burns, C. Delisle. *The Horizon of Experience: A Study of the Modern Mind*. London: George Allen & Unwin, 1933.

Cadogan, Mary. *And Then Their Hearts Stood Still: An Exuberant Look at Romantic Fiction Past and Present*. London: Macmillan, 1994.

Calhoun-French, Diane M. "Time-Travel and Related Phenomena in

Contemporary Popular Romance Fiction". *Romantic Conventions*. Ed. Anne K. Kaler and Rosemary Johnson-Kurek. Bowling Green, OH: Bowling Green State U Popular P, 1999. 100–12.

Carina. "About Us". 31 May 2011 <http://carinapress.com/blog/about-us/>.

Carina. "Submission Guidelines". 31 May 2011 <http://carinapress.com/blog/submission-guidelines/>.

Carter, Susan. "Coupling the Beastly Bride and the Hunter Hunted: What Lies Behind Chaucer's *Wife of Bath's Tale*". *The Chaucer Review* 37.4 (2003): 329–45.

Casteras, Susan P. "John Everett Millais' 'Secret-Looking Garden Wall' and the Courtship Barrier in Victorian Art". *Browning Institute Studies* 13 (1985): 71–98.

Cawelti, John G. *Adventure, Mystery, and Romance: Formula Stories as Art and Popular Culture*. Chicago: U of Chicago P, 1976.

Cawelti, John G. "The Concept of Formula in the Study of Popular Literature". *Journal of Popular Culture* 3.3 (1969): 381–90.

Chaucer, Geoffrey. *The Canterbury Tales*. Trans. Nevill Coghill. 1951. Harmondsworth, Middlesex: Penguin, 1986.

Clair, Daphne. "Sweet Subversions". *Dangerous Men and Adventurous Women: Romance Writers on the Appeal of the Romance*. Ed. Jayne Ann Krentz. Philadelphia: U of Philadelphia P, 1992. 61–72.

Clair, Daphne, and Robyn Donald. *Writing Romantic Fiction*. London: A & C Black, 1999.

Cohen, Julie. "From a Roller Coaster to a Mountain Road (with Klingons)". *We Write Romance*. 12 Mar. 2009. 12 Mar. 2009 <http://www.wewriteromance.com/blog/guest-blogger/julie-cohen-guest-blogger-from-a-roller-coaster-to-a-mountain-road-with-klingons/>.

Cohen, Julie. "Married in a Rush". 28 May 2011 <http://www.julie-cohen.com/books/rush/>.

Cohen, Ralph. "History and Genre". *New Literary History* 17.2 (1986): 203–18.

Cohn, Jan. *Romance and the Erotics of Property: Mass-Market Fiction for Women*. Durham: Duke UP, 1988.

Connors, Mary E., and Sue A. Melcher. "Ethical Issues in the Treatment of Weight-Dissatisfied Clients". *Professional Psychology: Research and Practice* 24.4 (1993): 404–08.

Conway, William G. "Argentina Protects Its Wildlife Treasures". *National Geographic* 149.3 (1976): 290–7.

Cook, Ida. *Safe Passage*. 1950. Rev. ed. Richmond, Surrey: MIRA, 2008.

Cook, Jon. "Fictional Fathers". *Sweet Dreams: Sexuality, Gender and Popular Fiction*. Ed. Susannah Radstone. London: Lawrence & Wishart, 1988. 137–64.

Côté-Arsenault, Denise. "Weaving Babies Lost in Pregnancy Into the Fabric of the Family". *Journal of Family Nursing* 9.1 (2003): 23–37.

Crusie, Jennifer. "Jennifer Crusie on Jane Austen as the Mother of the Modern Romance Novel". *The Friendly Jane Austen: A Well-Mannered Introduction to a Lady of Sense & Sensibility*. Ed. Natalie Tyler. New York: Viking, 1999. 240–2.

Crusie, Jennifer. "So, Bill, I Hear You Write Those Little Poems: A Plea for Category Romance". *Romance Writer's Report* 18.5 (1998): 42–44. Rpt. online at Jennifer Crusie's website. 11 Dec. 2009 <http://www.jennycrusie.com/for-writers/essays/so-bill-i-hear-you-write-those-little-poems-a-plea-for-category-romance/>.

Crusie, Jennifer. "Vince's Place". 10 Apr. 2010. 18 Apr. 2010 <http://www.arghink.com/2010/04/10/vinces-place/>.

Crusie Smith, Jennifer. "Romancing Reality: The Power of Romance Fiction to Reinforce and Re-Vision the Real". *Paradoxa* 3.1-2 (1997): 81–93.

Cuddy-Keane, Melba. *Virginia Woolf, the Intellectual, & the Public Sphere*. Cambridge: Cambridge UP, 2003.

Cunnar, Eugene R. "Donne's Witty Theory of Atonement in 'The Baite'". *Studies in English Literature, 1500–1900* 29.1 (1989):

77–98.

Curthoys, Ann, and John Docker. "Popular Romance in the Postmodern Age and an Unknown Australian Author". *Continuum: The Australian Journal of Media & Culture* 4.1 (1990). 3 Feb. 2010 <http://wwwmcc.murdoch.edu.au/ReadingRoom/4.1/Curthoys. html>.

Curtius, Ernst Robert. *European Literature and the Latin Middle Ages*. Trans. Willard R. Trask. 1953. Princeton: Princeton UP, 1990.

Dahl, Victoria. "Contemporaries". 9 Jul. 2010 <http://www. victoriadahl.com/books-Contemporary.php>.

Darbyshire, Peter. "Romancing the World: Harlequin Romances, the Capitalist Dream, and the Conquest of Europe and Asia". *Studies in Popular Culture* 23.1 (2000). 16 Feb. 2009 <http:// web.archive.org/web/20081121192951/http://pcasacas.org/SPC/ spcissues/23.1/darbyshire.htm>.

Davie, John. Note on the Text. *Persuasion*. By Jane Austen. Oxford: Oxford UP, 1980. xiii.

de Geest, Dirk, and An Goris. "Constrained Writing, Creative Writing: The Case of Handbooks for Writing Romances". *Poetics Today* 31.1 (2010): 81–106.

Devine, Fiona. *Social Class in America and Britain*. Edinburgh: Edinburgh UP, 1997.

Deyermond, A. D. *A Literary History of Spain: The Middle Ages*. London: Ernest Benn, 1971.

Dixon, jay. *The Romance Fiction of Mills & Boon, 1909–1990s*. London: UCL Press, 1999.

Dzaja, Nancy. "Lovesickness: The Most Common Form of Heart Disease". *University of Western Ontario Medical Journal* 78.1 (2008): 66–9. 14 Dec. 2009 <http://www.uwomeds.com/uwomj/ V78n1/Lovesickness.pdf>.

Eco, Umberto. "The Myth of Superman". Trans. Natalie Chilton. *Diacritics* 2.1 (1972): 14–22.

Editor, Mills & Boon Temptation. Letter to the Reader. *Night Watch*.

By Carla Neggers. Richmond, Surrey: Mills & Boon, 1994.

Ellis, Kate. Rev. of *Romance and the Erotics of Property: Mass Market Fiction for Women*, by Jan Cohn. *Modern Fiction Studies* 34.4 (1988): 749–50.

Ferriss, Suzanne and Mallory Young. Introduction. *Chick Lit: The New Woman's Fiction*. Ed. Suzanne Ferriss and Mallory Young. New York: Routledge, 2006. 1–13.

Fisher, Helen. "The Drive to Love: The Neural Mechanism for Mate Selection". *The New Psychology of Love*. Ed. Robert J. Sternberg and Karin Weis. New Haven: Yale UP, 2006. 87–115.

Flaubert, Gustave. *Madame Bovary*. Ed. Edmund Gosse. London: William Heinemann, 1923.

Fowler, Bridget. *The Alienated Reader: Women and Popular Romantic Literature in the Twentieth Century*. Hemel Hempstead, Hertfordshire: Harvester Wheatsheaf, 1991.

Freeman, Sarah. "100 Years of Romancing the Readers". *Yorkshire Post* 1 Jan. 2008. 8 Jan. 2008 <http://www.yorkshirepost.co.uk/features/100-years-of-romancing-.3631764.jp>.

Frye, Northrop. *Anatomy of Criticism: Four Essays*. 1957. Oxford: Princeton UP, 2000.

Fussell, Paul. *Caste Marks: Style and Status in the U.S.A*. London: Heinemann, 1984.

Gagne-Hawes, Genevieve. "Anatomy of a Romance: Questioning Genre Conventions in the Novels of Nora Roberts." *Modern Mask* 1.2 (2006). 10 Oct. 2011 <http://modernmask.org/Issue_II/modernmask_literature/anatomy.html>.

Gelder, Ken. *Popular Fiction: The Logics and Practices of a Literary Field*. London: Routledge, 2004.

Goosen, Gideon C. "Christian and Aboriginal Interface in Australia". *Theological Studies* 60 (1999): 72–94.

Greer, Germaine. *The Female Eunuch*. 1970. London: Paladin, 1971.

Gregory, Philippa. Foreword. *Katherine*. 1954. Chicago: Chicago Review P., 2004. vii–ix.

Grescoe, Paul. *The Merchants of Venus: Inside Harlequin and the Empire of Romance*. Vancouver: Raincoast, 1996.

Guiley, Rosemary. *Love Lines: The Romance Reader's Guide to Printed Pleasures*. New York: Facts on File, 1983.

Hackett, Helen. *Women and Romance Fiction in the English Renaissance*. Cambridge: Cambridge UP, 2000.

Haddon, Jenny and Diane Pearson, eds. *Fabulous at Fifty: Recollections of the Romantic Novelists' Association 1960–2010*. n.p.: Romantic Novelists' Association, 2010.

Hahn, Thomas. "The Wedding of Sir Gawain and Dame Ragnelle: Introduction". *Sir Gawain: Eleven Romances and Tales*. Ed. Thomas Hahn. Kalamazoo, Michigan: Medieval Institute Publications, 1995. 7 April 2011 <http://www.lib.rochester.edu/camelot/teams/ragintro.htm>.

Hallam, Julia. *Nursing the Image: Media, Culture and Professional Identity*. London: Routledge, 2000.

Hapgood, Lynne. *Margins of Desire: The Suburbs in Fiction and Culture 1880–1925*. Manchester: Manchester UP, 2005.

Hardy, Kate. "In the Gardener's Bed". 24 March 2010 <http://www.katehardy.com/books/in-the-gardeners-bed.html>.

Harlequin. "About Harlequin". 11 Oct. 2011 <http://www.eharlequin.com/articlepage.html?articleId=36&chapter=0>.

Harlequin. *Harlequin 30th Anniversary 1949–1979: The First 30 Years of the World's Best Romance Fiction*. Toronto: Harlequin, 1979.

Harlequin. "Spice". 31 May 2011 <http://www.eharlequin.com/articlepage.html?articleId=1263&chapter=0>.

Harlequin. "Writing Guidelines: Harlequin Blaze". 7 Sept. 2008 <http://www.eharlequin.com/articlepage.html?articleId=544&chapter=0>.

Harlequin. "Writing Guidelines: Harlequin Presents (Mills & Boon Modern Romance)". 14 Jan. 2008 <http://www.eharlequin.com/articlepage.html?articleId=547&chapter=0>.

Harlequin. "Writing Guidelines: Harlequin Superromance". 19 Sept. 2007 <http://www.eharlequin.com/articlepage. html?articleId=834&chapter=0>.

Harlequin. "Writing Guidelines: How to Submit a Novel". 5 Oct. 2007 <http://www.eharlequin.com/articlepage. html?articleId=564&chapter=0>.

Harlequin. "Writing Guidelines: LUNA". 6 Sept. 2007 <http://www. eharlequin.com/articlepage.html?articleId=698&chapter=0>.

Harlequin. "Writing Guidelines: Silhouette Nocturne". 10 Sept. 2007 <http://www.eharlequin.com/articlepage. html?articleId=1161&chapter=0>.

Harlequin. "Writing Guidelines: Steeple Hill Love Inspired". 9 Feb. 2009 <http://www.eharlequin.com/articlepage. html?articleId=559&chapter=0>.

Harlequin More Than Words. "Overview of the Program". 1 Feb. 2011 <http://www.eharlequin.com/store.html?cid=536>.

Harris, Heather. "Indigenous Worldviews and Ways of Knowing as Theoretical and Methodological Foundations for Archaeological Research" *Indigenous Archaeologies: Decolonizing Theory and Practice*. Ed. Claire Smith and H. Martin Wobst. Abingdon, Oxon: Routledge, 2005. 33–41.

Hewitt, Kate. "Kate Hewitt on Opposites: Do They Really Attract?" 16 Apr. 2010. 18. Apr. 2010 <http://www.iheartpresents. com/2010/04/kate-hewitt-on-opposites-do-they-really-attract/>.

Holmes, Diana. *Romance and Readership in Twentieth-Century France: Love Stories*. Oxford: Oxford UP, 2006.

hooks, bell. *Where We Stand: Class Matters*. London: Routledge, 2000.

"How Writer Spoiled A Good Story". *The Mail* [Adelaide] 10 Sept. 1938: 23. <http://nla.gov.au/nla.news-page4631105>.

Howatson, M. C. *The Oxford Companion to Classical Literature*. 2nd ed. Oxford: Oxford UP, 1997.

Jackson, H. J. "'Turning and Turning': Coleridge on Our Knowledge of the External World". *PMLA* 101.5 (1986): 848–56.

James, Henry. "Gustave Flaubert", *Madame Bovary*. Ed. Edmund Gosse. London: William Heinemann, 1923. v–xliii.

Janet. "REVIEW: *The Wicked West* by Victoria Dahl". 2 June 2009. 9 July 2010 <http://dearauthor.com/wordpress/2009/06/02/review-the-wicked-west-by-victoria-dahl/>.

Jensen, Margaret Ann. *Love's $weet Return: The Harlequin Story*. Toronto: Women's Educational P, 1984.

Johnson-Kurek, Rosemary E. "Leading Us into Temptation: The Language of Sex and the Power of Love". *Romantic Conventions*. Ed. Anne K. Kaler and Rosemary Johnson-Kurek. Bowling Green, OH: Bowling Green State U Popular P, 1999. 113–48.

Jones, Ann Rosalind. "Mills & Boon Meets Feminism". *The Progress of Romance: The Politics of Popular Fiction*. Ed. Jean Radford. London: Routledge, 1986. 195–218.

Jones, Malcolm. *The Secret Middle Ages: Discovering the Real Medieval World*. 2002. Thrupp, Stroud, Gloucestershire: Sutton, 2004.

Kaler, Anne K. "Introduction: Conventions of the Romance Genre". *Romantic Conventions*. Ed. Anne K. Kaler and Rosemary Johnson-Kurek. Bowling Green, OH: Bowling Green State U Popular P, 1999. 1–9.

Kalof, Linda, Amy Fitzgerald, and Lori Baralt. "Animals, Women and Weapons: Blurred Sexual Boundaries in the Discourse of Sport Hunting". *Society & Animals* 12.3 (2004): 237–51. <http://www.animalsandsociety.org/assets/library/539_s1233.pdf>.

Kelly, Brendan D. "Medical Romance". *The Lancet* 370.9597 (2007): 1482.

Kelly, Henry Ansgar. "The Metamorphoses of the Eden Serpent during the Middle Ages and Renaissance". *Viator* 2 (1971): 301–27.

Kenyon, Max. "The Danger of Constricted Repertoires". *The Musical Times* 77.1123 (1936): 785–7.

King-Gamble, Marcia. "From the Author". *Amazon.co.uk*. 1 Dec. 2010 <http://www.amazon.co.uk/Under-Spell-Arabesque-Marcia-King-Gamble/dp/1583140271>.

Knudsen, Eva Rask. *The Circle & the Spiral: A Study of Australian Aboriginal and New Zealand Māori Literature*. Readings in the Post/Colonial Literatures in English 68. Amsterdam: Rodopi, 2004.

Krentz, Jayne Ann. Introduction. *Dangerous Men and Adventurous Women: Romance Writers on the Appeal of the Romance*. Ed. Jayne Ann Krentz. Philadelphia: U of Pennsylvania P, 1992. 1–8.

Krentz, Jayne Ann. "Trying to Tame the Romance: Critics and Correctness". *Dangerous Men and Adventurous Women: Romance Writers on the Appeal of the Romance*. Ed. Jayne Ann Krentz. Philadelphia: U of Pennsylvania P, 1992. 107–14.

Kress, Gunther. "Textual Matters: The Social Effectiveness of Style". *Functions of Style*. Ed. David Birch and Michael O'Toole. London: Pinter, 1988. 126–41.

Lakoff, George, and Mark Johnson. *Metaphors We Live By*. 1980. Chicago: U of Chicago P, 2003.

Lakoff, George, and Mark Turner. *More Than Cool Reason: A Field Guide to Poetic Metaphor*. Chicago: U of Chicago P., 1989.

Law, Helen H. "The Name Galatea in the Pygmalion Myth". *The Classical Journal* 27.5 (1932): 337–42.

Leavis, Q. D. *Fiction and the Reading Public*. London: Chatto & Windus, 1932.

Lee, Linda J. "Guilty Pleasures: Reading Romance Novels as Reworked Fairy Tales". *Marvels & Tales: Journal of Fairy-Tale Studies* 22.1 (2008): 52–66.

Leidl, Christoph G. "The Harlot's Art: Metaphor and Literary Criticism". *Metaphor, Allegory, and the Classical Tradition: Ancient Thought and Modern Revisions*. Ed. G. R. Boys-Stones. Oxford: Oxford UP, 2003. 31–54.

Lerner, Alan Jay and Frederick Loewe. *My Fair Lady*. 1956. Harmondsworth, Middlesex: Penguin, 1980.

Luke, Brian. "Violent Love: Hunting, Heterosexuality, and the Erotics of Men's Predation". *Feminist Studies* 24.3 (1998): 627–55.

Lutz, Deborah. *The Dangerous Lover: Gothic Villains, Byronism, and the Nineteenth-Century Seduction Narrative*. Columbus: Ohio State UP, 2006.

Lutz, Deborah. "The Haunted Space of the Mind: The Revival of the Gothic Romance in the Twenty-First Century". *Empowerment versus Oppression: Twenty First Century Views of Popular Romance Novels*. Ed. Sally Goade. Newcastle: Cambridge Scholars, 2007. 81–92.

Macpherson, Ian. "Secret Language in the *Cancioneros*: Some Courtly Codes". *Bulletin of Hispanic Studies* 62.1 (1985): 51–63.

Magnani, Roberta. "The Mysterious Mrs Meeke: A Biographical and Bibliographical Study". *Cardiff Corvey: Reading the Romantic Text* 9 (2002): 113–37. 22 Nov. 2007 <http://www.cf.ac.uk/encap/romtext/reports/cc09_n04.pdf>.

Mangini, Elizabeth. "Pipilotti's Pickle: Making Meaning from the Feminine Position". *PAJ: A Journal of Performance and Art* 23.2 (2001): 1–9.

Margolies, David. "Mills & Boon: Guilt Without Sex". *Red Letters* 14 (1982–83): 5–13.

McAleer, Joseph. *Passion's Fortune: The Story of Mills & Boon*. Oxford: Oxford UP, 1999.

McAleer, Joseph. "Scenes from Love and Marriage: Mills and Boon and the Popular Publishing Industry in Britain, 1908–1950". *Twentieth Century British History* 1.3 (1990): 264–88.

Meisami, Julie Scott. "Allegorical Gardens in the Persian Poetic Tradition: Nezami, Rumi, Hafez". *International Journal of Middle East Studies* 17.2 (1985): 229–60.

Meisami, Julie Scott. "The World's Pleasance: Hafiz's Allegorical Gardens". *Comparative Criticism* 5 (1983): 153–85.

Meldrum, P. R. "Norway, Kate". *Twentieth-Century Romance and Gothic Writers*. Ed. James Vinson and D. L. Kirkpatrick. Detroit: Gale, 1982.

Memmott, Carol. "Romance fans: Vampires are just our type." *USA Today* 28 June 2006. 12 Oct. 2011 <http://www.usatoday.com/life/books/news/2006-06-28-vampire-romance_x.htm>.

Modleski, Tania. *Loving with a Vengeance: Mass-produced Fantasies for Women*. 1982. New York: Routledge, 1990.

Murray, Sandra L., Dale W. Griffin, Jaye L. Derrick, Brianna Harris, Maya Aloni and Sadie Leder. "Tempting Fate or Inviting Happiness?: Unrealistic Idealization Prevents the Decline of Marital Satisfaction". *Psychological Science* 22.5 (2011): 619–26.

Murray, Sandra L., John G. Holmes and Dale W. Griffin. "The Self-Fulfilling Nature of Positive Illusions in Romantic Relationships: Love is Not Blind, but Prescient". *Journal of Personality and Social Psychology* 71.6 (1996): 1155–80.

Mussell, Kay. *Fantasy and Reconciliation: Contemporary Formulas of Women's Romance Fiction*. Westport, Connecticut: Greenwood, 1984.

Nakamoto, Steve. *Men are like Fish: What Every Woman Needs to Know About Catching a Man*. 2002. Huntington Beach, CA: Java, 2006.

Neff, Lisa A. and Benjamin R. Karney. "To Know You is to Love You: The Implications of Global Adoration and Specific Accuracy for Marital Relationships". *Journal of Personality and Social Psychology* 88.3 (2005): 480–97.

The New Shorter Oxford English Dictionary. In 2 vols, Oxford: Oxford UP, 1993.

Newman, Karen. "Can This Marriage Be Saved: Jane Austen Makes Sense of an Ending". *ELH* 50.4 (1983): 693–710.

Nicholls, Jane. Letter to the Reader. *Would You Marry Me Anyway?* By Jo Ann Algermissen. Richmond, Surrey: Silhouette, 1991. 2.

O'Donnell, Mary Ann. "Aphra Behn: The Documentary Record". *The Cambridge Companion to Aphra Behn*. Ed. Derek Hughes and Janet Todd. Cambridge: Cambridge UP, 2004. 1–11.

Olivier, Séverine. "«Femme, je vous aime...»? Nora Roberts, une inconnue sortie de l'ombre dans l'univers sentimental". *Belphégor: Littérature Populaire et Culture Médiatique* 7.2. (2008). 30 Oct. 2008   <http://etc.dal.ca/belphegor/vol7_no2/articles/07_02_olivie_robert_fr.html>.

Opie, Iona and Peter. *The Classic Fairy Tales*. London: Oxford UP, 1974.

Orbach, Susie. *Fat is a Feminist Issue* ... 1978. Feltham, Middlesex: Hamlyn, 1979.

Osborne, Laurie E. "Harlequin Presents: That '70s Shakespeare and Beyond". *Shakespeare After Mass Media*. Ed. Richard Burt. New York: Palgrave, 2002. 127–49.

Ovid. *Metamorphoses*. Trans. A. D. Melville. Oxford: Oxford UP, 1998.

The Oxford English Dictionary. 2nd ed., in 20 vols, Oxford: Oxford UP, 1989.

Oxford Dictionaries. April 2010. Oxford UP. 13 March 2011 <http://oxforddictionaries.com/view/entry/m_en_gb0545930>.

Paizis, George. "Category Romance in the Era of Globalization: The Story of Harlequin". *The Global Literary Field*. Ed. Anna Guttman, Michel Hockx and George Paizis. Newcastle: Cambridge Scholars, 2006. 126–51.

Paizis, George. *Love and the Novel: The Poetics and Politics of Romantic Fiction*. Houndmills, Basingstoke: Macmillan, 1998.

Pantelia, Maria C. "Spinning and Weaving: Ideas of Domestic Order in Homer". *American Journal of Philology* 114.4 (1993): 493–501.

Patch, Howard Rollin. *The Other World According to Descriptions in Medieval Literature*. Cambridge, Massachusetts: Harvard UP, 1950.

Payne, Roger. "At Home With Right Whales". *National Geographic* 149.3 (1976): 322–39.

Pearce, Lynne. "Popular Romance and its Readers". *A Companion to Romance: From Classical to Contemporary*. Ed. Corinne Saunders. Malden, MA: Blackwell, 2004. 521–38.

Pease, Allison. *Modernism, Mass Culture, and the Aesthetics of Obscenity*. Cambridge: Cambridge UP, 2000.

Phelps, Ethel Johnston. "Gawain and the Lady Ragnell". *The Maid of the North: Feminist Folk Tales from Around the World*. 1981. New York: Henry Holt, 1982. 35–44.

Philpott, Trevor. "The Refugees—A World Survey". *The Rotarian*

97.6 (1960): 16–27. <http://books.google.co.uk/books?id=OjcEA AAAMBAJ&lpg=PA1&pg=PA16#v=onepage&q&f=false>.

Polan, Dana. "Brief Encounters: Mass Culture and the Evacuation of Sense". *Studies in Entertainment: Critical Approaches to Mass Culture*. Ed. Tania Modleski. Theories of Contemporary Culture 7. Bloomington and Indianapolis: Indiana UP, 1986. 167–87.

Priestley, J. B. "High, Low, Broad". *Open House: A Book of Essays*. London: William Heinemann, 1927. 162–7.

Radford, Jean. Introduction. *The Progress of Romance: The Politics of Popular Fiction*. Ed. Jean Radford. London: Routledge & Kegan Paul, 1986. 1–20.

Radway, Janice A. *Reading the Romance: Women, Patriarchy, and Popular Literature*. 1984. Chapel Hill: U of North Carolina P, 1991.

Regis, Pamela. *A Natural History of the Romance Novel*. Philadelphia: U of Pennsylvania P, 2003.

Reinhold, Meyer. "The Naming of Pygmalion's Animated Statue". *The Classical Journal* 66.4 (1971): 316–19.

Richardson, Samuel. *Pamela; or, Virtue Rewarded*. Ed. Thomas Keymer and Alice Wakely. Oxford: Oxford UP, 2001.

Roach, Catherine. "Loving Your Mother: On the Woman-Nature Relation". *Hypatia* 6.1 (1991): 46–59.

Roberts, Nora. "The Romance of Writing." *North American Romance Writers*. Ed. Kay Mussell and Johanna Tuñón. Lanham, Maryland: Scarecrow, 1999. 198–201.

Rogers, Edith Randam. *The Perilous Hunt: Symbols in Hispanic and European Balladry*. Studies in Romance Languages 22. Lexington: UP of Kentucky, 1980.

Romance Writers of America. "About the Romance Genre". 2007. 9 Oct. 2007 <http://www.rwanational.org/cs/the_romance_genre>.

Rougemont, Denis de. *Love in the Western World*. Tr. Montgomery Belgion. 1940. Princeton, NJ: Princeton UP, 1983.

Rowland, Beryl. *Animals with Human Faces: A Guide to Animal Symbolism*. Knoxville: U of Tennessee P, 1973.

Salovey, Peter, Alexander J. Rothman, Jerusha B. Detweiler and Wayne T. Steward. "Emotional States and Physical Health". *American Psychologist* 55.1 (2000): 110–21.

Saunders, Corinne. Introduction. *A Companion to Romance: From Classical to Contemporary*. Ed. Corinne Saunders. Malden, MA: Blackwell, 2004. 1-9.

Scheid, John and Jesper Svenbro. *The Craft of Zeus: Myths of Weaving and Fabric*. Trans. Carol Volk. Revealing Antiquity 9. Gen. ed. G. W. Bowersock. Cambridge, MA: Harvard UP, 1996.

Schell, Heather. "The Big Bad Wolf: Masculinity and Genetics in Popular Culture". *Literature and Medicine* 26.1 (2007): 109–25.

Scheper-Hughes, Nancy, and Margaret M. Lock. "The Mindful Body: A Prolegomenon to Future Work in Medical Anthropology". *Medical Anthropology Quarterly* ns 1.1 (1987): 6–41.

Seaton, Beverly. "Towards a Historical Semiotics of Literary Flower Personification". *Poetics Today* 10.4 (1989): 679–701.

Segal, Francesca. "Who Said Romance was Dead?" *Observer* 27 Jan. 2008. 23 Nov. 2011 <http://www.guardian.co.uk/books/2008/jan/27/fiction.features1>.

Seidel, Kathleen Gilles. "'I Can Pay the Rent': Money in the Romance Novel". *North American Romance Writers*. Ed. Kay Mussell and Johanna Tuñón. Lanham, Maryland: Scarecrow, 1999. 211–19.

Shanks, Lewis Piaget. "Gustave Flaubert". *The Open Court* 36.3 (1922): 129–45. <http://www.archive.org/details/opencourt_mar1922caru>.

Shaw, Bernard. *Pygmalion: A Romance in Five Acts*. 1916. Harmondsworth, Middlesex: Penguin, 1977.

Siegel, Jeff. *Second Dialect Acquisition*. Cambridge: Cambridge UP, 2010.

Snitow, Ann Barr. "Mass Market Romance: Pornography for Women is Different". *Radical History Review* 20 (1979): 141–61. Rpt. in *Powers of Desire: The Politics of Sexuality*. Ed. Ann Snitow, Christine Stansell and Sharon Thompson. New York: Monthly Review P, 1983. 245–63.

Sternberg, Robert J. *Love is a Story: A New Theory of Relationships*. New York: Oxford UP, 1998.

Sternberg, Robert J., Mahzad Hojjat, and Michael L. Barnes. "Empirical Tests of Aspects of a Theory of Love as a Story". *European Journal of Personality* 15.3 (2001): 199–218.

Stott, Annette. "Floral Femininity: A Pictorial Definition". *American Art* 6.2 (1992): 60–77.

Talbot, Mary M. "'An Explosion Deep Inside Her': Women's Desire and Popular Romance Fiction". *Language and Desire: Encoding Sex, Romance and Intimacy*. Ed. Keith Harvey and Celia Shalom. London: Routledge, 1997. 106–22.

Talbot, Mary M. *Fictions at Work: Language and Social Practice in Fiction*. New York: Longman, 1995.

Tatar, Maria. *Off With Their Heads!: Fairy Tales and the Culture of Childhood*. Princeton, New Jersey: Princeton UP, 1992.

Templeton, Karen. "'Tis a puzzlement". 24 June 2006. 29 Sept. 2008 <http://karentempleton.com/blog/?p=278>.

Teo, Hsu-Ming. "Historicizing The Sheik: Comparisons of the British Novel and the American Film". *Journal of Popular Romance Studies* 1.1 (2010). 31 Aug. 2010 <http://jprstudies.org/2010/08/historicizing-the-sheik-comparisons-of-the-british-novel-and-the-american-film-by-hsu-ming-teo/>.

Teo, Hsu-Ming. "Orientalism and Mass Market Romance Novels in the Twentieth Century". *Edward Said: The Legacy of a Public Intellectual*. Ed. Ned Curthoys and Debjani Ganguly. Carlton, Victoria: Melbourne UP, 2007. 241–62.

Tetel Andresen, Julie. "Postmodern Identity (Crisis): Confessions of a Linguistic Historiographer and Romance Writer". *Romantic Conventions*. Ed. Anne K. Kaler and Rosemary Johnson-Kurek. Bowling Green, OH: Bowling Green State U Popular P, 1999. 173–86.

"The Marriage of Sir Gawain". *Sir Gawain: Eleven Romances and Tales*. Ed. Thomas Hahn. Kalamazoo, Michigan: Medieval Institute Publications, 1995. 8 April 2011 <http://www.lib.rochester.edu/

camelot/teams/marrifrm.htm>.

"The Wedding of Sir Gawain and Dame Ragnelle". *Sir Gawain: Eleven Romances and Tales*. Ed. Thomas Hahn. Kalamazoo, Michigan: Medieval Institute Publications, 1995. 11 April 2011 <http://www.lib.rochester.edu/camelot/teams/ragnfrm.htm>.

"Thebes". *Encyclopaedia Britannica*. 1968.

Thiébaux, Marcelle. *The Stag of Love: The Chase in Medieval Literature*. Ithaca, NY: Cornell UP, 1974.

Thomas, Glen. "The Best Australian Romance Novelist: Emma Darcy". *Beautiful Things in Popular Culture*. Ed. Alan McKee. Malden, MA: Blackwell, 2007. 64–78.

Thurston, Carol. *The Romance Revolution: Erotic Novels for Women and the Quest for a New Sexual Identity*. Urbana: U of Illinois P, 1987.

Tiffin, Jessica. *Marvelous Geometry: Narrative and Metafiction in Modern Fairy Tale*. Detroit, Michigan: Wayne State UP, 2009.

Torstar. *2005 Annual Report*. 8 June 2011 <http://www.torstar.com/pdf/2005_annualreport.pdf>.

Torstar. *2006 Annual Report*. 2 Jul. 2011 <http://www.torstar.com/pdf/2006_annualreport.pdf>.

Torstar. *Torstar Corporation 2010 Annual Report*. 8 June 2011 <http://www.torstar.com/pdf/Final_2010TORSTAR_AR.pdf>.

Treble, Patricia. "Harlequin Thinks Unsexy Thoughts: Impotence is Just the Start: the New Romance Novels Put the 'Fun' Back in Sexual Dysfunction". *Macleans* 24 Sept. 2007. 13 Mar. 2008 <http://www.macleans.ca/culture/media/article.jsp?content=20070924_109276_109276>.

Trevelyan, George Otto. *The Life and Letters of Lord Macaulay*. 2 vols. London: Longmans, Green, 1876.

Vaz da Silva, Francisco. "Red as Blood, White as Snow, Black as Crow: Chromatic Symbolism of Womanhood in Fairy Tales". *Marvels & Tales* 21.2 (2007): 240–52.

Vivanco, Laura. "Birds of a Feather: Predator and Prey in *Celestina*". *Celestinesca* 26.1-2 (2002): 5–27.

Vivanco, Laura. "Feminism and Early Twenty-First Century Harlequin Mills & Boon Romances". *Journal of Popular Culture*. Forthcoming.

Vivanco, Laura. "Jennifer Crusie's Literary Lingerie". *Journal of Popular Romance Studies*. Forthcoming.

Vivanco, Laura. "One Ring to Bind Them: Ring Symbolism in Popular Romance Fiction". *New Approaches to Popular Romance Fiction*. Ed. Sarah S. G. Frantz and Eric M. Selinger. McFarland. Forthcoming 2012.

Vivanco, Laura, and Kyra Kramer. "There Are Six Bodies in This Relationship: An Anthropological Approach to the Romance Genre". *Journal of Popular Romance Studies* 1.1 (2010). 31 Aug. 2010 <http://jprstudies.org/2010/08/there-are-six-bodies-in-this-relationship-an-anthropological-approach-to-the-romance-genre-by-laura-vivanco-and-kyra-kramer/>.

Wade, Catherine. *A Straightforward Guide to Writing Romantic Fiction*. London: Straightforward, 1998.

Wainger, Leslie. *Writing a Romance Novel for Dummies*. Hoboken, NJ: Wiley, 2004.

Walbrook, H. M. "Happy Endings to Plays: Interviews with Lady Bancroft, Mr. J. Forbes Robertson, Mr. W. H. Kendal, and Mr. Robert Loraine. " *The Pall Mall Magazine* 43.192 (1909): 482–85.

Walker, Kate. *Kate Walker's 12 Point Guide to Writing Romance*. Abergele: Studymates, 2008.

Wallace, Ian. "Hall, Henry Robert (1898–1989)". Rev. *Oxford Dictionary of National Biography*. Oxford UP, 2006. 30 Aug. 2010 <http://www.oxforddnb.com/view/article/40694>.

Wardropper, Bruce W. "An Apology for Philology". *MLN* 102.2 (1987): 176–90.

Warner, Marina. *Alone of All Her Sex: The Myth and the Cult of the Virgin Mary*. London: Weidenfeld & Nicolson, 1976.

Watson, Daphne. *Their Own Worst Enemies: Women Writers of Women's Fiction*. London: Pluto, 1995.

Waugh, Patricia. *Metafiction: The Theory and Practice of Self-Conscious Fiction*. 1984. London: Routledge, 1988.

Weiss, Julian. Introduction. *Poetry at Court in Trastamaran Spain: From the "Cancionero de Baena" to the "Cancionero General"*. Ed. E. Michael Gerli and Julian Weiss. Medieval & Renaissance Texts & Studies 181. Tempe, AZ: Medieval & Renaissance Texts & Studies, 1998: 1–16.

Wendell, Sarah, and Candy Tan. *Beyond Heaving Bosoms: The Smart Bitches' Guide to Romance Novels*. New York: Simon & Schuster, 2009.

Whinnom, Keith. "Towards the Interpretation and Appreciation of the *Canciones* of the *Cancionero general* of 1511". *Medieval and Renaissance Spanish Literature: Selected Essays by Keith Whinnom*. Ed. Alan Deyermond, W. F. Hunter and Joseph T. Snow. Exeter: U of Exeter P, 1994: 114–32.

Wibberley, Mary. *To Writers With Love: On Writing Romantic Novels*. 1985. Leatherhead: Ashford, Buchan & Enright, 1993.

Williams, Anne. *Art of Darkness: A Poetics of Gothic*. Chicago: U of Chicago P, 1995.

Williamson, Margaret. "The Greek Romance". *The Progress of Romance: The Politics of Popular Fiction*. Ed. Jean Radford. London: Routledge & Kegan Paul, 1986. 23–45.

Wirtén, Eva Hemmungs. *Global Infatuation: Explorations in Transnational Publishing and Texts: The Case of Harlequin Enterprises and Sweden*. Section for Sociology of Literature at the Department of Literature, Uppsala University, 1998. <http://www.abm.uu.se/evahw/Global_Infatuation.pdf>.

Woolf, Virginia. "Middlebrow". *The Death of the Moth and Other Essays*. London: Hogarth, 1942. 113–19.

Zipes, Jack. "What Makes a Repulsive Frog So Appealing: Memetics and Fairy Tales". *Journal of Folklore Research* 45.2 (2008): 109–43.

Humanities-Ebooks.co.uk

All Humanities Ebooks titles are available to Libraries through EBSCO, Ebrary, and MyiLibrary.com

Some other titles

Sibylle Baumbach, *Shakespeare and the Art of Physiognomy**

John Beer, *Blake's Humanism*

John Beer, *The Achievement of E M Forster*

John Beer, *Coleridge the Visionary*

Jared Curtis, ed., *The Fenwick Notes of William Wordsworth**

Jared Curtis, ed., *The Cornell Wordsworth: A Supplement**

Steven Duncan, *Analytic Philosophy of Religion: its History since 1955**

Richard Gravil, *Wordsworth and Helen Maria Williams; or, the Perils of Sensibility**

John K Hale, *Milton as Multilingual: Selected Essays 1982–2004*

Simon Hull, ed., *The British Periodical Text, 1797–1835*

Rob Johnson, Mark Levene and Penny Roberts, eds., *History at the End of the World **

John Lennard, *Modern Dragons and other Essays on Genre Fiction**

John Lennard, *Of Sex and Faerie: Further Essays on Genre Fiction**

C W R D Moseley, *Shakespeare's History Plays**

Paul McDonald, *Laughing at the Darkness: Humour and Postmodernism in American Literature**

Colin Nicholson, *Fivefathers: Interviews with late Twentieth-Century Scottish Poets*

Pamela Perkins, ed., *Francis Jeffrey's Highland and Continental Tours**

Keith Sagar, *D. H. Lawrence: Poet**

Reinaldo Francisco Silva, *Portuguese American Literature**

William Wordsworth, *Concerning the Convention of Cintra**

W J B Owen and J W Smyser, eds., *Wordsworth's Political Writings**

Jared Curtis, ed., *The Poems of William Wordsworth: Collected Reading Texts from the Cornell Wordsworth, 3 vols.**

* These titles are also available in hard copy using links from
http://www.humanities-ebooks.co.uk

www.ingramcontent.com/pod-product-compliance
Lightning Source LLC
Chambersburg PA
CBHW030540030726
47495CB00004B/1074